THE
ORACLE

THE
ORACLE

A NOVEL

ARI JUELS

TALOS

Talos Press books may be purchased in bulk at special discounts for sales promotion, corporate gifts, fund-raising, or educational purposes. Special editions can also be created to specifications. For details, contact the Special Sales Department, Skyhorse Publishing, 307 West 36th Street, 11th Floor, New York, NY 10018 or info@skyhorsepublishing.com.

Talos® and Talos Press® are registered trademarks of Skyhorse Publishing, Inc.®, a Delaware corporation.

Visit our website at www.skyhorsepublishing.com.

10 9 8 7 6 5 4 3 2 1

Library of Congress Cataloging-in-Publication Data is available on file.

Cover design by David Ter-Avanesyan
Cover images: Greek coin by ArchaiOptix via Wikimedia Commons; crypto coin via Shutterstock
Part 1 title image: Planche XII. Temple du VIe siècle. Façade orientale restaurée in *La terrasse du temple*, Fernand Courby et Henry Lacoste, Fouilles de Delphes II.2 (1927)
Part 2 title image: Hanging Marsyas, 2019 by Lucas Werkmeister via Wikimedia Commons. https://commons.wikimedia.org/wiki/File:Hanging_Marsyas,_2019.jpg
Part 3 title image: Belvedere Apollo, 2009 by Marie-Lan Nguyen via Wikimedia Commons https://commons.wikimedia.org/wiki/File:Belvedere_Apollo_Pio-Clementino_Inv1015_n5.jpg
Part 4 title image: Greek coin by ArchaiOptix via Wikimedia Commons https://commons.wikimedia.org/wiki/File:Macedonia_-_king_Alexandros_IV_Philippos_III_Arrhidaios_-_323-315_BC_-_gold_stater_-_head_of_Apollon_-_biga_-_München_GL.jpg

ISBN: 978-1-945863-85-1
Ebook ISBN: 978-1-945863-86-8

Printed in the United States of America

AUTHOR'S NOTE

The Oracle is based on a research paper I coauthored in 2015 concerning the future risks of "rogue" smart contracts—blockchain-based computer programs that facilitate crime. The particular rogue smart contracts of that paper and the story here lie squarely in the realm of fiction. If the community takes due care, they should remain technically unrealizable for some time to come.

PART I

TEMPLE DU VIIe SIÈCLE

Trophonius and Agamedes, having built a temple to Apollo at Delphi, offered supplications to the god, and desired of him some extraordinary reward for their care and labor. They asked for no specific boon, only whatever was best for men. Apollo signified that he would bestow it in three days.

On the third day at daybreak, they were found dead.

—Cicero, *Tusculan Disputations* (I. 47)

ONE

Among the massive brick buildings in lower Manhattan that house the bright playgrounds of the tech industry, there's a bridge. This antique skybridge of glass and gray metal spans two buildings on opposite sides of the street. Its high arched windows run across what looks like a floating railway carriage, the elegant remnant of a forgotten era when feats of engineering still drew incredulous eyes to the sky. Thousands of tourists have photographed it as a picturesque backdrop to their selfies. Lit by the morning sun, it appears to be empty, shut up because it's too antiquated for foot traffic. Or maybe it was never more than an architect's flight of fancy.

After dusk, though, tourists taking in the city lights from the High Line or lingering office workers gazing idly out of a window see the bridge warmly illuminated. And there, hovering above the center of the street, barely visible from below, is a man sitting at a desk, oblivious to the teeming city, gravity, and time.

I am that man.

I build oracles.

TWO
Delphi, Greece, 405 BC

It is the seventh day after the new moon, one of the nine days of the year ordained for consultations at Delphi. A delegation of three envoys has journeyed here from Athens. They have come to the most famous oracle in the world to seek guidance from the god Apollo, for their city is in mortal peril.

Just after dawn, the Athenians purified themselves with water from the sacred springs. Led now by a Delphian host, they walk up Mount Parnassus carrying laurel leaves and leading a sacrificial victim, a snow-white goat kid. Among the other pilgrims there, they wend their way through the splendid buildings and monuments that fill the sanctuary dedicated to Apollo. They climb the winding road known as the Sacred Way.

Purple-shadowed mountains thrust skyward all around them, for Delphi is truly a place of eagles. To find the center of the world, it is said that Zeus released two eagles from the western and eastern extremities of the earth. Where they met he placed the oval-shaped stone called the Omphalos, the navel of the world. There Delphi came into being.

Perched above the envoys on the mountain slope is their goal, the great Temple of Apollo. It soaks the warm gold of the rising sun into its massive marble columns. The pigmented band of its lofty frieze above radiates brilliant red and blue. It looms over the other buildings, as great among them as a god among heroes, or a hero among men.

The envoys ascend past rows of statues frozen in valiant poses. They walk between the marble treasury buildings—shrines like small temples—that line the Sacred Way. Each treasury belongs to a different city of Greece and houses precious objects dedicated by its citizens.

The treasures at Delphi are of incomparable magnificence. Perhaps none more so than the massive, solid gold mixing bowl and lion given many years ago by King Croesus. Together, the two treasures weigh more than half a dozen men. Yet it is said that their gold represents but a fraction of Delphi's immense wealth. Of great renown too is the bronze serpent column that rises on high by the temple, its pinnacle bearing a gold tripod. Cast from the captured weapons of the Persians, it commemorates a rare moment of unity, the triumph of the Greek cities over an invading empire. Beckoning to the climbing pilgrims from the mountainside to the east is a shining colossus of the god Apollo, thirty-five cubits high. These are but a few of the wonders and masterpieces amassed at Delphi across the centuries. The sanctuary's peerless trove of silver, gold, ivory, bronze, and marble proclaims the towering importance of the Oracle of Delphi in the affairs of men. No Greek city embarks upon any great undertaking without consulting the oracle. No Greek colony is founded without the oracle's direction. Even the kings of distant lands pay homage to Apollo at Delphi and crave his counsel.

When the envoys arrive at the great temple, they find a crowd of pilgrims gathered in a nearby shelter, waiting to consult the priestess. The Athenians, however, have precedence over the other pilgrims and will be first to enter the temple. The Delphians have granted them this honor in gratitude for their lavish dedications to the sanctuary.

A priest takes charge of the Athenians' sacrificial goat and leads it to the temple. When the priest sprinkles it with water, the victim fails to shake off the libation. The priest sprinkles it again, with the same result. When the goat does not startle and bleat, the day is deemed inauspicious and no oracle can be given. The Athenians have brought rich new dedications with them, however, and the priest does not wish to deny them a consultation. He no longer sprinkles the goat, but deluges it with a libation that nearly drowns it. Only then does it relent, bleating and shaking away the water. It is led away, butchered, and sacrificed upon the Altar of the Chians. The god's portion is burned, dissolving in a column of smoke that twists as it drifts up to meet Him, the Radiant One.

The priest's coercion of the sacrificial victim has affected the Pythia, the priestess who gives voice to the god's prophecies. Or perhaps it is a divine sense of foreboding that has overcome her. She is unwilling to enter the temple. Only at the urging of the priests does she mount the temple steps and pass inside, there to descend into the inner sanctum, the adyton.

The Athenians soon follow, led by their Delphian host and a priest. As they pass through the portico, they look for the most famous of the inscriptions there. *Nothing in excess*, a piece of simple wisdom. More mysterious: *Know thyself*. And then the one most disputed by the sages: a lone letter "E" of shining bronze. They pass through the lofty doorway into the dim inner space. There burns the eternal flame, fed fragrant pine wood by an order of holy women. It throws dancing shadows onto the high walls.

They are led down a ramp, deep into the earth, toward the inner sanctum. Vast as the temple appeared when they threaded their way up the mountain, their descent into that darkling place, all but ignorant of the sun, is longer and steeper than they would have imagined possible. As they near the bottom, only glimmers from the gold and ivory of the great cult statue declare that they are still in the realm of the Radiant One. They might otherwise have believed themselves in Hades.

At the bottom, to the left, is the innermost chamber of the temple: the adyton. Within this small cave sunk into the wall, the Pythia sits upon her tripod seat of bronze. In one raised hand is a shallow libation dish filled with sacred spring water. In the other is a branch of laurel. A brazier illuminates only the craggy extremities of her hooded face. Sunk in darkness around her are objects sacred to the god: his armor and lyre, an altar, statues of wood and gold. It is the most ancient of these objects, the Omphalos, that the Athenians' eyes seek.

The Omphalos, which marks the very center of the world. The Omphalos, which the goddess Rhea used to deceive and destroy her husband Cronus. It was prophesied that Cronos, the primordial Titan king of the cosmos, would be overthrown by his sons. He tried to evade the prophecy by swallowing the infant Zeus, his son by Rhea. Aided by the earth mother Gaia, Rhea hid Zeus and caused Cronos instead to swallow a decoy, the swaddled Omphalos. The envoys cannot not be sure whether they see it there, flanked by its gold eagles, among the dim forms.

For a thousand years, the priestess has prophesied here, seated above a fissured patch of sacred ground through which vapors rise from the underworld. The Athenians smell the strange, sweet odor, which scents the air like a costly perfume.

The lead envoy of the Athenians takes a step forward and poses the question he bears from his desperate people.

"O God of the Silver Bow, God of Light and Truth! Terrible are your might and wrath. In our ceaseless war, you have aided our enemies, the Spartans. They and their allies now threaten us on land and sea with utter destruction.

"What must we do to appease the Olympian gods, who have stood watch over Athens for over one hundred generations? What do you command or counsel that Athens might yet stand for one hundred generations to come?"

They wait. The priestess stirs, then grows still. Then, as she gazes into the dish in her hand, she swells in size and her hair stands on end. She addresses them in a deep voice that belongs to no ordinary woman. They know that when the Pythia prophesies, hers is the voice of the god himself. But now her speech is harsh and rasping, loud then choked, as though the god possessing her has been seized by madness. "Fear—" she begins to cry out, but gasps and stops. The priests eye one another in alarm. "Fear not, Athenians!" she cries.

> Athens shall yet stand when this my wondrous hall
> Has turned to dust, the sacred springs have dried,
> My glittering bow's unstrung, my lips are cold.
> No more then shall my priestess sing the truth
> Of dooms spun by the fatal hands of three.
> The world shall far and wide with webs of lies
> Be then ensnared, as shall her purblind men,
> Who'd sell for gold the navel of the Earth.
> Once more then shall I rise—

The priestess breaks off and jumps from her seat, thrashing wildly. The dish flies from her hand and clatters away. Listing like a ship in a storm, seized by a mute, malevolent force, she topples the sacred objects around her. She shrieks and rushes from the adyton up the ramp to seek the daylight, but before she reaches the entrance, she throws herself to the ground. The Athenians flee the temple. So do the priests. A daemon has poured terror into their hearts.

When they return, they find her still conscious. Her eyes move, but the spirit has left her limbs, and her breath is weak. In whispers they discuss her dreadful prophecy. The god spoke through her of things that would come to pass thousands of years in the future, things that brought horror even to the god himself. This was more than her mortal frame could bear.

She lives for only three days.

THREE

The email from the FBI mentioned a rogue smart contract. That could have meant any number of things. It might have been what I'd warned people about years before. Or not.

I thought about it as I went through my late-morning routine. First the essential weekly bout with my personal trainer, who figuratively makes me jump through hoops for an hour. I feel less like a circus tiger than an obstinate rabbit. This year, she's pleased that I can now almost do a pull-up. A pity that next year I'll be too old to do one.

I'd almost trashed the email before I read it. My blog posts on oracles and smart-contract engineering are popular, so I get emails from all kinds of cranks and crackpots. Not many from purported FBI special agents, though, which was why I ended up reading this one. Of course, it wouldn't have mattered if I hadn't. Diane would have found me anyway.

After my grueling workout of multiple half pull-ups, I shoveled down a breakfast of yogurt with blueberries, hemp seeds, baobab, and ten other things with powerful health benefits demonstrated in scientific studies, mostly with rats. It's the one real meal of the day for me. I graze for lunch and dinner, and get a good chunk of my calories from dark chocolate. "Nothing in excess" has never been my motto. Good dark chocolate, though, has health benefits that may compensate for the extra fifteen pounds it adds around my middle.

I find that when email is bizarre and has evidence of human writing, not just an AI tool's, most of the time it's authentic. I gave my supposed FBI email a second read. Bizarre? Check. Plausibly human writing? Check.

Before I left for the day, I sprinkled the bonsai trees lining the window sill. *I'll prune you when I've got time.* They bowed in thanks. I bowed back. I felt bad. They really needed pruning.

I did an internet search on the FBI special agent who'd sent the email. Diane Duménil. Unusual name. There was only one on LinkedIn. She looked legit. Educated in France, at the École Normale Supérieure. A PhD in art and archaeology from Princeton, then a job at the Library of Congress, and now the FBI. A few years younger than me, but no photo. She'd turned her back on a solid academic pedigree. No professorship for her. I liked her already.

✳

My commute to work must be among the best in the world. It's a literal walk in the park (if a one-dimensional one). I exit my giant apartment building and head south on the High Line, the old elevated railway in Chelsea that's been converted into a walkway flanked with plantings. I barely even have to cross a street. It's fifteen minutes to work if I'm ready to dodge tourists, seventeen otherwise. I was tired that morning, probably from my workout, so it was seventeen minutes. As usual in springtime, half the tourists I elbowed my way past with a polite, if clipped, "pardon" were from France. I wondered if Special Agent Duménil was around somewhere, maybe hiding behind a tree.

People imagine that when you live in Manhattan, you're discovering a world of wonders through an ever-widening lens. The lights of Times Square. The Theater District. People-watching in Bryant Park. Galleries under the High Line. Museums on the Upper East Side. Stand-up comedy in the Village. Trendy basement restaurants in Brooklyn.

The truth, though, is that no matter where in this world you live, you focus on your own workaday life. Your pupils dilate and you forget to blink during the endless back and forth through a dim tunnel between work and home. If you've got the privilege of a high-paying job in Manhattan, it's even worse because you don't ever need to exit the tunnel. You can be lazy and have everything delivered. Everything. Even a pre-toasted bagel. Which I don't do, because I avoid gluten. But you get the point.

Just before noon, I strolled into the office. It's in a former cookie factory, a cavernous open office fully equipped for a space journey, with snacks, beverages, games, bathrooms, ample computing power, and a crafty crew. Alternatively, it can handle round-the-clock workaholism, which is what it's designed for. Were it not for the thousand and one delights of the Chelsea Market downstairs, I don't know if people would ever leave—except to indulge in the scant amount of sleep that passes for the norm at Adyton LLC.

Most of my colleagues were already there. Adyton employees aren't morning people, so the only lively presence in the office at that time was a giant inflatable sandwich cookie, a novelty item left over from the last company retreat. They're pleasant enough people, my coworkers, but not very communicative. Adrift in their individual, headphone-inflated acoustic bubbles, most of them ignored me. A couple of them nodded to acknowledge my arrival. They're decades younger than I am. They may have hair, but I have a magic bag of programming tricks.

Corinne, at least, gave me a conspiratorial wave of two fingers from her seat as I walked onto the Bridge. A trim and pretty redhead, with her forehead in a permanent inquisitive crease, she reminds me of Nancy Drew, updated in ways that Nancy's father would probably disapprove of. She's our best developer—or dev, as we call them—and my closest colleague. I'm also her company mentor. That means she keeps me educated about the constant ecosystem changes that make smart-contract programming almost impossible to master, and I reciprocate with wise platitudes.

I'm not very observant as a rule, but saw she'd been crying. I stopped next to her. I wanted to put my hand on or around her shoulder, but was paralyzed by Me Too uncertainty. She waved me on and snatched a tissue, so I sauntered over and took up position at my desk, at the midpoint of the Bridge.

*

When I first joined Adyton, the Bridge was sealed off. It was a disused skybridge from the 1930s abutting the company's large open workspace. Not unsafe, but expensive to maintain. I convinced Lukas, the company's CEO, to reopen it. I had to have it. I even offered to have the money for

11

the renovation taken out of my pay. When I see a neglected antiquity—the timeworn creation of some forgotten master—it pains me like seeing an aging cat neglected by its owners. I may be a techie by trade, but I like history too, and the past matters to me. I don't understand why people are so hung up on what happened in the last millisecond, second, or day, which is why I'll blog now and again but you'll never catch me on social media.

Adyton was short on space, Lukas wanted me badly, and there was enough money sloshing around in blockchain companies like Adyton to permit such little extravagances. So Lukas gave in. It helped that he was superstitious. He was already worried that a defunct passageway in the heart of the company's offices might signify death—or an oracle malfunction, which would be worse.

Oracles, you see, are bridges of a sort. Oracles in the ancient world, like the famous oracle of Apollo at Delphi, were bridges between man and the gods. They revealed divine truth in response to human questions about the present or future. Smart contract oracles are also bridges. They're a source of truth for questions asked by smart contracts about the real world. I can't understand, explain, or excuse the real world, but I can at least tell you what smart contracts and oracles are all about.

✳

It all starts with blockchains.

There's a lot of mystification around blockchains. You hear people rattling on about them in coffee shops, bars, dinner parties, and airports when they play games of intellectual one-upmanship, as though blockchains are some mind-bending phenomenon on par with artificial intelligence, quantum mechanics, or astrophysics.

Blockchains really aren't all that complicated, though—not at a conceptual level at least. In essence, a blockchain is just a digital bulletin board. A digital bulletin board with a few special features.

First, the bulletin board is *transparent*, meaning that anyone, anywhere, at any time can read all of the messages on it. It's also *publicly writable*: Anyone can post valid messages to it. And those messages are *immutable*. Once a message is posted, it can never be changed or erased. But the real beauty of this bulletin board is that no person, government, or corporation controls it. It's run by a worldwide community of thousands of computers, which makes it *tamperproof*—secure against manipulation and hacks or attacks.

OK. An armor-plated digital bulletin board. What's the big deal? To start with, imagine if the messages posted to the blockchain authorize transfers of money. A message might, for instance, say something like, "I, Alice, send $50 to Bob." Then what happens?

Boom! Suddenly you've got a powerful global payment system. Thanks to the transparency of the blockchain, the whole world can read its money-transfer messages and know the balance of every (anonymous) account. The blockchain's immutability means that if you receive money from someone, it can't be clawed back from you. The person who paid you can't stop payment, nor can any bank. Most importantly, as soon as a message appears on the blockchain, it moves money between people instantaneously—no matter where in the world they are. That's because the message *is* the money transfer. Try sending money across the globe using an international wire transfer in less than two days and without getting fleeced like a sheep at a shearing competition and you'll appreciate just what a blockchain can do for you.

Of course, I'm glossing over a lot of details. How does a blockchain ensure that Alice's money transfer is actually authorized by Alice? (Something called digital signatures.) Do people use their real names on blockchains? (No, for privacy they use anonymous account numbers.) Then there's the fact that money on the blockchain usually takes the form of cryptocurrency, not dollars, and that cryptocurrency has to be created somehow. What I've outlined, though, is basically how all blockchains and their cryptocurrencies work.

Blockchains, however, can do vastly more than just shunt cryptocurrency around. They can also run little computer programs called *smart contracts*—or just plain *contracts*. That's where things go from interesting to transformative.

Because a smart contract runs on a blockchain, it isn't like ordinary software—like, say, a mobile app. When you have a banking app on your smartphone, your bank controls the app. It can add new features whenever it wants, shut the app down, stop your payments, slap you with yet more fees, whatever. It's all up to the bank.

In contrast, because a smart contract runs on a blockchain, it's like the blockchain itself: It isn't controlled by a single bank, company, person, or organization. It's *autonomous*. It's like a bot. That's the "smart" part. Because it runs on a blockchain, a smart contract is also transparent and tamperproof. Everyone in the world can see and run its code, and that code executes exactly as programmed. Using a smart contract is like having a person of unimpeachable honesty handle the transactions in your system. It's like handing your money over to "Honest Abe" Lincoln, reincarnated in the twenty-first century as software.

Suppose someone codes up a smart contract for, say, betting on a baseball game. Assuming the code is correct, it will do exactly what it's designed to do: run a fair betting pool for the game. You can place a bet with it and be sure that it won't lose your money and will pay you fairly if you win. It will also have a critical feature that all smart contracts inherit from blockchains: They're *unstoppable*. Even a government intent on quashing sports betting will have no technical way to interfere with the contract. It will run forever on its own—for good or bad.

But here's the rub. Our hypothetical betting contract can only pay the winners if it actually *knows which team won the baseball game*.

You or I would just look up the answer on a website. But smart contracts can't trust people to report on the result of the game, because people are slow and prone to lying. It's also not possible for our baseball-betting smart contract itself to go ping a news or sports website to learn who won the game. That's because many thousands of computers make up the blockchain on which the contract runs, and it's not practical for all of those computers to connect simultaneously to a website and agree on what they saw.

Enter oracles, the magic missing ingredient. The rainbow bridge that connects smart contracts to the internet and so to the real world. If a smart contract posts a question on the blockchain—like "Which team won the Red Sox vs. Yankees game last night?"—an oracle will see the question, fetch the answer from the internet, and return it to the contract on the blockchain.

I'm simplifying a lot, of course. Fetching data sounds easy, but ensuring that it's correct and timely is a Herculean task. Oracles need to be as secure and tamperproof as the very best blockchains, which means they need to be bulletproof sources of truthful data. Someone who can hack an oracle today can steal millions or billions of dollars. But well-secured oracles are what enable nearly all interesting blockchain services today. Before oracles came along, practically the only thing anyone did with blockchains was move money around and breed ugly digital blockchain cats called CryptoKitties. When oracles first came on line, it felt like living in a primitive city that finally got electricity.

That's why oracles aren't just a technology. To their fans, they're the lifeblood of the smart-contract revolution. New financial services—money transfer, loans, and investment platforms—are gradually eating the banking world thanks to smart contracts. Those services are more transparent, flexible, and efficient than anything Wall Street ever created. Little by little, they're bringing financial inclusion to the billions of people neglected by the world's banks. Smart contracts are upending far-flung domains beyond finance too. They're authenticating luxury goods and suppressing blood diamonds, overhauling the lumbering insurance industry, and transforming art markets with blockchain-registered digital art called "non-fungible tokens" or NFTs. (NFTs alone are a big deal. When you move to the metaverse in a few years, don't be surprised if your house, clothes, toothbrush, and dog are all NFTs, if not your AI-powered spouse.)

Oracles lie behind all of these transformations. They're anchoring smart contracts—and the people they serve—in truth. That's why I believe in oracles as a force for good. Our society is being torn apart by income inequality and lies, populists and plutocrats, existential threats to justice and truth. Smart contracts and oracles might, just might, offer an answer to a few of these problems.

Lukas and the Priestess (as we call her) also believed in oracles in the early days when they founded Adyton. That's why I went to work with them. (I say "with," because I'm on a consulting contract. I refuse to work "for" anyone.) If we're going to smash the Wall Street machine, break the power of Big Tech, and rebuild a fairer world, oracles are the main tool at hand, the heavy wrench we need to do the job. (Disclaimer: This is just my idealistic view. The Priestess and Lukas are practical people. But I still like them.)

✺

Headphones in place, I was thirty minutes into an electrifying and grossly underappreciated Saint-Saëns piano concerto and a waist-high pile of other people's crappy, buggy code when a yellow polo shirt hove into view. The Shirt—as it's known to Lukas's fanatical band of followers. The shirt that launched a thousand memes. The shirt that's sold out several times online because Adyton fans—millions strong on social media—keep buying them up. Especially after Lukas gives yet another rousing conference talk about oracles becoming the new Delphi, the world's definitive source of truth. Steve Jobs had his trademark black turtleneck and Mark Zuckerberg his hoodies. Lukas has his short-sleeved yellow polo shirt. It's got thin white horizontal stripes, loose-fitting sleeves, and a crocodile sewn onto the chest, left of center—a style I've otherwise not seen since the 1980s. I hope he owns more than one, because he's always wearing it, possibly even to sleep. I often try to distinguish one shirt from others he might own by looking for distinctive stains or creases, but I never find any. After the Shirt, the rest of Lukas's body materialized in due course, including the glum face.

"I know what you're going to say." I smiled as I removed my headphones.

"No, you don't." He didn't smile. He never smiles. "Do you like thriller movies or novels? Like Michael Crichton?"

"No."

"I do. Because you feel the danger, the terror . . ." Unless you're paying very careful attention, you wouldn't pick up Lukas's hint of a German accent. His "the" sometimes shades into a "zee." "Zee terror."

". . . It's in your gut and your brain stem. Will they escape the dinosaurs chewing through the skylight? The clock is ticking. Seconds left. Will they defuse the time bomb? Will the motorcycle tear away from the explosion?

"But you *know* it's not real and the good guys will live," he said. "It's adrenaline without risk. Good stress. Entertainment. Good for my heart." He touched his chest, and the talismanic shirt, of course.

"To me, that sounds—"

"With you, it's the opposite. I feel the terror. Hours before we're supposed to start the final reviews and tests on a product release so we can go live. Everyone's watching. Is he going to finish that last, critical piece of code that no one else is smart enough to write? But I *don't* know that everything's going to be okay. Bad stress. Bad for my heart."

He looks like he's in his twenties. His smooth, young face is partially hidden beneath the goatee that I assume he's cultivated to make people think he's older than he is. Even before he cofounded Adyton, during the pandemic, he sold a company for trading carbon credits on blockchains that he cofounded as an undergrad. So he's already accomplished something important—more than I can say for myself.

"Your heart? How old are you? Twenty-nine? Thirty?"

"I felt young before you came along."

"I've never failed you yet. Look at it this way. The more pressure, the more productive I am. My productivity is the amount of work I have to do divided by the time I've got left to do it. So as that time drops to zero—"

"My stress goes to infinity."

"Anything else? I have work to do. I've got a deadline, you know."

"I don't get it," Lukas said. "You're afraid to drive. You're afraid to fly. You're afraid to eat gluten. But you're not afraid to dangle the whole company over a precipice. Think about it. What if you get hit by a bus before you finish?"

"Don't worry. I'm also afraid to cross streets." I stifled a crack about his not owning a black polo shirt with black stripes to wear at my funeral—one with a crocodile shedding tears. "And everything's backed up."

Believe it or not, Lukas, the Priestess, and I trust each other implicitly. There's a bond that comes from traveling a journey together, the journey from being lone believers in the wilderness to industry veterans with a shared vision. I think. The Priestess, frankly, intimidates me. Her nickname isn't ironic, like, say, Little John, the nickname of Robin Hood's sidekick, who was seven feet tall.

I was about to ask Lukas if he'd also been contacted by Diane Duménil, but remembered that she'd asked me to keep her email to myself. Unlikely she'd have divulged any secrets to me, but it would be best to keep things under wraps.

Ah yes, that email. Once Lukas had gone, I read it yet again. She'd said I should text her. I texted to suggest a brief meeting in Chelsea Market at two o'clock. I didn't have time to go farther afield. Her reply was immediate: "Yes."

I got back down to work. I needed to finish up my code and ready it for testing. I was responsible for the last piece of our upcoming Sanctum release. I had at most half a day if we were going to have time for the critical code review and testing. I wasn't actually sure I'd make it, particularly with odd distractions like rogue smart contracts popping up. But Special Agent Duménil had said her request was urgent.

FOUR

Knowing I'd need sustenance to get a monthlong job done in half a day, I went down to the market a little before two o'clock.

Chelsea Market is a huge indoor food hall, a gastronomic mecca of dozens of restaurants and shops. One of the shops there has a wall filled with chocolate bars, and many of them are good. No Domori, but other, lesser examples of the art. High-quality dark chocolate, for the record, has some four hundred flavor compounds, more than fine wine. So wine connoisseurs have nothing on me, except that they're better dressed and have a more florid vocabulary. I was in the mood for an adulterated treat—chocolate with something mixed into it—so I picked through the Cluizel. I was trying to decide between hazelnut and candied orange when someone tapped me on the shoulder.

I turned. "Sorry, am I in the way?"

There was an Asian woman, wearing glasses. Thick frames set with bulletproof-glass lenses. Her long black hair was streaked with white. She wore a smart suit of dove gray, accented with a silk scarf, a puff of scarlet and olive. Clearly a wine connoisseur. She didn't belong in the chocolate aisle.

"The wine aisle is over there." I pointed. I couldn't help myself.

"Excuse me?" She cocked her head and gave a bright laugh. "I'm Diane. Diane Duménil. Sorry to bother you here. I recognized you from your photo online." Unmistakable accent. Impeccable English, but her "here" sounded almost like an "ear." French. A wine connoisseur, as I said.

"Can we talk now?" she asked.

She chose to meet in the loud open area of the Chelsea Market, I suppose, so that we'd look like friends grabbing coffee and wouldn't be overheard. The swarms of tourists, though, left us almost nowhere to sit.

We ended up squeezed together on the end of a half-occupied bench, me clutching a mocha and her a cappuccino, an awkward centimeter between us. We strained to hear each other, so I guess that as far as eavesdropping went, she'd strategized well.

I observed her as she took her first sip. No wedding band.

"So, you're a special agent with the FBI?" I asked.

"Art Crime Team. Do you want my card?"

"Art Crime? I noticed that in your email signature." I didn't mean the question as a joke, so I was surprised when she laughed. "I don't need a card," I added.

Diane smiled and continued. "A few years ago you wrote an influential blog post on rogue smart contracts. That's how we found you. I'm not technical. A computer scientist at Cornell Tech who is a friend of mine said that you are the best person to talk to." She told me the name of the friend, a professor. He's okay, but I find his work predictable. I can guess what he's going to publish six months before it's online. But I didn't want to bad-mouth him.

"Your email mentioned a rogue smart contract," I said. "Did you mean that in the sense of my blog post?" In my post, I'd warned about how smart contracts could be used to facilitate a gamut of real-world crimes, including assassination. For contracts with such malintent, I'd coined the term "rogue" contracts.

"If I had given details in my email," she said, "you would think I was crazy. Maybe you will still think that. I *am* crazy—but only in other ways." She laughed again. I couldn't make out her expression behind the bullet-proof-glass lenses.

"People thought I was crazy when I wrote my blog post and warned that smart contracts could be used for serious crimes," I said. "Yet here we are. You included the blockchain address of the smart contract in your email, but I haven't had a chance to take a look at it."

"The rogue contract came out just a few days ago. Our people found a message in the code, with an explanation—if you want to call it that. Here." She showed it to me on her phone.

```
Claudio Viganò has blasphemed against the God and his
    oracle. May the God's glittering bow send him death.
```

"And the smart contract offers around $10,000 in cryptocurrency to kill him," she added.

"So it's happened . . ." I said. She crumpled her scarf and gazed into the distance.

When I'd written about the dangers of rogue smart contracts in my blog post, in the back of my mind I'd considered them improbable. Just a colorful yet disturbing example of the type of thing that *could* happen someday. I had never gone through the exercise of imagining, beyond the technical specifics, what it would mean for the world if they ever saw the light of day.

Any technology can be abused by people with evil intent. Smart contracts are no exception. Recent advances in blockchain design had merged with rapidly evolving technologies such as natural language processing—the part of AI that deals with human language. As a result, smart contracts had become a powerful tool for many different types of business. One such business, regrettably, was the business of crime. People could now in theory solicit crimes using smart contracts crafted for that purpose. That's what I meant by "rogue" contracts. The crime solicited by a rogue contract could be anything from website defacement to real-world vandalism to exposing secrets by hacking servers to assassination.

Of course, there's long been a market for crime of all kinds on the dark web, the shady part of the internet. But criminals and "contractors"—the people looking to hire criminals—often cheat one another. If criminals are paid in advance, they run off with the money. If they're paid after the fact, contractors refuse to pay.

Because rogue smart contracts could prevent cheating on either side, they raised the specter of a seamless market for crime. Like the dark web, rogue contracts could confer anonymity and global reach. Once a contractor created a rogue smart contract for a crime such as assassination, an assassin anywhere in the world could sign up to kill a victim. The assassin and contractor never had to meet or learn one another's real-world identities. At the same time, with their ability to prevent cheating, rogue contracts promised a leap beyond simple dark-web communications. A rogue contract would automatically and faithfully execute payment if and only if an assassin killed a targeted victim. Crime could now meet the standards of the Better Business Bureau.

However much smart-contract technology had advanced in theory, creating a truly dangerous rogue contract in practice was still a formidable technical challenge. Nobody had ever launched one. It was all hypothetical— until my meeting with Diane.

"What god are they talking about?" I asked her. "The message in the contract doesn't say God. It says *the* God."

"That is the crazy part. I think—we think—they mean Apollo."

Most people know that Apollo is the god of light, the sun, and music. But he's also the god of truth and oracles. I learned this when, as a thank-you gift, the Priestess gave me an ancient Greek silver coin set in a Lucite slab. I keep it on my desk on the Bridge. It shows Apollo sitting on the Omphalos, a marble stone at Delphi that marked the center of the world. I'm no expert, but no one had worshipped Apollo, to the best of my knowledge, for at least a thousand years.

"Why would—"

"There's a bit of history here," Diane said. "I will explain later. The point is, we need to protect Professor Viganò."

"I don't know who this Viganò is, but there's nothing I can do. My blog post only warned that this could happen, and that all technologies are dual-use. I wasn't even the first to point out the risk. I don't have a solution. I just urged people to think about countermeasures. I don't—"

"What I want is simple. My technical colleagues explained it to me. I don't know the details, but the rogue contract uses an oracle. I want you to help us create a tool so we can block the oracle or make it give false information."

"Whoa!" I put down my mocha on the bench. I needed both hands for this. "I can't do that."

"I know it's a big request." She continued to pluck at her scarf. I wondered how many she tore in a week.

"I mean if an oracle is well designed, it should be tamperproof. It's decentralized. That means distributed among a bunch of servers so that no one person or organization controls it. Even Adyton—my company—doesn't control its own oracles. Maybe there's a small chance I could devise a hack that would stop our oracles from feeding the rogue contract. But even if I could, I wouldn't."

"You wouldn't prevent a man from being murdered?" Even through her thick lenses, I saw her eyes narrow. "Why not?"

"Because it would be wrong. It would mean attacking my own system and undermining everything I do."

"It is wrong to let a man be killed."

"It *is* wrong. Abhorrent. But the greater wrong would be to take a system designed for individual empowerment, a system free from interference by any government, and subvert it. We're building oracles to be definitive sources of truth."

"I understand, but—"

"Couldn't you just stage his death?" I asked.

"What does that mean in an oracle system? I'm not technical."

"Remember from my blog post how a rogue smart contract works. The smart contract—"

"I didn't completely understand your blog post. Could you explain?"

"Of course. As you know, the rogue contract is holding a cryptocurrency bounty. That's the $10,000 on your Professor Viganò's head. The function of this rogue contract is to reward a successful assassin."

She nodded.

"Let's call our would-be assassin Ms. A, for 'Assassin.'"

"Ms. A," she repeated, a conscientious student.

"And we'll call the assassination target Mr. V. For 'Victim.'"

"Or Viganò," she said.

"Right," I said. "Or Viganò. Prof. V, I suppose."

"Mr. V is fine." She raised her cappuccino to her mouth.

"Our assassin Ms. A learns about the rogue contract and its bounty on Mr. V's head. She wants to do the job and collect the bounty. So she sends a message to the contract signing on to perform the assassination."

"What's in this message?"

"It includes a little bit of money—a cryptocurrency deposit—just to show that Ms. A is for real. The important part of the message, though, is a secret known as a *calling card*. That's some distinctive detail about the crime as Ms. A is planning it. Only Ms. A knows this detail, but when the murder happens, news articles are sure to report—"

"I see." She wrinkled her brow. "The detail could be the day or where it will happen or which poison Ms. A will use on Mr. V. Ms. A knows this detail in advance, but no else does."

"Exactly. To be concrete, this detail could be expressed as a key word or a small set of key words. Let's say that Ms. A is planning to murder Mr. V in some exotic way—say, having a piano fall on him from the fifteenth floor of a building. Then the calling card might just consist of the key words *piano + fifteenth floor.*"

"You said the calling card in Ms. A's message was secret. What do you mean?" Diane asked.

"To simplify things a bit, she encrypts the calling card *piano + fifteenth floor* in her message. So even though the contract stores her message on the blockchain, no one else can read it. Only Ms. A can decrypt it. It's as though she sends the calling card to the contract in a sealed envelope."

"So then the contract knows that Ms. A submitted the secret calling card before the assassination?"

"Precisely. Now let's suppose the assassination happens. Mr. V meets the instrument of his death. News articles report on the murder. Naturally, among the key words they use to explain what happened are *piano* and *fifteenth floor.* At that point, Ms. A can claim the bounty by decrypting her calling card. Think of it as opening the sealed envelope to reveal the calling card *piano + fifteenth floor.* Because Ms. A knew this detail in advance—which we know from her calling card—it's clear she was the assassin."

"But then the contract needs to know whether Mr. V was actually murdered with a falling piano, doesn't it?" She peered earnestly through her bulletproof lenses.

"And *that,*" I said, "is where the oracle comes in. When Ms. A decrypts her calling card, the smart contract calls the oracle. It asks the oracle if *piano* and *fifteenth floor* appeared among the key words in articles about Mr. V's death. The oracle checks using AI tools. If the oracle says yes, then the smart contract knows that Mr. V was murdered and that Ms. A was the assassin."

"I understand now. And then Ms. A receives her payment, the cryptocurrency bounty from the contract. Perhaps I should have learned all of this from your blog, but I think it was written for computer people."

I chuckled. "Sorry. I suppose it was."

"Isn't it a problem that Ms. A has to communicate with the contract? What if law enforcement is watching?"

"It's all done on a blockchain. Ms. A doesn't reveal her name. The 'A' in Ms. A could also mean 'anonymous.' The same goes for whoever created the rogue contract. They don't reveal their real-world identities."

"So everyone is anonymous except Mr. V."

"Essentially. Blockchains don't offer perfect anonymity. The criminals need to know what they're doing. And they need to be careful if they want to remain in the shadows. But you get the idea."

"OK. I understand now. So what then do you mean when you say that we should stage Prof. Viganò's death? Is that a blockchain term?" She took another sip of cappuccino. I realized I hadn't yet drunk any of my mocha.

"Not at all. What I mean is just that you—the FBI—pretend to be an assassin. You create a fake Ms. A. You pick your favorite calling card. Say you're going to pretend the professor was murdered by an exploding rubber duck in his bathtub. You can send a nice, distinctive calling card to send to the contract: *rubber duck + bathtub + plastic explosives*. Then you—the FBI—convince news outlets to publish a fake story containing the words in the calling card. You'll look to the rogue contract like a legitimate Ms. A. And the beauty of this ploy is that you not only neutralize the contract, but you get to claim the $10,000 bounty as though you were a real assassin. Yet the death was faked."

"*Voilà!*" she said. "Brilliant idea. So you mean we don't subvert the oracle. You think that is wrong. Instead, we subvert the press and produce fake news."

"That's one way of putting—"

"To me, *that* is wrong. It undermines everything *I* do. The press is a pillar of democracy. Oracles are not. What makes oracles sacred? They are just some fancy new technology."

"Sure. That's what people were saying six hundred years ago about an invention in Germany called the printing press. Just some fancy new technology. Yet it gave birth to your pillar of democracy." I smirked. "OK, so you don't publish fake stories. You fake the death itself. Blow up his car with a dummy in it."

"Oh, yes. Also brilliant. Then when the professor turns out to be alive, another rogue smart contract comes out, and now we have to kill him again and just hope the press is gullible beyond belief."

Her phone rang. "Excuse me. I need to take this." I was glad for the chance to collect my wits. I could make out a man's voice and later "*à tout à l'heure*," which anyone who's been on the High Line knows means "see you soon." A boyfriend, I figured.

She shoved her phone back into her bag. "You see the problem, yes?"

"No. Aren't you the FBI? Assign your professor a security detail. Find the people who put out the contract and throw them in jail. You're asking me to do your dirty work."

"Our dirty work?" I could see she wanted to make an angry gesture, but she was still holding her cappuccino. "A few years ago, we could have figured out who paid the money into the contract. We could trace cryptocurrency transactions. We could have discovered who the assassin was. But you and your friends used your 'moon math' to create technologies that conceal cryptocurrency transactions. Now criminals use them to hide from law enforcement. Is that another of your sacred principles?"

"It's called privacy. And it's a basic human right. Maybe it's not spelled out in the US constitution. Maybe it's not part of the FBI's remit. But—to use your term—it's a pillar of any decent civilization."

"So is the right to live in a society governed by rule of law, without assassins in the shadows. Freedom from fear."

I sighed. "Is $10,000 really enough to entice an assassin? It's not a lot of money. Isn't this whole thing just a publicity stunt?"

"Never underestimate the evil things people will do to each other," she said, obviously speaking with a whiff of personal experience. "Contract killings can involve even less money."

"Sorry, Diane. I can't do it. And I won't try to do it. I don't want your professor to be hurt, but there has to be another way. I respect the FBI, but it's a slippery slope. First you ask for a little favor. Then you ask for a bigger favor. Then you ask for lots of big favors. Then the Chinese and Russians come knocking on our door asking for the same favors. Either we refuse and look like a tool of the US government, or we accept and become some authoritarian regime's cat's-paw."

"And when a smart contract appears with a price on the head of a political dissident?"

"I'll donate to a bounty on the head of the assassin."

"I joined the FBI because I want to see justice. Real justice. Not your kind of barbarism."

We stared at each other.

"Thanks for the mocha," I said.

"Thanks for the lessons on truth and justice." She sprang up, holding her cappuccino at arm's length to avoid spilling on her suit, and marched off.

After she left I realized that I hadn't learned what all of this had to do with art crime. Or, for that matter, with the god Apollo.

In case you're wondering, I went back and bought both the candied orange and hazelnut bars.

FIVE

Suppose someone tells you that black cars are popular in Manhattan. You'll notice suddenly that every car trying to kill you when you cross the street is black. I couldn't tell whether there was an explosion of born-again disciples of Apollo on the internet, or I just had him on the brain after Diane's strange and unexplained mention of him. Delphi in particular was a cliché in our industry, with companies and products named Oracle, Apollo, Pythia, and whatnot. We at Adyton LLC were as guilty as any. But I observed—or thought I observed—references to the ancient Greek originals starting to creep in greater profusion across the internet.

For example, I was reading the *New York Times* online when I got an ad for an excursion to Delphi. And another for downhill skiing on Mt. Parnassus. (I guess it's not just popular with the Muses anymore.) Okay. Ads are targeted, and maybe my searches had let Google know I was in the market for Greek mysticism. But that wasn't all. Someone was buying up land in and around Delphi in metaverse platforms—that is, buying real estate corresponding to the site of the oracle in virtual worlds. And in the real world, I noticed that a gallery in midtown was having an exhibition on Delphi, and an online search showed that it wasn't alone. Four museums and galleries in the United States and three in Europe were holding exhibitions on Delphi. A little poking around revealed that in the year 2000, when the film *Gladiator* came out, so did themed exhibitions on ancient Rome and gladiators. But there had been no recent blockbuster Hollywood action flick about Delphi starring, say, Scarlett Johansson as the assassin-prophetess Pythia. So I didn't understand the sudden uptick in interest.

The rogue smart contract itself got scant press coverage. There were a few articles on trade news sites and a handful of blog posts about it, but they treated it as a joke. The god Apollo had awakened from a long sleep, one blogger remarked, only to make a pathetic discovery: His bow now shoots shoestring-budget cryptocurrency bounties instead of divine arrows. I learned from these articles that Prof. Viganò was a classical archaeologist. This fact, along with the "glittering bow" reference in the rogue contract, were what led people to conclude that "the God" in question there was Apollo and the "oracle" was Delphi. So Viganò and Apollo were in the same general line of business. Otherwise nothing about the whole business made sense. It had to be a bad joke indeed—or the work of a madman.

Still, I couldn't let it go. And I found myself wondering fancifully about it. What if the creators of the contract really did believe in Apollo? And what, for that matter, if they were right? If Apollo were to stir from his sleep in the twenty-first century and stride down Mount Olympus into the realm of mortals, how would he show himself? Not in the old places, surely. Not on a dusty field of battle, among the ruins of a Greek temple, or in a chariot in the sky. Maybe he would shimmer into view in cyberspace. Sensing his presence, disciples would arise. They would draw together in underground chat rooms and forums. They would worship and plan and rekindle in some new, disembodied form the eternal flame of Delphi. The idea had a perverse allure.

I was curious, and it's my business to understand oracles, after all. Once the Sanctum release was out of the way, I looked over the code of the rogue contract. As any hacker would, I tried to find a way to break it. I used a bunch of program analysis tools, and my own checklist of anti-patterns, as we call them. But the core logic was solid. It was written with extreme— almost absurd—care, and even sprinkled with bits of Greek. Often bugs take up residence in the cracks, the interfaces between pieces of code. But the contract's use of the oracle was also sound.

I did, however, discover something unsettling.

You can program a smart contract with a time limit, an expiration date. I expected to see one in the rogue contract. Since the bounty was small, I figured when I first heard about it that its creators didn't have money to waste. And I still thought the whole thing might just be a publicity stunt of some kind. I expected that if no one claimed the bounty after a few months, the contract would refund the money to its creator.

But there was no provision for a refund. The money would sit there until at least the day the good Professor Viganò died. It was cruel. Either he'd be murdered or he'd have the contract—the Sword of Damocles in his Apollonian world—hanging over his head for the rest of his life. Maybe the contract's real aim was plain psychological torture.

✳

I had more important things to think about.

Our Sanctum release had generated a lot of industry buzz because it solved a huge problem. As I've mentioned, smart contracts run on blockchains. That means that a smart contract is transparent, visible to the whole world. It's like a restaurant with glass walls around the kitchen. You can see everything that goes on there, which makes the whole operation more trustworthy. For smart contracts, though, there's a downside to transparency: They can't keep secrets.

There's plenty you can safely do on a blockchain without secrets—breed digital cats, trade assets where privacy isn't at a premium, and so forth. But without secret data, there's a lot that people can't or don't want to do. As I've said, smart contract *code* needs to be public so everyone—or at least some watchdogs with technical savvy—can read it and make sure it does what it's advertised to do. That's the only way people can trust a smart contract to hold their money. But there's no reason that the *data* handled by a smart contract needs to be public. After all, do you really want your transactions and account balances visible to the whole world on a blockchain? As a friend once put it years ago, blockchains are like Twitter for your bank account.

Sanctum was a powerful new system that could keep secrets inside an oracle. It could hide all kinds of private information used by smart contracts, from account balances to birth dates to health records. It could also run pieces of smart contract code faster than the blockchain, but in a way that kept them public and tamperproof. Its design was such that a smart contract's code and data could be split between Sanctum and the contract's native blockchain. The result was an ideal combination of speed, transparency—and, most importantly, secrecy.

An especially powerful feature of Sanctum was that it could generate "attestations"—some people call them "proofs"—about properties of the secrets it protected.

For instance, suppose Sanctum was keeping your cryptocurrency account private but you wanted a loan from some bank and needed to show you had at least $5,000 in assets. Sanctum could check your account balance and generate an attestation stating that you've got at least $5,000 worth of cryptocurrency. You could show this attestation to the bank. Because Sanctum ran code in a tamperproof way, the bank could trust that the Sanctum attestation was correct: You really do have at least $5,000 in assets. Apart from this one bit of information, though, Sanctum would keep your account balance secret. The bank wouldn't learn whether you have only $5,000 or whether you in fact have $100,000 or, for that matter, $20 million.

Sanctum was a big deal. The financial industry held hundreds of trillions of dollars in assets, but only a tiny piece was in smart contracts, in large part because of the privacy problems. We at Adyton were on a quest to turn the financial industry on its head and get a large segment—tens of trillions of dollars—into smart contracts. Sanctum was the key.

We had a Sanctum release party that Saturday night. Clear the furniture away, and the Adyton office is perfect for festivities. High ceilings. Open floor space. Wonderful views of the Hudson River toward the west. I arrived late. When I walked in, I was hit by a blast wave of music. As I tried to get my bearings, Corinne collared me and dragged me behind the now closed door to the Bridge, on which someone had taped a DO NOT ENTER sign.

"She's here, but still ignoring me."

"Who?"

"The Priestess."

"Of course she's here. But why—" I squeezed my eyes shut and then stared at her. "You don't mean . . . ?"

"You think I'm not in her league, right?"

"But—but you don't even know for certain she's . . . And how many times do I have to say it? I'm not that kind of mentor. Not for relationships. Unless you want a tested algorithm for divorce and a sad, solitary—"

"Tell me, why do so many people hate her? I've read things online, but I don't know what to believe."

31

"No. I can't do this."

"Please. Please. Please." She grabbed my arm and gave me a shelter-puppy look.

"No." I coaxed off her hand and tattooed forearm and swiveled toward the door.

"Forget it, then," Corinne said. "No love. Let's talk death." I turned back toward her. "I looked at the rogue contract." I'd mentioned it to her the day before. Told her how I'd failed to hack the thing.

"And?"

"It's strange code. Did you notice? High gloss. Someone spent a lot of time on it. Someone savvy. And there was Greek in it."

"I know. But what did you turn up?"

"Same as you. Nada. I couldn't find any bugs, let alone exploits. None of the obvious things. No reentrancy problems, access-control issues, or bad delegatecalls. And none of the less obvious things either. Transaction ordering, gas depletion. Nothing." Given the sophistication of the contract, there were some bugs we knew to hunt for that only first-rate devs could avoid. Even scanning tools wouldn't pick them up.

"Too bad." Again the puppy look. I hesitated, but what the heck. "OK. The Priestess. Certain people . . . certain people believe that in her position, she would have known that Cambridge Analytica was siphoning off Facebook data way back in 2016. But she didn't act. They blame her for Trump getting elected. That's it. Some say she started Adyton to redeem herself for propelling the world into the age of lies."

"And you?"

"It would be hypocritical to vilify her based on fake news, wouldn't it?"

＊

I got a glass of water from the bar, with a twist of lemon, which is alkalinizing and good for the digestion. I stood alone, sipping it, savoring the crowd that had come to celebrate our work.

In moments of triumph, I often experience what feels like a welling up of superhuman physical strength, as though I'm watching a superhero movie. That evening, though, I had a Greek god on the brain. Energized by the heavy bass of the music—he is, after all, the god of music—I imagined what it would be like to be Apollo himself. To feel my limbs thrum with Olympian power. To know that I could unleash a hail of swift and unerring arrows and fell an army of heroes. To possess vision so intense that it could pierce the mantle of mortal time and bore into a future that—

My vision didn't bore very far through the mantle of mortal time. The Shirt appeared beside me.

"Great job with Sanctum," Lukas said glumly. He seemed to have gotten over his coronary troubles. "Look at all these people."

We stood for a moment, surveying the room. There were clusters of devs from blockchain projects, prominent technologists, strategists from large tech firms, venture capitalists, economists, journalists, cryptocurrency traders, faculty members, graduate students. They were all enjoying themselves.

"I don't get all the technical details of what you did. I leave those to you," Lukas said. "But we're building something good, something they want."

A few partygoers came up to congratulate me. Some were decentralization purists, people leery of the insidious ways in which power can become concentrated in blockchain systems and erode the openness and egalitarianism that's the whole point of the exercise. It's not uncommon for such purists to reject what's called trusted hardware, the key technology that secures Sanctum. They'd rather place their faith in cryptography, with its mathematical foundations, than in the trusted hardware we were using for Sanctum. A few big tech companies had made that trusted hardware a standard part of servers in the cloud. You had to have a certain amount of faith that those companies had gotten things right and not planted any back doors—and that the trusted hardware wasn't vulnerable to hacking. Not everyone had that faith, so I understood the point of view of the in-cryptography-we-trust camp. But security is all relative, and I'd devised a special feature, a trick that I hoped would change at least some people's minds.

Vitalik Buterin, who was one of these people, wandered over to talk with me. He's the wunderkind creator of Ethereum, which is the most important cryptocurrency after Bitcoin and far more interesting. He's also one of the most popular people in the blockchain world, a star even among other luminary technology creators. You'd expect a universal obsession with money and tech in our community, but its greatest innovators could pass as textbook philosophers. Satoshi Nakamoto appears to have turned her, his, or their back on Elon Musk–level fame and a million Bitcoin, a fortune of dynastic proportions. Vitalik likewise stands apart from the rabble as a beacon of pure reason. He once destroyed most of a gift of seven billion dollars in cryptocurrency because he didn't want to be saddled with the power that kind of money comes with. In a field full of wacky ideas, I take his opinions seriously.

"Trusted hardware is useful, but it introduces assumptions some people are uncomfortable with," he told me in his distinctive voice, with its even pitch and humming overtone. His blue eyes flitted as we spoke. I looked at his famous unicorn-llama-ridden-by-a-cat-in-glasses T-shirt, which also features a rainbow and a squadron of UFOs. I've seen it a dozen times but haven't yet deciphered it. "Can you explain what you did?"

"It's a simple idea," I said. "As you know, trusted hardware allows a program to run in a protected environment. The program is both private and protected against tampering."

"If the hardware hasn't been broken by an attacker."

"Right. Now suppose that a program is run on two machines. The identical, deterministic program with identical data on both machines. On one machine, though, the hardware *has* been hacked, and on the other it hasn't. In that case, the two programs may perform the same computation but disagree on the resulting output."

"Let me see." He plunged into deep thought for a few milliseconds. "But two truth-telling programs can't contradict each other. So if they do disagree, you know for certain that the hardware was hacked on one of them. You don't know *which* of them was hacked, but you know one of them was."

"Exactly."

"Good idea," he said, "although it doesn't reinforce privacy directly . . ."

Vitalik has a finger in every pie, so I asked him about Viganò's rogue contract. He'd posted an interesting idea online, what he called a neutralization contract. It would pay a reward to anyone who managed to hack and disable the rogue contract. A kind of anti-rogue-contract contract. As far as he knew, no one had launched one yet.

Late in the evening, while I was chatting with some PhD students from Cornell Tech, I felt a gentle hand on my arm. The Priestess.

I've counted four distinct ways in which the Priestess intimidates me. (Corrine has rarefied tastes.) Number one, there's the British accent that lends such richness to her superfast, super-articulate patter. Two, she's been top brass at several big tech companies. Three, she's about my age, but fit and attractive. And finally, she's my boss. Not really my boss, but still my boss. I leave aside the understated haute couture clothes and the other ways she exudes wealth and breeding. ("Breeding." Who uses that word these days? Those who've met the Priestess.) Oh, and her mother was a dame, knighted for services to literature, I think. That we don't see her more than a few times a month at Adyton, where she of course has the sole fully private office, also adds to the mythological allure that wreathes around her. Hence her nickname: the Priestess.

"You've been in the office very late," she said.

"Who told you?"

"I worry about you. You're on the path to a solitary and nihilistic future. Some unpleasant drama is bound to ensue."

"I'm here late because I believe in what we're doing." I'm always a blithering idiot in her presence.

"That's the problem."

"Some boss you are."

"Were I your boss in anything more than name, I'd send you to a beach in Santorini for a month."

"Santorini? Why . . ." My eyes widened. "Why Greece?"

We were interrupted before she could answer. A tall, older man had appeared, trim and tan like an outdoorsman, with pale skin peeking out from the deep lines in his face. He wore a blazer of indeterminate, pinkish hue. With a chivalrous smile stretched just a quarter of an inch too wide, he handed the Priestess a plate of fruit. "I hope I chose to your liking."

"Let me introduce you to Professor Hévin," the Priestess said. "He used to advise my previous company."

"Call me Alexis," he said, still smiling as he shook my hand. "I'm in the States this month visiting academic colleagues. I've been learning about Sanctum. Most instructive. It's a great pleasure to meet you. I've known you by reputation, of course, and I've read your blog posts with delight for years. I've many questions of course if you would be so good as to *indulge* me." He wasn't a native English speaker, but his dramatic inflection made it hard to place his accent.

"I'm flattered," I said.

"You mention on your blog that you often work seven days a week, but I don't wish to *impose* upon you this evening."

"Not at all."

"Perhaps you're acquainted with my early work on machine learning," he continued, his voice dramatized for his intended audience, the Priestess. "Or more likely, my recent research on smart contracts."

I guess I was supposed to reciprocate. Someone with social graces might have. But I found his overdone friendliness to be off-putting. And I really had no idea who he was.

"I'm afraid not."

"Smart contract security. The same domain as you." His facial muscles were still propping up a smile.

"Sorry, Professor. I know a lot of people, but not you."

"Ah. A chemically pure developer."

"Meaning?"

"You don't read academic papers," he said. The Priestess's eyes widened as she choked quietly on a piece of fruit.

"I don't, huh?"

"To be fair, perhaps not those that must be *procured* with great trouble from a server across an ocean."

"That's right. I'm practically illiterate. I didn't finish my PhD." I almost added "because of people like you," but the silent, angry squint that replaced his smile told me I didn't have to.

✳

After the party, I sat on the Bridge and whipped up a smart contract implementing Vitalik's neutralization idea. I put thousands of dollars of my own cryptocurrency into it. If someone somewhere could do what Corinne and I couldn't, kudos to her or him—plus ten Ether, the cryptocurrency in Ethereum. I posted an anonymous note on Reddit under the name `assassin_samaratan`, pretending to have discovered the new neutralization contract. I upvoted the post with puppet accounts from my stash, fake users who'd boost the post's popularity. My neutralization contract might or might not work, but it was as far as I was willing to go. I dropped a note to Corinne about it.

I'm pretty careful about opsec. That's operational security, the steps you take to prevent adversaries from learning your secrets. I was sure I hadn't revealed my IP address—the internet coordinates of my computer—or any traceable cryptocurrency addresses or anything else that could be linked to me. I was sure I'd covered my tracks.

When I got home at two in the morning, I stopped by the front desk. I hadn't been expecting anything, but got email notification from my building at the beginning of the party saying there was a package waiting for me.

"Package? There's no package for you," teased Jazzelle, the night concierge—my favorite—now sporting dreadlocks. She morphs weekly.

"I'll just tell the management you lost it," I said, keeping up our usual banter.

"Oh, wait." She disappeared into the back room. "Here's a small one. Another brooch? Who's it for?" She held it in the air.

Attached was the customs form that had tipped her off about what was in the package. I'd forgotten about the Roman brooch I'd purchased in an online auction. One from my grandfather's dispersed collection.

"Not your style," I said. "It's for ancient Roman men, not stylish young women."

"The one you showed me last time was pretty," she said, handing me the package. "I liked the green stuff it had going on."

"If you like, I can show . . ." She had already turned to a woman in a fancy dress standing beside me. Even at two in the morning, Manhattanites really want their packages.

Back in my apartment I unwrapped the package and removed the small brooch it contained. The brooch was shaped like a fly, with traces of red and blue enamel, and was mounted on a white stand. I placed it in the glass-fronted mission bookcase where I keep my rescued antiquities, a couple of dozen Greek and Roman brooches from my grandfather's collection.

After my grandfather sold his lucrative candy business and went into retirement, he turned his ancient-brooch collection—perhaps the largest private one in the UK—into a full-time occupation. He hand-sketched every one of his thousands of specimens to bring out their distinctive details. He mounted them on stands that he made himself, little angular slabs of wood coated with glossy white paper, annotated with typewritten text. He published his sketches with accompanying scholarly descriptions in books with delightfully dry titles like *Ancient Brooches, A Second Collection*. With their pages of rows of brooches organized by type and arranged to show small changes in form over time, they looked like zoological treatises on the evolution of plankton.

When my grandfather could no longer hold a pencil steady, my uncle stepped in with his usual unsentimental efficiency. He sold off the collection and moved my grandfather into a nursing home. It was around that time that I spent a year abroad at Oxford, and I went down to Bournemouth every couple of weeks or so to see my grandfather. I asked the Ashmolean Museum at Oxford, to which he'd been a big donor of artifacts and money, if they could somehow employ him on occasion as a volunteer. He was so lonely.

They refused. He didn't have the right credentials. That was my first exposure to the Mariana Trench depths of academic snobbery.

Whenever one of his brooches comes up for auction, I buy it if I can. Reconstituting his collection brings him back to me in a small way. Pride of place in my collection belongs to the one brooch that isn't in the bookcase. Most of my brooches are bronze, and they have acquired a green or brown patina over the centuries. This particular brooch, though, is a piece of metal sunshine. It's bronze, but was dredged up from a river in Greece, cleansed of black crust and burnished shiny gold. It's shaped like a bow, with a hinged pin where the bowstring would be. The brooch is large— about three inches long—and the pin like a tiny stiletto. A dolphin glides over the back.

The brooch was calling out to me, my grandfather said when he presented me with it, the only piece in his collection he ever gave away. He removed it from its stand and told me the story of its period in history. He spoke of events and historical figures with such familiarity that it was as though he were reminiscing about his childhood.

Greece had been conquered by Rome. Rome was at that time the center of the world, but the Republic was collapsing. Julius Caesar, one of the greatest generals in the history of the world ("embarrassed he was balding, tried everything from comb-overs to sporting a wreath") seized power, becoming dictator for life. Months later, on the Ides of March, he was assassinated, stabbed twenty-three times by champions of liberty fighting to restore the Republic. Sadly, in vain. ("Marc Anthony displayed a bloodied wax statue of Caesar in the Forum during the funeral. Drove the rabble to burn down the Senate building and scare away the liberators, Brutus and Cassius. Caesar's partisans hunted them down in northern Greece, and poof! There went the Republic.")

I keep the gold-glinting dolphin brooch pinned to the inside of my jacket. It's a reminder that I am fighting against the dictatorial forces of a centralized internet and financial system. Probably in vain.

＊

After the mad, round-the-clock scramble to finish my part of Sanctum, I had sleep to catch up on. I was still in a catatonic state on Monday morning, in bed with my phone in do-not-disturb mode until ten. At a quarter past, the ringer punched through a warm, gauzy dream.

"You should come to our office." No greeting. Diane was breathless.

I yawned. "It would be pointless, Diane."

"I have been trying to reach you. Did I—did I wake you?"

"Yes."

"So you don't know yet. They created a new rogue contract. It has seven targets. With large bounties. $700,000. And you—"

"Did nothing to stop them?"

"—are one of the targets."

It took two minutes online to see that the rogue contract was already the talk of Reddit. Stunningly, I was too. Viganò had "blasphemed against" Apollo, according to the message in the original contract. It was hard to cut through the noise online, but I learned that the new contract bore a message saying I'd committed an "act of impiety" against the god. I also learned that the contract was running in Sanctum.

Oddly, my first thought wasn't fear of impending death. It wasn't the question "why me?" My first thought, and it infuriated me, was that mere days after its release, the bastards were using Sanctum. That meant I'd help forge the arrow destined to kill me. Sanctum would conceal if and when an assassin registered a calling card. No warning. Just Apollo's shaft through my crumpled body.

My second thought was that this was also going to be awfully bad for Lukas's heart.

SIX

As the subway car thundered down to the FBI's field office in lower Manhattan, my mind raced. The assassin's calling card. The key word or words the assassin registered secretly with the contract and revealed after the killing to claim the bounty. . . . What would the calling card be?

Subway? None of the people sitting on the subway car mesmerized by their phones looked like an assassin. Which meant everyone looked like a skilled undercover assassin. So maybe I'd be murdered on the subway. Calling card = *subway*?

My destiny was a problem in game theory. If multiple people submitted the same correct calling card to the rogue contract, they split the reward. Suppose people thought a real assassin would choose an obvious calling card like *subway*. Then opportunists might try to cash in by making guesses, submitting their own *subway* calling cards. To avoid sharing the payout with these cheaters, a real assassin might therefore instead plan my murder around an exotic, hard-to-guess calling card. Calling card = *bomb + subway + robot*. Or calling card = *falling refrigerator + penthouse*. Or maybe calling card = *garrote + piano wire + ballerina*.

Planning a murder with such exotic specifics would be hard, though. And then suppose everyone knew that a real assassin would choose an exotic calling card. Then no opportunist would waste money and submit the calling card *subway*. So a real assassin could in fact submit *subway* as a calling card and not worry about splitting the reward. A vague term like *subway* would give the assassin a lot of leeway in planning. Therefore, calling card = *subway*. But no, because if everyone expected the assassin to choose an obvious calling card . . .

Diane had insisted there was no immediate danger, which was why I took the subway to begin with. Maybe she and her friends at the FBI understood game theory better than I did.

✳

Up on the twenty-third floor of the FBI's offices, Diane led me through a warren of desks, chairs with blue FBI windbreakers hanging on them, fluorescent lights, large wall-mounted screens, and cheap carpeting. The view there was magnificent. On one side of the building were the mono-liths of the Financial District, thrusting skyward, mounting the arrogant challenge that gave rise to my life's work. Diane took me to her office, which looked out over a swath of Tribeca. Nearby loomed a windowless skyscraper, once a telephone exchange, now said to be a National Security Agency listening post. Behind it was the ultra-tall, ultrachic Jenga build-ing, a reckless stack of slip-sliding floors. Beyond were the Hudson River and the shore of New Jersey, yearning toward, and growing into, a shabby knockoff of dense, bristling Manhattan, the true center of the world. With that panorama and in the heart of that bustling office, one sensed the long arm of the Bureau. It would have comforted some people.

I slumped in a chair.

"I haven't changed my mind," I said. "I'm still not hacking any oracles."

Diane opened a laptop. "Our cyber people have performed a prelimi-nary analysis of the contract. There will be seven targets. Every twenty-one days—that's three weeks—a new target's name is revealed. In theory, the contract names the first target. Then, three weeks later, it activates the bounty on that person's head and reveals the next target's name. After another three weeks, it activates the bounty on that person's head and names the next target, and so forth—in a chain. But the old contract on Prof. Viganò that activated ten days ago apparently eats into the timeline of this new contract. In the new contract, the bounty on Prof. Viganò's head is already activated, and you've already been named. So unfortu-nately, you don't have three weeks for the bounty on your head to acti-vate. It activates next Friday. You have only eleven days." The threat for me wasn't immediate, just imminent.

"I'm a coward, but a stubborn coward," I insisted.

"*Il n'y a que les imbéciles qui ne changent pas d'avis,*" Diane replied.

"I only caught the word 'imbecile.'"

"That was the important part. It means something like 'fool' in English. Only fools don't change their minds. Either you need to change yours or I must change mine. Or both." More game theory. "I understand that you won't tamper with the oracle. But you can still help us learn why you were targeted and who these people are."

"The FBI will protect me?"

"If we work together, you will protect yourself."

"Even if we catch them, the contracts will still be there. I'll be a target until someone collects, at which point I'll be dead."

"They have an off switch in the contract this time," Diane said. "I don't understand how it works, but—"

"Diane, why Apollo? Why this insane business about Apollo?" I found myself leaning forward, my hands turned up toward my face and tensed into talons.

Diane plugged in her laptop, connecting it to a monitor on her desk.

"You have not had time to look at the smart contract yet, I assume." I shook my head. "*This* was in it." A slide appeared on her monitor with the words:

© *700th Olympiad* The Delphians.

"A copyright notice?" I asked. "In the rogue contract?" Diane nodded. "Is this a joke? What's it supposed to mean?"

"The date I can explain. The ancient Greeks calculated dates in terms of the Olympic games. The first games were traditionally dated to the summer of 776 BC. They happened every four years. If you do the math, the 700th Olympiad ended back in 2025."

"2025? I don't understand how they could have started work on it then. We didn't even have the oracle infrastructure to support a contract like this." Diane shrugged. "OK, then who are 'The Delphians'? People from Delphi?"

"That's one meaning. But more generally, 'Delphian' means having to do with Delphi or its oracle."

"So this copyright notice explains nothing about who created the contract or why."

"Maybe something." She flipped through her deck to another slide. "Target number one, Prof. Viganò." The photo was like the one I'd seen of him online. A man in his sixties, bald, heavy, with a white, fan-shaped beard, stained with nicotine around the mouth. Tired wrinkles around intense, stubborn eyes. What hadn't been visible in his headshot online was the electric wheelchair. "I've been using him as a source for years," Diane explained.

"A source? For what? That's why you're interested in the rogue contract?"

"That is why I'm leading our effort to stop it."

"I still think we should fake his death. It would buy time."

"Look at that face." She shook her head. "He's a fearless old goat. He won't let us intervene." So Viganò was uncooperative. That explained why she was eager to stop the oracle. "And we can't fake every target's death or—"

"Exactly what was he a source for?"

"He was helping with cases involving antiquities smuggling."

"Antiquities smuggling? Does that still happen? I thought museums and collectors avoid looted artifacts these days. I keep reading about artworks getting repatriated. Isn't everyone careful about checking that pieces are legit?"

"Of course they are careful," she said, "to make sure that falsified provenances are convincing. It's much better than it was, but it is still a dirty business. Many people have a romantic idea of antiquities smugglers—and their buyers—as harmless art lovers. But when they pillage a tomb, they destroy archaeological context, historical and scientific value. I don't know whether it makes me mainly sad or angry. After narcotics and arms trafficking, smuggling antiquities is the biggest form of international crime. Billions of dollars a year. It's much harder to prosecute than narc—"

"So this is all about smugglers trying to snuff out a source."

"There's another, deeper layer to the story. Are you ready to hear it?"

"Ready?"

"Calm enough?" I'd been interrupting her. I leaned back from the table and nodded. She did a web search and showed me a painting. A woman in a red, hooded garment, perched on a tall, three-legged seat over a crack in the earth through which rose curling smoke.

"Sources from antiquity said that the priestess at Delphi inhaled mysterious vapors from a chasm when she entered a prophetic trance."

I smiled for the first time that day.

"Why are you smiling?"

"One of our company's founders is nicknamed the Priestess. I imagined her inhaling Chanel No. 5—no, some posher perfume I've never heard of, maybe Chanel No. 7—before composing one of her mysterious emails to the company."

Diane huffed dismissively. "In the late nineteenth century, archaeologists from France located the temple of Apollo at Delphi. It was a sensational find. And even more sensational was what they found below the temple. Possibly the most mysterious place in the ancient world. The *adyton*, the holy of holies, the inner chamber where the priestesses delivered prophecies."

"Adyton," I murmured. "That's the name of my company. I only vaguely knew what it meant . . ."

"But my compatriots, the French, were disappointed. They found no chasm in the adyton. And no volcanic activity, which they thought would be needed to produce vapors from underground. They concluded that the Greek and Roman texts were wrong. There were no vapors. Delphi was a pious fraud. Maybe the priests fabricated the priestesses' prophecies to cheat people who consulted the oracle. For years, this was the dominant view."

"So Delphi just involved the usual religious hocus-pocus."

"No," she said. "They were wrong. For a century, archaeologists had it wrong. It is well known that Delphi is in a seismically active region. Earthquakes are still frequent there even today. But in the 1990s, an archaeologist, John Hale, and a geologist named Jelle de Boer made an astonishing discovery. They found that the temple at Delphi actually stands directly above the intersection of two geological fault lines. They theorized that geological features there caused hydrocarbon gases to be liberated in the adyton through fissures in the soil. The ancient Greek for 'chasm' can also be translated as a fissure, a crack in the ground, which the French team hadn't considered."

"So these two scientists found vapors coming through cracks in the ground?"

"Not in the present day. Not in the adyton. But chemical analysis of spring water at Delphi today shows traces of ethylene. That's a gas with a sweet smell that was used as an anesthetic many years ago. It's known to induce a trance."

"So you're saying the oracle at Delphi wasn't a fraud."

"The Greek and Roman texts preserved an accurate history at least. It's the geology of the region that made Delphi what it was. The priestess was inhaling vapors with the power to induce hallucinations."

"What's this got to do with Viganò?"

"Prof. Viganò is a specialist in classical and Hellenistic Greece and a scholar of Delphi. He opposes the ethylene theory. He says ethylene could not have accumulated in the concentrations needed to induce a trance. Also, he thinks that the ancient Greek—the word *chasma*—really meant a large crevice in the earth, which doesn't match what they found in the excavations. So he supports the old pious fraud theory: The oracle was nothing but theater and fabricated prophecies. While he's well respected for other work, most scholars dismiss his theories about Delphi. But his claims have received attention in the press."

"They can't be trying to kill him for that. That's crazy."

"We don't know who *they* are."

"You actually think these Delphians are worshippers of Apollo or something crazy like that?"

She bit her lower lip as she thought. Then she looked at me.

"How many colors are there in a rainbow?" she asked.

"What?"

"How many colors?"

"Seven. But what's—"

"You believe in the unseen, and the unseen is Apollo."

"You've lost me."

She laughed. "If you look at a rainbow and count—tak tak tak . . ." She counted the bands in an imaginary rainbow hovering above her laptop. ". . . you will find six colors. Most people don't see indigo. You *believe* there are seven because Newton said so. Newton said so because of the Pythagoreans. The Pythagoreans considered the number seven to be sacred because of its association with Apollo. Apollo's birthday was on the seventh of the month and there were seven strings in the lyre, which

Apollo invented. We still use scales with seven notes—do, ré, mi, fa, so, la, ti."

"But that's cultural residue, not worship."

"Cultural residue? No. These ideas were the philosophical seeds of our civilization. Do I think there could be worshippers of Apollo? Of course. I'd worship Apollo long before I'd join most sects of Christianity, although I'd rather worship a goddess, like his sister Artemis. What I want to know is why they are targeting you. Maybe as a caretaker for 'oracles,' you're like a digital version of a priest of Delphi." Then, in a subdued tone that reminded me of the way people had asked why my wife left me, Diane asked, "What was your act of impiety?"

I told her about my neutralization contract.

"Who knew you were involved?"

Only Corinne. Unless I was getting old and sloppy with my opsec.

✹

If you're looking to connect with old friends, estranged family members, enemies, and a gaggle of new acquaintances, it turns out that nothing beats a fat price on your head coupled with a newfangled technology like smart contracts. There were a dozen news articles about the new rogue contract that day on the heels of a *Forbes* piece, "Contract Killings Get Smart," and a *CoinDesk* article, "Greek God Swaps Thunderbolts for Smart Contracts." (Never mind that everyone knows thunderbolts were Zeus's business, not Apollo's.) Not much in these articles was superaccurate, but thanks to the copyright notice in the rogue contract, at least journalists could announce to the world an official name for the contract's creators: the Delphians.

Even my ex-wife read about the contract somewhere and showed something like concern. That's if I interpreted the subject line of her email ("Can I help?") the right way. I probably did, but I couldn't bear to read her email, so I deleted it.

Until there was an actual death, the press would treat the whole thing as a human-interest story, not as a landmark technological event. Some pundit told *Forbes* that there'd been assassination betting pools years earlier in a smart contract system called Augur, and they'd fizzled. But time had passed, I knew, and this was different. $700,000 in a cutting-edge, oracle-powered smart contract was far deadlier than what had come before.

I worried about professional assassins, but worried more that once the bounty on my head activated the next week, people would recognize me in public and some enterprising ignoramus, not understanding how calling cards work, would shove me under a bus. Idiots were suggesting as much in posts on various anonymous sites in the gutter of the internet. So I was glad that I don't have a distinctive face. I could be any middle-aged, middle height, pudgy, balding schlub, and the few photos of me online and videos of me giving talks showed a deceptively younger, fitter specimen. On the other hand, Diane had recognized me in Chelsea Market based on an online photo. So I decided to switch from contacts to glasses, which I didn't normally wear outside my apartment, and bought a baseball cap.

I'm terrified of little things. If I feel a stitch in my side, I'm sure it's terminal cancer of the colon or pancreas. If the cryptocurrency market, where I hold most of my money, plunges—for the fiftieth time, mind you—I'm convinced I'll soon be sharing scraps of discarded pizza with a rat in the subway. But true danger activates a different part of the brain. One summer at college, when my roommates were away, burglars smashed the glass by the front door to break into the house while I was sleeping. I tore out of my bedroom in my boxers, fire extinguisher in hand, howling and ready to clobber or freeze the intruders. They fled. I don't know what demonic force possessed me, but it left no room for fear.

My reaction to the rogue contract was similar, and it baffled me. At some level, I did feel terror, but it didn't paralyze me. I was determined to fight. The metaphorical hand tied behind my back—my moral refusal to attack the oracle network—somehow steeled me. The most unnerving part of the whole thing was having to do battle with forces beyond my understanding. Smart contracts and blockchain oracles I knew. The Delphians, whoever they might be, were another matter. We didn't know that their connection with the true Delphi was any more real than the Greek gods themselves were. But Diane had not dismissed the idea, and she had spoken of Delphi in tones bordering on religious awe. She had told me about mysterious vapors beneath the temple of Apollo giving rise to the oracle's prophecies. She had revealed to me the hidden imprint of the number seven, the sacred number of Apollo, in my own mind. No matter how hard I tried, I couldn't rid myself of the feeling that behind the appearance of Delphians, there were more things in heaven and earth than were dreamt of in my philosophy.

SEVEN
Delphi, Greece, fifty years later (355 BC)

Just before dusk, two ox-drawn carts lumber along the road. They are carrying dozens of amphoras, emptied of their grain and wine, ready for fresh cargo. One has a strange oval shape and is not of clay, but of white marble rubbed with dirt. They chose to hide it in plain sight. As the carts approach the gate, the lead driver tries to conceal his trembling. Still holding the reins, he buries his hands in his cloak.

The four soldiers on guard duty are short-tempered, weary of the occupation. They are Phocians, inhabitants from the region around Delphi. Their army has seized control of Apollo's sanctuary during yet another of Greece's never-ending wars. Under their hands now lies more gold than in all the rest of Greece, if not the whole world. But they have been forbidden to touch it.

When their leader Philomelus first seized the sanctuary a year ago, he announced that he would respect Delphi's sanctity. He refused to plunder its treasure, for fear of offending the god. His gesture of piety, however, meant little to the inhabitants of the city. He would have killed or enslaved the entire population had not a king of Sparta dissuaded him. He also threatened violence against the Pythia, forcing her to declare that "he could do what he pleased." He had her words inscribed on a stone tablet and placed on public view, as though they were a proclamation from the god himself.

To the soldiers of the Phocian army, the stone tablet does not signify the god's approval of Philomelus and his deeds. It reminds them of their own thwarted desires.

To the Delphians, it proclaims the Phocians' reign of terror.

✳

Many years ago, the Phocian occupation of Delphi would have been unthinkable. When part of the great Persian army of Xerxes marched to Delphi seeking plunder, the Delphians asked the oracle whether they should bury the sacred treasure. The god proclaimed that he would defend his own sanctuary. He unleashed an electrical storm upon the Persians and smote them with thunderbolts. He tore two peaks from Parnassus and sent them roaring down the mountainside to crush the enemy.

But in recent years, the oracle's powers have been waning. Since an earthquake destroyed half of the sanctuary twenty years ago, including the temple of Apollo itself, the omens have often been unfavorable, the god's voice faint. Now the Phocians have occupied Delphi for almost a year. It is rumored that other Greek cities are on the march against the Phocians. That Philomelus, despite his pronouncement when he first seized Delphi, now contemplates borrowing from the treasury. The priestesses have directed in secret that the most sacred objects be hidden.

It would be impossible to save the gold tripod atop the serpent column, the massive gold mixing bowl and lion of Croesus—any of the largest and richest offerings. Their obvious disappearance would visit savage punishment on the Delphians. But many sacred treasures could still be spirited away.

✳

The soldiers inspect the cart. They poke at the narrow-necked amphoras and peer inside. They rock one of them, but do not find the cloth-shrouded bundle stuck to the bottom with pitch and covered with clay dust. Nor do they notice the strange oval-shaped object made of marble. With bluff talk of Delphian wealth and a spear butt tapped menacingly against the wooden spoke of a wheel, they extract a piece of silver, one obol, from the driver—then another two.

The carts travel for hours, creeping in the dark, stopping, the drivers wary of unwanted followers and fearful of damaging their burden. They arrive at a small cavern hidden behind brush, thrust up from the underworld by the earthquake almost twenty years ago. It is redolent of the god's presence, sometimes emitting the same sweet smell as the adyton. There, the oldest Pythia awaits them with another priest.

A hidden spring is purling nearby. A nightingale warbles. Crickets sing an ecstatic paean to Apollo, the god of music.

They unload the amphoras and remove the small bundles within. They pry flat wooden cases from the undercarriage of the cart. They bury the most sacred objects from the great temple: the Omphalos and its woolen covering, the golden eagles, the god's lyre and dismantled armor. They have replaced these objects with replicas that are indistinguishable from the originals in the perpetual twilight of the adyton. Into two amphoras they consolidate scores of small gold sacred objects they have also smuggled out of the sanctuary. They bury these vessels in the cavern, the first and most important cache they will hide there.

"To move the Omphalos . . ." croons one of the priests. "It's as though the god has abandoned his temple."

The Pythia hears his voice catch in his throat.

"Not for many a year yet," she says. "But his presence wanes in these evil days. When I was young, his voice was clear, Delphi was in her glory, Sparta unbroken, Athens resurgent. Now we struggle to rebuild a sanctuary half in ruins, and Ares drives the Hellenes to their destruction. Soon barbarians from Macedon, posing as champions of Greece, will trample our ashes."

"How can we keep alive the memory of this place?" asks the other priest.

"As we tend and keep alive the eternal flame. It will be yet one more secret passed down among the Pythias." She clasps her hands. "But these holy objects will not return to the sanctuary in my lifetime or even yours. That future remains veiled even for me."

✳

The Phocians lose the battle of Neon to opposing Greeks. Philomelus avoids capture by jumping to his death from a cliff. His brother Onomarchus is elected supreme commander. Under his rule, the fiction of borrowing from the treasury gives way to naked looting, as the priestesses had feared.

The god makes one last attempt to save his sanctuary. When the Phocians try to seize the sacred treasures, Apollo shakes the earth, scattering the terrified soldiers. But their hunger for gold vanquishes even their awe of the god. The Phocians loot Delphi and melt down gold and silver worth ten thousand talents, the burden in silver of ten thousand men, the largest treasure in the world. Coins struck from their plunder pay for mercenaries to wage yet more war, grinding soldier against soldier, army against army, city against city, spreading dusty ruin across Greece. War does not save the Phocians. To punish their sacrilege, Philip of Macedon sweeps down from the north, crucifies Onomarchus, and crushes his successors. He becomes master of the exhausted remnants of Greece. He plants the seeds for his son, Alexander the Great, to conquer the world.

Thus does the desecrated gold of Delphi strip the cities of Greece of their freedom, plunging them into a fathomless night of thousands of years of bondage to conquerors, emperors, and kings.

PART II

As Apollo punished [the Satyr Marsyas], he cried,
"Ah-h-h! why are you now tearing me apart?
A flute has not the value of my life!"
Even as he shrieked in agony,
his living skin was ripped from his limbs,
till his whole body was a flaming wound,
with nerves and veins and viscera exposed.

—Ovid (trans. Brookes More), *Metamorphoses* (6.382)

EIGHT

"This is what smart contracts lead to," Special Agent Francis Walker said as we sat down. I guess I wasn't a victim in his mind, but a trouble-maker burned by playing with fire.

"Glad to serve as a warning to young children," I said.

He ran his tongue around the inside of his mouth, deciding what line to take with me.

Walker looked like he could be the heavy with the sawn-off shotgun. He was, in fact, the brains of the operation—the head of the FBI field office's Cyber Task Force. He had a shaved head and a blazer cut to show off his muscular bulk. He'll be a good test subject if anyone ever invents an experimental form of hand-reduction surgery. It surprised me when he pulled from an inside pocket not a revolver or brass knuckles, but a silver Rotring pencil. He spun this mechanical drafting pencil around his banana-sized fingers as we talked. It was hypnotic.

"Why did you publish your blog on rogue contracts way back when?" he asked, in his deep radio-announcer's voice.

"To warn the community," I said.

"So now you're a prophet. Great for your reputation."

"Now I'm a sacrificial goat. Terrible for my health."

"Mm-hmm."

"Come on. Are you suggesting that *I* created the rogue contract? Even if I had, I couldn't control it. I'd be putting a bounty on my own head. Why wouldn't I just target somebody else?"

He leaned back in his chair. The pencil kept spinning. The light glinted off the glossy dome of his head.

"We live in the age of advertising," he said. "More publicity is always good."

57

"At the cost of my life? Are you serious?"

"There's an off switch. You know that."

"Because Diane told me. I don't know how it works."

"Simple," Walker said. "The creators of the contract can trigger the off switch at any time. Once that happens, there's a wind-down period of twenty-eight days in which assassins can complete their work and make claims against any activated bounties. Afterward, the contract shuts down and refunds any unclaimed money to the contract creators."

This design made sense. The contract could be disarmed and unclaimed bounties would be refunded. But assassins wouldn't risk losing out while they already had plans in progress.

Walker—that's all I ever heard anyone call him, by the way—whipped out a small, immaculate, bright-orange notepad from another pocket. He wrote for a moment—perhaps just a page heading as he prepared to take notes. I couldn't remember the last time I'd seen an actual analog pencil in action.

"And what if a bounty hasn't yet activated?" I asked, wondering of course about the one on my head.

"Then that bounty just shuts down. No wind-down period."

"Can you tell me anything else?"

"One other detail," Walker said. "Before a bounty activates, the contract will accept outside bounty deposits."

"Great. So you're saying there's a short crowdfunding period to boost the contract's bounties?"

"Correct."

"Any other unfortunate discoveries?"

"Nothing useful. We've reviewed the code and understand the basic functionality. I'm working on this with the National Cyber Investigative Joint Task Force. I expect to know more soon. Can *you* tell *me* anything useful?"

"If the new contract is like the first one, it's solid code. Incredibly meticulous."

He nodded and made a note. "We can't spare a huge amount of resource for this. It's not a national security threat. Not yet. But I'm hoping the intel community will weigh in. They're interested. It may be a harbinger of things to come. You're going to help us."

A statement or an order? With Walker's deep, smooth voice, I couldn't tell.

"I'm not going to try to subvert the system, but I'd prefer to save my own skin and all that I've worked toward," I said.

"What's your role at Adyton?"

"I'm a developer."

"Yeah, and I work for the FBI," he said, crimping his mouth.

"OK. I lead the development of the Sanctum system. Do you know it?"

"I'm forced to know it now, aren't I? So you know the nuts and bolts of the infrastructure?"

"Yes. Why?"

"Who else does?"

"I don't understand what you're getting at. Whoever wrote the contract didn't need to know anything about the nuts and bolts of our system. We pride ourselves on clean and well-documented code and APIs."

"I'm sure you do, but who else works on the guts of the system?"

"I don't see how that's relevant."

"No?" He stopped spinning his pencil, thought for a moment, and stood. "For the record, I don't think you created the rogue contract. Too risky. We'll talk again and see where this goes."

"Am I supposed to work with you in some way?"

He tucked his pencil back into an inside breast pocket. Or maybe he had a little loop for it on a concealed gun holster.

"I'll see you later."

His deep voice made a simple goodbye sound like a rendezvous with destiny.

＊

I received email from Lukas offering Adyton's help—whatever I needed. I was sure people in the company were wrangling over what to do about the rogue contract. It might kill not just me, but the company's reputation. Sanctum was designed to prevent control by any one entity, especially Adyton. That was the project's strength and fundamental design goal: decentralization of power. I still believed this was the right way to build a system that would bring good to the world. And I held that conviction even when it might cost me my life.

If the community could get all the oracles supporting the rogue contract to agree to misreport or withhold data, the contract could be stopped. But this wouldn't happen. The oracle network was designed to prevent tampering. There were participants in the oracle network who would jump at the chance to advertise that they reported the truth come hell or high water. That was the whole point of the oracle systems, after all. Even if, miracle of miracles, the community could get everyone to agree to abandon the current version of Sanctum and switch to some new version—call it Sanctum v2—they'd have to figure out how to prevent the rogue contract from being relaunched in Sanctum v2. They'd have gained nothing.

The Delphians had been astute. They'd arranged to disclose targets one by one—a new one every three weeks—so only Viganò and I had been revealed at that point. They'd spent enough money and chosen targets with a profile just high enough to create a stir and raise their visibility—if that was in fact their goal. They'd avoided targets that might provoke a major backlash, however. No senators, presidents, famous actors, or pop idols.

I couldn't decide whether this whole rogue-contract business was in fact good or bad for Adyton. Lukas was surely having conniptions. But Walker was, in one sense, right. In today's world, all publicity is good publicity.

❋

After my conversation with Walker, I grabbed some food and headed back to Adyton.

Miss Manners probably hasn't written a column on what to say to a guy with a price on his head. Most of my coworkers, afraid of making a faux pas, pretended not to notice the dead man walking toward the Bridge. A few gave me their versions of pitying looks.

Corinne wasn't there, but her jacket was hanging over the back of her chair. I went around to the glassed-in conference rooms and stopped short. There she was, talking to a large suit, smooth head, and spinning aluminum pencil. I backtracked to my desk. Maybe the FBI were doing my work for me. Maybe.

She soon emerged onto the Bridge. She brought her hand to her mouth and stared for a moment, then walked over to me. "I'm so sorry. It's so . . . I don't know what to say."

"Show me your right arm."

"What?" She stepped back and drew her arm to her body.

"Your tattoo."

"Look, I know this must—"

"Show me," I said tonelessly.

She shot an anxious look past the Bridge entrance into the open-floor area, as though for help.

"You have a sun tattoo," I said.

"I have all kinds of tattoos."

"Apollo is the sun god."

"What? I'm Episcopalian, for Christ's sake. Oh, that didn't come out right. This is nuts. Here." She thrust out her arm and pulled up her cardigan sleeve. "It's not some Greek thing. I got it in fucking Queens." Her eyes widened. "But—but not in Astoria." Everyone knows there are a lot of Greeks in Astoria. "I mean . . ." On her arm was a sunburst tattoo, a dark green circle with wavy rays. She pursed her lips and her eyes bulged as she struggled not to put her foot in her mouth again.

"Who were you meeting with?"

"The feds. I'm not allowed to say anything about it. But they're talking to Lukas too."

"Did you tell anyone about the neutralization contract? Only you knew I wrote it. We were supposed to keep it that way."

"I— No one. Really, no one. I don't know how they found out. But it wasn't from me. I know what you're thinking, but I'm not a fucking Apollo cult member. This is crazy. I don't know how to prove it to you. Wait." She grabbed her laptop from her desk. She banged out a twenty-something-character password on the keyboard and tapped her thumb on the fingerprint reader—all in under a second. "Here, look if you want to."

"That won't help. Like you don't know any opsec? You don't use burner laptops?"

Her eyes glistened. "Look, maybe it wasn't even about the neutralization contract. Maybe the timing was just coincidence. Maybe it's because you wrote that old blog post on rogue smart contracts. Or maybe it's because you work at an oracle company. Greek oracles. Smart contract oracles. I don't get the connection, but maybe there is one. I don't know. How do I convince you I had nothing to do with it?"

She gave me a pleading look. I crossed my arms and let my head drop to my chest. We remained in silence for a while, long enough for me to cool off and start feeling embarrassed. Overcoming my Me Too qualms, I looked up at her and put a clumsy hand on her shoulder.

"I'm sorry, Corinne," I said. "It's all so unnatural. Maybe supernatural, with this Greek god stuff. I'm getting paranoid. I don't know who to trust."

She tilted her teary face back up at me. "I want to see you safe. I really do."

She knew how to make me feel like a cad.

"OK. Let's start again," I muttered. "Mentorship lesson one. Don't piss off Apollo."

✳

To my surprise, Lukas looked more cheerful than usual. Like his dog had vomited on him that morning, but only on his pants and not the precious shirt. Maybe he was happy the price was on somebody else's head.

"I'm so sorry about this. We're trying to figure out what to do," he said. I was mute. "Look, the reality is that my hands are tied. You know that."

"I know."

"And this isn't great for the company either."

"Unclear."

"It isn't. The Priestess and I agreed that we'll do everything we can for you. We're going to launch this thing called a neutralization contract. We're going to put a million dollars into it. Vitalik Buterin's idea. It—"

"Very generous. I know what it is."

"And we'll get you a bodyguard."

"Thanks, but my building doesn't allow pets over fifty pounds."

"That's very funny," he said earnestly. "I'm glad you still have a sense of humor. Give it serious thought. Or you could hide in a cabin in the woods somewhere, you know. Do you have any other ideas?"

"All I need for now is a couple of weeks' leave."

"Of course. It activates next week. Take all the time you need."

"How did you know?"

"When it activates? Let's say we had some visitors today. But it's not a secret. People just need to look at the contract code."

"I hope you didn't offer the visitors access to anything other than the coffee machine." His usual deadpan face went even more deadpan.

"You know I wouldn't do that."

"Can you spare some of Corinne's time if I need it?" I asked.

"Of course, of course," he said, his voice rising half an octave.

✻

Diane, like me, had noticed the Delphi exhibition at the gallery in midtown. The connection to our Delphians was tenuous. For Diane, though, visiting a gallery meant swapping the abstractions of cyberspace for solid ceramics, marble, and metal. I think she invited me along not for my advice, but to give me something to do, something to fend off the mental birds of prey gnawing at the condemned man's innards. There's a Greek myth about that somewhere.

I run in such frantic little circles—work, home, work, home—with videoconferences for remote collaboration—that before that morning, I hadn't taken the subway in months. Perhaps that's why I ended up boarding the wrong train. I realized my mistake at the next station just in time to dart through the train doors as they were closing. When at last I disembarked from the correct train and exited the subway, I had to walk almost ten blocks to the gallery. I was a quarter of an hour late. Diane was already there, window-shopping at the Helios Ancient Art Gallery.

Out of breath, I took up position beside her and gazed at the window. Her face and black-and-orange scarf, reflected by the glass, were superimposed over a large vase behind the window. On the vase, an archaic black-figured man hauled a kind of three-legged piece of furniture across a blank orange field.

"Sorry I'm late."

She continued looking into the window—avoiding my gaze out of annoyance, I figured. I bit my lip for a few silent seconds.

"I've been studying this vase with Apollo and the tripod," she said. "I don't think it's been robbed intact from a tomb. Look at the cracks."

It was reassembled from shards. Missing pieces were colored in.

"Cracks mean it wasn't robbed?"

"The cracks speak to you. Smugglers break intact contraband objects to make them easy to hide when they transport them. But they try to minimize damage to the value of the piece. This is a conservative restoration. The joins are visible and lacunae are toned, but not filled with imagery. You can see a join over his face and a missing foot. Those aren't breaks made by a smuggler. They're too obvious."

"Which tells us what?"

She turned toward me. "Interesting exhibition, but I don't see any reason to kill people for it."

The gallery itself wasn't large. Just two rooms, but chockablock with glass cases containing coins, vases, statues, jewelry, terra-cottas, helmets, swords, and spearheads. No one greeted us, so we walked over to the corner by the front window where the objects in the Delphi exhibition were displayed. We drifted apart. I took the amateur tour, Diane the professional one.

The glint of precious metal drew me to a glass case of coins. Most of them were silver, a few gold. They were accompanied by explanatory labels and photos of magnified details, most showing Apollo in various guises. The obverse of one coin bore his head, long-haired like Washington on the US quarter, but with a more abundant coif of feminine locks. Others had full-length portraits of the god on the reverse. One had him perched, painfully nude, on the cone of the Omphalos, clutching an arrow in his outstretched right hand. It was like the coin on my desk, but much crisper. You could even make out his six-pack. On another, he leaned against a column encircled by a corkscrew—actually a python, as the print label explained. This was Apollo as patron of the Pythian Games, his version of the Olympic Games.

God of the Sun, light, music, truth, prophecy, disease, and healing, and patron of countless cities, Apollo appeared on coinage throughout the ancient world. The glass case also contained a coin from a city in northern Greece with the god's lyre on the reverse. I counted the strings. Seven. *Doe, a deer, a female deer. Ray, a drop of golden sun . . .*

To me, though, the most beautiful object in the exhibition was a large vase whose ornate handles, conical lid, and dense riot of white, orange, and red figures didn't match my notions of the austerity of Greek art. A man clung to a large, rounded cone, clearly the Omphalos, his body slanted, leg hanging in the air like he'd lunged for home base in a game of tag. A white-haired woman, hands in the air, fled a wreathed figure in a panther skin, who warded her off with an outstretched palm. Another woman gazed into the distance, one hand on her brow, the other holding a pair of spears with familiar ease, her short dress blown back against her body, a pair of hounds at her feet. According to the label, the vase depicted Orestes seeking refuge at Delphi. The wreathed figure was Apollo.

As I tried to remember who Orestes was—or, for that matter, if I'd ever known who Orestes was—Diane materialized at my side.

"Ooh la la. Apulian," she said.

"Meaning what?"

"The best vases were from Attica. Athens. This one is from Apulia, in southern Italy. They created very ornate vases in very bad taste."

"Flamboyant, certainly," said a man behind us. "I suppose you prefer the spare artistic idiom of the Attic style?"

His rotund belly was shaped like the vases around us. His hair, in the spare artistic idiom of the Attic style, consisted of a few brown wisps, probably dyed, on a round head. He had merry little brown eyes.

"I suppose I do," Diane said with the obliging laughter I was coming to recognize as part of her standard repertoire. A way of setting strangers at ease. Or maybe just herself.

"Over here we have a beautiful Attic *phiale*." He gestured with both arms, comically short beside his belly. Using them to steer, he glided over to another case. He gestured toward a shallow dish with a knob inside in the center. "It's a libation vessel of the type held by the Pythia, a priestess of Apollo at Delphi, when she delivered her prophecies. And—"

"Why did you decide to hold this exhibition?" I asked. Diane shot me a look of annoyance.

"On Delphi? Why, Delphi was of enormous importance in the ancient world." His arms fell to his sides. He furrowed his brow. "A kind of Vatican of its day. More than that. In its heyday, Greek cities consulted the oracle about every important decision they made. Foreign states did too. It was a source of truth and wisdom for the whole Mediterranean." He looked over the oddly assorted pair of visitors standing before him. An elegant woman in a well-cut forest-green skirt and jacket, accessorized with a black and orange silk scarf. An ungainly guy in T-shirt, frayed jeans, and an olive-drab jacket. I think the silk scarf tipped the scales in our favor. "Shall I take this piece out of the case for you?"

"Thank you," said Diane. "We're still looking."

"My name is Max Venner. I'm the director of the gallery. If you need me, I'm at your service," he said, spreading his arms like a theatrical impresario before disappearing.

"I want to question him in private," Diane said.

We worked our way back through the gallery, glancing into cases as we passed them. Diane paused in front of a case of gold jewelry, window-shopping. It wasn't the kind of thing you buy on an FBI salary. I looked around and did a double take. Across the room was a brooch mounted on a white stand.

"Oh!" I made a beeline for it. It was one of my grandfather's. Given how big his collection had been, his brooches had a way of popping up in unexpected places. "Do you mind?" I asked Diane when she caught up with me. "I'm going to buy this. I need to."

"I didn't know that you have an interest in ancient art." She put her hands on her hips and peered at me through those bulletproof-glass lenses of hers. "Are you a collector?"

"I know next to nothing, but I collect this one thing."

Her smile suggested that I'd just evolved in her mind from four legs to two. "We probably shouldn't . . ." she said. But she saw it was pointless to try to stop me. "Unless you plan to pay cash, you should let me buy it and repay me. You don't want to reveal your name on your credit card." In my enthusiasm, I hadn't thought of that. And they say I'm in cybersecurity.

We found Venner all the way in the back of the gallery, in an office, standing by a desk and talking into a mobile phone. We waited by the open doorway. Behind him was a woman on a laptop. Venner raised a finger in our direction. "No," he said into the phone. "As I told you, he was right here, and I didn't *need* to ask him for ID. Did you read the name? It was Ralph Fiennes. The actor. Ralph Fiennes. It's spelled like Ralph, but it's pronounced *Raaaf*." He lowered the phone and made a face at it. "Absurd problem with a credit card charge," he said. "I'll be with you in a minute."

A few minutes later, Venner came out and unlocked the case with the brooch for me. I was tempted to boast about my grandfather. I remembered Diane's warning, though, and I do share my grandfather's last name. I gingerly removed the piece from the case and asked if there were other brooches from the same collection, but there was just the one. I was embarrassed about buying possibly the cheapest thing in the whole gallery. More embarrassing was the realization, when we read the label, that it was a stylized phallus. A flat little bronze thing, dark green with colored enamel highlighting the—never mind. From Roman Gaul, meaning Diane's native country no less.

We returned to Venner's office.

While Venner filled in a bill of sale on a laptop, Diane asked him, "Have you ever had an exhibition on Delphi before?"

"No. This is our first."

Diane laughed. "So why now?"

"It was long overdue." Venner looked up at her, an earnest crinkle above his eyes. "Delphi is a topic of perennial interest and offers an excellent opportunity to invest in objects of enduring interest and value."

"Our interest is a little different," she said. She reached into her purse and flashed her FBI badge. "Can we speak in private?"

"Natalie," Venner called to the woman in the back of the office. "Could you please give us a few minutes?"

Natalie left, and Diane sat across the desk from Venner. "Were you the one who decided to hold this exhibition or did someone suggest it to you?"

Venner pursed his lips. "Why does it matter? Surely holding an exhibition on Delphi isn't a crime?"

Diane laughed. "Of course not."

"All of our pieces are ethically sourced and carefully provenanced."

"That is very important to me personally," Diane said, "but is not why I'm here."

"I'll be happy to provide documentation." Venner gestured toward his laptop.

"Not necessary. There are three other galleries and museums in the United States holding exhibitions on Delphi now too. Why do you think that is?"

"As I said, it's a popular topic."

"Yes, but why now? Why is it suddenly so popular?" She leaned forward, chin on her hands, signaling earnest interest.

"I can't say what motivated others to stage exhibitions on Delphi."

"What were your reasons?"

"Delphi was of enormous importance in the ancient world. As I said, it was in a sense the Vatican of its day . . ."

Things were clearly heading toward an impasse. I drifted toward the back of the room. Something had caught my attention. Something that didn't belong there . . .

Five minutes later, Diane's unproductive verbal fencing with Venner was still underway. I interrupted. "If that documentation on your business is still on offer, I don't suppose you'll be willing to share your Bitcoin addresses?" Tucked away in a pile of items on his assistant's desk, I'd spotted the retail box for a cryptocurrency wallet. While Diane and Venner had been distracted, I'd popped it open.

"What do you mean?"

"You accept payment in cryptocurrency?" I pointed at the box.

"No. Why— That belongs to my assistant. I'm not terribly computer literate."

I picked up the box and made a show of photographing the barcode. Diane's hand floated up, as though to stop me—but too late.

"Thank you. This is all we'll need to trace the transactions," I said.

Venner stood, his eyes no longer twinkling.

"The Bureau will be in touch, Mr. Venner," I said gravely, tamping down my puckish mirth. Diane looked displeased. I guess only real FBI agents are licensed to talk like they're in TV police procedurals.

"I see," Venner said, lowering himself into his chair again. "I see." Meaning he didn't see, because, as I'd been hoping, he had no clue about cryptocurrency. "There's nothing inappropriate in our decision to hold the exhibition," he continued. "But there's the matter of client confidentiality. If I don't divulge a name, I don't see why I can't extend you the courtesy of explaining."

Venner now admitted that he'd been paid to stage the Delphi exhibition by "a serious collector" he'd never met in person. All contact had been by email. The collector had purchased a few pricey antiquities to be shipped to Europe. He insisted on using cryptocurrency, of course, and encouraged the gallery to get a crypto wallet. He later offered $150,000 to fund the exhibition. It cost Venner nothing. For him, it was pure profit. The whole thing was dubious, but I guessed Venner was right: As long as he reported the transaction to the right federal authorities, it was hard to see anything criminal in it. He agreed to cooperate by providing us soon with documentation and cryptocurrency addresses (just to save us trouble of tracing them, of course). He would redact the name of the client.

As we left the gallery and I clutched my prize in a beautiful little white Helios Gallery paper bag with silken cords, it occurred to me that I should change my will. I'd leave my brooch collection to Diane. Otherwise, in a week and a half, my brooches would go with all my other assets, mainly cryptocurrency, to my favorite charity, Save the Elephants. Elephants are among the smartest animals in the world, but they probably don't collect ancient brooches.

✳

"Why?" I asked Diane as we walked to the subway. "Why pay a hundred and fifty thousand dollars to have an exhibition staged? Is that normal?"

"You cannot do that again," she hissed.

"Do what?"

"You were there to observe. Even if he offered voluntary information, what you did was to conduct an unlawful search."

Hadn't I forced the critical confession out of Venner?

"But I—"

"We could lose evidence, and much worse."

"I'm sorry." It was a slap in the face. Here I was, planning to deprive the elephants of my brooch collection for her sake.

We walked for a while in such silence as the din of Manhattan affords. Without looking at me, her voice barely audible above the traffic, she asked, "Can we learn anything from their cryptocurrency transactions?"

"Maybe not if the Delphians are as careful as—"

"Wait. I don't understand. I thought cryptocurrency is private . . . But if the barcode on the box can trace transactions . . ." She stopped. Someone behind us almost ran into her. "Oh, how stupid of me."

"As you've guessed, the barcode is useless," I said. "But I figured Venner knows as much about cryptocurrency as I do about the spare Attic idiom."

She stuck out her lips and puffed in exasperation. As we started walking again, she turned her head away, but I saw a smile peek through. "It's still an unlawful search. I think." Still wrestling to contain a smile, she said, "The end doesn't justify the means."

"When the end is yours and it's coming in a week and a half, it does."

"We will find the Delphians."

"I'll applaud from wherever Apollo sends dead coders."

She opened her mouth to speak, then said nothing. We stopped short at a corner. The four seconds flashing on the walk sign wouldn't be time enough to cross. "You know, I was trained to treat art history as a science. That means not believing too much in instinct. But now the instinct is so powerful, I have to believe."

"Believe what?" I asked.

"Something ancient is coming to the surface. Something so big that they will not be able to hide for very long."

"This is just instinct?"

"The heart has its reasons that reason does not know."

"You think Venner could be a Delphian?"

"Antiquities dealers become blasé like everyone else. They talk like salespeople or clinicians. I did not like Venner, but I think his enthusiasm about Delphi was real. Unfortunately, it will be difficult to force him to turn over his email or to get a warrant. I wonder what the Delphians might have offered him . . ." Her voice trailed off as we started crossing.

"He won't tell us much after his assistant Natalie lets him know that I was fibbing about the barcode." I chuckled as we reached the opposite side of the street. "If she knows anything, she'll figure it out. He's having a painful discussion with her right about now."

Diane wasn't listening. She remained lost in thought until we reached the subway.

There was something I didn't tell her. Before drawing attention in Venner's gallery to the box with the cryptocurrency wallet, I'd opened it. I snapped a photo of a handwritten list, the so-called "seed words," basically the Helios Gallery's secret key for their cryptocurrency transactions. It was supposed to be kept in a safe-deposit box, but these people were amateurs.

I could now steal their money, which I wouldn't do, of course. Or I could trace their transactions, which I would do as soon as I left Diane.

I'm sure it wasn't legal, and Diane would have disapproved. But that's what you get for hiring a barely housebroken hacker who commits acts of impiety.

NINE

"It can't be real."

"It is real. It's live," Lukas insisted. "Look for yourself. It's those same fucking nuts who did the rogue contract."

During the mere two hours I'd been out at the Helios Gallery, Lukas had been alerted to a new Sanctum weapon created by the Delphians. Lukas claimed that the Delphians were now *predicting* attacks against smart contracts.

The true Oracle of Delphi made prophecies. But an oracle in a smart contract system only reports facts about the present or past, not the future. No prophecies. After all, it's not god-powered. That's why I thought Lukas was talking nonsense.

"That can't be," I said. "Let me see what's going on."

I looked online while Lukas stood and watched over my shoulder. There was a fog of misleading and hysterical news. But it didn't take much searching to find some expert analysis. The Delphians' predictions weren't the result of some godlike magic. They were worse than that. The Delphians weren't making predictions. They were using a Sanctum feature to generate proofs that they had cyberweapons capable of attacking vulnerable smart contracts. They called their proofs "prophecies." Sanctum let them generate their "prophecies" without revealing their cyberweapons' code to anyone. Sanctum ran the cyberweapon code in a simulated environment and then produced a kind of secure digital certificate—called an attestation, as I've mentioned before—confirming that the cyberweapon worked.

As I searched online and figured all of this out, Lukas stood beside me at my desk fidgeting with my Apollo coin. Luckily, they encase these things in Lucite specifically to protect them against the likes of Lukas.

"They've weaponized Sanctum," I explained, looking up from the screen. "Our proof features."

"Jesus."

The proof feature in Sanctum was one of the things we were proudest of. It wasn't meant to be a weapon. Just the opposite. It was meant to prove that certain types of risky-looking financial transactions in smart-contract systems were safe. For instance, this feature allowed people to do things like take out temporary cryptocurrency loans without collateral. Sanctum could prove that a borrower's smart contract would pay back a loan a short time later—an idea called a "multi-block flash loan." The Delphians had now subverted this very same proof feature in Sanctum to generate a completely different type of proof, namely their "prophecies" of destruction. They placed their attack code inside Sanctum, and Sanctum proved that the code worked correctly—meaning that the Delphians' attack, if launched, would succeed.

"And you know what's scary?" I said.

"Scarier than what you've told me?"

"Here's your Michael Crichton," I said, pointing at the screen. "There are smart contracts securing firmware updates for cyber-physical systems. Light bulbs, refrigerators, and I don't know what else."

"So they can prove—"

"That they can melt down your refrigerator and maybe start a fire," I said, "or make light bulbs strobe and cause seizures in people with epilepsy. There are technical hurdles. I'd have said the idea is far-fetched, but then again, a week ago I wouldn't have predicted I'd be a walking dead man."

"This is like COVID way back when," Lukas said with a sigh. "You think it's just a few people in China with sniffles. Then people start dying around you and the economy goes into a tailspin. At some point, the tech community's going to put us in lockdown. Why are they doing this? Is this really an Apollo-worshiping terrorist cult? They're that batshit crazy?"

"I don't know that any more than I know why they want me dead. Right now, from what I'm seeing online here, they've used Sanctum to prove that they've got a cyberweapon capable of destroying or stealing about $1 million in a second-rate synthetic asset system called GaiaX. I'd never even heard of GaiaX before this. In a way, that's good news. They had to go down-market to find anything they could attack successfully. So it's bad, but $1 million is peanuts. No cyber-physical attacks yet. No melting refrigerators."

"This is just the beginning. What if it becomes $10 million? Or $100 million? Or billions?"

"In principle, it won't be easy," I said. "Think about it. If it were, someone would already have stolen that kind of money."

"Sure. Assuming these people don't have powers that no one else does."

"You mean Apollo?"

"That kind of thing," Lukas said in an undertone, glancing around, probably looking for eavesdropping Olympians. Lukas's superstitiousness is legendary.

"And some of the damage can be avoided," I said. "Some of those contracts can be upgraded if—"

"Do we know where the bugs are? Or not really?"

"We don't. That's the problem."

"They developed all of this since we released Sanctum last week?"

"Probably not the cyberweapons."

"What about their use of the proof stuff in Sanctum?"

"It's hard to believe they managed to do all of it since last week," I said. Lukas cupped his forehead in his hand. "Could we have been breached? It's clear they've got a crack team of hackers. Maybe they're in our network."

"Look, the thing is that we've never worried that much about anyone stealing code. Our biggest concern has been people tampering with our stuff. It's open source. It's all made public anyway. So who'd steal it?" He raised his head and shouted, "Corinne!"

Corinne looked at us from her desk on the Bridge. She untucked the cinched-up sleeves of her cardigan and pulled them down her forearms. She clasped herself as she walked over to us.

"How long would it take to implement what we talked about yesterday?" Lukas asked her.

"Not long. Him—" She pushed her chin toward me. "Days. The rest of us, a week or two. Plus the code review and testing. We should do it. But—"

"What are we talking about?" I asked.

"An escape hatch," Lukas said. "You know, we let the community vote and appoint a committee—a committee of people who can turn off a dangerous contract in Sanctum or strip away its privacy if something catastrophic is going to happen."

"Sure." I said. "A couple of months to deploy your escape hatch. Then a couple of years of the community wrangling over who's on the committee. The worms in my coffin will have discovered fire and invented writing and income taxes by then. And in the end, instead of a council of elders, you'll just get a gang of the biggest loudmouths on social media. So what's the point?" Lukas and Corinne eyed each other. "Look. It's fine. I know you're under pressure. But so am I. I need to stop the Delphians—whoever they are—*now.*"

"The reality is that there's not much more we can do," Lukas said. "I'm sorry." Then under his breath to Corinne, "Let's talk in my office."

I walked over to one of the big arched windows by my desk and gazed at the High Line. Nameless thousands streamed by every day. On that warm late-spring evening, there was a torrent of them. The flow broke at that moment around yet another egocentric tourist planting himself in the middle of the walkway. Probably grinning as he put the world on hold to paste his face over my office windows in a selfie. *The guy thinks he's the Navel of the World*, I said to myself.

I'm no expert, but I'm sure that life was even more uncertain in the ancient world than in our crazy modern one. Medicine was primitive and people died young. Their plagues made our pandemics look like the sniffles. There were no weather forecasts. Science was primitive. Even the Greeks thought rocks fall faster than pebbles. There must have been comfort in the idea that the very center of the world was known. Marked by a sacred stone. Bubbling forth oracular wisdom.

What our latter-day Delphians had now realized is that smart contracts were propelling us into a different world. One with enclaves of determinism, digital realms in which outcomes were mathematical certainties, or at least measurable probabilities. In most big computer networks, programs interact unpredictably with one another. But smart contracts—and blockchains more generally—process inputs mechanistically. There's no roll of the dice. A given input to a smart contract can result in only one possible output. For a set of hypothetical inputs to a collection of smart contracts, therefore, it's often possible to compute a mathematical proof that certain results will or won't occur. If Apollo had really existed thousands of years ago, maybe this was what his gift of prophecy was like. He would execute bits of code in the Olympian gods' computer model of the machinery of the mortal world. He would forecast with divine certainty whether an army would conquer or a fleet founder, a city rise or a kingdom fall.

Usually, when I stared out the windows by my desk, my mind was a blank. Now, though, with just a week and a half to stop the rogue contract, Apollo and his Delphians could never be far from my thoughts. My mind was darting around the impenetrable surface of the Delphians' code, trying to learn its contours, desperate to find exploitable cracks. I was using all of the hacker's intuition I'd built up over the decades. But I had little to go on. Rogue contracts. The Delphians' "prophecies." And some cryptocurrency payments to Venner. Maybe.

✻

With the seed words I'd found in the box with the cryptocurrency wallet at the Helios Gallery, it was easy to reconstruct Venner's cryptocurrency addresses and find his transactions on the blockchain. In total, he'd received roughly $300,000 in cryptocurrency across four transactions, each for about $75,000.

I wanted to find the address or addresses that had sent the money. They could be a valuable clue, as it seemed almost certain to me that they belonged to the Delphians. After all, who else had that kind of money to throw anonymously at a bunch of exhibitions on Delphi? The Delphians were sure to have covered their tracks with extraordinary care when it came to the money in the rogue contract, given how public it was. But there was a chance that they were less careful with the Helios Gallery payments, which were done on the sly.

The money paid to Venner had gone through an anonymizing service called a "mixer." That meant that the Delphians had laundered their cryptocurrency to conceal its origins. A mixer is a big pot of money managed by a smart contract. Money is deposited into the pot by a bunch of users and blended together, so that one user's currency is indistinguishable from another's. A user who has put money into the pot using one blockchain address can withdraw from the pot using a completely different address. Using a mixer for cryptocurrency transactions is kind of like shaking a police surveillance team off your tail by driving into a big parking garage in a red Mustang and coming out in a black Prius (wearing a wig, of course).

Mixers have their limits, though. To continue with my analogy, suppose the surveillance team *knows* that you're swapping your car in the parking garage. And suppose that you're doing it at 2:00 a.m., when no one else is around. Then the trick won't work. It will be obvious to the surveillance team, when the black Prius comes out five minutes later, that it's you—bewigged.

Some mixers are like the parking garage at 2:00 a.m. They don't have many users, so they don't work well. Others are more like busy garages, with a lot of traffic. But even high-traffic mixers don't provide perfect anonymity, because they don't have *that* much traffic. Governments sometimes crack down on them because of their criminal uses, so many people avoid them. Also, sending large sums of money through a mixer—like the payments to the Helios Gallery—degrades the resulting anonymity. Laundering a big wad of cryptocurrency—hundreds of thousands of dollars, as the Delphians did—is a bit like trying the parking-garage maneuver with a whole circus troupe in a bus.

Adyton had access to a commercial blockchain analysis tool, the type of thing used by intelligence, law enforcement, and banks to detect money laundering, cybercrime, and sanctions evasion. A tool of this kind can't completely unwind a mixer. Given cryptocurrency transactions coming out of a mixer, though, it can compute a short list of probable originating addresses.

In all likelihood, the Delphians would have taken special precautions. They would have sent their cryptocurrency through the mixer more than once, or, more likely, through a chain of different mixers. Blockchain analysis tools can help even when that happens, if you know how to use them. I managed to produce a short list of originating addresses that I felt had a good chance of containing the Delphian address or addresses that had sent money to Venner. There was just one problem. My short list wasn't short. It had over two thousand addresses on it.

The FBI might have better tools, or have contacts at other three-letter agencies that did. I decided to see whether they could help me whittle down my short list and do something productive with it. But of course I didn't want to reveal my source—that is, explain how I'd gotten my information about the Helios Gallery transactions to begin with. The FBI has its own tricks to cover up methods and sources. One of their favorites is parallel narrative construction, aka cover stories. I decided to take a cue from the masters.

✳

I couldn't tell whether Walker bought my fairytale when we talked the next morning by video.

"So the guy trying to sell Greek pots to you and Diane just out and told you the dates and amounts of his transactions?" I could see him leaning back in his chair, one huge hand splayed on the table's edge. I expected to see a dent when he lifted it. The other hand was spinning a Rotring again. Black this time. I looked it up as we talked. Nice instrument. I wanted one.

"*Approximate* dates," I said. I figured Diane wouldn't know the technical details, so she wouldn't contradict me. "Venner's not technical, so he didn't know what he was doing."

"And you got enough information to find his incoming payments on chain?"

"Right."

"And then you used a blockchain analysis tool. Chainalysis or Elliptic or something?"

"I didn't get far. I'm hoping you have better tools. Or friends with better tools."

"I've got friends, but they don't tell me much. Now, those cryptocurrency transactions—"

"I'll give them to you. I also have a question about your friends. Or maybe for them."

"Shoot."

"The problem with the rogue contracts is that the Delphians just could launch them and walk away. We may never see another transaction from them going to those contracts. Can your friends retroactively trace the Delphians' transactions back to their servers?"

He looked away, figuring out how much he could say. "If they could have, they would have. But they've turned up—" He paused. "They aren't turning up much for you."

"If the Delphians now interact with Sanctum and we know which internet traffic is theirs, can we find them?"

"They could use Tor. I assume you know what that is."

That was like asking a carpenter if he knows what a band saw is.

"Yeah, I think I've heard of it. It makes internet traffic anonymous by routing it through a bunch of dummy machines. But your friends have ways around Tor, like EGOTISTICALGIRAFFE. You can thank Snowden that I know a little about the NSA's programs and their acid-trip names."

"Self-promoting little blowhard shit," he growled. "Not you. Snowden." He shook his head. "I doubt my friends can do what you want for past traffic. Only my opinion. I'm not part of the priesthood." He wriggled his fingers to signify magic powers, then revved up the pencil again. "If we could get your assassins to execute some fresh transactions that we know about, maybe. You know, like if we can get them to send some crypto when we know to watch for it. But I don't see how you're going to—" His pencil's motor jammed. "Hold on, my phone keeps buzzing." He pulled it out. "Holy shit."

He looked at me.

"Problem?" I asked.

"Diane's source. The professor. Vigan—"

"What about him?" I already knew the answer, but a seizure of fear made me want to slow the telling of it, if only for a split second.

"He's dead."

Suffice it to say that I didn't have a chance to ask Walker about his visit to Adyton.

＊

"Congestive heart failure," Diane said, pacing and mauling her scarf. Hearing Walker's news, I'd rushed over to her office. "Advance information from the coroner. They're not certain, but at this point it doesn't look like murder. They say the stress could have done it."

"I can believe it," I said. "My food intake has doubled, and my sleep has halved. I eat instead of sleeping. And I've noticed this itching on my arms that—"

"Claudio worked with me as a source for years. I thought of him as an ancient, knotty tree with a trunk of iron." She continued pacing. "The kind that has survived disease, insects, lightning, and axes. The kind that nothing can kill. But trees don't have hearts. And something stopped his heart. . . ."

Her eulogy for Viganò wasn't calculated to soothe the hypochondriacs in the room. My own chest felt funny. I noticed that her office windows were the type that don't open. They even had internal thermal panes to provide that extra little touch of claustrophobia.

". . . he was targeted by organized crime years ago. He was in hiding for years. He had an accident during an excavation that crippled him. He rolled his own cigarettes and smoked dozens a day. He survived all of that."

"Maybe it was that last cigarette that killed him," I said to comfort myself. I was a nonsmoker. "If the coroner is wrong and it *was* murder, we could find out in less than a day. The contract is designed to pay out a bounty publicly seven hours after a valid claim is submitted. If a bounty is paid, that means someone registered a valid calling card. And that would mean it was murder."

"Maybe Claudio's crazy theories about Delphi really were blasphemy."

"You mean Apollo—literally Apollo—killed him?"

"I mean— I don't know what I mean." She sat on the edge of her desk and patted her abused scarf back into shape. "I was responsible for his safety. But he wouldn't listen to me."

"I know."

She started pacing again, behind me. Her hands clapped suddenly onto my shoulders. I almost had my own heart attack.

"We should fake your death," she said.

I took a slow breath. "Well that's funny, because I now think we should find them. The Delphians. We need to find them, Diane. Otherwise, they'll just strike again. If there's a kill-switch—" That didn't sound right. "—an off switch, then there's a permanent solution."

"You aren't frightened. Why not?"

"Of course I'm frightened. What keeps me from dissolving into a puddle of panic on your office floor are occasional flashes of lucidity. I realize that until next Friday I'm worth more to an assassin alive than dead. If I die before the bounty on my head activates, they can't collect."

She wasn't listening. "Let's get out of here." She snatched her purse from her desk. I trotted after her.

At Maison Stern—the only place in New York where you can get real French pastries—she ordered both an éclair and a chocolate tart. That gave me license to get a massive almond croissant, the authentic kind that's stuffed with marzipan and has a truck backed over it to give it the right density. Stern's are so good that I'll even violate my prohibition on grains and take it over chocolate now and then.

"I'm French-American now," she said. "I eat French pastries, but I eat them to excess like an American." She noticed my already half-demolished almond croissant. "Sorry."

"Try harder," I said. "You need to eat a quart of ice cream at a sitting to pass the US citizenship test."

It was late morning. The restaurant's bistro mirrors reflected empty bentwood chairs and expectant place settings. After my conversation with Walker, I was itching to go scrutinize the Delphians' code again, but it was clear Diane had something to say. She alternated between her two pastries, carving off discreetly sized bites and chewing without hurry. Her chocolate tart looked even more enticing than my croissant.

"How did you end up in an exotic job in a foreign land, Diane?"

She laughed. "The foreign land, that was because of my boyfriend. I lived here for a year in high school. But I came here for graduate school because of him. He was an American."

"Was?"

"We lived together for years, until the pandemic. In quarantine, we discovered we hated each other."

"I'm sorry." I wasn't entirely.

"Art history and the FBI. That's—well, a longer story."

"I'm listening."

"When I was young . . ." She paused, a forkful of éclair hovering in midair. She was deciding how much she could trust me. She put her fork down. "I have never acted or felt completely French. My parents were immigrants to France from Hong Kong, you see. Our family name—my father changed it to 'Duménil' because he thought it sounded aristocratic. He took it from a bottle of champagne. I love the name, but it was a poor ruse. France is not like the US. The French have one route to assimilation, and that's through their culture. So I tried to become more French than the French. I studied art history at ENS, one of the *grandes écoles*. You know what that is?"

"No."

"The closest analogy is the Ivy League. But we have our own strange system in France. After years of study, I knew more about French art than the French people from rich old families who collect it in their châteaux."

"And that worked?"

She picked up her éclair-laden fork. "Knowing history isn't the same as owning it. I was young. I didn't realize that yet. I decided to go even deeper."

"So you went digging at an archaeological site."

"Metaphorically." She put her fork down again. "French is degenerate Latin. French culture is fundamentally the culture of the Romans and Greeks. In graduate school, I studied classical art and archaeology. You see, beneath everything in France there is a stratum of Roman civilization. Like my name, Duménil. It comes from the Latin *mansio*, a kind of official hotel in the Roman Empire. But then there is a deeper stratum, more sophisticated and mysterious. *That* is Greek."

"What happened when you learned this? Did you at last feel more French? Superior to the French?"

"I have never felt so French as when I moved to Brooklyn." She laughed. A genuine laugh, not one of her ingratiating ones. "So many French people. So open-minded and happy to be out of France. 'Très Brooklyn.' You know what that means?"

"No."

"Cool food. High quality. Hipster."

For the record, there is nothing cooler than a Frenchwoman uttering the word "cool." There's the catch of her tongue at the back of the mouth as she pronounces the "c," a coo, and then that long lingering "l." Her pronunciation of "hipster" ran a close second, though.

"So, anyway, you steeped yourself in ancient Greece."

"Drama, philosophy, democracy, trial by jury, medical science—all invented in a tiny area of the Mediterranean in an instant of historical time. It was an explosion of culture from a hot, dense core of ideas. A supernova. How did it happen? To me, that is *the* mystery of our civilization, of my life." She paused, gauging my reaction. I was reminded of how, when she first met me in the Chelsea Market, she told me she was crazy. I was chewing, but rapt.

"The key moment," she continued, "was when the Athenians abandoned their city to fight the Persians at sea, at the Battle of Salamis. They did it because of a prophecy: 'A wooden wall will save you.' No one knew what it meant, but the Athenians decided that the 'wooden wall' meant their fleet. Without that critical choice, Greece would have been swallowed up by the great Persian empire. No Pericles. No Plato or Thucydides. No drama or democracy. No Parthenon. Maybe no Western culture. That one prophecy changed the world. Where did it come from?"

I swallowed a last bolus of marzipan. "Delphi?"

"My colleagues don't care about all of this history. But when I saw you so desperate to have that brooch at the Helios Gallery—"

"Yes, about that . . ." I swallowed. "Honestly, when I saw it across the room, I didn't realize . . ."

She puffed out her lips and gave a dismissive wave. "The ancients loved male anatomy. I don't care. I thought you were just a computer person. But when that brooch called to you across the gallery, I saw that I was wrong. I thought you might understand."

"Understand what, exactly?" That fellowship of wistful souls whose polestar is the ancient world and whose members included both her and my grandfather? Had I unwittingly been inducted into it?

Smiling, she shook her head as if to dismiss a thought. "Viganò was helping me track something down before he died. Something on the underground market . . . new artifacts related to Delphi. Looted objects. They must be important, because one of my sources encountered them and contacted me."

"What are these artifacts?"

"That is what we are going to find out now." She glanced at her phone and pushed away her half-finished pastries. "We need to leave. We are going to visit a dying star."

TEN

I wonder if each of us has our own inner sanctum, our own eternal fire. A holy place in the mind, as it were, fed by some primal force, like love, loss, or the quest for belonging. A piano piece learned in early childhood. A long-unspoken language. A collection of memorized, oft-recited poems. Some nucleus of knowledge that has been etched into the brain so deeply by nostalgia that it's protected against even the diseases of old age that ravage thought and memory.

For Soren Mercator, this inner sanctum was the classical world.

The old man's face lit up when Diane shook his hand. I couldn't tell whether he recognized her or whether he just saw a pretty woman. He held her hand so long she had to pull it away in embarrassment.

I introduced myself and shook his hand. "I didn't recognize you," he said. His vague blue eyes tried to fix mine. Then they wandered instead to my lips.

"I don't think we've met before. A pleasure."

I'd have remembered meeting a billionaire. The only kind I'd encountered before were flash-in-the-pan cryptocurrency ones, the kind now missing insurance payments on their garagefuls of Lamborghinis. When Diane told me in the subway that we were visiting Soren Mercator, I tried to imagine the outsized splendor of his office. Marble porticos? Fifty-foot ceilings? Gold desk? Gold toilets? I remembered a campus building named after him from my undergrad days at Cornell. He was a real estate magnate who'd retired with a modest spot on the lower half of the Forbes 400 and then turned to philanthropy and expanding his collection of classical art.

When we exited the elevator on the twenty-seventh floor and passed through a nondescript glass door into his office, it seemed that the closest thing to a gold fixture was the Fifth Avenue address. Had it not overlooked downtown Manhattan, the office could have belonged to a tax accountant in Topeka in 1995. Everything was painted a tawny, almost flesh-like color, including the baseboards. The desk, wood veneer for all I could tell, was a mushroom patch of papers and bric-a-brac. The only clear sign that the occupant wasn't a Topekan tax accountant were the old photos on a window ledge showing Mercator in friendly poses with the Clintons, the Obamas, and other A-list celebrities from the intelligent half of the spectrum. Mercator's administrative assistant settled us into a drab seating area with a couch facing two armchairs across a coffee table. When we declined Coke, she served us soda water with wedges of lime.

"I— I remember now," Soren said when we sat. When I'd called him "Mr. Mercator," he'd insisted on Soren. "Glass. Not garnet. Glass. As good as semiprecious stones in the ancient world. A magnificent piece." His eyes wandered away.

I looked at what I took to be his personal assistant, seated across from me. "Soren's met all kinds of people," she said. "Are you a collector or with the FBI?"

"Neither," I said. "Not exactly."

Soren spoke to Diane. "Thank you for coming, my dear. I've forgotten your name. My brain doesn't hold new names anymore. But I remember you. So you've come again to have a look at my collection?"

"I've come to ask about a visit you had a few weeks ago."

"Visits are tougher than names. Maybe Meghan can tell you what you want to know." Meghan Maybell. Chief Investment Officer of the Sub Rosa Family Office, I learned from the business card she pushed across the table with a studied smile. I got the impression she'd mulled over the options long and hard when she picked out that smile, along with the nose and high cheekbones. She paid good money for a sleek, professional set.

"Delphi," Diane said as a cue to Soren.

"Ah, Delphi," he sighed. "The Navel of the World. I used to serve my guests water from the Castilian spring. One of the two legendary springs there. We ran out. Now you get fizzy water with lime."

"You gave me your last bottle of Castilian spring water," Diane said. "We drank it together. Do you remember? It was a few years ago."

"I'm giving everything away now." He smiled and closed his eyes. To remember that he was now one of the city's great philanthropists? To recall the taste of the spring water? To sleep?

"You contacted me about a visit a few weeks ago, Soren." Diane spoke to his inert face. "You were offered artifacts from Delphi."

We waited to see whether he would open his eyes. He didn't.

"A dealer sounded us out," Meghan said to Diane and me. "I don't know much about antiquities. But the dealer was offering some spectacular items, according to Soren. He wanted them."

"What happened?" Diane asked.

"Unacceptable terms," Meghan snapped. "We'd have to stage a public exhibition. Soren doesn't do that."

"Can you tell me the name of the dealer?"

"Not unless there's evidence of a crime. That's part of our agreement."

"With the dealer?" I interjected.

"With you," Meghan said. "With the FBI." Her annoyance suggested I should know. My half-denial that I was with the FBI wasn't sufficient.

"Not exactly," Diane said, "but fine for now. How can we find out what the objects were?"

"We went to their gallery," Meghan replied. "They had two items to show us there. I took a picture on the sly for you guys. They didn't want any photos circulating. They were super paranoid. Even checked my phone afterward." With a self-satisfied smile, she handed the phone to Diane. "I showed them the wrong album."

I leaned over. The Greek vase and silver cup in the photo meant nothing to me. Diane spent a few minutes scrutinizing them, enlarging details, looking things up on her own phone. Soren appeared to have fallen asleep.

"Can you reopen your discussion with them?" Diane asked Meghan. "Get us something more? Bring in your experts?"

"No. Sorry. That would look suspicious. We told them we don't do public exhibitions."

"Just say that you are thinking about it."

"Look, we already took a big risk. We don't burn our relationships with dealers. You know that."

"People change their minds."

"Soren doesn't."

I could see Diane's eyes behind her glasses. They flickered over to Soren, then lingered on Meghan. "Did they say anything else?"

"The pieces came from a major find near Delphi."

"I know that already. What else? What else did they find?" Diane persisted.

"The Omphalos." Soren had opened his eyes. "They've found the Omphalos."

"What?" Diane looked first at me, then Meghan. "What does he mean?"

"I know what the Omph— I know what that is," Meghan said, unmoved. "To be clear, they didn't *say* it's been found. That's Soren's guess. They claimed to know someone who said he'd made the 'find of the century.' It was thirdhand, and the usual dealer's hyperbole, I assume."

Diane leaned toward Soren. "You really mean the Omphalos? Soren, why do you think they've found it?"

He stared at the table, his eyes widening. His mouth trembled. "I don't remember."

Diane put her fingers to her temples, then started fingering her scarf. We were all silent. Then she stood up. "Soren, would you please show my colleague your collection?"

"He's tired, Diane," Meghan said. She was right.

Soren reached for the table, grabbed it, rocked forward, and fell back. On the third try, with a hand on one side from Diane, who'd run over to his side, and on the other from Meghan, he stood up.

He walked behind his desk, toward the back of the office. There was a door I hadn't noticed, painted the same tawny color as everything else. Automatically, as though attached to a younger body, his fingers punched at a keypad and his hand slid into a hand-geometry reader. The thick door swiveled open. As Diane walked over to him, I noticed how stooped Soren was, a good few inches shorter than Diane. And she's not tall.

When we crossed the threshold into what appeared to be a vault, we entered a different building, a different city, a different world. The ceiling rose, grand and improbable, to large, tinted skylights. The air was cool and dry and suffused with the subdued radiance of an artificial sunset. Matching marble columns with ancient weathering towered above us in the four corners of the room. On the wall opposite the door were huge slabs of stained marble, broken in places, their surfaces sculpted with a dreamlike procession of women clutching strange stalks, like staffs topped with large, spiky cones. Their garments clung to their breasts and sinuous bodies and swirled around their legs. Their heads, some bowed, some thrown back, bore flawless, dispassionate faces, frozen in a trance. Women have been sculpted and painted differently over the centuries, but never more beautifully.

In the center of the room and along its three sides were museum cases. Between them, pedestals holding sculptures and vases. On my right, a man's eyeless head communed with oblivion. On my left was the dark bronze bust of a matronly woman, the whites of the eyes glaring even in the hushed light. She sized me up. She didn't like what she saw. Too flabby for the Roman army.

Soren touched a button and the door drifted shut, sealing us in with a faint sucking noise. The dead silence cut us off from the city. The bowed, aged billionaire seemed to grow taller and he radiated triumph. Money alone could not have created this place, his face said. Only connoisseurship and an unstoppable force of will that sought out and compelled beauty from dealers, auction houses, other collectors, and maybe the earth itself.

Meghan stood, arms folded, gazing at the floor. Diane watched me. I looked around, dazed as if I'd emerged from a cave into sunlight. Even a troglodyte like me knew to marvel.

Soren walked over to one of the cases and waved me over. He was hovering over a small gold object, an elegant double knot formed of two thick, looped cords of gold oriented in opposite directions. The two strands of each cord passed through the teardrop-shaped loop of the other. In the center was what I took to be a red stone, smooth and ovular.

"Glass," he said. "Not garnet. I can show you in sunlight."

When he removed it from the case, with some help from Meghan, I saw the pin on the back and realized what it was. I don't know how to describe what I felt at that moment, except to say—in my own geeky way—that it was like the thrill you get when your code goes live. It's no longer just the code you plodded through and tested. You feel connections forming, hear electrons humming, sense your work becoming part of the fabric of the world. You feel more real, alive, at the center of things.

"Diane! It's a brooch!" I cried.

She laughed. "It's not for sale."

"No. I mean—" I turned to Soren. "Did you get this from—" He was returning it to the case. "—from someone with my name?" I stood there, the question warm on my lips as he shuffled away.

He moved to another case. The next object wasn't a brooch. It was a silver dish of some kind, with a big knob in the center circled by indentations in a sunburst pattern. "A *phiale*," he said to none of us in particular. "The kind of vessel used for pouring libations into the earth. You know the beautiful cup in the Delphi museum? It shows Apollo using one."

"Beautiful," Diane cooed.

"Meghan," Mercator called softly. She was now on the other side of the room, and may or may not have heard him. "I want her to get this when I go." The bowl was worth more than my whole brooch collection. Probably more than my whole net worth for that matter.

"Thank you, Soren," Diane said. "That is so kind. But . . . but I can't. I am not even allowed to."

"Too bad," he said, shaking his head. "Then I guess the Met gets it."

She put one hand on his shoulder and clasped his forearm with the other. "Soren, the Omphalos."

"They've found it," he barked. "I'm sure of it. Not that stupid thing in the Delphi museum that Pausanias saw. The real one. It should never be in a private collection. Not even mine. It would be a crime."

"I want to find it, Soren. A name, a clue would help. A guess, even."

"Diane," said Meghan, walking over to her and Soren. "He's tired. Another time."

"Soren—" Diane insisted.

"Ferrari," Soren blurted out.

"Ferrari? Something about the car?"

He reached across his body and clasped Diane's hand. His own hand trembled. "I can't— You know him. Ferrari. Ferrari. Something like that."

"Diane, please," Meghan insisted.

"Ferrari, Ferrari," Diane murmured. "Farnese! You mean Farnese."

"I'm not sure. I don't think it's his real name."

"The fake aristocrat. The Italian who always says he feels as though he is giving away his children. Him?"

Meghan put her hand on Soren's other shoulder. The old man wriggled away and said, pouting, "She wanted to see the collection. I'm showing it." He shuffled toward an open door.

He led us into a second room, with a ceiling rounded like a barrel, painted bloodred. The floor was a black-and-white mosaic, its regular pattern patched over with concrete in places where tiles were missing. There was a spartan bed toward the back. It was little more than a cushion on a wooden table with an elevated headrest. Were it not thousands of years old, I'd have mistaken it for a medical exam table. In front of it was either a footstool or a box hiding a chamber pot.

But those walls! It was the walls, covered on three sides by frescos, that turned the room into something otherworldly. What had looked at first like dark, polished stone columns running almost floor to ceiling turned out to be painted illusions. Between the columns were fantastical classical buildings, rising to impossible heights, in jarring, clashing reds, pinks, and yellows. Terraces, balconies, giant arches, groves, statues, fountains, and temples. Airy little rooms, with latticework open on three sides, cantilevered into space, like forerunners of my Bridge.

Even the common objects were artworks in their own right. Doors gaily patterned in red and yellow, flanked by columns and topped by lintels barbed with pigeon-proofing spikes. Vases of metallic gold, slender-footed, wide-necked, ornamented with ribbing. The perspective wasn't academically correct, but it didn't matter. It felt as though we were standing in the middle of an ancient city. Not a real one, but the one that some dream-struck Roman real estate developer, innocent of budgets, tried to sell his clients. Or maybe this really was the way the ancient world looked. It wasn't all cold, white, spectral marble, as in my synthetic historical memory, but a tumult of riotous color, with architects' creations luxuriating like hothouse plants.

"I slept in here when they used to let me," the old man said. "The buildings seep into your dreams. The statues too. Like people you used to know." He walked over to a fresco and met the raised hand of a tiny gold statue with a tender fingertip.

When we retreated from the vault back into the unremarkable office, Soren again sagged and looked off into space. After our handshakes with Meghan, he muttered what I took to be a goodbye. This time it was Diane who clung to his hand.

Afterward, back on the street, she explained his agreement with the FBI to me. Soren acted as a source. The FBI turned a blind eye to certain acquisitions. Some of what I'd seen was looted from archaeological sites. According to the FBI's calculus, a string of recovered treasures—and once in a blue moon, a convicted looter or smuggler—justified some rule-bending.

"It makes me a little sick," Diane explained. "But Soren Mercator is still the sweetest robber baron I know." She sighed. "At least it will all go to a museum."

ELEVEN

Different people see different things when they look at a piece of code. Ordinary people see technical gibberish.

Inexperienced coders see a puzzle.

A developer well versed in a programming language can spot patterns, big and small. Coding conventions, like common phrases in everyday speech. Macroscopic patterns, like the standard plot of a thriller movie or novel.

A true veteran coder, though, can go far deeper. Zero in by reflex on common blunders, "anti-patterns" as we call them. Intuit what's been generated by AI tools and what has sprung from a human mind. Ferret out clues about the personality of the creator. Code is like all writing, a form of self-expression. Admittedly, as coders collaborate more deeply with AI tools, stylistic decipherment is getting progressively harder. Still, with enough experience, you can absorb the general, conceptual approach to a piece of code, home in on the key bits that involve human craft, and quickly see whether a developer is sloppy or neat, terse or verbose, a technician or a magician.

The Delphians' code, especially in their second rogue contract, was like nothing I'd ever seen before.

The code structure was meticulously conceived, making it easy to grasp the way the code functioned. The repository structure, the composition of objects and methods, the names of variables, the comments (in English and Greek) throughout—all of it aimed at clarity. Excessive clarity. Showy clarity. As though the Delphian coders attended fancy finishing schools in Switzerland for programming, doing daily elocution lessons in Go, Rust, and Solidity (programming languages) for years before being permitted to touch a keyboard. When they'd finished their work, some ultra-persnickety master developer had gone over everything. He'd buffed every line to a high shine and stuck a lily in it.

Professional developers don't have time for this kind of spit and polish. AI tools can't give it to you. The closest thing I'd ever seen to it was code I encountered during my brief, failed stint in grad school at Berkeley. Most of the professors there were of the those-who-can't-do-teach school. But I worked in my first summer with one of the systems faculty, who enjoyed coding alongside her students as a kind of hobby. Writing beautiful code was in her eyes an art. (After my first year, of course, she quit academia for industry.)

But it wasn't just that the Delphians' code was polished. It was also a model of economy. Again, in a showy way. Clean and taut. They had written their smart-contract code almost entirely in a programming language called Yul that did away with the frills and inefficiencies of the "high-level," easier-to-use language Solidity. Again, in a showy way. Clean and taut. No wasted lines and no unnecessary storage or gas costs. Streamlined in strict adherence to the maxim Δαπανῶν ἄρχου: "Control your expenditure."

How did I know this choice bit of Greek? Because it was one of a bunch of proverbs from ancient Delphi scattered throughout the comments in the code. Every file had a copyright notice and a standard SPDX License Identifier, a short indication of the terms of use. (The Delphians went with the MIT license. They were graciously allowing everyone to make free use of their rogue-contract code with attribution.) The copyright notice included the phrase Πρᾶττε δίκαια. Easy to find online: The Delphic maxim "Practice justice." For the function in their code that paid out bounties, Δικαίως κτῶ, "Gain possessions justly." And in various places, general best practices for software, anticipated by Apollo thousands of years ago. Ἀποκρίνου ἐν καιρῷ, "Respond promptly." Ἄρρητον κρύπτε, "Keep secrets secret." Also a shout-out for my profession: Χρησμοὺς θαύμαζε, "Admire oracles."

Corinne and I had already gone over their first piece of code and both of us came to the same conclusion. More or less flawless. No vulnerabilities to sink our teeth into. But their second batch of code was at least a lot bigger and more complicated, so even in the face of our strange and powerful adversary, I had a morsel of hope. Everyone makes mistakes. Everyone.

Even formal verification, a kind of mathematical analysis of software correctness, misses things, because your theorems are only as good as your propositions. It was possible that the God of Light, or at least his followers, might trip up somewhere.

The way I solve problems is by internalizing them, committing details to memory. Then it's almost a tactile thing for me. It's like I've created a mental model in plastic that I can run my hands over, poke at, toss in the air and catch, reshape, and manipulate in my imagination. Stopping at home on the way back from Soren Mercator's office, I sat at the kitchen counter with my laptop and loaded the essentials into my little gray cells. Then I walked the High Line back over to Adyton, veering around the French tourists as I played with the Delphians' code in my mind.

✳

"Mister ———!"

When she called my name in the Chelsea Market, I turned. I held my backpack in place and secured it with my free hand. It was slung over one arm, so I could swivel it over my chest. They shouldn't have been coming for me yet, but at home I'd stuffed the bag with a metal oven tray, thick and heavy, thinking I could somehow use it as body armor. I'd entered the Chelsea Market through a little-used side door.

"Are you afraid you'll be next?" Microphone poking at my face. Videocam trained on her and me.

"I'm afraid *you'll* be next," I blurted out, lowering my bag. "Especially if you don't get that thing out of my face." I immediately felt embarrassed. But reporters eat abuse for breakfast, and she was unfazed. She had bobbed bleached hair, heavy makeup. Overdone look of seriousness. I don't watch much television, but thought I recognized her. Behind us, the baristas at the espresso counter were enjoying the pop-up live-studio show. I made for a nearby stairwell and ran up a flight of stairs. Breathless, I caught the elevator to my office on the second floor.

Viganò's demise had created a flurry of interest in my own impending death. I was already getting crazy emails. I was also getting requests from journalists and TV shows for interviews, both in email and through

Adyton's public-relations people. I wasn't expecting an ambush in the Chelsea Market, though. It hadn't even been a day since Viganò's death. I also thought my baseball cap and sunglasses were a good disguise, but reporters are used to that too.

In the elevator, I thought about a piece of email I'd just gotten, an invitation to give the keynote talk at a blockchain conference I'd never heard of—in Bulgaria. Everyone loves zombie movies, and I'd figured I got the invitation because they wanted an undead speaker to spice up a dull technical event. But after the reporter waylaid me, I realized it could well be a setup for assassination, this luring of a hapless techie to a lawless corner of Eastern Europe.

I just wasn't cut out for this sort of thing. The paranoia you need for digital opsec, the kind I have in my bones, isn't good for the real world. It helps you reason through dangers in cyberspace, but blunts animal instinct. You end up with an oven tray in your bag.

I entered the office weak-kneed. I walked the gauntlet of secret glances and pitying looks, past the inflatable sandwich cookie.

Someone called out. "*She's* looking for you."

I glanced at my smartwatch. I'd just missed her text, while my hooliganism with the reporter was being memorialized for the evening news in a ripe-for-social-media video clip. I headed to the Bridge, nodded to Corinne, dropped my bag, and went to the Priestess's office. Lukas's office is enclosed with clear glass. The Priestess's office, next to it, has frosted glass. It lets in light, but provides privacy. I knocked.

"Come in."

She was looking out of the window as I entered, her back turned to me, a graceful silhouette. She wore a turtleneck and slacks that flared at the bottom. Some kind of belt strap swung by her side. She turned.

"I told you I was worried about some dramatic episode upending your life. But you've exceeded my most cinematic expectations." She was backlit, her face unreadable.

"The result of my sad, solitary existence?"

"Which in turn leads to dangerous pigheadedness."

"So what's a lonesome pig to do?"

"My offer to send you to Santorini still stands."

"Thanks. I've always wanted a sandcastle mausoleum."

"This is all getting serious. Slipping in through a side door won't be enough." She might have seen me from the window. "Soon you'll be endangering the people around you."

It hadn't occurred to me that assassination might be contagious. But it was true that a bomb, stray bullet, or liberal dose of poison could cause collateral damage.

"I'll stop coming to the office."

"Permanently, if you're not careful. So, which will it be? Bodyguard or going into hiding?"

"I have over a week. No one should be in danger until then."

"That's not much time. What's your plan?"

"I'll find them. I'm starting with their code. And I'm getting help from—friends."

"Ah, 'friends,'" she said. "I see." She continued, "Corinne tells me that the rogue-contract code is flawless. Is that true? It can't be. Think of how hard it is for us even with access to the best smart-contract auditing firms."

"It's pretty remarkable code." The Priestess's doubts, even if she wasn't a coder, were encouraging. "I don't care if it was literally written by a god, though. Something that complex gives me a fighting chance."

She took a step toward the center of the room and leaned against her standing desk.

"They blindsided us by weaponizing Sanctum," she said. "Have you considered taking the same tack? For defensive purposes, of course."

How many years would it take for me not to feel like an idiot in her presence? I might not have many more.

"Weaponizing Sanctum? I—" Somehow it hadn't occurred to me. "Uh, no."

"I've been astonished by the community's quick development of new applications around Sanctum even before we released it. I won't presume to tell you how software works. But I've noticed over the years that complexity isn't the only source of vulnerabilities. New environments also cause them. And failures of imagination."

"That's true."

"Your 'friends' are notorious for failures of imagination, so don't rely too much on them." Of course she knew who they were. Maybe the incident responsible for her infamy had happened when she also trusted them in some way and they let her down too.

"I won't."

"If your hunt isn't successful, although I hope it is—no, I believe it will be—you'll tell me your decision before the end of the week. Agreed?"

As always when I was with her, I wanted to say or do something personal, warm, human—idolatrous. Particularly now that I was on the brink of disappearing forever. As always, I couldn't think of anything. At least, nothing—no chivalrous kiss of her hand, no parting embrace—that I could actually bring myself to do.

"Sure. Before the end of the week."

✳

"I have a theory," Diane said.

She was standing by her desk, yet another of those discouragingly fit people who don't need to sit. I was showing her the bits of Greek I'd found in the Delphians' code. I was trying to impress upon her the artistic perfection of the code itself, but she couldn't appreciate its significance. I had to remind myself that to her, exceptional skill of this kind might not seem so unusual. Unlike me, she was in regular professional contact with artistic masterpieces.

"A theory about their code?" I asked.

"About everything. I have been trying to project an ancient Greek mentality onto their behavior. To figure out what they want."

"Don't all people in the end pretty much want the same thing? Has it ever changed? Power, money, sex, fame. Maybe a bit of food and love if you're French."

"Power, money, sex, fame. Does that describe you?"

"My parents messed me up, so I just tilt at windmills."

"Like Socrates."

"Sure. Just like Socrates. Wasn't he also assassinated?"

"Executed by the state. Not assassinated. And you haven't been assassinated yet."

"Still, people share the same basic drives. Some just sublimate better than others."

"The ancient Greeks had corrupt politicians, class struggles, repression of women, religious fanatics, gullible, uneducated people led by demagogues. Terrible things familiar to us today. But in many regards they were very different from us. Think about it. Can you remember what the world was like before the internet?"

"You mean in ancient Greece? I think people used dial-up modems."

"*Voilà!* You were a child. You lived in that world, but today it is too strange to comprehend. Now imagine a world a thousand times stranger."

"Is strangeness really the point, or is similarity? I was always taught in school that the reason we study the Greeks is to learn eternal truths about humanity. Right? Like Homer. *The Iliad.* I remember a lot of spattered blood and brains. But also that what binds us together as human beings is that we all have to come to terms with our mortality. Some of us have to do that in less than . . ." I looked at my watch. ". . . less than ten days. Aren't you the one who said that when you pull back the curtain on Western civilization, there are the Romans standing in front of the Greeks?"

"Our cultural ancestors. But how much for that matter do you resemble your grandparents?"

"Good point." Betraying my trainer, who warns me against too much sitting, I dragged a chair from the front of her desk and plopped myself down. "So what's your theory?"

"The theory only makes sense if you accept that they believe in Apollo."

"Diane, I still think that's insane."

"Here in this office, a hundred meters above Manhattan, staring at a computer, it's insane. So is the religious right in this country. They believe the Bible is the literal word of God and Christ will rise again in a few years and carry all his believers into Heaven. They think that abortion is murder, but guns and eating meat are fine. And they regard Trump as God's—"

"OK. I get the point."

"They are in this office," she whispered.

"I get it. I get it."

"So why would somebody believe in Apollo? You will think I'm crazy. But let me explain." She sat behind her desk, opposite me. We were now teacher and pupil. "During the Peloponnesian War," she said, "the Spartans invaded the region around Athens. The Athenians took refuge within the walls of the city. They were crammed together, and hygiene deteriorated. A plague broke out, a horrible disease. It brought intense pain, a thirst that no amount of water could alleviate, and profound mental depression.

Some scholars think it was a kind of typhoid fever. There were piles of bodies in the streets. Healthy young people would die within days. Some believe it killed a third of the population. And all of this happened while the Spartans were burning the fields outside the city walls."

She drew her hand across the desk to illustrate an imaginary wall.

"People reacted in two opposite ways," she continued. "Some lost their faith in the gods, because the disease killed both good and evil people. But there were others who became more intensely religious and tried to appease the gods. The god of plagues above all . . ."

"Apollo, I presume."

"Of course. And then there was a psychological weapon of mass destruction pointed at Athens. An oracle from Delphi just before the war. Apollo declared that he would fight for the Spartans."

"And I guess he did."

"So I was thinking about the pandemic," she said. "Our pandemic."

"You think that's when Apollo reappeared?"

"I've been thinking about how it could create the preconditions for people to believe that was what happened. Imagine. You are an elderly Greek woman, maybe running a small family hotel near Delphi. There are no more tourists. You have lost your income, and you have no way of getting a job. Your friends have become sick. Some have died. Climate change, disease, economic collapse. It feels like the end of the world. It is testing your faith in God. Because you have no work, you begin to roam the countryside. It clears your mind, and you gather wild greens in the hills because you have no money for food. One day, you park your car by the road.

"As you are leaving the place, by accident you put your car in reverse. One wheel sinks into the earth and reveals a deep hole. You get out to look at it. It is unnatural, so you begin to dig. You think of your neighbor, who once found a cache of silver coins. He lived for months on the money he received for those coins on the black market. You use the little spade you brought for wild greens and dig until it hits a hard object. You pull it out. You wipe it down. Maybe it's bronze. A Gorgon? An eagle? You are unsure, but it looks ancient and is probably worth something. You dig further and find some rotting organic material. You almost stop, disgusted. Maybe there will be a corpse. But then you uncover a piece of marble. Not just a piece of marble. Your fingers tremble. You see the large egg shape forming as you claw away the earth with your hands. Even before it makes contact with the air for the first time in thousands of years you know what it is. Anyone in Greece would know."

She let this image hang in the air. "Wow," I said. "Your daydreams are in Technicolor."

"In the middle of all the suffering, you have found a miracle. You think at first about reporting it to the government. You will become a celebrity. They will show you on television. But no. Instead, there must be a rebirth of the ancient god you have known deep in your heart for your whole life. He led you to this sacred object. *You*. You will be the new Pythia."

"But how does this anointed peasant—you're basically talking about a peasant in rural Greece—start coding up rogue contracts?"

"She finds other artifacts. She sells them to feed her family. Small, gold votive objects. She doesn't think they are significant, but after some years have passed a dealer recognizes what they are. They are unlike anything he's handled before. He sells them on the underground market to a billionaire collector who must see for himself what the woman has found. The collector finds her and her ecstasy is contagious."

"This collector. We're not talking about Soren Mercator."

"No. Maybe in his younger days. But we know now that there are objects on the market, and Soren sensed the discovery of the Omphalos. This billionaire collector of my story, whoever he is, helps revive Delphi in his own manner. He becomes patron of a cult. Or maybe it's a woman for once."

"So where do smart contracts come in?"

"The cult can't rebuild the temple of Apollo at Delphi. And Olympus today is just a mountain. How can they channel this divine power when it comes again? Only in cyberspace. I don't know much about smart contracts. But they are roughly speaking like a force of nature, a way to project power that cannot be stopped."

"But why kill Viganò? And me?"

"Because they believe in Greek gods—or want to believe in them or make others believe in them—and that is what Greek gods do. They destroy those who oppose them. Above all, those guilty of hubris, arrogance.

Horribly. In Greek mythology, a satyr named Marsyas challenged Apollo to a music contest. To punish him, Apollo—" She scraped a forefinger down her arm.

"Skinned him?"

"Skinned him alive and nailed his skin to a tree."

"Diane, how can I put this?" She gave me an earnest look. "Did I actually commit an 'act of impiety'? You said Viganò's theories were wrong. I can't say I acted without some hubris. Was I defending a lie? Have I somehow deserved—"

"Of course not. Maybe you acted with hubris. I don't know. But even Marsyas didn't deserve torture. He died *pour encourager les autres*."

"Then I just hope I go like Viganò." She shook her head at me. I smiled. "So where does your theory lead?" I asked. "What's the endgame in the ancient Greek mentality?"

"Artificial intelligence," she said.

"AI?" I laughed and crossed my arms. "How's that?" Now she was in my wheelhouse.

She continued solemnly. "To reveal themselves, the Greek gods often replicated or took control of human forms. In Homer, Athena often appears to Odysseus disguised as a mortal—as a little girl, for instance. Zeus appears to Agamemnon in a dream as the wise man Nestor. At Delphi, Apollo possessed the priestess and spoke through her. The gods chose human form to communicate with us.

"Today, artificial intelligence simulates human intelligence. Avatars simulate human appearance. They are the perfect channel for the messages of a Greek god who has returned to the world."

"Wait a minute. Are we talking about a cult that believes in the Greek gods and creates avatars to embody them? Or are we talking about the actual gods of ancient Greece returning to Earth and somehow influencing the training of machine-learning models—basically injecting themselves into bots?"

"How could anyone distinguish between the two?"

Her question shouldn't have flummoxed me, but I had no answer. I gave a quick little shake of my head to reboot my brain.

"So let me get this straight. You mean a chatbot suddenly proclaims that it's possessed by the god Apollo? And people believe it?"

"They believe politicians who are more stupid than chatbots. So why not?" she said. "I meant, however, that they might start by revealing themselves to only a few people."

"But—"

"OK. Suppose *you* are the eccentric billionaire we are hypothesizing. You want to channel a divine power, one that is about to be reborn. What do you do?"

"I have no idea. You're the one who introduced me to all the billionaires I know."

"What would you do? Tell me."

I raised my hands, palms forward. "Search me. I don't have your imagination."

"Don't imagine. Just plan."

"I don't know. My reflex is to view everything through a blockchain lens. What would I do? What the Delphians have been doing. Except I'd play the long game."

"What does that mean?"

"I'd take your bot and bury it deep in blockchain infrastructure. I'd give it power. Let it control its own huge trove of cryptocurrency. I'd make it immortal. Turn it into a smart contract, so it couldn't be stopped or killed. Then I'd bide my time. If I wanted my god to give expression to his festering wrath after thousands of years consigned to oblivion, I'd plan and wait and have him unleash something immense. Sucker punch the whole world."

"Maybe they are doing exactly that. Maybe what we have seen is just the beginning." She patted down her scarf. "Anyway, it's just a theory. I have six more."

✳

Before I went too far down the rabbit hole, burrowing deep into the archaeological strata of Diane's mystical theories, there was another possibility I had to check on. I'd learned about it a couple of years earlier in Malta, at the Financial Cryptography conference—FC, as it's called.

I like FC. The talks are good, and it's one of the few research conferences where you can hear not just about the cloud-cuckoo-land blockchain systems they cook up in academia, but some practical, cutting-edge ideas. That's why I go, but I'm told most attendees like it because it's a big junket. It's always held on a warm island in winter or, as it was that year, early spring.

I attended practically all of the talk sessions, even the morning ones, sitting in a windowless conference room while half the attendees were in the "hallway track." At an ordinary conference, that means exchanging ideas and gossip outside the lecture hall. At FC, they're out together on the beach, a row of flabby nerds flopped on the sand, sunning skin that looks like the underside of a flounder. But who am I to talk? Unlike me, at least they air themselves for a few hours every year.

Malta was the perfect setting for FC. It's become a European Union cryptocurrency hub, and that's just the latest notch on the historical time line there at the crossroads of the Mediterranean. The island was owned centuries ago by the Knights of Malta, a powerful medieval order of warrior-monks. They still exist today. (What your modern warrior-monk actually does for a living, I can't imagine, but the Knights are alive and well and even issuing their own coins and passports.) In the sixteenth century, when all Christendom was imperiled by the Ottoman Empire, it was the Great Siege of Malta that turned the tide. Malta was also a staging ground for the Allied invasion of Sicily, one of the great strategic victories against the Nazis in World War II. The place is a wedding cake of civilizations and epochal historical events. We at FC could imagine that our charge over the hill, blockchain pennants flying and crypto battle cries rending the sky, was yet another great historical event, the crowning layer of the cake.

It was during a conference-organized tour of Mdina, a compact, fortified medieval maze of a city on the island, that I fell in with Alistair Llewelyn-Davies.

I'd seen him swimming in the hotel pool that morning, executing smooth, splashless laps when I left for the first sessions. He was drying off when I came back two hours later. He'd burnt every last molecule of fat off his tall frame. His head was shaved, probably good for cutting drag in the pool. It also perfected his resemblance to a hale mummy. Among the academics and people from technology companies at the conference, he was an outlier: He worked at a conventional bank, a big one, in their London office, doing something that sounded quasi-technical.

He and I met on the tour when we lingered to admire stone carvings of armor pointed out by the guide on one of the sandstone building facades. We fell behind the others.

"This city is extraordinary," I said as we began walking again and I tried to keep pace with Alistair's long strides. "It looks like it was conjured out of sand in a lost Arabian Nights story. I'm glad it survived."

"Survived what in particular?" Alistair asked. I hadn't yet pegged him as the kind of person who kept a mental catalog of military campaigns in Malta over the last millennium.

"Bombing. Malta was strategically important during World War II," I ventured knowledgeably. "It was bombed by the Axis powers. It must have been hard to defend, with Italy just miles away."

"It was," he said. "More bomb tonnage was dropped on Malta than Dresden. At the beginning of the war, the sum total of our defenses here against Italian airpower was a force of three biplanes: Faith, Hope, and Charity. And they largely succeeded."

"Three biplanes against Mussolini's air force? Really?"

"If you make a pilgrimage to a museum here, you can behold Faith."

Alistair, it turned out, was a font of surprising facts and views about everything. Malta and World War II: Malta was the base for air cover when the Allies invaded Sicily in 1943. But what really helped was the US government soliciting help from the Mafia. Cryptocurrency: Africa is now the best place to launch new cryptocurrency technologies because there's almost no regulation. Swimming: Human beings are genetically programmed to be underwater, a fact evidenced by what's called the diving response, a physiological reaction that automatically constricts your blood vessels and slows your heart rate. It took someone like him with an offbeat view of the world to tell me what he soon would. And it took my spending the day with him in a place like Malta to believe the outlandish things he said. In fact, some I didn't believe until later, when the Delphians made the outlandish all too real.

That evening, before the conference banquet (which we ate beside the Knights of Malta, unseen at a reception in a screened-off part of the restaurant), he and I booked a tour of the Grand Harbour. We took one of the traditional bright blue, red, and yellow Maltese boats, painted with eyes on the front as they've been for thousands of years and updated with an engine.

The pilot wasn't much of a tour guide. We swept across the harbor, and over the noise of the motor and wind he shouted the names of places and sites like bus stops. We relied on the guidebook on my phone for details. The pilot was lazy because he could afford to be. You don't need to know Malta's history. Just look around and it will steal over you, scouring away your self-important cares with its changeless honey-colored stone and sea breezes from places of legend.

We lingered near Fort Saint Angelo, a tiered bastion of irregular walls rising like a cliff from a peninsula thrust into the harbor, the headquarters of the Knights of Malta during the Great Siege. The low sun faceted its sheer walls gold and orange. All around us, crammed onto the spits of land flanking the harbor and stacked higgledy-piggledy up the surrounding hills, were the ancient buildings of Valletta and Vittoriosa, their stone aflame in the evening light. We were bobbing far from the glass towers of the world's banking centers, far from eavesdroppers, unmoored in time. It was a place for confidences.

"I need to tell you," Alistair said, moving close to me, "there's a powerful coalition growing, with a serious plan to destroy you."

"Me?"

"Your oracle network. There's a small cabal of major banks in Europe and Asia that worry they didn't embrace blockchain tech early enough. Now they want to see it fail."

"Fail? I don't see how they can possibly kill it off at this point."

"Just as the oil majors can't kill off renewable energy, but they do what they can to impede it."

"So you mean this cabal will just kneecap a few critical blockchain projects like mine and that will be a win for them?"

"And create short-selling opportunities."

"So what on earth is their plan?"

"Half is legal and—" My phone screen was still illuminated with the guidebook. Alistair gave it a sidelong glance. I took the hint—paranoid, perhaps, but then I didn't know what he was going to tell me—and turned the phone off. "—half is less legal. I don't know why, but I'm going to trust you. What they're doing is distasteful to me. If you're forearmed, perhaps you can stop it."

"Why not tell the authorities?"

"Unless there's clear criminal activity, whistleblowers fare badly. They'll think I've lost the plot."

He saw that I didn't understand.

"They'll think I'm batty," he explained. "In any case, I need your word that you'll keep this absolutely hush-hush."

"I can keep a secret."

"The legal part. First, there's the obvious stratagem of funding critics and negative publicity—all under the covers, of course."

"Isn't there a reputational risk if they're caught?"

"Of course. Second, they've begun to strike secret deals with data providers, here and in the States. Those agreements are meant eventually to cut you off from data and weaken your network."

"That's legal?"

"I don't see why not. They'll also secretly buy up decentralized financial instruments. As they erode your network, they'll take advantage of any hiccups to induce market chaos. Which, of course, will be attributed to you."

"Isn't that market manipulation? Surely *that* is illegal?"

"Quite legal, actually—on the face of it, at least—if part of a carefully documented arbitrage strategy."

"And then?"

"And then . . ." he said, raising his eyebrows. For all his surface aplomb, I think he was anxious. He stood up and stretched his back, one hand on a pole that held up the boat's sun canopy. His white linen blazer flapped like a loose sail.

"And then . . ." I repeated.

He sat.

"Just stay alert for a few things."

"We've been out for almost one hour," called the pilot. "We go back in a few minutes." I gave him a thumbs-up.

"You don't want to make that gesture around the Mediterranean," said Alistair, narrowing his eyes. "It doesn't mean what you think it does. Fine here, but trouble in the wrong places."

"Right," I said. *Something threatening? Vulgar?* I was too embarrassed to ask. "Stay alert, you were saying."

Alistair passed a hand over his smooth head and neck. "Unreliable nodes are not unheard of in your network. That's normal in blockchain systems." Nodes are the individual computers that compose a blockchain system—basically what you can think of as servers. They're run by individuals in the community—people or companies. When you've got tens, hundreds, or thousands of them, some inevitably fail. But a good blockchain system has enough redundancy to remain unaffected. Alistair added, "What would be unusual and dangerous in an oracle network is the sudden failure of some highly reputable nodes. Do you have safeguards?"

"Yes, but you're saying—"

"I'm saying nothing. Next, your oracles are public infrastructure. They can be used by anyone. Bad people could turn up doing bad things with their smart contracts. A selective kill switch controlled by someone trustworthy could be helpful."

"Some people like that idea, but that kind of centralization is never going to happen. Only the community can act. What else?"

"That's all."

He was suggesting that a group of major banks across two continents planned to jeopardize their reputations, if not businesses, by committing financial malfeasance and cybersecurity crimes to disrupt our network. It sounded like a conspiracy theory. And still I could tell he was holding something back.

"That's not all. What else, Alistair?"

"Look, for the rest I only have conjecture."

"A couple of friends are out on the water shooting the breeze after drinks," I said. At a cantina that afternoon there had been beer for him, water with lemon for me. "What's more fitting than wild conjecture?"

"Very well." He shifted on the bench, turning his back to the pilot. "These conferences. You know a journalist investigating government corruption was killed in Malta some years back by a car bomb? Members of the prime minister's inner circle were implicated, and the prime minister resigned."

"I didn't."

"Your conferences often take place in locales even dodgier than Malta and . . ."

Murder? I thought. *No way.*

Later I looked up some of the strange facts Alistair told me. The Mafia in World War II. Diving response. Car bomb. They were all true.

✳

After Malta, we met for coffee or a meal a few times when he visited New York City.

I'd sent him email asking to talk by video, but after a day, hadn't heard back. It was risky, and frankly Alistair intimidated me, but time was short and I had his telephone number. Although it was late, I knew he was often in the United States. Anyway, he once told me he didn't sleep much. I texted him.

(Me) *Hope you're well. History question for you, if OK.*
(Alistair, a minute later) *Of course. Good to hear from you— given situation.*
(Me) *Remember tour boat under Malta fortress? Talked about Turks' plan to destroy Christendom.*
(Alistair, after a long pause) *Yes.*
(Me) *The rogue contract on my head. Something Turks would have done?*
(Alistair) *No. Crazy stuff. Too Byzantine. Not Turkish.*
(Me) *Would Turks have been happy about it?*
(Alistair) *No. Imams found new religious doctrines dangerous.*
(Me) *OK. Thanks.*
(Alistair) *Frightfully sorry. Ping me if I can help. Good luck.*

I didn't know exactly how to interpret Alistair's reply about imams. It could mean Greek religion was too outlandish for a bank. Or, in keeping with the bank/Turk metaphor, it could mean the banks didn't want smart contracts to create trouble outside the financial realm and spook their customers.

The specifics didn't matter. Only the upshot was important and it was clear: Banks weren't going to go near a rogue contract. I'd already figured bankers are just money-crazed, not the Delphian kind of crazy. Alistair confirmed it. The only god they believe in is Mammon. Still, I did have to check.

TWELVE

Diane had gotten a name from Soren Mercator while we were in his vault. A name connected with Viganò's work for her. *Farnese*. There was just one problem: She'd already had that name for years.

She and counterparts in Europe had long wanted the police in Switzerland to raid Farnese's house or some office he had there, but never managed to gather enough evidence. She suspected Farnese of being behind some of the most important looted Greco-Roman antiquities coming into the United States. Most were sold using triangulation, meaning that the vase, or whatever it was, was sold to a museum or collector through a middleman. Farnese's name never appeared in the suspicious transactions, just the squeaky-clean ones.

Diane explained all of this in a video call late that evening in which she updated me on progress—mostly a lack of it—stemming from our visit to Soren Mercator.

Before he died, Viganò had made some progress in linking tainted pieces of art to Farnese by tracing auction sales. Dealers like Farnese try to launder their looted wares through Sotheby's, Christie's, and the other big auction houses. They buy and sell them through fictitious owners, and even buy their own pieces from themselves. Laundering a piece through an auction house creates a pedigree. Cleansed of its dirt, fresh loot from a grave in Greece or Italy, like a silver cup—or chalice, or whatever they call them—is reborn as a clean piece when it's discovered in an attic and becomes "a fine example acquired from the collection of the Schmidt family of Zurich in a sale at Sotheby's." A ring of shills, dealers buying and selling from one another—again, through fictitious owners—can make certain pieces seem to be in high demand and jack up their prices.

Diane believed that Farnese ran a sophisticated international operation, called a *cordata* in his native Italy. Like any criminal network, it was a hierarchy. Farnese was at the top. Grave robbers were at the bottom. Middlemen, front men, smugglers, shady dealers, forgers, and other seedy characters were somewhere in the middle.

Diane convinced Meghan Maybell to give her the photos of the silver cup and the vase she'd shot on the sly, and in the end, even got the name of the dealers who'd approached Soren. She managed to find traces of what might be a fresh encrustation of dirt on the objects in the photos, an indication of looting.

But there was no smoking gun. The objects didn't appear on the Interpol database of stolen works of art. If they were fresh from the ground, there would be no record of their existence. Not only that, but Soren's dealers, like Farnese himself, were based in Europe. Their galleries were in Paris. Even with Diane's strong connections, she'd need ironclad evidence to get the French authorities to raid their gallery.

Even if that happened, we'd only get one plodding step closer to Farnese. And even then, Farnese's connection to the rogue contract—the thing I cared most about—was purely circumstantial. There was Viganò's investigation of tainted artifacts that might be connected to Farnese. There was also Soren's apparent mention of Farnese in connection with the Delphic artifacts that had recently surfaced. In the very best case, *if* we managed to bag Farnese by going after Soren's dealers and *if* he was connected to the rogue contract, results would at best take months or years, not the week and a bit we had before Apollo nailed my skin to a tree.

Diane's job was always tough. She explained that antiquities smuggling is an orphaned branch of law enforcement, hard to prosecute. It's not like, say, heroin smuggling. The customers aren't junkies, buying a toxin that rots the body. They're the cream of society, buying art that enriches the soul. No one sees or pities the archaeologist shedding hot tears down a borehole punched into a pillaged tomb.

To add insult to injury, Faranese was friendly with prominent collectors and museum curators in New York and Los Angeles. He frequented both cities. Diane showed me an old photo of him beaming beside a big Greek vase he'd donated to the Getty Museum. She'd met him several times.

"He's supposed to be an expert, but I don't think he knows much. Which convinces me even more that he's the *capo dei capi*. He reminds me of my director at the Bureau."

So the name Soren gave us was a dead end. It was up to me to find another way.

✳

Most everyone I know invests in cryptocurrency. Betting on its insane market gyrations is addictive. Some of the people at Adyton have price tickers visible at all times on their monitors. One has his smartwatch buzz whenever his crypto portfolio value moves a percentage point. As you'd guess, he gets a lot of stimulation. People with a tad more discipline just reload prices in their browsers all day to get their little dopamine hits. I've got bad habits, but usually don't behave like a frenzied, button-pushing lab rat. Viganò's death turned me into one.

The rogue contract was programmed to pay out a bounty hours after a valid claim was made. *If* Viganò had in fact been killed, it could come to light whenever the assassins claimed their reward. Any minute. Or next week. Or never. I coded up an alerting program that would send a text message to my phone the second a bounty payout was detected.

But that wasn't enough. What if there was a bug in my code? What if the text message got delayed? I checked on the bounty status in a browser window. I checked on my phone. I checked during my meeting with Diane while she told me about Farnese. I checked whenever there was a lull in my work going through the Delphians' code that evening. I checked, and between the lulls in my checking, I went through the code. It became an itch, a reflex, a compulsion. Hour after hour. I tried to stop but couldn't. It got into my nervous system. I couldn't sit still. To distract and wean myself, I played a shooter game in VR, the most immersive experience I know. Big mistake just before bed. Throughout the night, my hypervigilant body twitched sleep away like it was a buzzing housefly.

I blame what I did the next morning on sleep deprivation, desperation, and the Devil.

✳

"You want to use cracked trusted hardware?" Corinne whispered with a look of innocent horror. I couldn't tell if she was reacting to my request or the state of my face after an ugly night. "Are you serious?"

"Yes, me. The guy who's fighting for his life."

She typed out a smart-contract command, one phased out years ago because devs deemed it too dangerous: "`selfdestruct(owner);`". Her message was clear. What I was proposing to do could get me fired, if not destroy my reputation in the community. Worse still for an ideological purist like me, it seemed to contradict everything I stood for.

"That's one way of putting it," I said. Sanctum relied on trusted hardware for its nodes. I intended to inject cracked trusted hardware into the network to create a back door I could use to find the Delphians. Verboten on every level, but I told myself that it would be a temporary, itsy-bitsy, dollhouse-sized back door.

"It's just so unlike you," Corinne insisted. "You're the one who always talks about oracles being incorruptible like it's religious doctrine."

"This wouldn't change that. I'm the one who designed half our safeguards. Remember? It would only help me find out who they are."

"That's not true. You know it isn't. If there are enough broken nodes, someone can falsify—"

"There won't be. Just one."

"And you realize that if you're caught . . ."

"It will ruin what's left of my beautiful career. All nine days of it. I know."

"Don't say that. Please don't say that." She looked at the floor. "I don't know anyone useful anyway. I hear trusted hardware's gotten much harder to crack."

I shook my head. I was avoiding naming Mork because I didn't want to hurt her feelings. "I'll find someone myself, then. I just thought you'd have better connections."

"Don't do it."

"I've got to."

"I don't mean using a broken node. I mean talking to *him*."

"I'm sorry, Corinne. I was trying to—"

"That only makes it worse."

"I'll be honest then. I wanted to find another way. But he's already emailed me."

Mork Lupu was an old boyfriend of hers. Old on the time scale of a rotting fish, which is to say their relationship had ended—for good, I hoped—a couple of weeks earlier. There were only two things more incredible than the year Corinne spent tethered to an object she outclassed in every way. First, according to her, when far from the madding crowd, Mork was somehow a charming and tender mate. Second, there was the way it ended. *He* dumped *her*. Given what I knew of him, it was no wonder Corinne then ditched the male half of the species and reverted to what I think was her original orientation.

"Don't do it," she said. "I'm not saying this just because I hate him. He sucks people's souls out of their bodies the way he sucks secret keys out of computers."

"What choice do I have?"

"He'll make you regret it."

"If I let him. I've dealt with him before."

"You think you're smarter than he is, and you are. But you're too nice. He'll stoop lower than you can imagine. You're dealing with Beelzebub. Believe me. Please. If you have to do it, then let me help."

"Help me create a back door? That's not like you."

She squeezed her eyes shut. "There's just no winning."

"Look, I'm sorry. If there were any justice in the world, they'd be offing Mork, not me. Then neither of us would need to bend our principles."

❋

Mork suggested we meet at a coffee shop in Hudson Yards, near his start-up and, coincidentally, my apartment. Not that my convenience entered his mind. I had to wait twenty minutes—Mork was always late, so I'd at least gotten my mocha—before he even texted.

I sighed, downed the chocolaty dregs from my cup, and left with the cappuccino I'd ordered for him.

"Well, well, well," he said, shouting over the wind as he holstered his phone in a belt case. "If it isn't my friend Victor." He pronounced it "Vik-tour." He claims to have gotten his doctorate at Cambridge, but he's clearly not British. No one, not even Corinne, knows his real nationality.

I was still out of breath. The elevator was full, so I made the mistake of climbing to the top of the Vessel, the outdoor sculpture that's a two-hundred-million-dollar set of copper-sheathed, interlocking stairways to nowhere. Then up a flight of stairs and down, up and down, winding around the top level looking for him, living the physics of bad dreams, where you can't seem to guide your steps in a straight line, only toward something unpleasant.

"Victor? Who the hell is Victor?" I asked.

"Victor Frankenstein. The one who created the monster that murders people. Sanctum, I think they call it. That's you, right?"

"Glad to see you too, Mork."

"You can see my office window up there." He pointed at the top of one of the thousand-foot buildings, hard on the neck even at 150 feet above the soulless, windswept plaza. The wind fluttered in our ears.

"Here's a cappuccino for you."

He pushed back a mop of dirty blond hair from his fleshy, overgrown boy's face. The wind tousled it again. He popped the plastic lid off the coffee cup, gave the contents a suspicious look, and gulped down most of them. There'd been plenty of time for the cappuccino to cool.

"I like coming up here," he said, foam clinging to his mouth. "It's awesome. Like being in an Escher."

"Lucky you. A perennial tourist."

"I've already guessed what you're trying to do." He laughed, as he always does, with a kind of hissing and spluttering that always makes me wonder if he's going to start foaming at the mouth. And that's without a cappuccino.

I gave a stony stare. "What's the price?"

"Who says I'm selling?"

"Come on. *You* contacted *me*."

"But I've realized you may not have that kind of money."

"Look, you know why I need it."

"The Delphians are stupid. Everyone knows that trusted hardware can be broken."

"Outside of maybe some big intelligence agencies, Pandemon is the only organization I know that's done it recently." Pandemon was his semi-corporate hacker organization. They call themselves a "pirate hacker collective," whatever that means. "And you haven't even told me if you've got some fancy new side-channel attack to crack the latest version."

"Correct and correct. So Apollo had the professor killed, huh?" The wind jerked at the plastic cup cover he held loosely between his fingers, threatening to waft it to New Jersey.

"We don't know that he was murdered," I said.

"Prices for Delphian-themed NFTs shot up after he died yesterday. There was an NFT of you I thought about buying, but I hesitated and lost it. Stupid mistake. You haven't officially endorsed any yet, have you?"

"No."

"Doesn't matter, apparently. Someone flipped the one I'm talking about and made fifty thousand dollars."

"Can we get back to the matter at hand?"

"Sure. The Delphians' 'prophecy' thing is interesting. I've been following it. They run an exact simulation of an attack on trusted hardware to generate a proof that it works. So you know, with broken trusted hardware, we could fake the proofs and generate bogus attacks that everyone thinks are real. We would scare the shit—"

"Yes, Mork, impressive. What's your price?"

"I'll have to think about it." He hissed as a prelude to another laugh. There was still a bit of foam on his mouth and a strong wind, so I took a step back.

Though he was well known for his technical chops in certain circles, I'd always heard Mork was more of a broker than a doer. Maybe he was still trying to clear something with the real brains in Pandemon. I didn't care. Half the time, when I wanted something just this side of the law, he could get it for me. And sometimes I didn't even come to regret it. When he finished laughing, I said, "I don't have much time."

"I know." He downed the rest of his cappuccino, then licked his lips. "Interesting they chose *you* as a target."

"The price of impiety."

"Now you're famous."

What was it with people and my lethal fame? I think he was actually envious.

"Sorry they passed you over," I said. "I was just complaining to some-one that there's no justice in this world."

"I'll let you know when I've decided what I can do for you. Maybe later today."

To ensure secure communication up to our paranoid standards, we verified one another's Signal safety-number QR codes on our phones before I left. I last glimpsed him snapping a photo of his office in the sky, carefree like a tourist. My turn to be envious.

✳

When developers analyze the security of smart contracts, we assume that attackers are "rational actors." That's a fancy way of saying their goal is to make money. Sometimes people just want to smash up the world a bit. That's pretty rare, though, and almost never true of sophisticated hackers. They're either in it for the money or working for a government to advance its political objectives.

I didn't know how to reason about the Delphians' behavior. It's not obvious how you make a profit spending hundreds of thousands of dollars to snuff out an archaeology professor or a harmless drudge like me. A few people thought that the Delphians' goal was to show how dangerous smart contracts were and destroy confidence in them. That would tank the cryp-tocurrency markets and enable the Delphians to make money with short selling. But that didn't make sense. Historically, attacks haven't moved cryptocurrency prices in a predictable way.

To find the Delphians' motives and their weaknesses, if they had any, I was coming to realize that I needed to learn—not just learn, but under-stand intuitively—how they thought. Given the references to ancient Greece in the Delphians' code and now bubbling up all around the inter-net, it was clear that I needed to understand the original Delphi.

Props always help. Someone had re-created ancient Delphi—moun-tains, buildings, sacred objects, and all—in virtual reality. A brand-new addition to a metaverse world. It had launched just the day before, so it was almost certainly inspired by the Delphians, if it wasn't their handi-work. I threw a virtual reality headset into my backpack and went over to the FBI building.

"I want to learn what Delphi was about," I told Diane in her office. "How the Delphians think. What they want from the world. I need to apply your theories to my understanding of their code."

"Wow! This is fun," Diane said, looking around the interior of the Temple of Apollo with the headset strapped on. To my surprise, she'd never before experienced the metaverse—or virtual reality in any form. "But it's wrong. The temple is beautiful. Look at the marble and those high coffered ceilings. But it is so empty. There are no votive offerings. And what is that thing? They have a silly little garden house for the Pythia in the adyton." She started toward it and tripped over my bag on the floor. I caught her as she stumbled. Instead of chewing me out, she dissolved into laughter. "This is crazy!"

I was steadying her when Walker appeared at the door.

"I heard you two from down the hall. What the hell are you doing to her?"

"She had a bad trip," I said. "Must be the ethylene."

"Huh?"

I led Diane to a safer part of the office and backed away. Walker loomed over me as we watched Diane take mincing steps. "Why don't you just show her how to make the VR image transparent?" he asked me. "Anyway, I had a question for you."

"The Omphalos is wrong too," Diane insisted. "It should have a kind of wool covering."

"What's she talking about?" Walker asked. "The French Snuffleupagus?"

"I think they modeled it after the one in the museum," Diane continued. "Also, there are no golden eagles."

"What's the question?" I asked Walker.

Walker watched Diane feeling her way around, shook his head, and turned back to me. "Again, why did they target you?"

"Again? I never told you why."

"So tell me."

"It happened after I set up my own contract to neutralize the first rogue contract. The one on Viganò. I set up a bounty, payable on successful neutralization."

"Your money?"

"My money."

"Why?"

"Seemed like a nice gesture."

"Awfully nice. You do that often?"

"No."

"Can I move without walking?" Diane asked. "I want to go outside."

"Yes. Extend your hands like wings and you'll fly," I said, "or poke the map in the—"

"How much was the bounty?" Walker asked.

"I don't remember. Maybe ten ETH." That's Ether, the cryptocurrency.

"That's not chump change," Walker said. "That's thousands of dollars. Many thousands of dollars."

"*Voilà*! The map. It worked!" Diane exclaimed.

Walker continued. "So you're a crypto millionaire?"

"I've made money. I'm not one of the crypto elite."

"But you can drop thousands of dollars to help out some shaggy old professor you never heard of. You understand why I'm having a hard time with this?"

"I'll make it easier, Walker. I donated $50,000 to an elephant conservation fund just last month. Not for the first time. I once calculated that I spend more than $3,000 a year on chocolate and $15,000 a year on a personal trainer who, thanks to the chocolate, hasn't been able to get me past the overweight 'before' results you see in front of you to the 'after' results that will only come in my afterlife next week. I paid $400 yesterday for a flat, cracked bronze phallus brooch not much bigger than your little American flag lapel pin there. I've got most of my money in the cryptocurrency market, and it's a gambling parlor. It could all vanish tomorrow. So I don't spend my money in the typical way. I don't hoard it and don't have a family to lavish it on except my bonsai trees. I don't have a car and am wearing the same T-shirts my ex-wife bought me twenty years ago to supplement a bunch of conference freebies. I wouldn't know what else to do with the money I blew on a bounty to satisfy my curiosity about whether someone else had the brilliance to punch a hole in a piece of code that it turns out was maybe crafted by an Olympian god. Clear now?"

"Got it," Walker said, wide-eyed. "Answers my question. Thanks, man." We both looked at the floor. Then at Diane. She was craning her neck toward the ceiling and pointing.

118

"It's there! The golden letter E!"

"Let me guess," Walker said. "She's on the set of *Sesame Street*, right? As in . . ." He slipped into a sonorous announcer's voice. "*Sesame Street* was brought to you today by the letter 'E' and the number 5." He didn't wait for a response. "Sorry. I'm late for a meeting." He turned and headed to the door.

"Didn't the Greeks call that letter 'epsilon'?" I asked Diane.

"Nope," Walker said over his shoulder, half-turning. "Only since the Middle Ages." Through the glass office walls I saw him glance back and wink as he strolled down the corridor.

Diane removed the headset, laughing and shaking her head. "Cool, and beautiful, but you won't learn anything from this."

"No good?"

"I hope they don't use it in classrooms."

I sighed through my nose. "Then forget it. Let's just do things the old-fashioned way."

"And what is that?"

I sat and gestured at her chair on the other side of the desk.

"So," I said, "what do the god and his minions want?"

"Light and truth."

"Meaning?"

"Meaning I can't tell you what they want or wanted. It's complicated, and often ambiguous. Have you heard of the famous prophecy to King Croesus?"

"No."

"Croesus was the ruler of a kingdom called Lydia, famous for his wealth. He had a brilliant idea. He tested all of the major oracles to learn which were trustworthy. He sent envoys to each oracle. He instructed the envoys to ask, exactly one hundred days after they departed, what the king was doing back in his kingdom. The oracle at Delphi was the only one that answered correctly."

"What was the king doing?"

"Eating tortoise soup."

"Good job. I wouldn't have guessed that."

"Croesus became one of Delphi's greatest patrons. He consulted the oracle often and made huge gifts of gold. When the rising Persian Empire became a threat in the east, he had to decide whether to raise an army against it. Naturally, he consulted the oracle at Delphi. The priestess told him that if he went to war, he'd destroy a great empire. He did go to war. And he did destroy a great empire. But the empire he destroyed was—"

We said it together. "His own."

"Maybe I read it while I was poking around," I said. "So the moral of the story is that the oracle's prophecies could contain veiled truth. But I'm a computer scientist. What I need to understand are the *rules.*"

"That's what I'm saying. There wasn't a religious law like the Ten Commandments. There were strict formulas for their religious rites and consultations at the oracle, but most are lost and there were dramatic changes over the years. We don't even know when Delphi was established. Maybe three thousand years ago. There are different myths about its founding."

"I read about it in Wikipedia. Apollo founded Delphi after killing a giant python guarding the oracle."

"Some scholars interpret the story to mean that the cult of Apollo displaced a more ancient religion, perhaps centered on an earth goddess, Gaia."

"Gaia. I forgot about Gaia . . ."

"And they believed that a shepherd—"

"This is very bad," I said. "And I read something about Gaia."

"Why is Gaia bad?"

"The Delphians attacked a system called GaiaX."

"That makes sense from a mythological point of view."

"But I thought they attacked that system because it's the only one they *could* attack. I assumed that their technical capabilities were so limited that they didn't have a choice and just attacked the most vulnerable system. That wasn't so bad. But now what you're telling me means the attack must have been targeted. They decided what system they *wanted* to attack. To attack at will, they'd have to have powerful tools. That's far more serious than I thought."

"I'm sorry. So I can help explain some of their behavior after all, but—"

"Shit."

✳

I'd already banged my head against the Delphians' code as hard as I could. Now I could only trust that hidden forces were advancing my cause. My subconscious mind beavering away at my mental models. Mork doing whatever Mork did. I wasn't sure which I trusted less, Mork or my subconscious mind, but neither was likely to listen to me, so there was no point in pleading for results. Walker's grilling might mean he and his friends weren't making headway, although he could have been toying with me. I didn't forget his parting shot and wink as he left Diane's office.

Diane was reviewing bits of Greek I'd extracted for her from the Delphians' code. She was trying to figure out what historical sources our latter-day Delphians were using, whether they identified with a particular time or place in the ancient world. And she was putting out feelers, hoping another source would yield up more than Venner or Mercator. A hot tip from the fast-paced world of classical archaeology. I wasn't holding my breath.

It may sound crazy, but I thought about working on the next generation of Sanctum, on Sanctum v2. It's not that I was being tempted back into an abusive relationship with a blockchain. If I was going to leave a legacy, I'd need to seal it quickly, and I could see no better path. If nothing else, the Delphians had demonstrated Sanctum's power, and it was my success, in effect, that was my undoing. So what if my brainchild had a touch of Oedipal complex and wanted to kill me? My fingers were itching for my keyboard, a way to do something and distract myself.

But Diane's question about what I would do if I were a Delphian nagged at me. I told her I'd be sowing the seeds for something tremendous. I shouldn't assume the Delphians only poked their heads above the rampart to loose their arrows. It might be worth sifting through nutty online rumors to see if the Delphians were there somewhere, spreading silently through cyberspace. Maybe those ads I saw weren't as targeted as I thought.

Adyton's followers are a ferociously loyal fan club. Their memes often feature Pepe the Frog—a humanoid green frog with broad popularity in crypto circles. Pepe grinning, smoking $100 bills rolled up into a cigar after he's made a fat profit trading our tokens. Pepe sitting in a yellow Lamborghini, wearing Lukas's famous shirt. Pepe in a Santa Claus suit, lavishing gifts on Adyton's faithful. These people wanted to help me and were hunting for clues with furious energy. I felt some comfort in knowing that the Delphians had kicked a hornets' nest. But others—the kind who'd sell their grandmothers for a few likes on their social-media posts—created memes about me featuring a golden-orange Pepe. That's the color of a species of frog that secretes a lethal toxin, the kind used in poison arrows.

Anonymous claims, theories, and counter-theories about the rogue contract and the Delphians' "prophecies" were swirling around in social media and online forums. There were thousands of repostings and likes, which could mean this stuff was being read by hundreds of thousands of people—or more. It was mostly the usual vicious rumors and FUD, as they call it: Fear, Uncertainty, and Doubt.

```
Insider here. The dev at Adyton had a fight with
Lukas their CEO. They were punching each other
and the guy literally drew blood. I saw it. Lukas
is behind the rogue contract. Its all gonna come
out and hes going to prison and everyones gonna
dump. Short their token, screenshot this, and
thank me later.

$1mil to neutralize the rogue contract. $700k to
kill the guy. Even genius autists can't collect
the $1mil. But a brainlet like me can tell you
how to make the $700k.

Apollo is Satoshi Nakamoto. Trust me. He's mad
because Bitcoin was taken over by Wall Street.
His next brainwave is going to obliterate all
the fucking devs and scam artists who betrayed
him. And I'll be laughing my head off.
```

Plus plenty of tripe about the Jews, the Illuminati, and I don't know what else. I'm a quarter Jewish and a quarter Illuminati, so I found this stuff particularly offensive.

I'd already read every blog post on the Delphians' code by every technical expert I trusted. Nothing useful there. Someone observed that the times at which the rogue contract and the Delphians' "prophecy" system launched were often between 9:00 a.m. and 5:00 p.m. Beijing time, suggesting Chinese intelligence was behind it. But the Delphians knew what they were doing and wouldn't have made such an obvious slip. So another theory was that the launch times were a false flag, cover for some other intelligence agency. Another was that they were a double blind, and it really was the Chinese. Yet another was that it was a triple blind, and it was really the Russians.

A few people posted stylometric analyses, attempts to identify the authors of the Delphians' code. Stylometry involves computer-based statistical comparisons between pseudonymous content and content that has known authorship. It's been pretty successful in unmasking pseudonymous authors. It once outed a fresh new literary voice named Robert Galbraith, author of a novel called *The Cuckoo's Calling*. Galbraith turned out to be a pen name for J. K. Rowling. In the case of code, the idea is to find a stylistic match between a piece of pseudonymous code and a code sample with known authorship. While it's not good for basic code, most of which is AI-assisted, it seemed promising for the Delphians' rogue contract. The harder the coding task and the more experienced the coder, the more distinctive the result, and the better stylometry works. But maybe it doesn't work so well for a god. Stylometric analysis of the Delphians' code attributed it variously to me, an experimental code-synthesis program from a European university, and Pepe the Frog. No one had anything solid.

At least I wasn't alone in finding the Delphians' code a little otherworldly. One well-known smart-contract researcher drew an analogy to Crusaders first encountering Arab military technology. The Arabs forged their swords of a legendary substance called Damascus steel. To the Crusaders, these weapons were familiar in form and function, yet alien, superior, tinged with magic. Strong enough to cleave a Crusader's clumsy weapon, yet sharp enough to slice through a piece of silk wafted into the air. (Modern analysis has found carbon nanotubes in Damascus steel.) And the Arabs' weapons were beautiful too, like the Delphians' code. You had to wonder why someone would devote such elaborate craftsmanship to a functional object. The pattern of rippling water on the surface of a Damascus-steel blade so mesmerizes with its loveliness that you forget the thing was meant to inflict death.

However you look at it, it wasn't surprising that the Delphians' following snowballed. There were plenty of people outraged about the rogue contract. They posted rants online—some frankly hard to dispute—about the excesses and perils of cryptocurrency and public blockchains. Others spouted nonsense about how rogue contracts were a giant step toward the artificial-intelligence apocalypse. But on the other side were people seduced by the Delphians' power. Lacking a direct connection to the god, they formed a community of would-be disciples. And not a small one.

Even if an online post is written by an obvious nutjob, it's hard not to see a grain of truth in it. So I'll admit it: The Delphians mob's online rants really shook me.

```
We don't know what terrible things the professor
and the Adyton guy did. Plenty probably. And
GaiaX was a known shitcoin. Apollo's followers
believe in truth and they're on the bleeding
edge of tech that will change the world. Don't
assume they're evil.

In Greek religion, Apollo represents Truth.
Dionysus is his opposite. He represents
slobbering drunks. Choose your side, frens.

i need to be a part of this. i cant say why but
i need to be. if youve made contact please help
me. i sent a message but i didnt get an answer.
please. i made a lot of money in crypto and im
willing to pay.
```

There was a way to make contact, in principle. The Delphians' smart contracts were launched from blockchain addresses under the Delphians' control. You could send a message to one of those addresses. You could even encrypt your message, since every address has a public cryptographic key associated with it. I saw lots of messages sent on chain, some encrypted, some not. People sent money to the rogue contract for the bounty on my head, but far more money directly to the Delphians' addresses. They also sent virtual art and goods in the form of NFTs—the digital equivalent of the golden statues and jewelry and whatnot once offered to pagan gods. A virtual pile of shimmering coins and precious artworks. Millions of dollars' worth.

Blockchains' main feature is their transparency. Everything that happens on them is visible forever to everyone. That's why I could see people's encrypted messages and virtual tributes. And I could see that the Delphians didn't reply on the blockchain to anyone's message. Or touch any of the offerings to the god.

The cryptocurrency community was already long steeped in mythology and cultlike behavior. It all started with Satoshi Nakamoto, as Bitcoin's creator is known, the Homer of cryptocurrency. As the original poet of decentralization, he bestowed his gift on the world and then vanished from the internet.

"Satoshi" is like "Homer" in another way too: It's just a name. No one knows who she, he, or they are or were. At least if anyone does, they're not saying. Theories abound. Maybe it was Hal Finney, an early cypherpunk— meaning a believer in cryptography as a world-changing force. He died of a terrible degenerative disease and is now frozen in a ten-foot-tall tank of liquid nitrogen in Arizona. Or Nick Szabo, another cypherpunk who invented smart contracts and a proto-Bitcoin called Bit Gold. Or both of them. Or the National Security Agency. Or extraterrestrials.

Before Bitcoin, the very best academic researchers tried for two decades to create a viable cryptocurrency. All of them failed. Whoever Nakamoto was, his invention cracked the social, economic, and technical problems needed to make it happen. Bitcoin might just as well have just dropped from the sky.

This previous history of crypto mythmaking was perhaps why the community of Delphian hangers-on had no trouble devising their own mythology. The central idea was something known as the Great Return. It spread virally and I couldn't trace its genesis. As best I could make out, Apollo is the sun god. He is born as the rising sun, scoops his arc across the sky, dies in the luminous blood of twilight, and is reborn as the next sunrise. This is a metaphor for his cycles of ascendancy on Earth, which span many centuries, followed by equal periods of darkness, when the god departs for Olympus or to live among a mythical people called the

Hyperboreans. (The god's true dark-period vacation home and its cosmic address were the subjects of acrimonious online debate.)

Another cycle on Earth was beginning now. His disciples were readying themselves, turning to the metaphorical east in the glimmering minutes before dawn, ready to receive and be blessed by the first rays when the newly resplendent god shone again upon the earth.

In this idea and under the surface of everything I read was a collective holding of the breath. I could feel everyone—coders, yearning disciples, onlookers, and my phone—waiting, waiting for that one transaction claiming the bounty on Viganò, if it ever came. Waiting to see whether a piece of code had, for the very first time in history, reached its baleful hand into the world and taken a human life. Only then would it all be real.

```
The future is here. If you stand in the way of Truth,
        Apollo will delete you.
```

THIRTEEN

"**G**ood news," Mork's message read. Time received: 2:42 a.m. I saw it when I woke up and messaged him throughout the late morning. I got ahold of him by video just after one o'clock in the afternoon.

"Hey, Victor," he said, his face pressed up to the camera, too big for the screen. "I've got the key you wanted."

He meant a secret cryptographic key. A sequence of hundreds of random bits (usually 256, to be exact): 1100101001110 . . . The type of secret key he was talking about was supposed to be protected by special security features in the CPU, the main chip on a computer, and more or less impossible to extract. But nothing is impossible in the world of security, and Pandemon had refined their key-extraction hacks over a number of years.

Pandemon could sell their hacks—or the secret keys they extracted with them—to international intelligence agencies. Instead, they usually played nice and warned the manufacturer of the CPU about the dangerous vulnerabilities they'd uncovered. Not always, though. And even if they did, until a security patch came out, Pandemon's hacks amounted to a secret weapon.

The secret keys that Mork now claimed Pandemon could extract were associated with a security technology known as trusted hardware. As I've mentioned, this was the critical technology behind Sanctum. Trusted hardware is present in many cloud servers. It creates what you can think of as a black box in which it's possible to run computer programs. The trusted hardware can "attest" to exactly what program is running in this black box—i.e., send digital proof over the internet—so that a hacker can't tamper with the program or swap in fake software. The trusted hardware also ensures that the black box is opaque, meaning that it conceals both programs' code and data. The black box created by trusted hardware is so secure that it can protect programs even against the very owner of the server.

Trusted hardware, though, relies critically on cryptographic secret keys. If one of these keys can be extracted from the trusted hardware environment, the result is fatal: The key can be transferred into a *hacker's own piece of software*. The hacker can then create software that looks to all the world like it's running securely on trusted hardware and protecting users from attack, but actually isn't.

When this happens, unsuspecting users of an internet service or a blockchain system might think they're sending their sensitive data to an ultra-secure software application protected by a piece of solid, honest-to-goodness trusted hardware. Instead, they could be sending their data straight into a hacker's own computer program.

All security technologies of course evolve in a game of cat and mouse. Trusted hardware had been improving over the years. We'd reached the point where experts believed that only the most well-resourced organizations (read US government intelligence agencies) could crack it, and only under limited circumstances. We at Adyton thought that trusted hardware was finally beyond the reach of the likes of Pandemon. Plus we'd developed some technical tricks—like the one I'd told Vitalik about at the Sanctum release party—to bolster trusted-hardware security against at least certain types of attacks. That's why we believed that trusted hardware made Sanctum safe for users.

If Mork was telling the truth, though, we were wrong. Ordinarily, this would have panicked me. Now, though, it might prove to be my salvation. With one of Mork's extracted keys, I could play the role of the hacker. I could set up a fake server in the Sanctum network with my own home-grown software, instead of the real, privacy-preserving Sanctum software. Smart contracts in Sanctum migrated around the servers in the network. So with luck the Delphians' rogue smart contract, along with any secret data it contained, would soon find its way into my fake server. The Delphians would drift into what they thought was an opaque black box protecting their secrets, but was in fact my own personal transparent cube. And there I would be, squashing my nose up against one of the cube's crystalline walls, peering at the Delphians' juicy secrets within.

At a minimum, if things worked out, I might be able to see the names of the five assassination targets that their rogue contract hadn't yet revealed. Also, any submitted calling cards—although those might mean little, since they were encrypted and could come from anyone, not just real assassins. But if I got really lucky, I might learn secrets about the Delphians' setup that I could use to hack and terminate their contract.

"Enough with the Victor stuff," I said to Mork. "But thanks for the key." I hesitated. "How much?"

"Seven ETH." (He pronounced it "Eeeth.") Seven Ether.

The talismanic number shouldn't have crossed Mork's lips. The arch smile that formed on his face didn't fit him. It was too knowing. The buffoon had turned into a creepy clown.

"Seven," I said, studying his face. "Why seven? What's the story, Mork?"

He gave me a grave look. Then, reverting to buffoon form, he burst into laughter. I was glad the plastic laminate on my laptop screen was there to protect me from his spittle flying over the internet. The hissing trailed off.

"Too much?" he asked. He grinned and hissed a little more.

He could have read about the number seven anywhere, I told myself. It didn't mean he was a Delphian.

"Seven ETH is dirt cheap," I said.

"Seven's lucky. You're just a lucky guy."

"Yeah, my first thought when I fell out of bed this morning."

"Maybe you want instead to officially endorse one of those Delphian NFTs some people have started selling. If you tip me off beforehand, I can make a killing. Then you can keep your seven ETH."

"No thanks."

"That's too bad because—"

"What's going on, Mork? What's the catch?"

"You know the terms. Tell anyone, leak the key, or screw up in any way, and we boil you alive."

"You'll have competition." I had a bad feeling about the whole thing, but that's pretty much what I expected. "Fine. Terms accepted."

"Hey, does Corinne still miss me?"

"The terms are seven ETH and my soul, not the right to malign your betters."

"Yes, in other words. That's what I thought."

"When will I get the key?"

"Already sent. Check your email for something from ProtonMail. We'll bill you for consulting services."

I guess nobody's ever faulted Beelzebub for poor customer service.

✳

In the dark days of World War II, on the eve of the Allies' invasion of Sicily in 1943, the British mounted one of the most successful covert operations in military history. On the corpse of a fake Royal Marine, (Acting) Major William Martin, they planted a fake letter from the British high command. The letter indicated that Sicily was a feint, and the Allies really planned to invade Greece. The British arranged for the major to wash up on a beach in Spain and fall into the hands of the Germans.

On the face of it, the deception was simple. To get it right, though, they needed Major Martin to be thoroughly convincing to the Germans. They created a fictional London itinerary for him covering the week before his discovery and stuffed his pockets with a paper trail. A receipt for a new shirt, a threatening letter from Lloyd's about an overdraft, stubs for theater tickets, a bill for lodging at the Naval and Military Club. He carried a photo of his fiancée Pam—in reality the coquettish beach photo of a beautiful clerk from an MI5 typing pool—along with two love letters and a receipt for a diamond engagement ring. The pièce de résistance was his underwear. To reflect the prevailing shortage of military underwear, the fine woolen garment was supplied by a civilian, none other than the late warden of an Oxford University college.

Martin's body found its way to a German agent. Hitler received photos of the major's documents a week later. He swallowed the deception "hook, line, and sinker," British intelligence informed Churchill. The Führer redirected German army troops and panzer divisions from the eastern front and France to the Balkans. Major Martin saved tens of thousands of Allied lives.

The whole episode may sound like it belongs in a Bond novel. That's not a coincidence. A certain Lieutenant Commander Ian Fleming helped hatch the plan.

Why do I mention Billy Martin? Because he looms large in my mind every time I need to cook up a deception in cyberspace. Billy has a critical lesson to teach: In war, successful deception requires utterly meticulous planning. To deploy Mork's key in a fake server that would fool the Delphians, I'd have to plan down to the underwear.

I named my fake Sanctum server the Magic Crystal, because it was magically transparent to me. When the Delphians' rogue contract hit the Magic Crystal, they'd think it was running safely in Sanctum, shielded from the world. But of course I'd be spying on them.

I didn't know what I'd see. As I've said, I was hoping at least to discover the names of the assassination targets that the Delphians' contract hadn't yet revealed. There was no guarantee I'd learn those names or anything useful, for that matter. But the Magic Crystal remained my best hope—as long as the Delphians didn't figure out what I was doing.

Mork's extracted key was critical to my plan, but it wasn't enough. Launching the Magic Crystal in a way that could deceive the Delphians, with their technical sophistication, presented some technical challenges.

Sanctum had a default security option known as "moving-target defense." To evade attack, as contracts ran, they hopscotched around a cluster of Sanctum servers maintained by different organizations. This perpetual movement helped protect against slow leakage of secret data from any one server to a particular organization—a potential security concern. Additionally, if servers in a cluster failed, the code on the cluster would automatically migrate to a new one.

The first technical challenge I ran up against was that Sanctum concealed which contract code was running in which cluster. So it wasn't clear where to find Delphians' code and launch the Magic Crystal. But here I lucked out. I checked public registrations of code "fingerprints" in Sanctum, used so that people could be sure of which code the various contracts were running. I learned that the Delphians had loaded their rogue contract code within an hour of the launch—before their contract went live several days later. Sanctum had been heavily subscribed and all of its clusters at launch time had been reserved for use by smart contracts developed within the blockchain industry. I deduced that the Delphians' code had to be in the first new cluster spun up after the launch.

Another problem was that a piece of code will run in different ways depending on its environment. It exhibits different "jitters." That's what I call the minute, random variations in operations and timing that happen as a software application interacts with a computer's hardware and other software. I wanted to be sure that the jitters of the Delphians' contract code running in the Magic Crystal would mirror that of their code in a genuine Sanctum server. I burned out not a few gray cells devising tricks to do this. The Magic Crystal's job was to create a fake Sanctum server with fake trusted hardware. Paradoxically, I had it perform this fakery while running on real trusted hardware—just to make its jitters look authentic.

These things were subtle—possibly overkill—but could be important. The underwear, as it were.

There were other technical stumbling blocks, but none bothered me as much as a nagging thought. Corinne had warned me that Mork would stoop lower than I could imagine. In the past, letting me down meant not following through on his promises. Now, though, things were different. He was certain to have kept a copy of the key he sold me. Once the Magic Crystal was launched, if Mork could breach Sanctum and hijack traffic in its network, he could siphon off all kinds of data into his own Magic Crystal, duplicating my power of spying—or even tamper with contracts. Some of the contracts that had launched with Sanctum ran valuable financial applications. I could be opening the door for Mork to rob our users.

But breaching Sanctum in this way would be difficult for Mork to pull off. We'd worked hard to ensure it would be hard for anyone, except perhaps an organization like an intelligence agency. And it wasn't about attacking trusted hardware. It would require a different set of technical skills than Mork and the crew at Pandemon had. So I was willing to take the risk. Besides, I was finding that when a god ordains a target on your back, you become philosophical about trifles—such as jail time for abetting larceny.

I thought about asking permission for my little caper from Lukas or even the Priestess. But I was sure Lukas would say no. His success as a CEO owed a lot to his relentless minimization of risk. And such was their working relationship that if he said no, the Priestess would agree with him and scotch the Magic Crystal. That would be the end of my only idea for finding the Delphians. In my defense, I knew my project was too unethical and dangerous to involve Corinne. I just told her that when I'd met Mork on the Vessel, there'd been no key.

As it would turn out, this half-truth probably saved my life.

✳

When I saw Walker again at Adyton, it was a rerun of the first time. There he was again in one of the glassed-in conference rooms, his back turned to me. The besuited Goliath, dome of a head, with a spinning Rotring. And there was Corinne.

During Walker's first visit, when I half suspected Corinne of being a Delphian, I figured he was interrogating her. Now I didn't know what to think. He could have been questioning her about me. He knew I was nearby, but it seemed typical of Walker to hide an investigation in plain sight.

"Feds again?" I asked, sidling up to Corinne after she returned to her desk. She flicked away a browser window.

"I wasn't supposed to tell you the first time."

"If it has to do with me . . ."

She bit her lip. "It may have to do with me."

I glanced down at the arm with the sun tattoo, now covered.

"No," she said, "not because I worship Apollo."

"Anything you can talk about?"

"No." She crossed her arms. "Are you sure there's nothing going on with Mork?"

Corinne makes me feel like I've got a transparent skull, like my brain's running in a Magic Crystal. I can never tell her a wholesale lie, not even a white one. But I can usually slip a wafer-thin truth by her, so I stuck with my story.

"As I said, there was no key when I met with him," I said. "And I won't talk to him again if I can avoid it."

She nodded and turned back to her monitor. For some reason, she was too upset to talk.

✳

Late that night, alone on the Bridge, I put the finishing touches on the Magic Crystal and the attack code needed to launch it. Floating there above the silent, throbbing city, armed with my stolen key, I might have been one of just a handful of people awake in the dark neighborhood.

133

Normally, I like working in the dead of night, on weekends, and on the few holidays when the people at Adyton take a real vacation, like Christmas and New Year's Day. The rest of the world is frozen, motionless, while I am activating my special skill. My brain and fingers spin out code. I feel like a speeding superhero. I'm a streak of light like the Flash, so fast I defy the laws of physics. Or a superhero who can stop time, like Sway from the X-Men. No one sees me flatten a gang of bank robbers, scoop up children to save them from oncoming cars, snatch two time bombs planted by terrorists in buildings on opposite sides of the city and hurl them into the sky just as they blossom into searing white light.

But things were different now. It might take a superhero to bend the arc of destiny and defeat the enemy I was up against. But I wasn't feeling so super. In the Magic Crystal I had a secret weapon. But I wasn't fighting a cartoon enemy, I was fighting something more sinister. The only good news was that I couldn't make things much worse for myself. Still, I hesitated a long time before I pushed the button and launched my code. The last time I was alone in the Bridge confronting the Delphians had been the night when I launched the neutralization contract. The start of my troubles.

"I'm not your enemy," I whispered to the small figure on the coin on my desk. The coin was a bit primitive, to be truthful, the god almost cartoonish. He sat in the nude on the Omphalos, grasping the middle of an arrow as long as his head and torso. He looked to me like he was about to give it a clumsy toss at a dartboard. But maybe that was just my hubris.

The god didn't reply, so I pushed the button. Then I packed my bag and left for home. Another restless night as a true denizen of the City That Never Sleeps. If all went well, the Delphians' code would enter the Magic Crystal within at most a day, probably within hours.

FOURTEEN

I checked every hour or so during the night. Smart contracts swam into the Magic Crystal as predicted. My setup was sound. But the Delphians' code didn't appear.

Diane texted me the next morning.

"I don't know if it will help," she said on a video call. "But I've realized how you can begin to understand the Delphians."

After our failed educational jaunt into the metaverse with the virtual-reality headset, she'd tried to get me to read specialist material on Delphi. I was supposed to ingest some poem called the Homeric Hymn to Apollo, topped with the meaty scholarly book *Delphi*, and with lashings of the Greek tragic playwright Aeschylus. The only thing I could get myself to read were the first few lines of the hymn:

> *The gods tremble before Apollo as he strides on Olympus.*
> *He approaches their seats and they leap up,*
> *All of them, as he stretches back his glittering bow.*

Nice to know he terrified not just me, but also his coworkers.

I consider myself a bit of a history buff, but didn't have the patience for the rest of Diane's syllabus. Too long, too tragic, too scholarly. My already short attention span was shrinking with my days of grace. But Diane had seen me perk up in the Helios Gallery and Mercator's vault when there were gleaming artifacts and not just ancient texts. I think that's what gave her the idea of using show and tell.

She fussed with something and raised a finger. "Listen."

I admit that my taste in music is a little narrow. I don't get rock music. I don't get jazz. I don't even get contemporary classical. I don't understand why, when there exist sublime creations like the second movement of Mozart's A Minor Piano Sonata, people instead subject themselves to the dull, strident, esoteric exercises in self-indulgence with which orchestras feel compelled to lard their programs in a hopeless quest to attract listeners besides me under the age of sixty. I've suffered through a lot of that stuff between the Bach and Tchaikovsky at Carnegie Hall.

I certainly didn't get the music Diane played for me.

There was no melody. It was all eerie, experimental-sounding scales and tempos. A little like certain types of world music, maybe in some classical Eastern tradition, but austere and primitive. I could sense a kind of sophistication in it, a complicated structure that was unintelligible to me. A small male chorus sang in a language I couldn't identify—Greek, I assumed. A string instrument was plucked to mark syllables or words. A drum materialized, also beaten syllable by syllable. Then a singer declaimed rhythmically, reminding me of the half-sung, half-spoken parts of an opera. But something was missing. There had to be some emotional content to it, some mood. It was music, after all. But was it tragic? Melancholy? Joyous? Contemplative? Angry? I couldn't tell you. It left me feeling musically autistic.

It lasted for five minutes. When it ended, Diane broke into a proud smile. "This is better than virtual reality. Now you have a real idea of the religion practiced at Delphi."

"How strange it was, you mean. Or is, if that's what our latter-day Delphians are practicing."

"And rational and complex and beautiful."

I grimaced.

"It's not that I want to praise your enemies. But we need to understand them. Apollo was the god of reason and intellect. There was beauty— We don't even know—"

"So archaeologists dug up this ancient recording of a Greek rock band?"

"It's called the First Delphic Hymn to Apollo. It's the oldest surviving piece of music in the world where we know the name of the composer: Athénaios. The notes and lyrics were inscribed on the wall of the Athenian Treasury at Delphi."

"Are the lyrics as strange as the music?"

"Not so strange. They call the Muses to—" I think she considered try-ing to ram the whole hymn down my throat, but thought better of it. "I will give you the short version. 'Come with songs to celebrate golden-haired Apollo as he visits his mountain oracle.'"

She was trying to sketch a rich background story. True to form, I latched on to a detail. "Golden-haired? Apollo was blond? What kind of Greek is blond?"

She laughed and gave her head a quizzical tilt. "I guess you wouldn't expect it. But Greek gods and heroes were blond. The goddess Artemis, Apollo's sister, was also blonde. And Aphrodite and Athena." She consid-ered. "And Achilles, and Helen—"

"*That* is strange."

✳

I had a Google alert set for news on the terms "Apollo" and "Delphi."

A lot of random stuff turned up. News about companies and prod-ucts with Apollo or Delphi in their names. Reviews of an *Apollo 13* movie remake. A profile in a local newspaper of a cat named Apollo, "Cat of the Week" at the Merrimack River Feline Rescue Society in Salisbury, Massachusetts (a light-ginger cat, blond like the god).

Amid this miscellany were items of apparent but unclear significance, coincidences teetering on the edge of plausibility.

Cryptocurrency prices had whipsawed over the previous week. Not unusual, but their recent volatility was extreme. An article in the popu-lar crypto trade rag *CoinDesk* speculated that the Delphians' contract was the cause. When I glanced at a chart in the article, I noticed something I'd missed before. A major plunge in the price of Ether happened in the very hour we learned of Vigano's death at the FBI. His death only became public knowledge a couple of hours afterward. Was information leaked by the coroner or the FBI? Were the Delphians capitalizing on their inside knowledge? Was it coincidence? Impossible to say.

In other news, a bronze statue of Apollo on loan to the Getty Museum from the National Archaeological Museum in Greece toppled overnight during a minor earthquake. No other artworks were affected. An article in the *LA Times* noted that earthquake damage at the Getty was almost unheard of. In fact, the Getty was a pioneer in seismically stable mounts.

The *New York Times* reported that a large silver coin from an ancient Greek city in Sicily had appeared from nowhere as the featured lot in an auction in Zurich. "Arguably the most prestigious and important coin in existence," it was among just a dozen surviving examples of the so-called Akragas Decadrachm. On the obverse was Helios, Apollo as sun god, driving a four-horse chariot through the sky. One could see fire in the steeds' eyes, their heads tossing wildly as they cleaved the air with a thicket of legs. The god hunched his giant, nude body in a racer's crouch, reins in hand, whipping the chariot past a startled eagle. It was an entire sculptural group compressed onto a small silver disk. Masterful. Or so I thought. But of course Diane has established that I have bad taste.

This particular coin last appeared at an auction in Switzerland in 2012 and sold for over $2.7 million. Rumor had it that the money was never paid and the coin never delivered.

This time, it sold for $11.7 million, the largest sum ever for an ancient coin.

✳

I was beavering away at Magic Crystal monitoring code on the Bridge in the afternoon when I glimpsed a flash of yellow off to the side. Lukas's shirt. I turned to see him standing in the middle of the office, in line of sight of my desk. He met my eye, glanced at the floor, met my eye again, and marched over. He's not what I'd call athletic, so when he hustles, you know it's bad tidings. At first, I worried he'd gotten wind of the Magic Crystal.

"They hacked GaiaX," he said.

"When?"

"And they burned over a million dollars. They could have stolen it, but they destroyed it."

"When?"

"I just heard. GaiaX's devs were seconds away from upgrading the contract." An upgrade meant an update to a smart contract on the blockchain—usually to fix a dangerous bug. It could have prevented the attack.

"Seconds? Did GaiaX advertise what they were doing?"

"No. But maybe those fucking Delphians somehow intercepted their upgrade transaction, instantly reverse engineered it to find the bug it was fixing, and front-ran it. I don't know. Who cares? It gets worse. At the same time, the Delphians announced a bigger hack. 'Prophecy.' Whatever." He gave an exasperated huff, his version of a sigh. "Listen. Is it okay that I'm bothering you with this stuff? It's bad enough for you. I don't want to pile it on, but—"

"Why not? These could be clues. I'll take anything I can get at this point."

A quick intake of breath. "Thanks. Now they can destroy almost $50 million," he said. "Not even steal it. They published proof that they can hack one of the contracts on a list of fourteen. Just one, and they're not saying which. They're toying with us."

"Not toying, Lukas. Strategizing. Any one contract has small odds of being the real target. So it will be hard to get the people behind any one contract to take emergency measures. It's only $50 million and there's only a one-in-fourteen chance of getting hacked. That's around 7 percent. As far as motivating people to act, that's bad for the defenders."

I was again struck by how masterfully the Delphians were calibrating their attacks. They were doing just enough damage to draw a flurry of attention in the press and social media, but not enough to provoke a massive counterreaction.

"Bad for the defenders means bad for us," Lukas said. "Eight of those contracts belong to our customers. Eight. They want us to do something." He rubbed his eyes. "I mean we, not you. I don't think our customers understand that bugs in their contracts aren't our fault. I wish—"

"You wish I hadn't drawn their fire."

"I wish we hadn't launched Sanctum. But there's no turning back now. Why are they doing this? To fucking short Ethereum?"

"We've already rejected that hypothesis. And I don't think it's the big financial institutions. I've checked."

"I didn't think it was. You know, my grandmother's been following this stuff online. She doesn't buy the whole Delphi thing. She thinks it's some evil computer genius advertising his superiority to the world. She's usually right."

"Your grandmother? Your grandmother surfs the web? How old is she?"

"Ninety-five."

"Wow."

"She didn't shave years off her life running this company," Lukas said. "Or being me."

"She lived through other crazy shit. Worse shit, like a world war. Half the men in her family died on the Eastern Front, crushed between Stalin, the enemy, and Hitler, the lunatic friend who's worse than your enemy." This was Lukas's version of a pep talk.

He reached for my Lucite-embedded coin. Instead of using it as a fidget toy, he held it at eye level, scrutinizing it. I'd never seen him do that before.

"Is there anything I can do to help you?" he asked, still looking at the coin. I think he wanted my advice but felt too guilty to ask.

"No, but maybe I can help you." I remembered Diane's mention of Apollo displacing the earth goddess Gaia. "It turns out that GaiaX has a mythological connection with Apollo. If you want, I'll run the new targets by a friend and see if any has another mythological X painted on its back. I want to know anyway."

"Thanks," he said. "Only if it's convenient. I'll stop bothering you." He sighed, then turned to leave.

"Lukas, the coin."

"Oh, yeah. Sorry." He gave it another look before putting it back on my desk. He started walking away, then pivoted and returned. He aligned the coin's Lucite against the back edge of my desk with millimeter precision, shook his head, and again walked away.

✳

Throughout the time that the Delphians' sword hung over my head, all kinds of people sent me email. Cranks. Crooks. Kooks. Friends, or at least what passed for friends in my life. The two members of my extended family I wasn't estranged from. A life insurance salesman (I kid you not). Spiritual counselors. An elementary school student writing an essay about me. ("Are you scared?") A graduate student writing a scholarly paper about me. ("On a scale from 1 to 10, with 1 being the lowest, how would you rate your fear?") All of this email went into the trash.

I was also invited to speak on television news programs. CNN, MSNBC, Fox News. I turned them all down. I don't like the major networks and didn't want to advertise my face. I said no also to National Public Radio, which I even listen to on occasion.

The only place I agreed to talk was a popular blockchain podcast called *Rattling the Chain*. The host, Molly Aksoy, was a snarky venture capitalist who offered up a weekly milkshake of crypto ideology sweetened with wormwood and bile. Hers was a typical crypto journey. In 2008, she was poised to graduate from an elite university and launch herself on a smooth professional arc of exorbitant, ever-rising pay in the world of finance. Then the meltdown came. Plum job offers at investment firms dried up, a torrent of bailout dollars flowed to the big banks, and her eyes opened to the devil's bargain that is Wall Street. When Bitcoin dropped from the heavens, she became a bitter apostle of the crypto world's rage against the machine.

Her podcast was more cultural and financial than technical, but smart and addictive—the guilty little pleasure of some top blockchain devs. I agreed to be a guest because I liked her show. I was also hoping there might be some genius savior among her devotees, someone who'd come out of the woodwork to fight the Delphians or at least go after the rich bounty in the neutralization contract Adyton was setting up.

Molly, as always, cranking up the vocal fry as she introduces the podcast. "Welcome to *Rattling the Chain* . . ." Sexy, groovy music with a heavy beat. We could be at a rave or a clothing store. A man's voice issuing a warning: "Please be advised that the show's contents don't constitute investment advice and that Molly has invested personally in many of the crypto assets discussed with her guests."

Molly: Thanks for joining me. I've wanted to have you on the show for a while. I'm so sorry it took this terrible thing to get you here.
Me: The will of the god.
Molly: Yeah, the god. Some god. Let me nerd out for a second to get our listeners on the same page. Apollo was the ancient Greek god of archery, healing and diseases, music, poetry and dance, prophecy, and—am I forgetting anything?

Me: Truth.

Molly: Right, Truth. Just a little thing. He was also patron god of the Oracle of Delphi. You're one of the main developers at Adyton, working on a different kind of oracle, smart contract oracles. Now there's some group that call themselves "Delphians"—supposedly a cult of Apollo. They've launched a smart contract that's offering a reward to kill you.

Me: Fair summary.

Molly: I've done some crazy episodes, but this is *definitely* the craziest. We'll get to some technical stuff, but there's one thing I really want to know: Given all that's happening, do you—how should I put this? It seems nuts to ask, but do you believe in Apollo?

Me: Honestly, I don't know. But it seems that Apollo believes in me.

Molly: Good answer. So who do you think these Delphians are? Real worshippers? Or are they after something else? Like what happens if you play investigator and follow the money?

Me: I've tried. The money leads to my grave. Six feet under, a dead end.

Molly (with a snort): You mean you can't see who profits from your being gone?

Me: No. I'm not an especially important person. The contract says I'm being targeted because of my impiety. I don't know what it means, but it may be because— Well, here are the facts, with a little simplification. The contract reveals a new target once every three weeks. The first target of the contract was an archaeology professor. He's dead, but we don't yet know whether he was murdered. I tried to save him with a neutralization contract, a kind of anti-contract that offered a reward to hack the Delphians' contract.

Molly: Which didn't work.

Me (pausing to look at the Magic Crystal): Which didn't work, but may be why I'm now a target.

Molly: So there's a tragic irony here. You spend years building a platform that's supposed to be a definitive source of truth. And now it's killing you. You must really, really want your oracle to lie now, because that could save you.

Me: It would also kill me to see it lie. That would mean my life's work as a technologist has failed.

Molly: So what now? You're crushed between the weight of the truth and the awfulness of a lie?

Me: There are only two ways to stop the contract without subverting the oracle. The contract's got an off switch. Somehow that gets flipped. Or the contract gets hacked. I'm here on your podcast because I'm hoping to encourage people to hack the Delphians' code.

Molly: But then the contract could be launched again and you'd have to start all over. Are public smart contracts just a bad idea? Too dangerous?

Me: Yes. Like cars, kitchen knives, balconies, ladders, staircases, and swimming pools—not to mention the ocean. We should get rid of all of them.

Molly: Or make sure the people who use them are professionally licensed. And keep kids away. I'm not advocating for that personally. It would just hand control of smart contracts over to big companies. But some people are.

Me: I know. And if there's anyone who understands the temptation, it's me. But I still think it's a bad idea.

Molly: Life and death. Liberty and crime. Centralization and decentralization. It seems like civilization can only exist on a tightrope, doesn't it?

✳

Late that night I sat alone on the Bridge, waiting for the Delphians' code to enter the Magic Crystal. Only hours left, if it was going to happen at all.

I watched as my hope slipped through the hourglass. At two in the morning, I gave up and walked home.

As I passed the front desk in my building, Jazzelle held up a small package. I shook my head—*not now*—rode the interminable twenty floors up to my apartment, and threw myself face down on the sofa.

✳

I spent a restless night half-suffocated by a sofa cushion and rose late even by my standards. I didn't leave for Adyton until noon.

I was looking down at the sidewalk as I walked, trying to figure out how the Delphians could have discovered and avoided the Magic Crystal without genuine, Olympus-grade oracular powers. Only when I was several yards from the side entrance to the building did I notice the wooden passage, the kind that protects pedestrians around construction sites. It had gone up overnight. Odd on a weekend. I hesitated, but an annoyed workman in a bright yellow vest waved me in.

A few steps into the dark passage, I was seized from both sides. I tried stamping on their feet and dropping my weight, but they were fast and strong. They pulled down my jacket. A needle was thrust into my arm.

Before I swooned, I had two thoughts.

Calling card: "Kidnapped."

Idiot.

PART III

With Apollo, the highest conception of ideal male youth has been made into an image; he combines the strength of a perfect age with the tender forms of the most beautiful spring of youth. . . . Apollo was the most beautiful among the gods.

—Johann Joachim Winckelmann,
Geschichte der Kunst des Alterthums

FIFTEEN

I awoke with a jolt from the first deep sleep I'd had in a week. I was in the back of a truck, strapped to a gurney. I tried to loosen the straps cutting into my arms and legs. It was hopeless.

"Yikes! Sorry. They're kinda tight." The words were shouted from above my head, toward the front. By a girl. And I don't mean a young woman. I mean a girl.

"Dooo yoooo tink ooo cooo loooo duh swaaaa?" I said, or thought I said. My mouth was dry and my tongue malfunctioning. I felt carsick. Or truck sick. Or maybe drugged-bound-and-abducted sick. My lower back was spasming. I tucked my hips the way my trainer was always telling me to do and felt a good half percent better.

The truck was rumbling down a highway, jouncing as it hit small craters, patched and unpatched. Atrocious roads meant we could be anywhere in the tristate area, except maybe Connecticut.

The girl appeared nurse-like over the gurney. She was pretty, with light brown skin, incongruous under her blonde hair, and owlish, large-lensed glasses of a kind I didn't think opticians had carried for forty years. A small gold cross swung from her neck. She was sixteen, seventeen years old, I guessed. She struggled with the straps and loosened them a bit. They still chafed my arms.

"Better?" she shouted. Rather: "Beddah?" Her Jersey accent jarred me even more than the thudding and rattling of the truck.

"Not weally," I said. I'd limbered up my tongue a bit. "But tanks."

"I could loosen them more, but I'm afraid you'll fall."

"Aw 'scaaa?"

"What?"

"Aw 'scape?"

"You can't escape. We— there are two men up there." She pointed toward the front of the truck and lost her footing, catching herself against the truck wall. "We're almost there anyway."

"Ah you—"

"We're almost there." She put a hand comfortingly on my chest, again lost her balance, giving me a chest compression ("Sawrry!"), regained her footing, and made her way to the front of the truck.

The truck's growl rose to a whine as we turned and exited a highway in what I guessed was New Jersey. I lapsed back into sleep, so I don't know how long it was before we stopped.

The two men emerged from behind my head and opened the rear doors. They set up a ramp and wheeled me down. I couldn't see the ground from the gurney, only the ceiling and shelves filled with boxes in what I guessed was a warehouse. I was rolled into a modular office inside the warehouse, a kind of white, flat-topped cabin ribboned with windows. The girl watched as the men lifted me from the gurney and plonked me onto a chair. She winced as handcuffs were clicked onto my hands behind my back and long-chained leg cuffs onto my ankles. My arms were swollen from the chafing of the straps on the gurney. I smelled—somehow coming from my insides—a mixture of mucus and rubbing alcohol.

I felt for my phone in my jacket pocket with the inside of my arm. It wasn't there. On the other side, I felt for my dolphin brooch, which was. MacGyver could use its inches-long, thick pin to pick the handcuffs, short a circuit, trigger a blackout, and jump-start a stolen truck behind the warehouse. For me, it was just a comforting accessory.

The taller of the two men had dark hair and eyes. His scowl told of a life of pain, the pain of unacclaimed talents or unrequited love—or maybe just his masochistically tight ponytail. He dropped my bookbag on a desk and rifled through it. He removed the oven tray, turned it over, and rapped it with his fingers.

"What the hell is this?"

"An oven tray."

I flinched as—clang!—he struck it with the head of a screwdriver snatched from an open toolbox on a low metal cabinet. He nodded with head and body, as though he'd just improvised a groovy solo. He continued searching my bag, fishing out a bar of Amano Madagascar chocolate and my Cluizel hazelnut bar. He sneered at the price tag on the Amano and unwrapped it. Instead of breaking off one of the small, molded tasting squares, he chomped on the bar, chewed, and puckered. With a dubious squint, he continued chewing.

"Sour. They should've used more sugar."

It took talent like his to provoke my contempt under the circumstances, paralyzed as I was with terror. "Yeah," I almost said, "connoisseurs prefer M&Ms."

I said nothing, but the thought must have flickered across my face. He glared at me, then shot an angry glance at the toolbox. The second man smiled and wagged a finger at him. The smaller of the two, he had a cowl of stubble, recessed behind a shiny forehead. His piggish nose made him look playful—in a pigletty sort of way. If he was one of the two who'd grabbed me, though, he was one strong piglet.

The Lord Byron wannabe left the room, while the piglet fiddled with his phone. The girl sat at the desk and took out a laptop.

"Could I possibly have some water?" I was so parched I could barely get the words out.

They looked at each other. The piglet went and got me a cup of warm tap water. I could just manage it with my shackles. It was the most restorative elixir ever extracted from a Jersey tap. The blessed liquid demummified my throat.

They removed my handcuffs, but kept the cuffs on my legs. I studied the office for clues about who my captors might be, but it was a barebones affair. An L-shaped desk in a corner, empty except for a wooden box not quite two feet high, incised with the script word "Pearl." A virgin bulletin board. A low metal cabinet with a toolbox on top. A small circular table with two chairs. Outside in the warehouse were rows of tall shelves crammed with cardboard boxes.

"Where am I?" I asked the piglet. "What do you want from me?"

He smirked. "You're the golden goose. What the hell do you think we want?"

"Look, I—"

"Relax. You'll find out soon."

So they knew who I was. Whoever they were, their kidnapping made no sense. Why didn't they just keep me drugged, tide my body over until the contract on me became active, and then snuff me out? And why on earth send a teenage girl after me?

All I could do was wait.

✳

A faint clang of metal announced someone entering the warehouse. Heads jerked up from phones. A little later two sharp raps sounded in the distance. The piglet grabbed the wooden box from the desk, planted it on the floor, and sat on it. He started working it with rhythmic, caressing slaps. His percussion was met by keening song floating in from the warehouse. The song grew gradually louder and the box-slapping continued until the singer was close upon us. The piglet burst into a percussive frenzy, then slashed the music dead with silence.

A man appeared in the doorway. He wore a blue blazer and leather vest. His red cravat was studded with a huge diamond that glinted like a lighthouse beam. He was a good eighty years old, and with his fedora and cane and proud, upright bearing, he would have looked more at home in sepia. Another two men stood well behind him in the warehouse, just in front of the high metal shelves.

"*This* him?" he said, pointing at me with his cane. I couldn't get a good fix on his accent. Maybe the part of New Jersey by the Mediterranean. "I expected him to look like he has brains. You guys lose his glasses?"

Actually, I'd switched back from glasses to contact lenses. I guess I'd forgotten my propeller beanie.

"What was the tune?" I asked. "Big step up from shave and a haircut." As a security guy, I had to admire their musical password system, if that's what it was. It was hard for intruders to replicate. In my fear, I also wanted to please my captors.

The man's head and chest swelled and he wailed a brief snatch of song, tapping different rhythmic parts with his cane and left foot. "Flamenco music," he said, "my love." He turned his diamond lighthouse beam toward the girl. "My other love, Julia." *Hoo-lya.* She gave him an adoring smile. His granddaughter, I was hoping.

"You're the boss, I assume?"

He stared at me and blinked.

"If you are," I said, "just to clarify, to offer some advice on your investment, you know you can't kill me for six days, right?"

He walked over and leaned on his cane, breathing souring sugar and a lifetime of decaying teeth into my face. Carb addict. He patted my cheek. "Kill you? I'm not gonna kill you. Like you say, you're an investment. Who kills an investment?"

"That's a relief. But I don't—"

"You can thank Julia I keep you alive."

"You mean you'll let me go?"

He righted himself. His face was shadowed by his fedora. His diamond sparkled as he spoke. "You owe me money. Seven hundred thousand dollars. A lot of money. A lot of interest to pay."

"If you let me go, I can pay—"

"Julia says you're a Bitcoin brain. Easy for you to make money."

"It's not so—"

His cane struck the floor. "You pay or I call in the loan. Understand?"

"OK." My throat had shriveled up again. "I understand."

"Starting tomorrow. You got more to say?"

"Only that to do what you're asking, I'll need my phone and a computer."

He shook his head and tsked. "You trying to fool an old man? Not nice. You do everything through Julia. She's *my* Bitcoin brain. Smart as you. Maybe smarter. Definitely prettier."

I looked at her. She shrugged and made a sorry-not-my-fault face.

So I was to be a digital-cash cow, milked by a pretty dairymaid, and made into hamburgers if I ran dry.

※

The boss left with the piglet. With the same tenderness he'd shown the oven tray, Byron shoved me in my chair next to Julia. He sat on the edge of the desk and chomped on my other chocolate bar, which was more to his liking.

Julia's job was to execute my cryptocurrency transactions for me and make sure I wasn't trying to summon help from the outside.

I could see no good way to conjure up the shovelfuls of cryptocurrency demanded by this farcical gang or Mafia or nontraditional investment firm or whatever they were. It wasn't clear whether they knew I couldn't, and figured they'd milk me as dry as they could before they killed me, or whether they actually believed I could deliver the goods. Or maybe they just kidnapped me because they figured I'd yield a guaranteed return, alive or dead.

Sure, I'd had some shower thoughts about new forms of gambling I could launch with Sanctum. Fair online blackjack, to start with. There were plenty of online blackjack games, but the house could cheat you. Using Sanctum, I could create a blackjack game that would be provably fair. You couldn't do this with a basic smart contract, because the contract couldn't keep the cards secret. After all, blockchains are designed to be transparent. But I could code up my blackjack game in a day with Sanctum, and I was sure it would be popular. Apart from the flat illegality and societal worthlessness of such schemes, though, they're always hit or miss. Once I launched my game, someone else would copy it in the blink of an eye, so there would be little money in it. My best hope of salvation was instead to dupe a teenage girl as soon as possible into broadcasting an unwitting SOS to the authorities. Lovely.

They'd called Julia a "Bitcoin brain." I figured she wasn't expert in smart contracts, which go far beyond simple cryptocurrency. Coding a smart contract with her help would be about as efficient as punching it into a keyboard in binary, using just the 0 and 1 keys. But her inexperience would work in my favor when I tried to finesse a secret distress signal past her. I figured my odds weren't much worse than Princess Leia's when she hid her message in R2-D2's memory. Leia managed to slip the droid by the imperial forces in an escape pod, and it worked out pretty well.

My first plan was a simple one. I would send transactions from an Ethereum address I often used for testing. I'd used these addresses before in my work with Corinne, so there was a chance she would spot them on the blockchain and know to alert law enforcement. If this gang then went to cash out their cryptocurrency for dollars at an exchange, the FBI could subpoena their transactions and collar them.

"I have a hardware crypto wallet in my backpack," I said to Julia. "Not much in those addresses, but it's a start." Enough to pay my "interest" for maybe a day.

She emitted a nervous peep, like a small bird at an audition, then said, "I didn't mean for it to happen this way.

"I'm sure it was the boss's decision."

"They were just gonna kill you. I convinced them to do this instead. I know who you are. I read your blog—"

Byron slapped the desk. "Come on, Julia!"

"No need to get salty," she grumbled.

"You're making my job harder," Byron said. "You know you're not supposed to get cozy with him." Julia gave him a defiant look, with a dash of menace. I could guess which of them the boss would side with if it came down to a fight.

"Do you want to get my hardware wallet?" I asked her. I told her where in my bag to find it, stashed in a mint tin. I gave her step-by-step directions on how to use it. She kept looking at me, sweet and owlish, wanting to say something, but Byron loomed.

"I've got ETH in a few different addresses. We'll start with that one." I pointed at the screen. "The 0x0d one. That's how addresses in Ethereum are formatted."

I watched with surprise and not a little dismay when she popped open a tab and traced the transaction history. "I watched you, so I know your PIN now," she said. "I'll move the funds. You haven't mixed your crypto, and law enforcement must know you got— They're probably watching your addresses now, and I don't want them tracing us."

So much for my original plan.

"How on earth . . . how did you learn this stuff?" I asked.

"About crypto?"

"Yes. In school?"

"School?" She giggled. "No way. My teachers don't know crypto from a knock on the head. My friends think it's cringy or they're just in it for the money. I learned from Isaac." *Eee-sok*. She lit up. "My father's hacker. He does all our . . ." She caught Byron's aggrieved eye roll. "And I've taught myself a lot."

Time for Plan B, which involved Sanctum. I proposed to code up my blackjack game and make money by taking a cut as the house. I needed to connect to an Adyton Sanctum node. We had a hidden function in Sanctum for generating trustworthy random numbers, good for card shuffling, and not yet publicly released. I could send a secret signal to Corinne by using that function in the blackjack game before anyone was supposed to know it existed. Corinne would surely then get law enforcement to trace my traffic.

"Cool idea!" she said. "I wanted to learn how to code really advanced smart contracts. I mean, you can learn a lot online, but it's way better to have someone to talk to, a teacher . . ." Then in hurried defiance of Byron, "I've read your blog. It's straight fire. I've always wanted to meet a top dev like you." I felt a touch of the adoration she'd shone on the boss. It was hard not to be charmed by it.

"Lucky you." I shook my feet, rattling the cuffs. "You've got a pet dev on a chain now."

"Let me start writing some code," she said. She shifted her laptop to plug my hardware wallet into the USB port. She tilted the screen away from Byron, who showed no particular concern, and typed:

```
   i didnt want this but they were going to kill u.
ill do whatever I can to help but i cant get my family
                 into trouble. ok?
```

"I understand your code. Very clear," I said, as she deleted her message.

It's amazing how small compunctions, guilt or embarrassment, can override even your survival instinct. Deceive her and save myself. It was the obvious and right course of action, yet I felt some relief mixed with my dismay when she torpedoed my stratagem.

"We'll use Tor to connect to Sanctum," she said. "But I've heard the feds own a lot of those nodes. Is that true? I've set up my own extra proxy servers. You can rent cloud servers and pay with crypto. How cool is that?" Cool indeed. With a bright smile, she sent my second distress-signal plan to the ocean floor.

Julia wasn't a Bitcoin brain. She was post-Bitcoin. It turned out I was dealing with a sixteen-year-old crypto-prodigy gangster girl.

✸

We worked on my blackjack game through the late afternoon. Julia first showed me some basic smart contracts she'd already coded up on her own. There were rookie mistakes, but not many. She avoided the gotchas that ensnare nearly all beginners: thinking "private" functions are secret, not optimizing gas costs, and whatnot. How much was instinct and how much careful study, I couldn't tell, but it impressed me.

Sanctum brought a whole new level of complexity to the proceedings, but she soaked up my crash tutorial on trusted hardware, privacy-preserving computation models, and secure random number generation like the Berkeley PhD student I wish I'd been. It's not that sparks of brilliance flew from her cranium. It all came naturally to her. She wasn't aware of how astonishing her abilities were, so there was no pretense. She'd just emit one of her nervous little peeps, followed by a perky, matter-of-fact summary of what she'd learned. It was yet one more surreal experience in a week abounding with them.

By convincing Byron it would get the money spigot flowing faster, we got permission for me to type under Julia's supervision. I started some patter running about a fictitious buggy piece of code. With this cover, I typed a covert question for her. She grasped the idea, and we alternated typing as we talked about our work, a brain-twisting exercise.

Me: Julia, why are you doing this?
Julia: so you can stay alive
Me: I mean, who are they? Why are you involved in all of this?
Julia: theyre my family.
Me: Who
Julia (nudging me aside before I finished typing): i hate it but theyre my family.
Me: The guy here now?
Julia: earlier. my father.

Her father? The piglet? Surely not the old man.

Me: Which one?
Julia: you called him the boss.

❉

Byron was oddly solicitous about my dinner. Maybe feeding hostages in style was a point of honor among thugs in his set, the way the British insist upon serving tea to their guests or Arabs offer lavish meals.

"We'll do takeout," he said. "What'chu want? Greek? Italian? Tapas? Japanese? Your choice. I know a great little Japanese place. Real good eel. Melts in your mouth. Not too heavy on the sauce."

Japanese was the easiest way to avoid gluten and other poisons, and to judge from his enthusiasm, maybe the best way to make a friend.

"Japanese sounds great to me . . ." It sparked an idea. "Hey, if you like Japanese, I know a place in the Chelsea Market in Manhattan with incredibly fresh fish."

Based on his reaction and, if it worked out, the delivery time for the order, I could gauge how far from Manhattan we were. If I could get him to order from the place I had in mind—it was a wild idea, really—I'd ask for a special item. I was a regular customer, and often ordered something I was pretty sure no one else did: raw quail eggs with my mackerel. Since there was no good way to balance the eggs on the fish, they'd had to devise a special nori wrap for me that became a running joke with the chefs at the counter. "Sushi engineering!" Once news of my kidnapping got out, maybe, just maybe, if Apollo was looking the other way, someone would wonder who was ordering the quail-egg mackerel.

Byron thought about it. "The eel's good?"

"Excellent," I said. "Pricey, but—"

"Fuhget it. I don't like pricey. My place is good. Not pricey."

He walked out of the office as he made the call. If he left to pick up the order, at least I'd have a chance to talk with Julia. Maybe, if I made the right promises, and she knew how to get the key to my cuffs, she'd even let me escape. Maybe.

Half an hour later, Byron got a text message and left again. I expected Julia to start conferring once he was out of earshot, but she continued typing.

"How long do we have?" I whispered.

She made a strained little peep and said, "He's just meeting someone at the door. He had a runner get our dinner."

"Quickly then. Where are we?"

"I—" she hesitated. She made a rapid mental calculation of what it would mean to answer. If I ever managed to communicate with the outside world and led the police to the warehouse, I'd endanger her family. "I don't think I should tell you that." She touched the back of my hand. "I'm sorry."

We ate dinner at the small table. Byron even condescended to release my ankles, which were by now rubbed raw. Unwilling to stoop, he shoved the key at me across the table. There was little to discuss apart from the overabundant meal, but this was enough for his monologues. He didn't particularly listen to me or Julia. "They're Japanese beans. You bite and suck, like this . . ." He fished a bottle of sake out from a desk drawer and plied me with some, which I didn't feel it wise to refuse. "You hardly drank," he said, concerned by my moderation. "This is good stuff." I didn't have the stomach to eat much either.

I assumed Byron and Julia would leave after dinner, but Byron threw the remnants of dinner into a plastic bag, tied it up, tossed it out the office door, and started on the rest of my chocolate bar for dessert. He kindly offered me a piece with only a small bite mark. I declined. Julia took up her post at her laptop. Since we'd spent the afternoon having me teach her about Sanctum, it was only now that we could start working in earnest on the blackjack idea. We began with a simplified smart contract for dealing cards. The Sanctum part—needed to keep the dealer's cards secret—would come later. Even though Byron was allowing me to type, and speed was a matter of life or death for me, I left Julia at the helm. Given my hopeless situation, her goodwill meant more than speed.

I don't know whether it was Byron's unwinding over dinner or the hamster's portion of sake I'd drunk, but I lowered my guard.

"You know, it seems unlikely," I said to Julia in a conversational tone to avoid sounding secretive, yet softly so Byron couldn't make out my words. "But maybe I'll somehow come out of all of this alive."

She gave an unhappy smile. Byron glanced up from his phone.

"If I do," I continued, "I was just thinking. You should come do an internship at Adyton."

"Really?" she squealed, wide-eyed. "Honestly?"

"Why not? You're—"

In one smooth motion, Byron bounded past the girl, seized my collar, and whipped a knife up at my jaw.

"Sweet-talk the girl," he growled, "and I'll slice off your face." He let me feel the tip of the blade.

"I was just—"

"They told me I got to keep you alive for a few days, but no one said you need two fucking cheeks."

"A few days?" Julia cried. "What do you mean?"

He ignored her and stood. "You got that?"

Julia screeched, "What the hell do you mean?"

"'Til Isaac takes over," Byron said, snapping his blade shut and starting back toward his perch on the desk. "That's the plan."

She jumped up. "No. That's got nothing to do with keeping him alive. Who said a few days? You touch him, Antonio, and—"

"He won't make his payments for more than a few days." He squinted. "*That's* what I mean."

Antonio, the artist formerly known as Byron, stood opposite me, facing Julia.

"I'm calling my father," she yelled and stalked out of the room, phone in hand.

Unconcerned, Byron—he was still Byron in my mind—strolled back again to the edge of the desk. He sat and took out his phone. He tapped at it with his usual intense focus, replying to posts on mafioso chat boards or doing whatever he did during the hours Julia and I worked. Julia's plaintive voice carried from the warehouse. She returned, put her laptop in her bag in silence, and wiped a wet cheek with her sleeve.

"I'll see you tomorrow," she said firmly.

First, she went and got two cups of water for me. Byron gave me a sleeping bag and a bucket. He took a wireless videocam from a desk drawer and plugged it in. Leaving the office lights on, he tucked me in for the night by checking the irons on my ankles and cuffing my right hand to a leg of the desk, which was bolted to the floor. He would have cuffed both hands, looping the chain around the desk leg, but Julia insisted that it would be impossible for me to sleep. He grabbed the toolbox as he left. Then he returned and snatched up my backpack.

SIXTEEN

When I heard the distant slam of the metal warehouse door, I sprang into action. Byron had placed the camera at the opposite end of the desk from the leg to which I was cuffed, near the crook of the "L." He'd misjudged its distance, or hadn't cared, but it was close enough that I might be able to get at it.

I wouldn't be able to lift my entire body from the floor. I tried to climb my legs up the desk and get a purchase on the top. With full freedom of movement, it would have been easy, but the chain on my shackled legs made it difficult to maneuver my feet. Several times I got close to hooking a foot on the desktop, but slipped and dropped to the floor, clanking the chain with an "oof." In a final, supreme effort, I caught a foot on the handle of a desk drawer and strained so that I felt the veins in my temples ready to burst. I managed to lodge part of my left foot on the desktop and then secure my right foot. My upper back remained on the ground, so that I was executing a kind of supine plank. I slid my feet toward the camera. It was barely within reach. Only the top was visible from my position on the ground.

As I nudged with my foot, tension from the unseen power cord caused the camera to swivel in the wrong direction, toward my head, and slide away from me toward the back of the desk. In desperation—I might get only one shot at it, and my strength was ebbing—I aimed a kick at the front edge. I nicked it, and it swung back where I wanted it just before I had to let my body go and slammed to the ground, knocking the wind from my lungs with a grunt of pain. I created what I hoped was a blind spot around my head.

I'd chosen not to kick the camera to the back of the desk because that would take me completely out of its field of view. Then Byron or whoever was on surveillance duty might come to the warehouse to fix it. I was hoping I'd swiveled the camera before they started using it to watch me. Then they'd think Bryon had simply gotten the angle a bit wrong—annoying, but not worth the trouble of fixing. I could then work at my handcuffs in the dead of night, when no one would be watching, and couldn't be sure what I was doing if they were.

Next, I needed to find a tool. Amateurish as Byron was, he'd remembered to remove the toolbox. I had my brooch, but the bronze pin was fragile and liable to snap. I opened the desk drawers nearest me. I could see inside if I squatted, but found it too painful, so I rooted around with my free hand. I dug out some spare furniture parts: a couple of casters, a big black plastic grommet, and some bolts. I found wrenches, but with my rotten luck they were Allen wrenches. Useless for unscrewing the solid bolts securing the desk leg to the floor. One of them was about a quarter inch in diameter, the other sized less than a millimeter. They probably came with some piece of assemble-it-yourself furniture in the office.

If Byron was going to check on me using the camera, I figured he'd do it soon. Even if he could see only my legs, he might get suspicious if they were jerking around as I wrestled with my handcuffs. Best to try to free myself in the dead of night. In any case, I felt a powerful wave of fatigue. Even the wrenches wouldn't have been enough to prop my eyelids open. I stretched out in the sleeping bag across the field of view of the camera. Before conking out, I checked whether my watch detected any nearby devices I could pair with and possibly use to issue an SOS. Another longshot idea that didn't pan out.

It was just past 9:00 p.m. I set an alarm for 2:00 a.m. With my limbs still quivering from trauma, fear, and desk gymnastics, I passed out in the sleeping bag, my head lolling on a pillow mashed together from my jacket and the top of the bag.

✳

A playful dolphin was biting at my hand and my ankles and chirruping at me as I swam. My arms were fatigued, my legs unresponsive, the shore ever-receding. I tried to fend off the strange yellow creature by batting at it between strokes. It swam a short distance away, circled, and glided back, still chirruping. I soon realized it was trying to save me, urging me to grasp its fin or climb onto its back. I lacked the strength.

I don't know how long I lingered in this dream state before my vibrating watch finally roused me. In a groggy panic, I fumbled and turned it off. *No*, I said to my pounding heart, *they didn't hear it. It was only vibrating.*

I tested one of the bolts securing the desk leg with my fingers. Solid. I tried loosening it with the bend in the larger wrench against the hexagonal bolt head. It didn't move. No surprise.

I only needed to free my hand from the desk. The chain between the cuffs on my ankles was long enough so I could walk. I knew this because I'd already been frog-marched to the bathroom outside the office by Byron during the day. How I'd escape the warehouse, I didn't know. The doors were probably locked. But forcing them open had to be easier than freeing myself from the desk.

I pushed the shaft of the wrench through a link of the chain on the handcuffs and secured the tip against the edge of the metal plate at the base of the desk leg. Levering it away from the desk, I tried to pry open a link in the handcuffs. With only one hand free and the metal biting into my palm as I pushed, I couldn't generate much force.

I'd once seen someone open a pair of handcuffs with a bobby pin. All I remembered was that he'd inserted it into the keyhole. The smaller wrench was less than a millimeter in diameter, the closest thing I had to a bobby pin. I pushed it into the keyhole, feeling around the edge for a piece of moveable metal. I had no idea what I was doing. I tried bending it to create something like the tooth on a key, but couldn't kink it, even when I shoved it into the crack between drawers and bent downward. I scraped around the hole, hoping for some effect. Again and again I tried. In the end, the best I could hope for was that I hadn't broken the lock and doomed myself to a few final days shackled to the desk.

With the right tool and a little training, I was sure it could be done. Had it been a digital device, not an analog one, I'd have beaten it.

I returned the wrenches to the desk drawer and nestled myself into the sleeping bag. In a short several days, I'd be culled from the face of the Earth for my uselessness. Deep in a pit of helplessness and despair, I laid my head down and went off to find the friendly dolphin.

✴

"Look at you." Byron stood over me and grinned. "And they told me you're a fucking genius."

It was late afternoon, probably after school let out for Julia, and the two of them had just returned. Byron had gone through the camera footage, seen my contortions, and guessed what I was up to. He gloated, but perhaps because Julia was there, he didn't thrash me.

They'd left me no food. Because I ate almost no dinner the previous evening, I felt famished by morning. While they were away, once my hunger pains passed, I just lapsed into and out of sleep. Byron now uncuffed my hand and gave me a paper bag containing a bagel sandwich with lox and cream cheese, a banana, and a small container of yogurt. I devoured them under Julia's sorrowful gaze.

"I got the money out of your crypto wallet," she said. "It's enough for three days. Don't worry. We'll get the contract done by then." There was more in the wallet than I remembered. It still wouldn't buy me much time.

She and I continued with our pair programming of the previous day. She did most of the typing, and I supervised.

I tried to imagine that it was summer, and she'd taken the internship I promised. We were at Adyton, on the Bridge. Lukas was wringing his hands because Corinne and I were wasting time tutoring the girl when there were urgent product features to get out. But we'd show him what she could do, and then disappoint him when he tried to hire her straight out of high school. We'd be her computer-science fairy godparents, getting her into a top university, maybe Princeton if her family wouldn't let her leave Jersey . . .

When Julia went to the bathroom, Byron stood up and sauntered over to me with a malicious smile. I looked up at him, keeping my body angled away for protection. He slipped his phone into his pocket. With a nonchalant swing of his arm, he slapped me.

"Houdini, huh?"

I'd never been slapped that hard before. It turns out the pain isn't too bad. Not as bad as the shock—or the shame.

"Tonight we'll see how you sleep with both hands cuffed tight," he said. "I'm curious. I hear it can fuck up your neck with pain for years."

He frowned. "But I'll never find out, 'cause you won't be around very long."

✳

Julia was optimistic, but to me it was clear we wouldn't complete and launch our blackjack game in the two days before my funds ran out. Left to do it on my own, I might have managed. I suggested they leave me with a laptop and turn off the warehouse Wi-Fi, but even Julia didn't like the idea and wouldn't tell me why. My guess was that we were in range of other Wi-Fi signals, a sign that there were other buildings nearby, which wasn't surprising, although a helpful surmise. Julia approved of my next suggestion, that we pry open a laptop and remove the Wi-Fi card. She and Byron argued about it, then referred the idea for arbitration by text message to the famous Isaac. He quashed it.

When we ordered dinner, Byron was again oddly hospitable, but this time I was leery and silent. That didn't stop him from giving another masterclass, this time on the pizza we ordered for dinner. His monologue offered a clue about who he and his gang were. He talked about how pizza shops in New Jersey had once been forced by the Mafia to buy a particular brand of mozzarella, but continued even when the Mafia's grip relaxed.

"It's good. It's good cheese. I'm not saying it isn't." He held a slice in one hand, dripping grease over his paper plate, and gesticulated with the other hand. "But we're talking about the fucking Italian Mafia. If they would've done it right," he said, "they'd have chose buffalo mozzarella. The real stuff. " He took a bite. "And San Marzano tomatoes," he said while chewing. "Like this. That's why those guys are disappearing. No pride. No sense of quality." He licked his lips. "More territory for us."

I have to admit the pizza was rather good, and I was still famished. I figured the gluten and other assorted toxins were the least of my problems.

Julia and I continued working after dinner the way we had the day before. We again exchanged typed messages.

Me: Your friend here is threatening bad things tonight. Could you possibly stay until he leaves?

Julia: hes usually not this bad. my fault for getting excited before. he thinks youre trying to pull a fast one on me.

Me: Not your fault.

Julia: ill stay. but he could come back later. ill think of something.

Me: Thank you!

They were preparing to leave when Byron got a call. Swearing, he stomped out of the office, phone to his ear.

"I'll stay until he leaves," Julia whispered. "And I've got a plan to make sure he doesn't come back. I'll get access to the video camera and let him know."

Byron stalked back into the office. "We got to move him. *Fast*. Isaac will take over."

"Who said?" Julia asked.

"Listen, kid. we don't have time—"

"Don't 'kid' me. Who said?"

Byron grabbed my arm and yanked me to my feet. As he pulled my arms behind my back and cuffed them, Julia grabbed my shoulder, starting a tug of war. As Byron yanked me away from her, the chain on my feet threw off my balance and I fell. Because I couldn't break the fall with my hands, I twisted in mid-air to take the impact on my side and avoid smashing my head.

It was only when they sat me up that I felt pain. Julia, crouching beside me, first noticed the blood.

"Oh my God!" she cried, holding up her bloodstained fingers and glaring at Byron, who protested innocence with raised hands.

I saw my brooch, undone, glinting on the floor. The large pin had gouged my flank when I fell. So much for friendly dolphins.

"We need to find a first aid kit." Julia scrambled to her feet.

"We don't have time." Byron bent and reached for me. I didn't know what his game was, but I clutched my side and, not needing to feign much, cried out in agony. Better to delay and let Julia work things out.

"Where's the first aid kit?" Julia hunted around the office. Byron thrust his hands under my shoulders to hoist me up. I let out my best-effort howl of pain.

"If you want to get out of here," Julia yelled at Byron, "find the first aid kit."

"Fuck," he spat, and left the office at a trot. She followed.

In retrospect, I think Byron chose not to tell Julia the truth because he didn't trust her. That he didn't drag me screaming along the floor also meant he misjudged the urgency. Julia returned before he did, first aid kit in hand.

"Is it bad? It seems deep. Can you pull your arm away a bit?" She ripped open some gauze pads. "Shit!" she said, as I struggled to elevate my cuffed hands. "Those cuffs are totally unnecessary." She lifted my shirt and pressed the gauze pads gently on the wound. She gradually increased the pressure, until I winced and sucked in sharply. "We gotta stop the bleeding."

When Byron returned with another first aid kit, she demanded he remove the handcuffs. She swabbed my wound with an alcohol wipe. She secured some fresh pads by wrapping gauze ribbon around my torso. Byron watched, impatiently shuffling and kicking at the desk with his heel in frustration.

"What is that thing anyway?" Julia asked. "It looks like a hairpin. Is it gold?"

Byron cocked an ear.

"Bronze," I said.

"OK. Enough." He grabbed my shoulder. "The man's good. Time to go."

"Can you stand?" Julia asked.

We heard a bang in the warehouse, like the telltale noise of the metal door, but somehow wrong. Julia looked at Byron, who froze. We listened. Even I was hoping to hear flamenco music, because I couldn't imagine what the alternative might be. We heard nothing. With a slow, silent motion, Byron slipped a pistol from a shoulder holster.

He crept toward the office door, keeping his body just behind the wall as he peered out. He glanced back, giving the two of us an evil look. Our fault for dallying. I wondered if these were rescuers, if Julia had somehow arranged a way for me to escape. But no, the surprise and terror on her face were real.

Byron was poised on his toes in a runner's crouch, about to plunge into the warehouse, when a black object darted into view. High above the ground, just under the steel roof truss, between two rows of shelving. A drone, hovering, executing a side-to-side sweep.

Byron shot twice at it. He missed. A clomp of boots echoed as an unseen mass of men rushed close to us. From behind the tall shelving, an order was barked. Byron swore, and I missed the first words.

". . . drop the gun! Get down on the floor, hands on your head! Now!"

Byron spun his head wildly, a cornered beast. The office was a trap, the only exit the door. Julia spread herself prone on the floor, hands on her neck, murmuring, "Oh my God, oh my God." My wound was excruciating, but I also dropped onto my belly.

"On the floor! I won't say it again! You've got three seconds. Three, two, one . . ."

Byron lowered himself onto his knees, shoved his gun away, and clapped his hands behind his head.

My flank was toward the door. Tilting my head, I saw them. Half a dozen men in military fatigues, body armor, and helmets, laden and bristling with tactical gear. Rifles raised, they rushed toward us.

SEVENTEEN

"You're in a shit ton of trouble," Walker said, pointing his silver pencil at me. I could feel the table vibrate with his subwoofer voice. "Different shit ton than I thought you were in. But still a nice, sticky shit ton of trouble."

I'd already been debriefed by agents for three hours. After my kidnapping and captivity, that felt like a day spa. Walker's voice, now booming out notice of my federal felonies, felt like a caress.

"Just a pleasant interlude between being kidnapped and assassinated," I said.

"I get that you're desperate," Walker rumbled, "but what the fuck were you thinking?" He rapped his notebook on the conference room table. I flinched, but was still in the throes of giddy relief.

"Wouldn't you have done the same in my shoes?"

"I've done stupid shit, but not like that. Maybe we're both cybersecurity guys. But I know trust is about people."

"Meaning?"

"Technically, what you did makes sense. Hack a system. Surveil the enemy." He was referring to the Magic Crystal. "We do it all the time. But did you seriously think Mork Lupu wasn't going to screw you over?"

"You forget. I still don't know how he screwed me over."

Walker raised his head, nodded, and curled his finger at someone in the corridor behind me.

Diane entered as though tiptoeing around a sickbed. She peered through her thick glasses into my face and looked me up and down. "I'm so sorry." She plucked at her scarf, unsure how to offer sympathy. She settled for a look of anguish. "Are you okay?"

I rolled up my sleeve and displayed the seven rainbow colors around my left wrist from sleeping handcuffed. "Not too bad," I said. I considered showing off the ugly gouge in my flank, a manly trophy, but that would mean exposing my belly fat, which was anything but. "It was a mild flaying."

The bruises horrified her. Even Walker winced. "Mild?" he said. "You look like you've been eaten by a wolf and shit off a cliff."

It looked worse than it felt. I pulled my sleeve down and tried to appear perky. Walker and Diane eyed one another, unsure how to proceed decently.

Walker chose to restore normalcy, such as it was. "OK. Now that we're all on the same team, it's time to talk about Sanctum. I wanted to make sure Diane's in the loop."

"Can't that wait?" she asked. "Shouldn't he be getting medical treatment? Psychological counseling?"

"They gave me a physical last night," I said. "And there's counseling on offer. It's okay, Diane."

"Who did this to you?" she asked.

"I don't know. I was debriefed, not briefed. No connection to the Delphians, though. Just criminals going for the bounty. Pretty amateurish criminals. A teenage girl and some clownish thugs."

"I'll tell you who was responsible," said Walker. "Bin Laden."

Diane raised her eyebrows.

"It has to do with the Mafia." He leaned forward. "People don't realize this. Or they don't remember. The Mafia was still powerful and dangerous in our lifetime. We didn't start getting them under control until we began taking down the Five Families in New York in the late eighties. By the nineties, we made real headway. The Mafia was crumbling.

"But then came 9/11. Our anti-Mafia people got repurposed for anti-terrorism. We lost a lot of ground, and organized crime sprouted again like weeds. Not the same people. Not the old Mafia. Different ethnicities, more sophisticated, lower profile. Less violent. Usually. This was one of those newer groups. They don't do much abduction—maybe this gang have never done it before—which is why they fucked it up so much. Made our job easier."

"But they knew in advance about the raid," I said. Walker squinted. "Have they infiltrated the FBI?"

"Nah. We do joint operations with local law enforcement. I'd say that's where the leak was, if there was a leak. Or it could just have been a tactical fuck-up. We'll know soon enough."

"He's still not safe," Diane said. "As long as the rogue contract is active, others could try to kill him. Right?"

"Right," said Walker, "which is why we need to get back to business. I was going to explain the story with Sanctum."

"OK, Walker," Diane said, putting her hands on the back of a chair. "But remember, I am not technical." He nodded and gestured at the chair. "I'll stand," she said, peering into my face again.

"When this whole thing started—I mean the rogue contract—the intelligence community had a careful outside look at Adyton's systems. We saw traffic from serious threat actors. I'm talking nation-states."

"What kind of traffic? Communication with C&C servers?" I asked.

Diane crossed her arms. "*Aeì koloiòs parà koloiôi hizánei.*"

"Huh?"

"Ancient Greek," she said. "It means computer people flock together like birds."

"I get it. Sorry," Walker replied in his soothing bass. "I mean hostile nations were trying to compromise Adyton's computer systems. And from what we could see, it looks like a couple may even have succeeded."

"Jeez," I said. "I thought we were doing a good job. I can't tell you how hard I worked with our CSO. But maybe the intelligence agencies got the wrong idea, because they don't know what countermeasures we have in place. We built honeypots for this kind of thing. We have a complete parallel software development environment and . . ." I gave Diane a sheepish smile. "We have strong defenses."

"Anyway, with the rogue contract, it was all too weird," Walker said. "I couldn't be sure you were on the level."

"While I was working with Diane, you thought *I* might have orchestrated the rogue contract?"

"No. But something was wrong. The truth only came out when I interviewed your colleagues."

"I saw you with Corinne at Adyton."

"You know why she dumped Lupu?"

"She didn't. *He* dumped *her.*"

"That's what she told people. Otherwise, she was afraid the guy would take revenge."

This was a slap in the face. There weren't many people in my life. Corinne was one, and I'd have expected her to confide a thing like that in me. But I guess I hadn't exactly been honest with her either.

"She dumped him," Walker continued, "because she caught him breaking into her laptop. The bastard had her password and swiped her spare hardware security key. He must have lifted her fingerprints. He admitted to peddling your company's data on the black market, probably to foreign intelligence services. He even tried to blackmail her."

"That explains—"

"So when we found out you met with him . . ."

"You concluded he and I were in cahoots. But why would he have stolen data from Corinne if he had me on the inside?"

"He got caught. Maybe he wanted to get caught. Maybe he was building a cover story for the real inside man. You."

"But then why the rogue contract?"

"A way of blackmailing you. Or maybe you screwed up and your handlers had to get rid of you. They decided to enter the twenty-first century. Use something less messy than Novichok. The professor was a decoy, collateral damage."

"Of course. Why assume a simple explanation when a surreal conspiracy theory will do?"

"There's no simple explanation for any of this, man. Apollo. Rogue contracts. Blackmail. All psycho stuff. And you need to think about the backdrop. There's a fucking war going on in cyberspace. Us versus the Chinese and Russians—for years. You know that. You wouldn't believe the shit that happens: proxy wars, back doors into back doors, cyber-physical attacks, secret channels in video games, deep fakes, electromagnetic weapons. It's my job to be paranoid. Sometimes I do my job too well."

"Why do you trust me now? The kidnapping doesn't debunk your theory."

"Not the kidnapping. After you met with Lupu, you lied to Corinne about it. She saw through the lie, but didn't know what you were up to. We told her to keep her eyes peeled, and she saw your server spin up." He meant the Magic Crystal. "Some weird-ass thing about the hardware registration tipped her off. She told us about it. She figured it had something to do with the meeting with Lupu. That raised a red flag, and that's when we put you under surveillance. We know you paid the guy and we know other stuff. You weren't working with him."

"What other stuff?"

"Once he gave you the key and you installed it in the infrastructure, you made his investment pop. He had a back door he tried to sell on the market. Seven ETH?" Walker curled his lip. "Heh. Try a hundred Bitcoin for one of those keys. At least. Millions of dollars. That fucker is slicker than pig snot on a radiator. He was negotiating to sell his back door 'exclusively' to at least three intelligence agencies. Man, you at least deserved a commission."

"Walker, I set up a server in Sanctum as a trap for the Delphians. It failed. I assume you know that. I don't understand how the Delphians could have learned about it. Did they also buy the key from Mork? It's either that or Apollo is real. Because I don't see otherwise how they could have—"

"Think about it. They didn't need to buy anything. If they're deep in the dark markets—maybe they're ex-intelligence—they see a Sanctum key for sale. They know there's a trap somewhere. If you know there's quicksand around, but you don't know where, what do you do? Stay put. That's good enough. They made sure their code didn't migrate into any new servers. So they didn't fall into your trap."

"You're right." I saw now that my rescue had only thrust me back to an earlier, pre–Magic Crystal stage of peril. Worse than that. Corinne, my most trusted ally, had betrayed me. And she'd been right to do it.

As Walker and I talked, I grew more and more agitated. I noticed my trembling hands. "Could I trouble you for some water?"

Diane hurried out of the room. I closed my eyes and lowered my head. She returned with a small plastic bottle of distilled, remineralized water. Nasty stuff, but I wasn't going to quibble. I drank it all in one go and dabbed my mouth with my sleeve.

"I assume the surveillance is how you homed in on me after the kidnapping?" I coughed. I'd drunk too fast.

"Uh-huh. Those guys may have been clownish when they were holding you, but when it came to grabbing you, they were pros. One of them got into your office and threw your phone behind a desk." He reached inside his blazer and handed it to me. "If you weren't under surveillance, it might have been hard. But we knew the score in minutes. We had video of you wheeled into the ambulance, before they switched to the truck. The rest was legwork. The court warrant and prep to raid the place were what took so long."

"So in the end, Mork saved my life." Walker gave me an are-you-kidding look. "Accidents happen." I smiled. "Did he do any obvious damage to Adyton?"

"Corinne said the Delphians may have gotten Sanctum code before you released it. That right?"

"Maybe. So they bought it from Mork?"

"Who knows? All I know is that your buddy's not going to be selling anything for a long time now." Walker's pencil had been unusually inert, but he now pointed it at me. "You see, it all comes down to people. That's why I don't buy all this 'trustless' crap you people spout about blockchains. There's no 'trustless' in this world. If you didn't have a bunch of devs jabbering, scrabbling, and losing their shit like scared monkeys every time a blockchain system goes haywire, the whole thing would fall apart."

"If it weren't trustless, I wouldn't have ended up as trussed-up goods in a warehouse in Jersey."

"Ohhh . . ." Walker said, chin up, lips rounded. "Yeaaaah . . ." He widened his eyes in a mock epiphany. "Now that's a great advertisement for smart contracts."

"Why is 'trustless' good?" Diane asked.

"We use that word to describe blockchain technology," I said. "It's mystification, like everything else with blockchains. It means the opposite of what it sounds like. In a blockchain system you don't need to trust a person, company, or government. You just need faith in the blockchain."

"Sounds like a religion," she said.

"Yup," said Walker. "I grew up African Methodist Episcopal. I know about religion. Apollo. Bitcoin. Blockchains. All religious sects."

"You said I'm in a shit ton of trouble, but we're all working together. Which is it?" I asked.

"Both," he said.

"So I can go?"

Diane looked at him.

"You can go." He repressed a smile, like a father scolding a clever child. "You've been through enough. But we're not going to be keeping an eye on you. Your company arranged some executive protection."

"What's that?"

"A bodyguard."

"OK," I said, still a little giddy, "but thanks for your help. I've been happy with the FBI service. I plan to give you a really good Yelp review. Should that be under 'Blockchain Services' or 'Kidnapping'?"

Walker rolled his eyes. "Try 'Babysitting.'" He reached over and enveloped my shoulder in his hand. "Get some rest, man. When you're ready, we'll get you back to work."

I was walking through the office and halfway to the elevator when I stopped and slapped my hand to my forehead. I turned around.

"I almost forgot," I said, popping my head back into Walker's office. "I need a favor." Walker was showing Diane something in his little orange notepad. "There was a high school girl in the warehouse where they held me. Julia. I don't know her last name. She tried to help me. Could somebody look after her?"

"Julia," Diane said. "OK. We will take care of it."

"She's something special, and—they're her family." I was babbling.

"We got it," Walker said. Then he rumbled, "Go home."

✸

Someone had charged my phone. The screen lit up with a string of text messages and voicemail from the Priestess's admin. My "executive protection" would meet me downstairs. I left the elevator and went up a flight of stairs to the building's entrance pavilion, a bright, high-ceilinged space where people wait in line to endure a security screening that's like an annual physical. I looked for a beefy guy in a dark suit with sunglasses, an earpiece, and a former career as a linebacker. The one who met my gaze and walked over was wearing jeans and a trim brown leather jacket stitched with ribbing to enlarge the shoulders. A wiry super-featherweight. I'd have to hope he was a top-notch marksman, or else Bruce Lee's cousin.

Bruce Lee's cousin from Brazil, I thought, as I got a closer look at his features. He gave me a cockeyed smile. Knowing, guileful, or awkward, I couldn't tell, but I didn't like it. He offered his hand.

"My name's Ray. They let you know I'd meet you here, right, sir?"

If the Priestess was in any way involved in hiring him, he'd have to be first rate somehow. Maybe he was a terror with a Glock. Could warn you off at fifty paces by blowing away an earlobe.

"They let me know." I shook his hand. "Good to meet you."

Outside, he shepherded me at a trot across the pink and white stone cobbles and marble slabs of the plaza, past the scrub-and-tree-adorned dollops of public park and the bollards lining Lafayette Street, into a waiting car.

"They said I should take you home. Then we'll figure out where to hide you." He'd already slid in from the opposite side of the car by the time I reached for my seatbelt.

"I'm going to Adyton."

"I don't think—"

"Sorry, Ray. I don't want to be offensive. But I need to understand the terms of engagement here. Who calls the shots? The people who hired you? You? Me?"

"You do. I need to tell you what I think, and I think we should get you out of New York. But it's your call, sir."

He told the driver to head west. He whipped out his phone and updated the rideshare app from memory with my office address.

The car nosed into traffic. It kept pace with the pedestrians for a few blocks west. Then it crept north along the river in the daily mid-afternoon molasses flow of commuters avoiding rush hour traffic. Ray pored over floorplans on his phone. Presumably for my building. I couldn't tell.

I shouldn't have asked in the car, in front of the driver, but was too tired to suppress the impulse.

"Just curious. Are you carrying?"

"You mean a handgun? No, sir."

"No gun at all?"

"My job's to look, plan, think fast, and keep you out of danger. If I need a gun, I've already failed."

"Proactive defense," I said, nodding. "Sensible."

Skepticism seeped through my agreeable words. Ray flashed his unnerving smile. "I get it. You look at me and think, 'This here's the kind of pipsqueak who got his head sat on every day as a kid in school. Doesn't even carry and *he's* gonna protect *me*?'"

"I wasn't—"

"Everyone thinks that. It's okay." He smirked. "They did sit on my head. That's how I ended up in this job. But I train so hard, nobody's gonna sit on my head anymore. I do hand-to-hand combat, weapons training, surveillance, sprinting, even my own parkour routine. And they'll *never* touch my clients. That's the important thing."

I disliked his smiles a little less.

The car dropped us off at the back of my office building. As we crossed the crowded sidewalk, Ray somehow managed to be on both sides of me at once. When I went to get him a guest badge at the front desk, we found he'd already been registered for the day. The Priestess or her admin had guessed I'd be pigheaded and come to the office.

Ray negotiated the tortuous way as if he already knew the building. As we walked through the Adyton office, he gave everyone and everything the once-over, especially the inflatable cookie. People glanced at him from their desks, unaccustomed to anyone around them taking such an active interest in meatspace.

The rank and file hadn't been told about the kidnapping. There was no reason to advertise the discovery that the danger for me began before the contract activated. But Corinne knew, of course. She intercepted me before I made it to the Bridge and threw her arms around me. Stunned, I let my own arms hang in the air until it became less awkward to succumb and hug her. We stood like this for a minute. I could feel rumor-seeking stares warm my back.

When we disentangled ourselves, I found that Ray had dropped his backpack by my desk and was already darting around the Bridge like a terrier in a new house. He poked behind my desk, stood on tiptoe to peer into the street from a window, and took photos with his phone. He examined the sealed door at the end of the Bridge opposite the office. Corinne pointed a thumb at him and raised her eyebrows.

"Corinne," I said as he walked back, "this is Ray, my . . ."

"You can say 'bodyguard.'" He put his phone away and shook Corinne's hand. "We need to cover some windows here or move you. Not now. In a few days." Someone had briefed him on how the contract worked. Unless I'd again made a stupid miscalculation, the only immediate concerns were kidnapping or someone planting a time bomb. "I'm going to check out the rest of the office and some other stuff and fuel up. If you want to leave the office or anything comes up, you text me, okay?"

"Got it. Could you give me—" My phone pinged.

"Yup. Sent." He reached into his jacket and handed Corinne a card. "You should put my contact info in your phone too. Just in case."

Corinne and I drifted to a window. We watched cars whiz under the Bridge and pedestrians spill out from the market below. Around lunch or at dinnertime, we often stood like this. We played the game of guessing where people had eaten or gotten takeout. We rarely agreed with each other and rarely got to confirm our guesses, because from the Bridge, it was hard to make out logos on paper bags. But the game was a good way to figure out what we were in the mood to eat. ("The woman in the middle there. She's got that happy hummus-and-pickled-cabbage look. I wouldn't mind being her.")

Now we stood watching in silence.

"I—" we both began.

She looked down. I chewed my lip.

"You did the right thing," I said.

"I agonized." She was still looking at the floor. "I totally agonized. I thought about whether to go to you first. But you stopped telling me the truth. I knew you were losing control. They promised me they wouldn't do anything to you."

She still didn't know I was working with the FBI. Did restoring trust now mean telling her? Or would it make things worse?

"I didn't want to involve you. I was entering dangerous shoals," I said.

"I tried to warn you."

"I should have listened. But I was desperate. Am desperate."

"Did they hurt you?" she asked. "The kidnappers?"

"I can't tell you how much white flour I had to eat, and the ugly things I learned. Turns out pizza tastes awfully good."

She laughed.

"I don't know what I'm going to have to do next," I said. "I don't know if I can involve you. I'm on a highway to hell and don't want to take you with me."

"I thought I was the risk-taker."

"In a placid world without vengeful gods, you are, and I admire you for it." I decided I shouldn't tell her about how Diane, Walker, and possibly the intelligence community were failing me. Not yet. But I had to say something. "Corinne, there are things I can't tell you," I said. "Not yet. But I promise to be honest about what I can."

"So what's next?"

"You and I put our heads together. This time, for real."

EIGHTEEN

We combed through the rogue contract code again, the "prophecy" system code, and Sanctum logs.

Ray went out for a few hours, texting us for dinner orders before he came back. He walked into the office with a gym bag in one hand and a clutch of take-out bags in the other. He was sheepish about joining us in the Adyton kitchenette, but we twisted his arm. I ate a big salad freighted with tea eggs and avocado, while he slurped at a bowl of hand-pulled Beijing noodles with hot sauce. Corinne got sushi. I didn't tell her, but I'd now developed an aversion to the stuff. I hoped it wouldn't last long.

For me, a meal wasn't a welcome break from our intense yet fruitless work. The pain in my flank was a relentless spur to action.

"I feel like a fool for eating dinner. I should be scrambling to preserve my life."

"You have to eat," Corinne said.

"I imagine a wall of clocks—like one of those setups with different time zones—Beijing, San Francisco, New York, London. Except on my surreal wall, the clocks are ticking at different rates. There's the clock that telescopes through history from ancient Greece, ticking once a decade. There's the clock measuring my progress finding the Delphians. It's got a cranky, creeping second hand. And there's the clock showing how much time I have left. It's spinning backward like the altimeter in a crashing jetliner."

Ray wore his jacket while he ate. He seemed to hover half an inch off his seat, ready to swivel from noodle to action. He slurped up a noodle's tail end. "Time and money." He chewed and swallowed. "It's all about time and money. Can't change the flow of time. But we *can* change the flow of money. We're gonna make sure no one claims that bounty."

"Time and money are strange things in our world. The blockchain world," I said.

"'Cause you can make money so fast?"

"It's about more than that. Flash loans are a great example."

"Sounds like money for superheroes."

"They're cool. They're magical," Corinne said.

"Imagine if you walked into a bank and asked for a million-dollar loan without any ID or collateral," I said. "The loan officer would go for the little red button under the desk, right?"

"Probably."

"But you can do crazy things like that with smart contracts. You just need to complete everything in a single transaction. That's why it's called a flash loan. Your smart contract borrows the money, uses it to do whatever you want, and then repays the loan. Boom. Boom. Boom. It happens instantaneously. If you don't repay the loan, the whole transaction aborts. Time rolls back and the loan never happened. So it's impossible for the lender to lose the money. It all works because all the operations take place on a blockchain and involve blockchain assets."

"If you can only keep the money while you blink, why do it?" Ray asked. "'Cause then you can say you were once a millionaire? Can I be a temporary billionaire? Or the richest man in the world? 'Cause I'm not making it into *Guinness World Records* for my height."

Corinne and I laughed. "We can make you a multimillionaire," she said.

"That should still impress my mom."

"You might think you can't do much in a single transaction," Corinne explained. "But in a smart contract system you can. You can trade and make money by taking advantage of price differences. Alice buys a crypto asset for two dollars on Exchange A, sells it for three dollars on Exchange B, repays the loan, and pockets a dollar. It's called arbitrage."

"Arbitrage happens on Wall Street all the time," I added. "But only firms with deep pockets can do it. Flash loans democratize the process. People do use them to make money. You don't need capital, just good ideas implemented in code."

"I got all kinds of ideas," Ray said with a crooked smile. "But I'd need a loan for like a year."

"Sorry. I'm afraid we're only up to seconds. We're like physicists creating subatomic particles. It all decays quickly. And it only works on a blockchain. Our big idea was extending flash loans a little beyond a single transaction. Multi-block flash loans, we call them. Seems trivial, but it's a big deal. As I said, time and money are strange things in our world."

✳

After dinner, Corinne and I continued to sift for clues in the Delphians' code and Sanctum. I didn't realize how much time had passed until Ray checked in on us. It was almost midnight.

"You gonna be long? Don't want to rush you. Just need to plan."

"Sorry to keep you. We wanted to work a little longer, Ray." I hadn't thought through the implications of having a bodyguard. "But you escort me home, don't you? Then what?"

He clutched his forehead. "Sorry." His cockeyed grin appeared. "I didn't tell you. I'm staying with you."

"Ah, okay. I hadn't—"

"I got my toothbrush and PJ's." He pointed at his gym bag. "Just need a pillow and a corner. Really sorry. Don't know how I could have forgot to tell you."

"No problem. But we could be here for another hour or two, if that's okay. You can meet me—"

"Got it. I'll leave you guys alone. Let me know when you're ready."

✳

Corinne and I knocked off a little after one in the morning. We found Ray in the kitchenette, working on a tiny laptop. He led us downstairs, along a corridor inside the building between two shops in the marketplace, to an exit I'd never used before. As Ray peered up the street through the glass doors, a car materialized. He motioned to us to stay inside, went out and opened the near door of the car, and ushered me in. I felt ungentlemanlike leaving Corinne to fend for herself, but Ray's job was to protect the target.

We dropped Corinne off at her building a few blocks away. There was no one around, so we waited until she entered the foyer, where there's a night concierge. After she'd gone in and we pulled away from the curb, I looked through the rear window and saw she'd reemerged onto the sidewalk. She held the door with one hand and waved with the other as though I was heading off to the airport for an international flight. I felt a surge of—something I didn't want to feel.

We circled the block and raced up an empty Tenth Avenue to my building, hitting a succession of green lights just as they turned yellow. Normally, I like being out in Manhattan in the early hours of the morning, owning the empty streets, being among just enough other lone wayfarers so it doesn't feel postapocalyptic. But I usually walk home, rather than clutching my insides in the back of a car while the driver drag races himself. Ray, unaffected, looked out the window. Slight movements of his head suggested he was making mental notes along the route.

We got off at the far entrance of my building. The electric eye on that side never sees me on my first try. The doors retract only after I've humiliated myself by dancing back and forth a few times. When we hustled in from the car, they instantly parted for Ray in a gracious welcome. Maybe it was that there were two of us, or maybe it was Ray's quantum trick of being in multiple places at once.

Primary colors streaked by as we passed the front desk. Jazzelle had bright new hair ribbons. Ray gave her a thumbs-up.

"Hi, Ray," she said. Then to our retreating backs, "Goodnight, you guys."

"You know her?"

"Came by while you were working. Wanted to make sure she knows what to do if someone comes and pokes around."

"Does she?"

"She does now. Don't worry. She likes you. She's got your back."

Ray rebuffed my offer of the sofa for the night and insisted on the floor. Good for his back and staying alert, he said, and also "primal." That's exactly what my trainer says of the crawl she exhausts me with on the gym floor to show me evolution has done me no good. Ray accepted a pillow and towel. I left him an optional blanket at a primally safe distance away, on the sofa.

"I'll be ready before you get up," he said.

"Help yourself to anything in the fridge."

"Thanks. Got breakfast in my bag."

When I shuffled out of the bathroom after brushing my teeth, he was staring out the window. We nodded to each other in the reflection over the jagged, light-studded nightscape of Manhattan.

Barely more than three days before the contract on my head activated. I lay awake for a long time, playing with my mental model of the Delphians' code. I was missing something. I could feel it. But where? Somewhere the plastic-like material of the model was thin—too thin—and pliant. I rotated it and pressed and rotated and pressed but found I was instead pressing my mind down beneath the logic of code, below consciousness, into the realm of illogic, the kaleidoscopic place of dreams.

✳

The next morning, Corinne was staring at her monitor.

"They're sailing so close to the wind. Somebody likes speed and danger. It's actually kind of beautiful."

Her face was tilted upward, her lips parted. She would have resembled a saint or the Virgin Mary in an old painting, kissed by a golden shaft of light from Heaven, were it not for the purple streak in her hair.

She was talking about the Delphians' code, admiring their daring minimalism. To add insult to injury, it now seemed like Apollo was exercising his fascination over the women I knew, edging them in subtle ways ever closer to worship. *First Diane*, I thought, seeing Corinne's face aglow, *and now Corinne*. According to Diane, the Greeks considered Apollo to be the most beautiful of the Olympian gods. I didn't see it, but for Diane and Corinne, it was as though his beauty radiated through his works. For Diane, that beauty was in the art and culture of ancient Greece evoked by glimmers of the god's return to earth. For Corinne, it was in the Delphians' code.

At least Apollo didn't always get the girls. Diane told me that one once ran away and turned into a tree.

"Strange and beautiful," Corinne said, still staring at the screen.

But there was a third woman. Never fascinated, only fascinating. The Priestess. She was immune to the god's charms. Because she was older? Because she was the Priestess? Then it hit me. She'd asked me something.

What? About weaponizing Sanctum. An interesting idea. More than an interesting idea.

"Corinne!"

She turned to me with unfocused eyes.

"Scroll up. Up, up. No, not—yes, near the top."

The cursor hovered on a variable declaration, a line of code that hadn't meant anything special to me before. "Sorry. Let me do it." I took the trackpad. I examined scattered bits of code. I read through the documentation for a Sanctum feature.

"They *are* sailing close to the wind," I said with a demonic grin. "And I think I know how to conjure up a storm."

All I needed was a few billion dollars. And I knew just where to get it.

In their quest for showy economy, the Delphians had kept the data storage in their contract to an absolute minimum. They'd set variable lengths in many cases to only four bytes—i.e., thirty-two bits—instead of the usual thirty-two bytes. They'd made an assumption: Bounty funds would never be more than about $4 billion dollars. To put it in nerdier terms, 2^{32}, an upper bound on the amount you could represent in thirty-two bits. A safe assumption a couple of months earlier, when the only way to get that kind of money was with a flash loan. A flash loan wouldn't work with the Delphians' contract. To prevent an assassination bounty from sitting unclaimed forever, a depositor of bounty funds could specify a delay, called a "lockup period," after which the depositor could withdraw the money. This period ranged from seconds (presumably so crowdfunders could test it) to years. It could even be forever, as with the Delphians' deposit. But a flash loan needed *instantaneous* repayment. In other words, the Delphians' contract wasn't compatible with the "flash" part of a flash loan.

Apollo, the god of prophecy, had somehow failed, however, to foresee the advent of *multi-block* flash loans in Sanctum. Multi-block flash loans lasted longer than flash loans. As their name suggests, they lasted the length of time it takes for a blockchain to generate multiple blocks. Usually only seconds in wall clock time, but in computer time, that's an eternity. Multi-block flash loans would last long enough to ride out the shortest lockup period in the Delphians' contract. That meant I could turn them into a weapon.

You'll remember that the Delphians' contract had a kind of crowd-funding period before a bounty activated. Crazy people were already contributing to the bounty on my head. I was going to do the same. I'd make my own contribution to the bounty on my head. A very big contribution. In fact, I'd hit the Delphians' contract with so much money that I'd cause a critical piece of it to fail. The idea was like artificially running up the odometer in a car to the point where it rolls over past zero and erroneously indicates that the car has almost no mileage on it. My attack would cause the bounty balance recorded in the Delphians' contract to roll over and go to $1. Then I'd withdraw the $1, causing the balance to hit $0.

If a withdrawal caused a bounty balance to drop to $0, that would normally mean that a bounty was claimed or monetary support for it vanished. So the contract was programmed to treat the bounty as terminated. My attack would use this fact to trick the contract and permanently end the bounty. No more calling cards or assassination claims. No more price on my head.

Multi-block flash loans enabled me to make all of this happen with borrowed money. I worked out that I could scrape together the roughly $4 billion I needed by simultaneously borrowing from an assortment of multi-block loan contracts launched when Sanctum was released. After terminating the bounty, my attack code would withdraw all of the money—still possible, even with the bounty balance out of whack—and make the necessary repayment of the loans.

My flood of money would only terminate the bounty on my head, not destroy the Delphians' contract. The Delphians could create a new bounty on the same Apollonian timeline and even transfer their old bounty deposit to it. But then I could just mount the same attack again. There was only one way for them to stop me from doing so repeatedly. They would need to upgrade part of their contract, a so-called code "library" that handled new deposits. By sending a special transaction, the Delphians could modify this library so that the contract would accept only their deposits and reject deposits from everyone else—including yours truly.

The critical thing—the whole point of the attack—was that if the Delphians did send transactions to fix the contract, we'd know about them in advance. Walker had said that maybe, just maybe, the intelligence agencies could trace transactions with advance warning. At best, we'd only get one shot at it. But that might be enough.

Whether the Delphians didn't respond and left their contract in its broken state or whether they chose to fix it and launch a new bounty—and even double the price on my head—it would be a victory. I'd found a chink in their armor. If I was right, my blade would draw blood from mortal flesh.

What all of this might mean about the god, I didn't know. Maybe after thousands of years in a faraway place, Apollo had lost his touch. Or maybe he'd tripped up the Delphians with an ambiguous prophecy, the way he did that king of old. Or maybe, just maybe, the world was saner than it seemed, and Apollo didn't exist after all.

NINETEEN

I've done it dozens of times—at conferences, workshops, and Adyton.
Still, giving presentations jangles my nerves. It doesn't matter that the
stakes are low. If I make a mistake, at worst some of the audience will think
I'm an idiot. They already do.

When Walker had me give a presentation in a secure videoconferencing facility in the FBI offices, though, it was a literal matter of life and
death. In his thunder-in-the-mountains voice, he warned that I'd better not fuck it up. There would be technical directors there—big muck-
ety-mucks in the shadowy world of US government cybersecurity—or at
least their deputies. I had just days before contract activation, and we'd
managed to get them assembled on a few hours' notice. Only they could
bless my idea.

So it was odd that I didn't feel nervous. The excitement of being on the
cusp of victory against the Delphians changed things. My hands trembled,
somehow not with my usual panic, but eagerness. Mastering the pain in
my flank gave me a sense of control. Diane was there beside me, so I was
particularly happy about putting on a brave show.

There were three other groups in the video conference with us. Two
were identified on-screen as "Department of Defense." The National
Security Agency, I figured, and another of DoD's other countless intelligence units. It turned out I was right: The other was the Defense
Intelligence Agency, military intelligence. The third group was CIA.
Only two people at DIA, a woman and a man, wore military uniforms,
of the camouflage type. Nearly all of the dozen odd others were in suits,
apart from a couple of the men at NSA, who were wearing short-sleeved
Oxfords, probably techies. The videoconferencing system was so good it

was like sitting across the table from them, this gang of spooks holding my destiny in their hands.

Walker introduced me and reminded everyone that I didn't have a security clearance. The DIA people introduced themselves with their full names and titles. Among them was their Cyber Branch Chief (who left after fifteen minutes). The CIA people introduced themselves by their first names, like restaurant servers. The NSA people didn't introduce themselves.

Walker's pencil remained hidden and I saw Diane self-consciously pull her hand away when it was about to pluck at her scarf.

I had only thirty minutes. I presented slides I'd made fairly nontechnical on Walker's advice. I explained in layperson's terms the structure of the Delphians' code and its exceptional polish. I explained oracles, Sanctum, and flash loans. I squeezed in everything from a mini intro course on smart contracts to a master class on rogue contracts.

I was interrupted only twice. The first time by a heavy graybeard in a gray suit at NSA. Reclining far back in his chair at the end of a conference table, he asked, "What's your adversarial model?" It wasn't the kind of question meant to clarify anything technical, just the pecking order around his table. The second interruption came from a woman at the CIA. "What's your theory about who these people are? Terrorists? A cult?" A nontechnical analyst, I guessed, at sea without clear sociohistorical background. *Welcome to the club*, I thought.

"Dr. Duménil here is from our art crime unit," Walker answered. "She's the expert on that angle." Then he whispered to Diane, "Targeter."

"We don't really know who they are," Diane explained. "I can only give you my hypothesis." The hypotheses I'd heard from her privately carried a whiff of Apollo worship, suitable only behind closed doors. She was more clinical now. "We have intelligence about the discovery of some artifacts from Delphi. That is why I'm here. It's possible that they are a cult, but—"

"What are we talking? Like the Moonies? Branch Davidians? Scientologists? QAnon?"

"That is not what 'cult' means to classical scholars. Ancient Greek cults revolved around codified sets of practices and worship of specific deities, not ideology. These Delphians are using language and showing patterns of behavior that draw on mythology and religious ritual from ancient Greece. What they really practice or believe, we don't know."

"What about their organizational structure? I did some research. I couldn't find anything." If the video link wasn't playing tricks, I saw her glance at me. "Even on the high side."

"Nothing yet," Diane said.

"No social media presence? No known leader?"

"No." Diane opened her mouth again, but thought better of whatever she was about to say. I resumed my presentation.

It was only when I finished that the grilling came in earnest. Surprisingly, it didn't come from the NSA, who'd probably figured out all the technical details already. It was "Jeff" at the CIA who served up a heap of smiling skepticism. His shiny pate heliographed evidence of a former military career. I don't know much about the armed services, but Jeff had a cherubic look that I'd have expected his commanding officers to browbeat off the face of a career junior officer. So I pegged him as at least a colonel.

"Even if you crack their contract, why do you think the Delphians will try to fix it?" He had a hint of a southern drawl, friendly yet menacing.

"I don't have a technical reason," I said. "They've shown extraordinary capabilities. They've created a mystique. If they walk away from their contract, they'll lose it."

A woman beside him whispered in his ear. He nodded. "If we can locate one of their servers, then what?"

"That's up to you. If you can use it to find their real-world identities, it may save some lives."

"If we can't? Or don't?"

"If not . . . I can't say I have a plan. I can only tell you my gut feeling. If we can shatter the Delphians' mystique, and find bugs in their code, then we're operating in familiar territory. Maybe it's just my hubris talking, but if that happens, I have a hunch they can be beaten."

"A hunch. Heh." Jeff laughed softly. "I'm an amateur astronomer. When I'm out at night with my telescope in a field in Virginia with the stars tickling my head, I have a hunch I'm going to be the first to make contact with an alien lifeform. Hasn't happened yet. Is there a reason we should believe in your hunch?"

"Because if this works—if—then we're no longer looking for Apollo in the heavens. We're looking somewhere on earth for some guys like—" I was going to say like the two guys in short-sleeves over at NSA, but thought better of it. "Like me. Plain terrestrial techies."

"Plain terrestrial techies." Jeff smiled. "OK."

"That was fine," Walker said afterward when the screens went dim. Diane had hurried off to another meeting. "You were a little mouthy, but I think it went okay."

"Sorry about that."

"Lucky thing the cybersecurity coordinator from the NSC didn't show." He gave the screens a wary glance. "She's a real hard-ass and—"

"When will we get the thumbs-up or -down?"

"It doesn't work like that."

"How do I know whether to go ahead?"

"You should go ahead. If they need to be ready, they're ready. You may hear something, or not. Maybe you find an IP address in a fortune cookie. Maybe you see a message spray-painted on your building. Maybe you wake up and it was all a dream."

"They'll conceal sources and methods, you mean."

"Yup. Their shit is so secret that even the way they hide their secrets is secret."

✸

Rain was gusting across the plaza when Ray and I left the FBI building. He snapped open an umbrella and covered my head as we prepared to cross. Already I disliked having a bodyguard, playing the dignitary. Ray with his umbrella now reminded me of the servants in Victorian costume dramas dashing out to shield their masters' heads across the ten steps from horse-drawn carriage to manor entrance.

"Ray," I said, "let me hold the umbrella for you."

He smirked. "You trying to take my job?"

"No. It would be safer for me to look like the bodyguard and you to look like the target." That flummoxed him. "Besides," I said, "I don't have hair to get wet. You do."

His mouth hung open for a moment. But we stood exposed at the building entrance, with no cover, and he had to act.

"The point's that the umbrella hides your face," he said.

I hadn't thought of that. I bowed my head and let him hold the umbrella as we scampered through fresh puddles to the car waiting to take us to Adyton.

✻

Rain lashed the windows behind us on the Bridge as Corinne and I set to work. It cast a gray shroud over the street in front, relieved only by the red of taillights and yellow of taxis, indomitable in the gloom.

We knew what to do, and worked together in silence. I told Corinne that I had a friend who might be able to trace the Delphians if we broke their contract and they sent a transaction to fix it. After I swore up and down that the friend wasn't Mork, Corinne didn't pry.

An hour later, it began to thunder. When that happens, I can feel the steel girders of the Bridge stretched taut between buildings like the strings of a musical instrument. The floor vibrates. There's the thrill of a dangerous harmony with nature, but without the risk. I think.

When our code was complete, we tested it as thoroughly as we could before going live. We might not get a second chance. I prepared our custom attack contract.

Twice before on the Bridge I'd executed a fateful piece of code. The first time I created the neutralization contract. The second time I launched the Magic Crystal. Both times, I'd unleashed a torrent of trouble. This time, I worried less about trouble than failure. I hesitated and sighed. Corinne watched me.

"Want me to do it?" she asked.

I was tempted. But the wrath of the god had been on my head. It needed to stay there. The date with destiny was my own. I set the attack to launch on a seven-second timer and hit the Return key. I walked across the Bridge and pressed my forehead to the cold windowpane. I closed my eyes. I could feel the rain hammering on the glass.

I wanted to postpone the moment of reckoning. I thought about Jeff from the CIA beneath the stars, his feeling of imminent contact with aliens. For our trick to succeed against the Delphians would mean something similar, contact with an otherworldly force, perhaps an equal impossibility. Yet if I failed now, I couldn't imagine how I'd ever succeed. I'd run out of time and ideas. At best, I'd have Ray as a roommate for the rest of my life. At worst, the rest of my life would be the summer of a fruit fly.

There had been times before in my life when I had crossed the threshold into unreality. It happened with my first professional success. I wrote a popular piece of code a year after I left Berkeley—a computational puzzle generator to slow down attackers. I was stunned to see it proliferate and get used to secure websites visited by millions of people. It happened again when I walked straight into a movie to meet and embrace the cinematic beauty who became my wife. (Never mind that the reel ended and I was thrust back in my solitary seat, watching the projection machine sputter glyphs onto the screen.) It happened too, of course—in a nasty way—when the rogue contract on my head came out. I wondered, could it once again—

"Whoo-hoo!"

I turned to see Corinne beaming at me. "It worked!"

"Worked?"

"It's totally wedged!"

"You're sure?"

"Yes! I tried to make a bounty deposit. It failed!"

She raised her hand. I gave her a limp high five. I didn't believe it yet. I looked at the contract's transaction history. I glanced at its code again, although I nearly knew it by heart. I started coding up my own test.

"Come on!" Corinne said. "You don't trust me? I can show you the bounty balance and the status flag. Move over."

She took control and showed me the balance for the bounty on my head. $0. That could only mean we'd terminated the bounty. I was convinced.

The spanner we'd thrown into the works didn't mean I was safe. The Delphians could fix their contract at any time. But that was the point: We'd created bait that I didn't think the Delphians could refuse. It was all now in the hands of the intelligence agencies.

That left me in the quiet eye of the storm. If they relaunched the terminated bounty, I'd still have only three days until activation. But for the first time since my ordeal had begun, I realized, I didn't have to think, I didn't have to scramble. In fact, I couldn't. At that moment, there was nothing else I could do. I was helpless. And it was a relief.

*

Corinne insisted on a celebration. Good for my morale, she said. I wasn't in the mood, but gave in. There was a chance it would be our last meal together. I thought of Diane and her chocolate tart. I wanted to invite Diane, but it would be too complicated. Her chocolate tart, at least, could join us. Corinne and I ordered pastries from Maison Stern.

It didn't take long for someone out there to notice what we'd done to the Delphians' contract. Social media was soon abuzz with the news. We watched a stream of rants rush by and swell into a river. I expected our attack to tear away the Delphians' mantle of invincibility. For a few people, it did. To my surprise, though, Delphian sympathizers and conspiracy theorists doubled down. The mass of money we'd used to attack the contract was a desperate move by the world's governments to stop the god and his disciples, they claimed. We would fail. The contract was still running and hidden code, planted by the Delphians in anticipation of an attack, would fix it. The attackers would soon feel the vengeance of the god.

"These people are nuts," Corinne said.

She was right, but the spectacle of a horde of half-brained people baying for my blood was irresistible. It took the goods arriving from Maison Stern to peel me away from my monitor. In the kitchenette, Corinne and I disassembled the boxes carrying the precious pastries, nudging open the curved white cardboard panels that Maison Stern architected to protect the glazes and decoration. I was now so sensitized to danger that even pastries, coming as they did from the outside world, made me nervous. I had to remind myself that the bounty hadn't activated, and even if would-be assassins didn't know we'd terminated it, I couldn't be kidnapped by a box or chocolate tart. Ray was sitting with his laptop at what had already become his habitual table.

"Sure you don't want any, Ray?" I asked.

"No, thanks. Too fancy for me. Mind if I do push-ups by your desk?"

I'd seen eyes bug out of heads around the office when he did push-ups on his fingertips in the kitchenette, with one foot on a chair and the other lifted toward the ceiling. The Bridge was more secluded than the kitchenette.

"Go for it. While you do, I'll sit here and gorge on pastries to keep the universe in balance."

Ray grinned. I'll never get used to that grin, I thought. He took his bag and left.

As Corinne and I ate, my phone kept buzzing. I couldn't face any more of the commotion around the Delphians' contract, so I ignored it.

"What's next?" Corinne asked.

My chocolate tart was good, but I noticed that her dark-chocolate mousse cake, with its shiny glaze and circlet of cocoa nibs, looked better.

"I don't know," I said, "but I'm sure the Delphians will immediately grasp what we've done."

I caught a strange glance from a dev at a nearby desk. She couldn't have heard what Corinne and I were saying sotto voce. She was new, so maybe I was just a novelty to her. I ignored her.

Corinne poked her cake. "You know, this whole thing has highlighted for everyone all that you do around here. You mean more than you think to the company. Lukas says they think of you as a cofounder. And the Priestess . . ."

Another person, another strange glance. Then another.

"Corinne, have I sprouted horns or something? Have you noticed—"

A yellow warning sign appeared. The Shirt. Lukas huffed up to us.

"You've still got the bodyguard, right?"

"Why?"

He eyed our half-eaten desserts and my phone.

"I guess you don't know. They just claimed the bounty."

My tart clung to the roof of my mouth. Corinne swallowed. "The bounty. You mean—"

"I mean it's certain now. The professor was murdered." Lukas avoided my eyes and looked at Corinne.

Ray walked over. "I heard what happened. I think we should leave the building soon."

I gestured toward him. "Lukas, meet my bodyguard Ray."

"Your bodyguard Ray's right," Lukas said.

"Why? We've still got days," I objected. I didn't bother telling them about the bounty termination, since it might only be temporary. "I'm not worried about assassins until then."

"Me neither," Ray said. "At least I know what assassins are gonna try to do. But there's worse than assassins. There's crazy people. And reporters."

✳

For all of my wondering and waiting and agitation about Viganò's bounty, when it was claimed at last, I'd been caught flat-footed with a fat mouthful of chocolate tart. I felt regret that we'd been unable to terminate it—even temporarily—since it had already activated. By now, though, Viganò's murder didn't surprise me. Before I was kidnapped, the Delphians were an abstraction, an amorphous pall of terror created by a piece of code. My ordeal in New Jersey changed things. Whenever I thought about the rogue contract, I felt the tip of Byron's knife on my face, the bruising cuffs, the pain in my ribs.

How stupid I'd been not to realize that someone might try to abduct me. How idiotic to fall for the fake pedestrian walkway. My mind reverted constantly to that moment, projected me back into something like a waking dream, and tried to rewrite it. If only I'd let Adyton hire Ray beforehand. We'd have arrived in a car and scuttled across the sidewalk before the gang from Jersey even noticed. If only I'd had the sense not to be lured into a closed passage, a plywood box, practically a coffin. I'd have walked right by, cheating my captors of their prey. Their patriarch (had the FBI caught him?) would have been left to scold Byron in a cloud of fetid breath. If only I'd not been fool enough to disregard the Priestess. I'd have fled the country to sit incognito on a beach in Santorini. The sun god's flaying would have been at worst a sunburn.

The fact that the bounty for Viganò had been claimed, though, was frightening for a different reason.

It wasn't a coincidence that the claim happened right after we hacked the Delphians' contract. Our attack wasn't fatal. The Delphians could circumvent it. But once a piece of code starts showing cracks, it draws hackers' scrutiny. They apply their ingenious armamentarium, their toolbox of twisted instruments. They probe and find subtle flaws and before you know it, they've cracked the code and left it in pieces. I didn't think this would happen to the Delphians' almost impeccable contract, but you never knew. Adyton's neutralization contract, with its million-dollar reward, was a powerful incentive for more hackers to try. So it was sensible for Viganò's assassins to claim their bounty while they still could.

It wasn't the fact the assassins had cashed out that was frightening. It was the fact they'd waited so long to do it. Why would they wait for a week? There was no technical or financial rationale. There was only a strategic one. They'd wanted to delay revelation of Viganò's murder to the world in order to hide their existence from their next targets. These weren't amateurish kidnappers. These were professionals who'd swiftly orchestrated Viganò's murder with such finesse that they'd even deceived coroners primed to find evidence of foul play. Without intending to, I'd flushed them out of the shadows.

Now I knew they existed. And I knew they'd be coming for me.

TWENTY

Ray walked with me to the Bridge. I scooped up my backpack and started back toward the office. He shook his head and pointed behind me.

"Other way."

"What other way?"

He meant the opposite, sealed-off side of the Bridge. There was a door on that side, but it was an emergency exit. It was barred with an alarmed exit device, a metal push bar with a red-lettered warning: PUSH TO OPEN. ALARM WILL SOUND. I'd never gone through it and had no idea what lay beyond.

"We're going to set off the alarm?"

"Nah. It says 'Push to Open.'" He grinned. "We ain't gonna push it."

"Then—"

"Don't want you to see this. Give me a sec," he said. Hiding the cylinder lock and edge of the door with his body, he fished out his wallet, took something out, and popped the door open without touching the bar. The alarm didn't sound.

"This is exciting. Can I come?" Corinne appeared beside us.

Ray looked at me.

"I assume it's okay?" I said.

When we passed through the door, I felt the way I do when I see a new refit of the USS *Enterprise* in a *Star Trek* movie. The office we stepped into felt familiar, was somehow like Adyton, but there were differences in the people, layout, and visuals. The windows were bigger, the lights brighter, the decor more lavish. It was clearly a tech company, with its industrial ceilings and standing desks and double and triple monitors riveting the gazes of twenty- and thirtysomething employees. (Fast-moving tech companies euthanize employees by age forty.) Juvenile touches were everywhere. In the primary colors of the ceiling panels, carpets, and upholstery. In the Miro-shaped sofas and armchairs of the meeting nooks. In the six-foot-high Lego model Empire State Building and the snacks and jumbles of stuff on desks. I discovered that I'd led my last few years of unwitting existence on the Bridge within a stone's throw of a giant aquarium and an appealing if bizarre grove of little padded tree houses with hammocks.

We'd swung the emergency door open behind a standing desk. The lanky woman there had headphones on and didn't hear us. She jumped when we materialized from nowhere and strode past her.

"Sorry to disturb you," Ray said, half-turning and pointing at the door as we walked away. "That door violates the fire code." He spoke in a voice of crisp authority I didn't know he had in him.

We tried to look purposeful as we wandered the office looking for an exit. We hit a dead end, a wood-paneled library that could have been transplanted from a nineteenth-century estate in Boston. Brimming with leather-bound books, I guessed it served as a quiet room for employee-laptop dyads. I wondered if the kids who used it knew how to operate a book.

We backtracked, found the elevator, and descended to the ground floor, where Ray and I dashed from the building through light drizzle into a waiting car. Corinne went back across the street to Adyton.

Coasting down the street, I saw that Ray was right. There was a camera crew in front of an entrance to the Adyton building, and onlookers waiting to see why the crew was there. Ray had positioned me on the far side of the passenger seat, so no one noticed me.

"It's time to get real careful," Ray said. "I don't like what happened to the professor."

"You think he was poisoned?"

"I don't know much about poisons, but maybe."

"Do you know just how slow-acting a slow-acting poison is? Could I already be poisoned?"

"Don't think so. I've already been taking steps against that," Ray said. I now understood why the Maison Stern bag had a name written on it that I didn't recognize. "The assassins don't want things getting messy. If they accidentally kill two people at the same time, everyone knows immediately that it was murder. That makes poisoning tricky. I heard the professor didn't have protection."

"He refused it," I said.

"Heard you did too before you got kidnapped."

"I was reckless in my youth. Maybe still. But now you've cajoled me out of the office."

"Yes, sir. I have."

I turned and peered out the rear window through the haze. Far down Tenth Avenue, just above the glassed-in part of the High Line that over-looks the traffic, I glimpsed the fast-receding brick corner of the Adyton building.

I wondered: Would I ever return?

✻

There were reporters in front of my apartment building too. They didn't know it shared an underground amenity floor—where the gym, pool, and bowling alley were—with the building next door. We slipped in through this secret passage.

I didn't have to wait long for the Delphians to respond to our hack. Within hours they took the bait. They sent transactions to turn off deposits other than theirs, so that we couldn't mount our attack again, and to freshly reinstate the bounty on my head.

Now the game was on—if the intelligence agencies chose to play. Theirs is a delicate calculus that often involves cyberweapons to locate and spy on adversaries. Cyberweapons aren't like most conventional weapons, like bombs, guns, and missiles. A bomb doesn't vanish if the enemy learns of its existence. It will still detonate. But a cyberweapon exploits critical flaws in software. Once deployed—or after persistent use—it may be observed, and once observed, it may be nullified by software updates that eliminate the flaws.

The intelligence agencies stockpile cyberweapons laboriously and at great cost. They probe software, penetrate companies, influence technical standards, and otherwise engage in a multipronged campaign of armament. Before they use a cyberweapon, they estimate the chances it will be nullified or made visible to the enemy and decide whether it's worth the risk. Their decision about whether to go after the Delphians involved a metaphorical pan balance. One pan held a shiny cyberweapon. The other held the featherweight life of a grubby software developer. Happily, the intel community also cares about things like preserving national security, which added a little weight to my pan.

The Delphians had made a similar calculation. They used their own arsenal of technologies to conceal their computers, their servers. The fact they'd taken my bait meant that they bargained they wouldn't be caught, that the intelligence agencies couldn't track them down. Or they wouldn't, because a shiny cyberweapon cost too much.

✳

Three more nights before the rogue contract flipped off the safety on the gun pointing at my head.

I avoided reading emails with troubling subject lines or looking at news sites. On my way to the kitchen for a snack, I couldn't help overhearing the evening news as Ray listened in the living room. I didn't see the screen, but the woman's TV-anchor lilt was unmistakable.

"We've all seen it in science fiction movies. A rogue computer programmed with artificial intelligence murders innocent victims. So far, it's only happened in movies. But today, tragedy struck when the computer technology called *blockchain* did the unthinkable . . ."

HAL 9000, move over.

The tempestuous day left me exhausted. I went to bed early—early for me, that is, which is to say eleven o'clock. I knew it was a mistake. I awoke a few hours later and lay in bed, prey to the psyops of the mind in the dead of night. My heart pounded and my chest tightened. Flashbacks to my abduction popped up, taunting me to try and rewrite the script, screaming that it would happen again and this time I would die. I could have gotten out of bed but kept telling myself the terror would abate and I'd sleep. I tried again and again to calm my mind. At last, as the late May sun outlined my blackout shades, I slid into a deep pool of oblivion.

I flew upright at 7:30 a.m. My phone, which I'd kept on just in case, was ringing. It was Alistair Llewelyn-Davies.

"This is a little impromptu," he said. No greeting. "But can you meet today?"

"You realize I'm not in London? It's seven thirty in the morning here." I blinked hard. "Did you say meet you?"

"I'm in New York, as it happens. I thought we might meet in person."

"Sorry, but—"

"We've been doing some testing of Sanctum at the bank. There's a small problem you should be aware of."

"I don't know if you saw the news yesterday, but I'm not thinking much about Sanctum. You should talk to—"

"I think you'll want to hear about this."

✳

Ray cleared a face-to-face meeting with Alistair, but insisted we stay in my building. I met Alistair a few hours later in the Stratolounge.

In addition to the glorious High Line commute, the Stratolounge is the main reason I chose my building over the other dozen possibilities near Adyton. It's on the sixtieth floor, many hundreds of feet above the ground—far higher even than my apartment—with wraparound, floor-to-ceiling windows. Gravity is a little weaker up there. You hover over the city's landscape of rectangular stalagmites, punctuated by its great buildings—One World Trade Center, the Empire State Building, the gold-pyramided New York Life building—visible at last in their full glory. At dusk, it's as though sharp-elbowed New Yorkers vanish from the reeking sidewalks and the restaurants and shops to become lesser angels, mere lights glowing in distant buildings. Even on wet, hot days, the excellent ventilation makes the air crisp, clean, and invigorating, almost Alpine. In the far distance, above the shining Hudson, are tracts of forest, hints of a beautiful hinterland.

Of course I'm always at Adyton, so I almost never use it.

Alistair didn't give the view a second glance. He did show some interest in the lounge's pool table, a rather good one, he said. We sat across from one another by a window with a clear view of the Empire State Building.

Crossing one leg over the other and clasping his knee, Alistair asked, "So, how are you?"

His posh accent and steel-trap memory seemed to endow even his simple questions with many layers. His voice lacked the consoling tone everyone else used around me. As always with Alistair, I felt I couldn't ever respond with enough wit or sophistication, so I swallowed and gave the obvious answer.

"Fine, all things considered."

"You have plenty to consider," he said. I nodded. "But perhaps we can help. As I said, we've been experimenting with Sanctum at the bank."

"And you found something?"

"Yes." He stood and turned to the window. He gazed at the Empire State Building. His jeans and green blazer hung loose on his skeletal frame, not slovenly but dégagé. "That building," he said, waving at it. "I fail to understand the popular obsession. The Chrysler Building is far more exciting. A soaring Art Deco jewel and after a century still the world's tallest brick building." He sat. "In London, we live with the Gherkin."

"Alistair, what did you find?"

One leg again crossed over the other and he clasped his ankle. "Our people installed the Sanctum development environment. I don't know if it's back-doored or the system we got it from is compromised. We found our server infected with malware soon afterward."

"That shouldn't have happened. I'm sorry. I'll let Adyton know."

"No harm done. We take precautions. Our security operations center is aggressive. They traced the C&C server." C&C stands for "command and control." A C&C server is the mothership that hackers' software calls to relay data and get instructions.

"You should report it to the authorities."

"I thought I'd do you the courtesy of holding off."

"Do me the courtesy? What do you mean?"

"The server is running a log analysis tool, you see."

"That's not surprising, but how do you know?"

"Whoever set it up misconfigured it. Apparently, it's publicly accessible. So our people were able to collect a record of traffic to the server. That led them to some other servers in the same network. One of those servers had the same configuration error, and someone noticed requests for some rather interesting files, including one called `BelosTouApollona.sol`." He pronounced it slowly ("Bellows Too Apollona . . ."), but I'd only seen it written, not heard it spoken, so I didn't grasp the name until he got to the file extension ("dot sol").

"A copy of the rogue-contract code."

"So I'm told."

"Interesting," I said, "but the source code is public." I was surprised Alistair didn't realize this, but I didn't know how deep his technical knowledge was. "What you saw probably isn't original. It could have been copied."

"No, I don't think so," he said coolly. "The request we saw for the contract code came four days before the contract actually went live."

Only the Delphians could have been handling the rogue-contract code four days before the rest of the world saw it. Alistair was putting me hot on their trail.

That it was Alistair who'd made the discovery might have been a coincidence. But there was another possible explanation. I remembered Walker's words about how the intelligence agencies might communicate with me. *Maybe you find an IP address in a fortune cookie. Maybe you see a message spray-painted on your building.*

Hypotheses starbursted in my mind. Alistair might be working directly for the intelligence agencies in Britain or the United States. Or he might be their pawn. The NSA might have located the Delphians' server and found a way to use Alistair to pass information on to me. Knowing that Alistair and I were friendly, the NSA itself introduced the malware into the bank and the configuration error into the Delphians' servers. Or maybe the C&C server was a complete NSA fabrication, a way to point to the Delphians with an unseen hand. Or maybe Alistair's discovery really was a coincidence—an idea just plausible enough to cast doubt on my cloak-and-dagger hypotheses.

If I'd never learn the true backstory, I could at least ask. Alistair might think I'd lost the plot, as he would put it, but so be it. Ray was out of earshot, by the elevators.

"Alistair, is this coming from an intelligence agency?"

He laughed. "Why are my American friends always hoping I'm James Bond? Sorry to disappoint you. I don't work for MI6. I'd make a poor civil servant." Exactly what I'd expect him to say if he was working for MI6. Or for GCHQ, the British counterpart to the NSA. Also exactly what I'd expect him to say if he wasn't.

He handed me a slip of paper. On it were written two IP addresses.

"The address of the server with the rogue-contract code," he said. "And the one that made the request, just in case." He told me other details we'd need to get started. "I'm sorry, but I can't give you the C&C server. I'm told we want it uncontaminated for now. You have a day to probe before we report it to the authorities. They might end up dismantling other parts of the network, so you'll need to move fast."

"Thanks, Alistair. Who knows? This may just save my life. If it does, I owe you. If it doesn't, it was a nice try. I'll save you a seat in the afterlife."

He gave a mirthless smile, as though he wasn't sure where I'd be going in my afterlife and whether he wanted to join me there.

✳

Corinne joined my feverish work at the kitchen counter in my apartment that afternoon. On the server that housed the rogue-contract code—and was controlled, we assumed, by the Delphians—we found the configuration error that Alistair had indicated in the log-analysis tool. That allowed us to start mapping interconnections among other possible Delphian servers.

On one of these servers, thanks to the same error, we made a critical discovery. An unusual file request led us to a so-called "tarball" file named `snapshot.tar.bz2`. This turned out to be a software backup that we were able to access. Most of it was boilerplate stuff, but there was also some tantalizing residue. Web3 code, meaning blockchain software. Files with Sanctum extensions (`.sctm`). Filenames containing words with Delphian associations: lyre, Helios, Adyton, Pythia. We found nothing unusual about the way any code here was written, no evidence of the extraordinary polish of the smart contracts. But we didn't look closely. That's because we also found monitoring scripts, little programs to check the correct functioning of the system. And in the scripts were clues—clues that proved to be pure gold.

One of the scripts sent system-failure alerts by text message to a list of four mobile numbers—belonging to the system administrators. All of the numbers had a +7 prefix. Not Apollo. The international code for Russia: +79. Russian mobiles.

We also found Unix usernames in the scripts: `thelyov`, `pinkyclyde`, `meRelyt`, `dedShell`, `lechamois`. They were embedded in comments in the source code and in commands to change file ownership, meaning they belonged to whoever controlled the server. They were almost certainly hacker handles, the names these Delphians went by in cyberspace. They were even more useful than the mobile numbers, because hackers may change phones, but to build up their hacker cred, they keep their handles for years.

I thought about going to Walker at this point, but Corinne had already started Googling the admins' mobile numbers.

She found one of them in an ad. It was for a pair of sphynx kittens, a black male and a pink female. ("Pure pedigree. Fully immunized. Playful and funny.") The sphynx is a hairless breed. The kittens in the ad photos were little gremlins, cute in an ugly way to Corinne, but to me a source of terror. The contact information included not just one of the mobile numbers, but an email address: `thelyov@yandex.com`, a city, St. Petersburg, and a name: Igor.

The ad gave us a first name, city, and email address for the handle `thelyov`, and one of the mobile numbers. A good start, but not enough for us to learn their real identities.

Next we looked for the Delphian hackers' handles on social media. We found accounts for the first four handles on some video-sharing sites and VK, the Russian version of Facebook. The hackers were careful enough to make their profiles private, though. All we got were a bunch of public-facing photos and another three first names: Vlad, Anton, and Kirill. Common and therefore useless.

Igor had the most interesting set of photos. In many, he appeared with the same woman, a bleached blonde with a classically Slavic face, broad and high-cheeked. She had a distinctive dark tan and style of eye makeup, which made it easy to identify her in photos. Igor's partner, we assumed. At first, we gleaned little except that the couple frequented beaches and mountains all around Europe—Croatia, the Amalfi Coast, the mountains of Switzerland, and at least a dozen other places I'd never been. Cross-matching with the photos on Vlad, Anton, and Kirill's sites showed that the group traveled and socialized together.

The breakthrough came in a photo from Igor's profile taken at a conference. Either Igor or his girlfriend was in another line of internet business.

The conference turned out to be an "adult webmaster" (aka online porn) convention in Prague. We enlarged the photo. The woman's badge was visible. With the help of some convolution filtering, we sharpened the text. Out popped a name. Anastasia Arkhangelskaya.

There were only a handful online with that name, and we soon found our woman. Ms. Arkhangelskaya had a wide social media presence, and—we couldn't believe our luck—no privacy options activated for her accounts. Her abundant selfies came with a treasure trove of information.

She posted often about her cryptocurrency investments and transactions, money she'd made on trades, the Mercedes she'd bought with Bitcoin, hot new crypto tokens she wanted to promote. In one post, she included a Bitcoin address so that a friend could pay back their shares of a dinner tab. That address had recently received two large payments. We matched the transaction amounts against fiat currency prices at the time they were made. Each of the two payments had a value roughly matching the round figure of 100,000 Euro, suggesting a European origin. With a transaction-tracing tool, we were able to trace the payments to a US cryptocurrency exchange that's popular in Europe.

Cryptocurrency exchanges don't publish account holders' names, balances, or physical addresses. They're all hidden in databases somewhere. But given a subpoena, they'll divulge them to law enforcement.

To agencies like the FBI.

※

Walker couldn't stop chuckling as I told him in a videoconference about my conversation with Alistair and my legwork with Corinne. I shared the photos we'd found.

"Porn conventions and demon-spawn kittens. Man, you're a magnet for weird-ass stuff."

"Not your typical FBI cyber investigation, I take it."

"There's no typical. But there's weird-ass. That's you and your Delphian friends."

"Things lined up a little too well. The intelligence community's fingerprints are all over this, aren't they?"

"Not for me to say. And things may have lined up nicely, but it could take a while for us to do anything about it. We can probably track down the members of this hacking group now, but I hope you're not expecting help from the Russian government." He smirked. "That dog won't hunt."

"Why not?"

"They'll say we don't have convincing evidence. And if these guys turn out to be mixed up with the GRU—that's Russian military intelligence—or the FSB, forget it. Anyway, Article 61 of the Russian constitution prohibits them from extraditing their citizens."

"So what are our options?"

"The good news is that your little gang likes to travel. We're entering peak travel season for Europe. The courts will give us a sealed arrest warrant so we don't tip them off. That Arkhangelskaya woman"—her name rolled impressively off his tongue—"she looks like a sun worshipper." A worshipper of Helios, I thought. "So maybe we get lucky and they're getting a head start on their tans on a nice beach on the Mediterranean. Maybe I get lucky and they let me go help with the arrest. The beaches over there are all pebbles, but the water," he said, kissing his fingertips, "perfect." He saw my bemused look. "Anyway," he continued, "in theory we can grab them from most places in Europe."

"What about the crypto transactions?"

"Definitely interesting. We'll look into them. But you need the hackers if we're going to deactivate the contract."

"I assume so."

"These are your plain terrestrial techies, man. It may take some time, but we'll get them. Hang tight and play it safe until we do."

One thing gnawed at me. It was just a gut feeling, so I didn't tell Walker. Everything I saw in the Russians' servers painted the same picture. Young men in their twenties or thirties with a reckless streak. A familiar species of hacker, the kind who flies by the seat of his pants. The kind who lacks the chops to craft the code in the Delphians' contract. That required specialized expertise. It involved technical advances of the type that need focus, self-discipline, a knack for research, and that dose of delusion or megalomania that says you've been anointed to create something genuinely new under the sun. The exact qualities I was missing early in my career, and something I sensed these hackers also lacked.

My thoughts dwelled on one of the handles in the Delphians' scripts. The only one with no trace online: `lechamois`. French for "the mountain goat."

TWENTY-ONE

It wasn't Walker I heard from early the next day, but Diane. I don't know if it was an effect of the lighting or her lapis scarf or some quality of the video connection, but I was struck by her smooth complexion, something I'd noticed in person.

"You're a genius!" she said.

"What did I do?" I puffed a little with pride.

"Those crypto payments, to the Russian woman." Her nose twitched with distaste. "Guess who made them?"

"Igor, I assume."

"No." She laughed. "It was— You're alone?"

Ray had gone down to instruct a new concierge. Corinne wasn't arriving for another hour.

"Yes."

"It was Farnese. Giuseppe Farnese." She beamed.

"The crooked art dealer?"

"I'm not sure I should be telling you, but I have to. Everything is starting to make sense. The job of the Russian hackers is to stimulate the market. For artifacts from Delphi, I mean. It doesn't matter that what they are doing is criminal. It's working. It's all over the news."

"And Farnese is bankrolling them?"

"If he has looted artifacts from Delphi to sell . . ."

"So why pay the girlfriend?"

"Who knows? Igor—it's Igor, right?—Igor wants to hide transactions or impress his girlfriend. Or maybe she's a hacker too. Do they all have handles? Or maybe she manages the operation."

"She might."

208

"It's not important. We applied for a search warrant. We should receive it within hours." She glanced heavenward. "Finally, after all these years. You don't know what this means to me."

"The warrant's for Farnese's gallery in Paris?"

"No, Switzerland. Genève. He lives there and meets with clients in an office in the *Port Francs*—the Freeport. I've learned that the Swiss pay lip service, but don't care much about contraband artworks. I have tried to get search warrants before. But they do care about money and murder. They took the crypto transactions connected to Viganò's death seriously. They are efficient and less strict about admitting evidence than we are in the US. In France this would take months. But we heard back from the Swiss Federal Office of Justice today."

"When do you think—"

"I'm flying tonight," she said.

"And I'm going with you."

"Going with me? Are you crazy?"

"My bodyguard has been trying to get me out of the city. Where better to hide?"

✳

Ray had been trying to get me out of New York from the beginning. He didn't like the idea of my holing up somewhere remote, say in a cabin in the woods, as Lukas had suggested. In that case, the secret of our location alone would protect me. If assassins found me, they could overpower us and escape without a trace. Ray wanted us to relocate to another city. Given that Viganò had been murdered outside of Chicago, suggesting his killers had a domestic network, Ray didn't think it was a bad idea to go abroad. The problem was that Ray's firm wouldn't allow him to travel to Europe that evening.

"I just need a day," he said. "If you wait—"

"I can't."

"I need to get approvals lined up. We ask our clients for a couple of days' notice. I'm doing everything I can. The firm knows we need to move fast."

"If I fly tonight, it'll need to be even faster."

"OK. Can't convince you. I know that by now. I'll get there before the contract starts." We had little more than a day. "Never been to Europe before," he said with that grin of his. "I hear Switzerland's nice."

＊

Waiting for Ray would have been the sane thing to do. You'd think the flashbacks and my still smarting flank were sufficient reminders of my close brush with death. But I couldn't sit and wait. Inertia was torture, motion liberty.

I'd stay safe by staying close to my personal FBI agent, I figured. At least she'd protect me from violent art crimes. Plus I still had a whole day left.

PART IV

For five days before Helike disappeared all the mice . . . and every other creature of that kind in the town left. . . . After the afore-said creatures had departed, an earthquake occurred in the night. The town collapsed, an immense wave poured over it, and Helike disappeared.

—Aelian, *On Animals* (11.19)

Warnings are wont to be sent by the god before violent and far-reaching earthquakes. . . . blasts of wind sometimes swoop upon the land and overturn the trees; occasionally great flames dart across the sky.

—Pausanias, *Description of Greece* (7.24.7–8)

TWENTY-TWO
Six days earlier

Breathless and bowed under his knapsack, his shirt soaked with sweat, Giuseppe Farnese finished the final ascent to a clearing on the mountain. There, near the lip of a precipice covered with grass and limestone, waited a tall older man, carving slices from an apple with a penknife as he gazed out over the green slopes of the Jura Mountains.

"You're driven by the devil," shouted Farnese. He swung off his backpack and planted it in the middle of a small carpet of deep blue wildflowers. He took a deep breath, grabbed a bottle from his bag, swigged some water, and wiped his mouth with his sleeve. "I couldn't figure out until today why you do what you do for us, but *mamma mia*! You're driven by the devil."

The apple eater, whom Farnese simply called "Professor," glanced back and chuckled. "Now you know, my dear Farnese."

Farnese was a demonstrative man. He would have clapped a hand onto the taller man's shoulder were it not for the risk of sending him headfirst into the valley below. Even so, he was tempted. Instead, he hung back from the sheer drop. "Really, why do you do it? Like this, to make fools of the rest of us?"

"Because I failed to win the Nobel Prize."

Farnese edged closer and lowered his bulky body onto the grass. He squinted up at the professor. "Were you nominated?"

"No. Another mistake." The professor sat beside Farnese. "Computer scientists don't receive Nobel Prizes, only Turing Awards. But I was also overlooked by the Turing Award committee." He started on his last slice of apple.

"I don't understand your riddles."

The professor swallowed. "There is a thing known in Switzerland as *retirement*. Faculty at our illustrious federal institutes are encouraged by an inviolable rule to take this *appealing* option at the age of sixty-five. Today, I publish papers, I advise students, I teach—tak, tak, tak—as efficiently as ever. I don't even have to power the engine with coffee, as you have observed. Soon . . ." He swept the air with his cupped hand, uttering a sound like "shoooup." "Soon they'll expel me as a kind of birthday present. But the university permits Nobel laureates to stay until age seventy. More brain cells, slower senility. You see?"

"You've already told me about your forced retirement. It's the same in Italy. It doesn't explain why you refuse money."

"But it *does*, my dear Giuseppe. Once my services at the university were no longer required, I could have spent all my days hiking like this, until one day perhaps I *retired* down a crevasse or over a precipice. But now, with these projects of yours . . . I've never before felt so alive. Never before seen the future—no, never before shaped the future like this. I can't help myself. Money would spoil it."

❋

As retirement neared, he'd considered the standard ways that graybeard professors faded from computer science departments. There were consulting appointments at the university, development of new course materials, or partnerships with universities in the Middle East or Asia. The dross left over when you took away research, the only fire that burned in the belly of a high-powered academic. There was also the option of exile. A friend had put off retirement by becoming a dean, at the cost of disappearing to Australia. Or maybe work as an expert witness in patent cases, odious hours billable for fantastic sums of money in the service of patent trolls or tech giants steamrolling over the competition. The most exciting possibility was launching a start-up. But he'd done that before, exulted in the brief moment of revolutionary technical possibility that came before probable failure as you scrambled madly to stay afloat, bastardize your ideas, and ship a product.

He was slipping down this incline of poor options into a dark pool of despondency when Farnese posed his challenge. Couched at first as a joke. Those smart contracts you're working on, if they're so powerful, can they clear up a little business problem of mine? Farnese laughed as he, the professor, cocked his head in thought.

He noodled on the question. It wouldn't be easy, but it was possible. He synthesized and coded up parts of the first contract as an exercise. A prototype just to test the idea. If it worked, it would realize something dark and alluring, a new way to project power into the world, raw and unadulterated power. A way to aim his decades of brilliant, unrealized research at a focal point. His academic papers and open-source tools were already being forgotten—too hard for developers to master—but no one would forget the thing he considered doing now.

He shadowboxed with his prospective enemies, those who would try to stop or find him. Rogue contracts for assassination became a running joke between him and Farnese for months. An idea to float in the rarefied air of the mountains when they met, which they came to do several times a month. He brought his prototype contract just up to the point of launch. He let his finger hover over the return key, get within a centimeter of a power that no one would suspect him of creating and possessing. He'd launch his contract with a small bounty and target a right-wing politician, maybe in the *Front National*. The contract wouldn't be for real. Just a statement and demonstration. His code at least would awe the cognoscenti.

But I'll bankroll it, Farnese said. I'll fund a team. I'm a rich man. It will be the best PR campaign in the history of the world. Prices for my Delphian artifacts will rise to the skies and join the gods. Laughter again. It was like a courtship. Jokes, feints, and hints. Embarrassment and retraction. A sense that it couldn't become real. But it did. And if it was a little sordid, not quite what he'd hoped, it was still thrilling, a stirring and revival of feelings he'd thought long dead, and some he'd never felt before, laden with mystique, impossible to stop once that first contract went live . . .

*

"Money spoils nothing," Farnese said. He plucked one of the blue flowers beside him. "I find it sinister that you take none."

"*Sinister*? You?" He laughed. "Not principled?"

"What we're doing isn't exactly pretty."

"I often drive by the Swiss headquarters of a company known as British American Tobacco. It's near the lake in Lausanne. I'm sure you've seen it."

"Of course."

"I've calculated that every employee there is individually responsible on average for fifteen deaths a year caused by smoking. Murders. Not for religion, art, or to create the astonishing things we are creating. All for profit.

"Besides, what would I do with money? I already have this." His outstretched arm took in the grass, forests, and green mountains. Beyond were tiny fields, tessellated yellow, green, and brown, clustering around towns shrunk in the distance to small pebbled patches. At the horizon, masquerading as a thin band of cloud, were the snowcapped peaks of the Alps. The crisp air carried birdsong and the tinkle of cow bells.

"You love the opera," Farnese said. The two shared a singing teacher. This was how they had met. "Enjoy the best seats at La Scala. It's not far. Live a little. I would, if I had the time. Take a diva as a mistress."

"You know what they say about the romantic lives of men over sixty?"

"I'm not even fifty."

"When a man over sixty propositions a lady and she accepts, he is *flattered*. When she refuses, he feels *relieved*."

"You have a uniquely depressing view of life." He chuckled. "If you prefer, I can give you a beautiful gold artifact. I've just started moving them in from our mysterious Grotto. It would feel like I'm giving you one of my children. But for you, Professor . . . You'll feel the power of our patron god. Do you understand how magnificent these objects are? Think about it. Artifacts dedicated thousands of years ago to Apollo. Artifacts used by his high priests at the center of the world." He stood up, extended his arms toward the precipice and shouted, "Apollo! God of the Golden Arms!"

"Olympus is that way," the professor said, pointing to Farnese's left. "A hill by Swiss standards. Less than three thousand meters, I believe."

"You really don't care about art or ancient history, do you? But you could at least feast your eyes on your retirement fund. Or think of others. Don't you have children, grandchildren, a wife?"

"My dear Farnese, we're not in nineteenth-century Sicily. I don't live in a house filled with my offspring and wailing *bambini*. My family tree will flourish without me. And you and your colleagues love your gold and money so much that I dare not *impose* upon your love story. My interest in Apollo is very different." He wiped his pen knife on his trousers and snapped it shut. "Enough about money. I'd rather discuss how my plans are unfolding."

"Beautifully, my friend," Farnese said. "Beautifully. You know that. You're doing far more than we could have hoped for." The professor stretched his arm behind his head. "Apollo and Delphi haven't been this popular for two thousand—"

He flinched as the apple core whipped out over the abyss. The two men watched it—falling, falling—until it dropped out of sight below the lip of the cliff.

"As I was saying," Farnese continued, "It's all going beautifully. Exactly as planned. The little exhibitions I've quietly funded. The strategic bidding in auctions. And all you've been doing online, of course—I can't say I understand it, your 'prophecies' and buying things in the metaverse. I understand the rogue contract, of course. Brilliant idea of yours. Brilliant. It's all working. Prices for Greek artifacts are rising across the board. Rich collectors are begging especially for anything Delphic. It's all thanks to our Delphians, to the mystique we've created."

The professor either smiled or grimaced, Farnese couldn't tell which. "Yet," the professor said, "I sense some *dissatisfaction* on your part."

Farnese gaped at him. "Dissatisfaction? With you? Of course not. Never. I just wonder if we might perhaps consider—might think about a slightly different approach. For the rogue contracts—so well done, by the way. You are a maestro. . . ." The professor was expressionless. "But I'm wondering. Why not choose more prominent targets? A senator. A famous actor. President of a small country. We have the money. Spend it to make it, I always say."

"I've already explained. Smart contracts can't be stopped. Or oracles. Except if the community collectively decides to do it. Then it can happen. It happened once before in the dawn of smart contract history. A contract called The DAO held 15 percent of all the currency in Ethereum and was hacked. Before the hacker could drain the funds, the community modified the contract to return the money to the victims. To do that, they had to reconfigure the entire system, which created an uproar. Blockchains are supposed to be tamperproof, a sacred principle that the community violated. Nobody wants to do that again. But if we go *too* far, they might consider it."

"OK. So no senator. Honestly, I was glad to get Viganò out of the way." He flung up an arm. "A risky move, but the way he was poking around was dangerous. I'm glad about his silly ethylene theory. But you never told me how you chose the tech wizard."

"He works for the best-known company building smart contract oracles. For your purposes, the connection between ancient and modern oracles creates more mystique."

"Agreed."

"For my purposes, it was a personal *gesture* of admiration, but that is of no consequence."

"Personal? You didn't do anything that would lead back to us, did you?" He put a hand on the professor's shoulder.

"Not at all."

"Excellent. Excellent." Farnese smiled. "I trust you, Professor. The technical stuff, it's all a mystery to me. I leave it to the brilliant ones like you."

The professor shrugged, at once acknowledging and dismissing the compliment.

"How are your hackers?" Farnese asked.

"Fine, but not outstanding. They're ex-Russian intelligence, so I expected more. Good coders. Strong offense. But weak defense and no formalism. I have to orchestrate everything. Teach them how to use the tools I developed for code synthesis and formal verification. That means nothing to you. Let's just say that while the field moves at inconceivable speed, I've still been years ahead of my time. We're even using some tools my group at the university created several years ago and never released. I experimented painstakingly with a little invention of mine to refine the smart contract code before we launched it, to give it a touch of elegance. But just as I can't grow excited about your gold artifacts, you can't grasp the significance of my work."

"A new Delphi, you tell me. But to me, Delphi is its people, the splendid works of art and architecture dedicated to the god there, the mystery of the oracle."

"Not in the twenty-first century, my dear Farnese. Oracles mean something different, but even the people building oracle systems don't understand. They call them 'middleware.' To them oracles are a *banal* incarnation of an old story. No. These new oracles are the source of truth for a new financial system. And money, as you know better than I, is power.

"Oracles are more than a conduit for the truth. They *create* truth, as our rogue contract is doing. And in this new world, with its mechanics defined by code, with its mathematically definable rules, its logic, oracles can in some cases even predict the future and prove their predictions. What we're doing now is primitive. Someday—"

"Your students must enjoy your lectures. But I don't know anything about computers." Farnese placed his hand on the professor's shoulder. "This is what the ancients got right, my friend. Their gods had different aspects. The god Apollo is both your Apollo of mathematics and my Apollo of beauty. Two of the god's many faces."

"I wonder if he recognizes himself in the mirror in the morning."

"Do you recognize yourself, Professor?"

"I avoid the mirror. It depresses me. I see my father there."

They took snacks from their backpacks, Farnese his butter cookies and the professor a bag of nuts and a bar of chocolate. These they shared along with a bottle of wine. When they'd emptied it, they sang together, a Bizet duet, *au fond du temple saint*.

Farnese took a short nap, while the professor meditated on the slow sweep of cloud shadows across the mountains. Farnese stirred and stretched and the two men stood and shouldered their bags. The tall, lean one shook hands with the short, stout one. Abbott and Costello in the wilderness.

"By the way," said Farnese, who would descend as the professor continued hiking, "I cannot tell you what pleasure these little hikes of ours bring me. I'll see you next week at the Dent de Vaulion. Our usual spot. But perhaps we should climb separately." He bit his lip thoughtfully, then broke into a smile. "Less risk of being seen together."

TWENTY-THREE

The plane banked and made its descent through the golden early morning sunlight. As we approached Switzerland, I gazed past Diane out of the window.

I don't understand how the French keep their country so tidy. Their farmland has been landscaped into an irregular but neat patchwork of green and brown fields, the boundaries between them stippled with mellow trees. Even the forests are packed into neatly carved parcels. This gentle cultivation, so different from the untamed streets, buildings, people, and woods of the New York tristate area, felt reassuring. I've heard Switzerland even takes a broom to its mountains in the spring to clear off old snow. Never mind that most of Europe is fertilized with the corpses of two world wars.

We flew over the low contoured ridges of deep green near the Swiss border and landed at Geneva Airport. Diane awoke when the plane hit the tarmac and jostled her head on the dwarf pillow nestled into her headrest. She'd slept for nearly the entire flight, stirring earlier when the seats were raised for the landing but then nodding off again. The overnight flight offered my first opportunity to study her face. Most passengers' mouths hung open as they snored in harmony with the engines, but not Diane's. Her mouth twitched from time to time, as though she was reacting to a dream movie. Her face was strangely bare without the thick glasses. Her smooth complexion contrasted with her white-streaked hair. She wore a touch of eyeliner, but no other makeup that I could see. She didn't need it.

With my name all over the news, I expected to be questioned at passport control. But they stamped my passport with barely a glance. Diane whisked through on her French passport, so I met her on the other side of customs.

When Ray had resigned himself the day before to my traveling without him, he tutored me on how to protect myself from abduction before he could join us in Geneva. We should avoid hotels, he said. They'd force me to register and their databases are sieves. Because they're all chains, a criminal ring needs just one employee on the inside to gain intelligence on guests across the globe. Diane and I instead booked a rental apartment under her name. There weren't many choices in Geneva with two bedrooms on a day's notice, and Ray didn't like some of them. We ended up with a designer attic, near both the city center and the site of our rendezvous and priced like the Ritz. I insisted on paying for it myself, which led to wrangling with Diane. In the end, I don't know if it was the magnificent roof deck that convinced her to allow me to pay or seeing the sofa bed to which the FBI's travel policy and Ray's vetoes would otherwise condemn one of us.

Diane punched an address into her rideshare app and called a car to take us to the place. As we were about to leave the airport, she gave the driver new directions. They spoke in French, so I didn't understand, but the driver tapped a new address into his phone. We drove for ten minutes along a highway lined on one side with trees, crossed the Rhône, and entered a pleasant residential neighborhood. Then suddenly we were in a zone of the city showcasing the high Swiss industrial architectural style: functional, clean, and ugly. We turned into a small parking lot in front of a brown building with vertically striped windows, a little less offensive than its neighbors.

"The apartment is here?" I asked.

"We're doing a tour first."

"Not a very scenic one."

She turned toward me. "Where is the greatest art collection in Europe?"

"Art collection? I don't know? Paris? The Louvre? But why—"

"And the second greatest?"

"I don't know much about museums. The Vatican? The Prado?"

"It's right here."

"In this office building?"

"We are at the *Ports Francs de Genève*. The Geneva Freeport. The greatest museum in the world that no one can visit. There are warehouses back there. That's where we will go in a couple of hours. But I wanted to show you first. That way you'll understand why it's been so difficult to stop Farnese, why the stakes are so high. Even the owners of the building don't know what's here."

"How can that be?"

"We should go. I'll tell you on the way."

We drove off. I glanced back at the greatest museum in the world no one can visit. Yes, pretty ugly.

Superrich people store their fine art collections in the Geneva Freeport to avoid import duties and taxes, Diane explained, or to hide them for even more unsavory reasons. Items in the Freeport are considered not to have entered Swiss territory. It's a kind of no-man's-land outside national borders.

Over the years, artworks seized by the Nazis from Jews have been found there, as well as illegally excavated antiquities, valuables hidden from creditors, and an assortment of other tainted objects. They may be a small minority among the vast holdings, and Swiss laws around the Freeport have tightened over the years. In principle, objects stored there must be inventoried and can't remain for more than six months. Antiquities in particular require documentation. But there are loopholes, and plenty of ongoing mischief. The Swiss have resisted calls by the European Union, among others, to shutter the place.

"The Swiss value the kind of privacy you do," Diane said, with a residue of bitterness from our first encounter. "There are well over one million works of art in the *Ports Francs*. It's not as sinister as it used to be. In the past, they didn't even know who was renting space here. Now they know who's there, just not what they're hiding." She breathed in between her teeth. "The economy of Switzerland is all about discreet hospitality. The Swiss are famous for their hotels, and not just the ones for people. Their banks are fancy hotels for money. And the *Ports Francs* are a grand hotel for art and luxury goods." The driver's phone pinged. "Anyway, we've arrived."

＊

After showering and breakfasting on food grabbed at the airport, with half an hour to spare before we met the Swiss authorities, we sat in the living room of the apartment we were renting. Diane had also unpacked, but I kept my clothes in my suitcase. Even Switzerland has bedbugs. That's because they allow New Yorkers to visit.

"I keep a mental list of the great lost treasures of the ancient world," she told me. "The ones I have always dreamed of finding."

The room was ingeniously constructed with custom-carpentry niches and cabinets as well as skylights. It felt bright and luxurious despite no windows at eye level. In the niche opposite me was an artwork of sorts, a giant plastic apple core, its top and bottom ruby red, its column a nude woman's torso. Probably not one of Diane's lost treasures.

"The Omphalos is on your list, I assume."

"Maybe top of the list."

"What else?"

"So many treasures at Delphi," Diane said, her face and gold-hoop earrings twinkling. "All of the finest works in gold were stolen, almost certainly melted down. I still like to imagine some survived. But I'd be content just finding the small statue of Apollo mentioned by Pausanias, a Greek author. It was believed to be the first dedication ever made at Delphi. That would be an astonishing find."

"And beyond Delphi?"

"So many things. Let me see. . . . The tomb of Alexander the Great. His crystal sarcophagus. The tomb was last seen over five hundred years ago in Egypt. The Egyptian government has tried a hundred times to find it."

"How do you lose something like that?"

"Time passes. Shorelines drift. Monuments sink into the earth. People forget."

"Even the greatest conqueror in the world?"

"Even Alexander. Everyone. De Gaulle once said 'les cimetières—the cemeteries—are filled with indispensable men.'"

"An epitaph to aspire to. But who's de Gaulle?"

She rolled her eyes at my flippancy. "Even greed, for all its power, cannot preserve memory. Metal objects were melted down for reuse or as bullion. But so many famous artworks in stone have also been lost. Like the famous cup the emperor Nero bought for a million sesterces. It was murrhine ware, a kind of polished semiprecious stone. How does a treasure like that just disappear? Only one comparable piece has survived. A carved cup called the Tazza Farnese. It's magnificent."

"Farnese? Any connection with our Farnese?"

"It's named after the once powerful Farnese family. I think he claims descent from them." Her eyes dropped. Then she looked up at me. "And then so much lost literature. I would kill to find just one new poem by Sappho."

"I've heard of—"

"A celebrated lesbian poet. In fact, bisexual." Her mysterious smile gave me something new to consider. "Or *Margites*. A famous lost work supposedly by Homer. A comedy. Can you imagine?"

"Not Homer's comedy. But I understand lost treasure in my own small way." I thought about my brooch collection. "I know the obsessive drive to find and possess certain objects. For some people, it's about riches, but for a true treasure hunter, I suspect it's something different."

"What?"

"A treasure is a talisman. When you hold it, you're in communion with all of the others who've touched or gazed upon it. The urge to find or possess it is like the desire to return to some paradise, the place you hear in a piece of music when it wrings your heart with nostalgia. It's like a longing to recapture your lost youth."

"Or the lost youth of the world."

"And you expect to find that at the Freeport?"

"I have always wondered about the place. It fascinates me. And I hate it. If any of my dream treasures have been rediscovered or survived in the shadows, it would not surprise me if they were in the Freeport. Now there is a chance that the most mysterious of all awaits us there today. The Omphalos. That would be a miracle."

＊

You'd think a giant vault brimming with $100 billion worth of artworks would be ringed with barbed wire, armed guards, and Swiss-German shepherds. From the outside, though, the Geneva Freeport resembles any other warehouse, apart from the thin angled windows in the main building, like floor-to-ceiling arrow slits. The place is an enormous, high-security complex of armored spaces for rent, room-sized safe-deposit boxes for the world's elite. But it's also a strange hybrid. A number of the rooms also house art conservation labs, galleries, and dealers' offices, like Farnese's, that have sprung up around the treasures.

We met a posse at a security checkpoint: three officers from the Swiss federal police (FedPol), one of whom was an inspector, a forensic photographer, the deputy director of the Freeport, and an archaeologist working with law enforcement. A public prosecutor was also there to oversee the raid on Farnese's office and broader investigation. Prosecutors have wide-ranging powers in Swiss criminal law, Diane explained. They both conduct criminal investigations and bring prosecution.

The archaeologist, Prof. Hélène Dassault of the University of Geneva, was the lone woman of authority among them. A full head shorter than the grim, besuited men and two officers in azure and dark navy uniforms (one woman, one man), she wore jeans, a floral-patterned shirt, and a black cardigan. As we shook hands, I saw sunny climes in her warm, attractive smile and in her thick, dark eyebrows and black hair set in a wavy bob. She was from Bordeaux, Diane later told me, the region of France where the world's best wine grapes ripen under abundant sun.

The Swiss police had Farnese under surveillance. Otherwise he'd have been there with a lawyer and, according to Diane, howling in protest.

We walked through the drab main building together. It bristled with cameras, sprinklers, and fire extinguishers. On the fourth floor, in Corridor 16, behind a blank gray metal door identical with the others in the building, was our destination: Room 25. Beside the door was a compact black console with green-glowing indentation. The deputy director inserted a finger and entered a PIN. Diane held her breath.

Behind the armored door was a showroom. The exterior wall consisted of overlapping panels, each with a small protruding side containing one of the arrow slits visible from the outside. Two other walls were lined with tall cherrywood cabinets, spotlit from above. Off to the side were a couple of settees around a piece of ancient stone carved with human figures and carrying traces of blue and red pigment—evidently a coffee table. In the middle of the room, centered on a Persian carpet, was a table whose base consisted of a giant capital—an ancient column carved with vegetation, some three feet in diameter—supporting a surface of clear glass. Around it were four antique French chairs of ornate gilded wood. This, I guessed, was the place where Farnese hammered out his deals. Each of the furnishings might have been beautiful on its own. Together they looked like a rummage sale at the Louvre.

Behind the showroom was an office. It contained a desk, a couple of metal bookcases and cabinets, a large safe, and a worktable strewn with small objects, some glinting gold.

We began with the showroom. The two tables were the only antiquities in immediate view, but as the police opened the cabinets, an entire gallery materialized. Shelf upon shelf was filled with ceramic vases and more vases, bronze statuettes, carved stone fragments, ancient armor, glass vessels, and jewelry. In niches created where shelves had been removed, there were even small frescoes. It was all very tidy, but with the sheer profusion of objects—there were hundreds—it was hard at first for me to grasp the rarity and quality of the collection.

Diane and Prof. Dassault saw it instantly, of course. Their excitement turned into rapid-fire French. They pointed and waved their hands as they spoke until they reached an agreement of some kind. They put on nitrile gloves and separated. Prof. Dassault began to remove the contents of a cabinet one by one, starting with the vases. She placed them on the large table and typed notes on a tablet while the photographer documented them. The prosecutor steered clear of anything fragile, observing us from the safe distance of the settees. The police went back to the room serving as an office, presumably to confiscate papers. The deputy director hovered near the outer door, ready to tackle anyone who tried to bolt with a vase. Diane moved from cabinet to cabinet, hunting high and low. But the Omphalos, if that's what she was looking for, couldn't be in the showroom. The cabinets weren't deep enough. She soon scuttled into the office in the back.

I drifted over to a glossy row of vases with fresh-looking reds and blacks. I made sure my shoelaces were tied and kept my hands behind my back. On close inspection, even I could tell that the workmanship in Farnese's trove was superb, a big step up from even the goodies for upper-crust Manhattanites in the Helios Gallery. My untutored eye sought anything with an obvious connection to Delphi, but apart from the Omphalos, I didn't know what to look for.

I was locked in a staring contest with a bearded man on a long-handled cup when Diane rushed back into the showroom. At first I thought she'd found the Omphalos. Then I saw she was clutching a circle of gold.

She waved Prof. Dassault and me over.

"Come look!"

She set a gold dish on the center table.

"This was in the safe. They left it open. Incredible!"

The dish was maybe eight or nine inches in diameter. Sculpted in relief on the inside were two birds facing one another, their great wings outstretched. Between them, a raised cone in the center bore what I now knew to be the telltale crosshatch pattern in representations of the Omphalos. Everyone clustered around us.

"A libation dish, used to pour offerings to a god," Diane said. "The two birds are the eagles released by Zeus to find the center of the world. It's ingenious. The boss in the center, the raised knob, is typical of this type of dish. In Greek it was known as an *omphalos*, a navel. In this dish, it's *the* Omphalos. And there's an inscription." She held it up and pointed to Greek letters etched crudely near the rim. "'Leonidas dedicated this bowl to Apollo.' It *could* be from Delphi. If these thieves hadn't looted it, we'd know where it was found. If it's real, it's an astonishing find."

Prof. Dassault picked up the dish and held it out with her thumb on the rim and fingers under the knob. "Yes," she whispered.

"How much would it fetch in the underground market?" I asked.

The professor raised her eyebrows. "Millions. Many, many millions," she said in a heavy French accent. "But it doesn't matter. It will go to a museum."

"Officially, we are here to find evidence tying Farnese to Viganò's death," Diane said, addressing the prosecutor. "This piece," she said, gesturing toward it with both hands. "If it is what we think it is . . . It's already a motive."

Our excitement soon turned to frustration. None of the objects in the room turned up in the Interpol database of stolen artworks. That meant Farnese's wares had to have been looted from new sites. But where? The problem was that nothing was labeled. Was the libation dish truly from Delphi? We had no way of knowing. The police found no paperwork worth mentioning in the office, no catalog or photographs as we were hoping for. There was no dirt or other telltale signs of looting on any of the objects. It was almost as though Farnese had prepared for just such a raid. When it came time to interrogate him, everything would turn out to have come from some of those eighty-year-old private Middle Eastern collections that surface whenever a convenient provenance is needed. He'd probably even have ironclad documentation somewhere.

Diane handed me Farnese's tablet.

"Can you hack it?"

"No. Even Walker and his cybersecurity experts can't hack these things."

"So we'll have to get the password from Farnese. That will take an eternity, if it ever happens."

"I'm sorry," I said. "But I—"

The police inspector interrupted us. In good professional form, he'd been eavesdropping.

"You're authorized to inspect the artworks, not electronic devices. Only we are . . ."

Roger Parmalin—he'd introduced himself at the entrance—was somewhat older than I am, his face encircled by a thin charcoal beard iced with silver and rising to a thinning crown of unkempt hair. There was something impish in the lively eyes behind his steel-rimmed glasses and the not-quite-garish orange stripes on the necktie he wore with his sober light gray suit. His British-inflected English was excellent.

"But I may be able to help," he added.

"How?" Call me a nationalist, but I couldn't imagine the Swiss out-hacking US law enforcement.

"We obtained the PIN for his phone during our surveillance. We find that people generally use the same PIN for other devices."

"How did you do that? You infected his phone with malware?"

Smiling gently, he shook his head. Those Americans are so heavy-handed. "We have simpler methods."

"Like what? It's not as though he'd be entering his PIN very often. Phones use face recognition."

"We jammed the face scanner with an infrared laser. That forced him to use his PIN." Embarrassingly simple. My face said as much. Parmalin chose to rub it in. He raised an eyebrow and said, "It's a well-known technique."

He made a brief call and took the tablet from Diane. We watched him tap in a PIN and heard the sound of a lock clicking open.

I think Diane felt as stupid as I did. The PIN was 7777777. Of course.

✳

Prof. Dassault guided Parmalin as he searched the tablet, while Diane and I stood at a respectful distance. Farnese's recent browser history revealed frequent access to a spreadsheet in the cloud. In that spreadsheet were meticulous records of his finds, including photos of objects prior to cleaning and repair. Some vases were in fragments, three-dimensional jigsaw puzzles encrusted with the telltale dirt of freshly unearthed objects. Diane wreaked havoc on her olive-colored scarf as the professor and Parmalin scrolled and looked for the golden dish. We soon glimpsed a tiny photo of it.

"Gold *phiale*," Prof. Dassault said. "There's a notation here. Maybe the name of the site where it was found. I don't know what it means." She paused.

Diane pressed her. "What does it say?"

"It's in English. *Delphi, Grotto*. That's Delphi, Greece, of course, from someplace called the 'Grotto.'"

So it *was* from Delphi. But what on earth was the "Grotto"?

There were photos showing the dish stained with some tarry matter, before it had been cleaned. But beyond the notation in the spreadsheet, there was no information on where it had been recovered. Diane and Prof. Dassault again conferred. They discussed two questions, Diane told me later. Could the "Grotto" be a well-known mountain site near Delphi called the Corycian Cave? (Conclusion: no, that site was for locals too poor to offer gold.) Was the Leonidas named on the dish the famous Spartan general who fell at Thermopylae? (Conclusion: no, the style of the dish was too late.) Meanwhile, Parmalin searched Farnese's calendar.

"Your report," he said to me. "I remember one of the names because it was French."

"*Le Chamois*?"

"That's the one."

"One of the hackers. What about him?"

"I'm looking at the calendar. Farnese has a meeting with this Chamois in a few hours."

"Where?" I exclaimed. "Can we intercept them?"

"The calendar doesn't say. Maybe . . ." Parmalin skimmed through Farnese's email and text messages. He shook his head and said, "Look. I don't see anything right now. But we'll catch him. We're following Farnese. Even in the mountains we can—"

His mobile rang. A brief, angry exchange ensued. Parmalin shot an evil look at the deputy director, but he was staring at his feet and didn't notice. Parmelin's people intercepted a call. Someone had tipped Farnese off to the raid.

The police had photographed everything in the showroom before touching it. That way they could leave everything exactly as they'd found it, keeping signs of their entry to a minimum. But they were already prepared to bring Farnese in if he noticed traces of the raid when he visited his showroom.

"We didn't want him to warn others and destroy evidence," Parmalin told me, lowering his phone, still on the call. "So we just arrested him at his home."

TWENTY-FOUR

Parmalin had raised my hopes and summarily dashed them. Just as we were on the verge of finding Le Chamois by following Farnese, the arrest appeared to snuff out the trail. Happily, in my roller-coaster world, I only had to wait a minute for my hopes to rebound.

Parmalin finished the call and pocketed his phone.

"Farnese was about to drive off when we arrested him," he said. "But he entered his destination into a navigation app and the surveillance team captured it. The Dent de Vaulion. That's in the Jura Mountains, by Lac de Joux, north of here. We need to leave now. He was driving from Lausanne. It would have been only an hour by car for him. It will take longer for us."

Parmalin, a uniformed officer, Diane, and I scrambled into a police car. The siren gave a high-low European wail as we tore off, the uniformed officer driving. From the passenger seat, Parmalin issued instructions over the radio.

"If we're going to observe inconspicuously, we don't want to arrive in a police car," he said, raising his voice. "There will be an ordinary car and hiking clothes and equipment waiting for us. And backup."

I'm always slumming it as far as clothes are concerned, equally ready for an all-night coding session or a light hike. Diane wore jeans, which was good, even if they looked freshly pressed, but her ensemble was otherwise too chic. She could shed the blazer and scarf and cover the blouse, but the sparkly metallic silver sneakers with wedge heels looked like trouble. The soles would crumble within sight of the first sharp rock.

"Do we need to get hiking shoes for you?"

"There is no time for that," she said, "and these are very comfortable."

"For a hike in an art gallery, they are."

"How many times have you hiked in the Jura Mountains?" she asked, squinting at me.

"Whenever I visit Switzerland."

"You said it's your first time in Switzerland."

"It is."

"My family hiked often on the French side. I know what it's like. And I have seen Farnese." She outlined a potbelly with her hands. "I doubt this hike will be challenging." The photos I'd seen were of a shorter man built a bit like me. I guess it was good that the hike had a kiddie-level difficulty rating. After all, I still had the war wound in my flank.

Geneva is a small city. Traffic in the center was light by New York standards. It was still congested at streetlights, though. Without the police siren carving our way through, things would have turned out very differently that day. We recrossed the river and headed back in the direction of the airport. Parmalin issued instructions and received reports on the radio. About ten minutes out from the airport, he turned off the siren, but I saw our still-flashing lights reflected in the vehicles beside us.

We emerged onto the A1 highway, which circumnavigates the lake. It's designed for efficiency, not beauty, and lacks the spectacular views I'd later gawp at elsewhere. The Alps were visible in the far distance on one side, though, and the Jura Mountains on the other. Even at high speed, the smooth surface of the highway was a pleasant respite from the insults dealt to the spine by our universally rutted American roads.

"Let me explain the situation," Parmalin said, turning to me. Diane was sitting behind him. "Farnese was about to leave fifteen minutes ago, a little past eleven thirty. He entered the address for the *buvette*—a kind of little restaurant—at the Dent de Vaulion. But his calendar says he was going to meet with Le Chamois at two o'clock. Since he was driving to the restaurant, it may be that he meant to eat lunch beforehand. In that case, he would have had his rendezvous with Le Chamois at the restaurant or a short hike away. The peak is only fifteen minutes away on foot."

I gave Diane a look. She'd been right about Farnese's physique.

"The problem with the Dent de Vaulion," Parmalin said, "is that it's a popular place. There are several paths up to the peak. It may be crowded on a beautiful day like this."

"So how will we find Le Chamois?" I asked. "How will we even recognize him?"

"We don't have to. We'll photograph everyone. If we're lucky, we'll have drones up soon over the trails. We can sort things out afterward. But I want to be on the ground. Drones are good, but I don't entirely trust them. Aerial surveillance misses things, especially in the mountains and when there's forest."

I'd gotten maybe four hours of sleep on the flight. I was cranky. The fear that had taken up permanent residence in my chest was tightening its grip. "We need to catch him today," I snapped.

"It's possible. But I can't guarantee—"

"Fourteen hours. That's how long I've got until the contract on my head activates. For you this is just another police case. For me it's life or death."

"We can give you protection. That would be more practical. How do you propose we find your Chamois today? Look for a little man with fur and curved horns? Pin up an advertisement on the trails for a master hacker?"

"I don't know. How are you going to sort things out afterward?"

"We'll show faces to Farnese. We use eye tracking devices. When people recognize faces, their eyes make saccades: small, reflexive movements that we can detect. I've looked through Farnese's calendar. He knows Le Chamois. This isn't the first time he's had a rendezvous with him. He's had many. If we can show Farnese a photo of his face, I think we'll know."

"So why not show faces to Farnese in real time?"

"We can't immediately do whatever we like with him. Like you, we have something called due process. And even if we can obtain a photo or video of Le Chamois, then comes the hard part, matching the face to his identity. Not to an animal. Not to a hacker handle. A real identity. Maybe Farnese will cooperate. Maybe not."

"We don't need him to. We may just need to match a surveillance image to a photo of him on the internet."

"That's possible. But not easy or reliable in my experience. We need time."

"You have it, I don't," I was about to say. But I realized that Parmalin was being reasonable. I wasn't.

"What worries me," Parmalin continued, "is how many variables there are. It's possible that plans changed and Farnese was going to have lunch with Le Chamois at twelve thirty, for instance, but didn't update his calendar. We have people heading up from Lausanne, so in that case we'll still catch him. But other things could go wrong. That's why I want to be on the ground myself."

Diane wasn't listening to us. She was staring out the window at the distant mountain peaks capped with snow, where the gods dwell. The gold dish had stirred something in her.

✳

Half an hour later, we exited the highway onto a small road that took us past vineyards and orchards into the small town of Aubonne. Neat but drab gray, pink, and ochre plastered buildings roofed in terra-cotta lined the steep, winding streets. They presented a solid front of weathered and patinated prosperity. The town dwellers did allow themselves a few lively touches: bright red and green exterior shutters, antique signs and lamps hanging from delicate metal brackets, and window boxes overflowing with improbably healthy red and pink blossoms. We exited the town on a narrow road flanked by a mossy stone wall that gave way to terraced vineyards. We were soon surrounded by farmland.

The road climbed through fields, some bare, some filled with corn and sunflowers. Dark green mountains swelled on our left and woods gathered on our right. I turned to see Lake Geneva now in view behind us, spanning most of the horizon. The road passed through a village and then wound into a forest. Parmalin talked on the radio and his mobile phone every few minutes. Otherwise we all sat in silence, as though only collective concentration could ensure we made it in time.

As we climbed higher and higher, the two-lane road leaned against a rocky rise on one side. Trees ran down the slope on the other, dropping away now and again to reveal the deep valley and distant forested mountains hidden elsewhere from view. We passed rock faces covered with netting to catch tumbling stones, triangular signs with exclamation points and squiggles representing the road's dangerous contortions, and red-and-white-striped reflectors, reminders of the upland hazards of fog or dark. On we went, up and up. The road looped and the sun swung around and lit up the trees beside us. I couldn't believe I was on a quest for the secret of a smart contract in this place.

Still surrounded by forest, we emerged onto a crossroads studded with signage: large blue arrows pointing to Vaulion, Orbe, and Yverdon, and towns in France and a board with a cheery cartoon mountain welcoming us to the Vallée de Joux. We turned onto a gravel clearing on the right, across the road from a larger, half-full parking lot.

A red Volvo station wagon was waiting for us, two plainclothes detectives leaning against it. We got out and did a hasty round of introductions. Parmalin and the uniformed officer went into the woods to change their clothes discreetly. The detectives outfitted me and Diane with large-frame backpacks, loose, long-sleeve shirts, hiking poles, and caps containing hidden video cameras. The one helping me with my equipment glanced inquiringly at my wrists. As a professional, he may have recognized the signs of overzealous handcuffing on my still livid skin. I didn't want to explain, but also didn't want my bruises misconstrued. "Kidnapping," I muttered. He nodded as though this was the only natural explanation. Maybe he didn't know the word in English.

Once Diane and I had been outfitted, she began a conversation in French with the detectives. Parmalin and the uniformed officer were still changing. I was getting anxious. I wandered toward the road to distract myself.

I was surveying the cars in the parking lot opposite us, still bleary from the red-eye flight, when a mass of black swept past my face. A black bird with a four-foot wingspan drifted just yards away. It was an awe-striking sight. I spun around to see it alight on a rock next to a signpost topped with yellow arrows. A trailhead. The glossy black creature cocked its head and fixed a black eye on me.

I was matching my two eyes against the bird's one when a tall man with a deeply lined face approached and started up the trail. He was equipped like an inveterate outdoorsman, in old hiking boots, gray technical pants with zip-off lower legs, a faded T-shirt, and a tan cap with a neck flap, like something worn by a desert corps. The thick waist belt on his hiking backpack was undone, but the sternum strap lay tight across his chest. His lanky frame and smooth, pole-driven stride completed the look.

We made eye contact for just a second, but within that second, a drama unfolded. Recognition. A cringe and shrinking within. A gaze steadied to deny and provide cover. These things happened on my side, but I thought—I could not be certain—that they also happened on his.

"*Bonjour*," he said with a slight nod.

"Bonn-jore," I replied.

A stranger. An instant of recognition. This was one of several preludes to death I'd rehearsed in my imagination. As the man disappeared up the trail, I stood, frozen, awaiting another surprise that might end my life. I half believed that if I turned, I'd see Diane and the Swiss police lined up behind me, guns aimed at my chest. I had to talk myself through it. *The contract doesn't activate until tonight. I'm not yet the quarry. I'm here as the hunter. I'm not going to be kidnapped by the Swiss police. Perhaps the man recognized me. But I also recognized him.* Some of my imagined deaths involved a stranger recognizing me. They didn't also involve him allowing me—and therefore the Swiss police—to recognize him. That made no sense.

I turned. There was no one behind me. I dashed back to the cars.

Parmalin and the officer, transformed into day-trippers by hiking pants and T-shirts, had joined Diane in conference with the two waiting detectives.

"The man who just passed," I said, breathless. "I'm not sure— Yes, I am sure. I recognized him. Diane, did he look familiar?"

She shook her head. "I didn't see him. But what do you mean? You mean you know him?"

"Maybe, but if so, I don't remember who he is. Does this trail go up to the peak?" I asked Parmalin.

"Yes," he said. "The long way. Maybe an hour on this trail. You think he might be—"

"It can't be a coincidence. Not right here and right now," I said. "We've got to go after him."

"I agree," said Parmalin. "Especially because we don't know precisely where the rendezvous is supposed to happen." He stroked his beard— clutched it, really. "Whoever he is, he's seen the police car. Maybe it's okay. He may not have noticed that we're federal police and even if he did, it may mean nothing to him. We are wearing hiking clothes after all. Still, it's a risk. If this is Le Chamois and he grows suspicious and tries to contact Farnese . . ." He crossed his arms and bowed his head. "No," he said, look-ing up at me, "we can't just take him into custody. Not yet. Look, it's only another twelve minutes by car to the *buvette*. I'll drive there as planned. There are more of us up there, ready to deploy across the trails. But if this is Le Chamois and he turns back or takes a detour, it's best to track him from behind too. Bernasconi," he ordered one of the detectives, "you go with him." Meaning with me.

"I'll go with them too," said Diane.

"Fine," he said. "Be careful. And Bernasconi . . ."

"Yes, sir?"

"Don't lose him."

He and the two other officers tore off in the Volvo, spitting gravel behind the rear wheels. Diane, Bernasconi, and I started up the mountain.

TWENTY-FIVE

The trail curved away to the right through the dense woods, around a low rocky rise, so that by the time we set out, the man was already gone.

Bernasconi spoke softly into a radio hidden in his shirt. He was a young fellow, slender and just a couple of inches taller than Diane. His youthful naivete and the dark hair tumbling over his eyes seemed out of place in a police detective.

He handed me his backpack.

"I want to look ahead first," he said. "You should keep walking."

He jogged off. I slung the second backpack over my shoulder as best I could. Diane whipped out her phone and typed as we walked. The trail consisted of two dirt strips separated by a width of grass. Perhaps it doubled as a logging road.

"We just left Pétra Félix," Diane said. "'The Happy Rock.'" She paused. "It's about three hundred meters of elevation to the summit. As Parmalin said, it should take us less than an hour."

"It's one o'clock now, so if this is our man, I guess Farnese's calendar was right."

"We still don't know where they were going to rendezvous." She cocked her head. "Doesn't it seem strange they wouldn't hike together? How sure are you that you recognized him?"

"I couldn't tell you his name. I've been racking my brain. But faces I remember."

Bernasconi returned at a jog.

"He seems to be alone. He's fast." He took his backpack from me, flipped open the flap on top, and loosened the drawstrings. "Do you want to give me your heavy items? Canteens?" I pulled a face. He added, "I assume you don't normally hike in the mountains. I do trail running here."

"Good idea," Diane said. "I haven't used those muscles in a long time." She and I ceded our canteens, which were heavy with water. My bag grew noticeably lighter.

We pressed ahead. It was ideal hiking weather. The afternoon was cool and the forest percolated up its own lightly chilled air. After ten minutes of climbing, though, I was already warm.

"Shoes okay?" I asked Diane, breathing hard.

"Very comfortable," she said.

"You should use your sticks," Bernasconi called back. "Like this." He curled his biceps to lift his poles. His tutorial wasn't particularly helpful. I tried instead to imitate Diane. It took some doing to get a feel for skiing uphill on dirt and grass, but once I eased into a rhythm, I found that the poles did help.

The trail kept climbing. The only sounds were birdsong, light rustling in the upper trees, and our shoes scuffing the dirt. A line of sky showed through the tree canopy on the lower trail, but the trees gradually joined overhead. Raking sunlight made the treetops glow. I couldn't imagine that drones would capture faces here. Bernasconi continued his smooth mechanical ascent, dragging us—me, mostly—in his wake. I was sweating under my backpack. Diane smiled encouragement.

"I think I'm getting altitude sickness," I said to her.

She laughed. "No, you are not. We are barely above a thousand meters."

"A thousand meters? Just imagine a skyscraper that height."

"Only in a nightmare. But wait until you see the view. It will be worth the pain. From the top we'll see lakes on three sides, Lac de Joux, Lac de Neuchâtel, and Lac Léman—or Lake Juhneeevah, as you would call it." She chuckled and glanced at me, then did a double take and turned serious. "Do you need some water?" I shook my head.

A short while later, Bernasconi weighed me down again with his backpack and bounded ahead. This time, he took longer to return.

"We are falling behind," he said, catching his breath. "But we have someone descending from the summit now and the drones are over the mountain. Fortunately, there are only a few trails that lead from this one."

I pushed hard. I was desperate not to lose my shot at finding Le Chamois. But about twenty minutes into our climb, I was sweating, my legs were wobbling, and Bernasconi's gentle patience was giving way to worry. I just couldn't keep up.

"Go ahead without me," I said, bending with my hands on my knees.

"I was just going to say—" Bernasconi said.

"Yes," Diane said. "You should go ahead."

"You did well. Both of you." Bernasconi handed us back our canteens. "Follow this trail to the restaurant. I'll text you if anything changes." He launched into a near-vertical sprint and disappeared.

"If this is Le Chamois we're after," I said, "we now know how he got his name."

More than twenty minutes later, still at a forced march, if a slow one for Bernasconi and our quarry, we reached a junction of two trails. Diane checked a trail map on her phone. We made a sharp right.

"It's good that Bernasconi went ahead," she noted. "There are two trails detouring from this one. One goes down the mountain, the other leads to the *col* of the mountain, the ridge."

We pressed on until at last we emerged from the woods onto an area of tufted grass surrounded on three sides by pine trees. Like the trails, the grass was strewn with white rocks, large and small, the bones of the mountain poking through holes in its soft covering.

Diane's phone pinged.

She glanced down and wrinkled her brow. "He has turned away from the restaurant, Bernasconi says. And the peak."

"Where's he headed?"

"We don't know."

✳

The path continued steeply along the rock-strewn glade until it ended at a small gap in a metal-wire fence. This led us onto a paved road, barely the width of a car. Diane consulted her phone and we turned right. The road tunneled through yet more woods. Behind the dark tree trunks on our right, bright leaves shimmered. On our left was a steep bank of impenetrable forest, its mysteries illuminated a few yards deep by the high sun. We walked for five minutes and entered a small clearing. I would have stopped to admire the view of a valley that emerged here, but Diane hastened onto an unpaved road leading up and away on the left. Behind a barbed wire fence on the side of this road was a grass-covered slope studded with more white mountain bones. A herd of cows grazed in a narrow flat area beside us, working patiently around the rocks in their dinner.

We again entered the woods and climbed for several minutes, then switchbacked onto a path. This was hard going. The path was steep and rocky and climaxed in a hill that it might have been easier to climb on all fours. At the top, Bernasconi was waiting. He put his finger to his lips.

"Just down there." He pointed down the path. We descended in silence. He raised his hand and we stopped. I thought I'd heard something at the top of the hill, and I was right. Orchestral music and singing. We listened.

A man sang in a deep, plodding voice of foreboding. Another man replied defiantly in a higher register. Or maybe there were three men. It was hard to tell. The singing sounded as though it were live, accompanied by music from an electronic device, maybe a phone. Faint, but familiar.

"*Don Giovanni*," I whispered.

"Of course!" Bernasconi said. "I should have recognized it. I *thought* I heard Italian."

"The end of the dinner scene," Diane said. "Is someone with him?" she asked.

"No. It's just him."

We listened, aided by our familiarity. The singing quickened, slowed, quickened. The opera approached its climax. Don Giovanni sang in mounting agony and terror as the orchestra drummed a death march and the earth shook, as bows scraped frantically across strings and flames shot from the underworld. The hollow-voiced chorus chanted, "Eternal torments await thee!" The Don gave a final cry of despair. Then his voice faded away.

"He has plunged into hell," Diane whispered. She asked Bernasconi, "Are you armed?"

He patted his left flank. Diane gave a brisk nod and we emerged from the woods.

We weren't at the peak, but even in that secluded place the view was as Diane had promised. Spread at our feet lay all that we'd conquered. The mountain swooped down to grassland, then rose again to a low forested hill. Above this hill was a light brown speckling, like coarse sand. Distant towns pressing against the shores of Lake Geneva. The lake sparkled blue, a band across the horizon, swallowed up on one side by towns and fields and eclipsed on the other by a neighboring peak. Beyond the lake were the Alps, small but clear, crushed green velvet beneath a chain of noble crests, gray-blue in shadow, tinged orange where the sun struck the still-thick snowcaps.

And there, in a glade bright with wildflowers, was a lone man. The possible author of my nightmare. He smiled or scrunched up his face against the sun. Diane, Bernasconi, and I approached him.

"I'm a baritone," he announced as we grew near, "so please excuse my *lamentable* Commendatore." I was now certain I'd met him somewhere before. He and I eyed one another. "Yes, it *is* you," he announced. "I thought it might be."

"Who are you?" I crossed my arms.

"*You* of course are the famous one now," he said, waving his hand at me. "My name is Alexis Hévin. We met in New York."

The one the Priestess had introduced me to. The arrogant professor whose papers I was supposed to have read. All along I'd assumed it was my neutralization contract that had angered the Delphians and drawn their fire. But my enemy had never been faceless. In this fresh encounter with Hévin, I felt what I did the first time: pure chemical hostility. He and I were meant to fight. Meant to lock horns in combat as surely as the kind of solitary male animals that gave rise to the name Le Chamois. I was just glad Bernasconi had taken care of the actual physical side of things.

"And two 'undercover' police with you," Hévin added. Bernasconi was a short distance away, talking on his radio.

"Who is he?" Diane asked.

"Dr. Duménil," I said, "meet Prof. Hévin. Or is it Prof. Le Chamois? He's a distinguished faculty member in computer science somewhere, probably here in Switzerland. He does impressive technical work. He's best known for his killer apps."

"*He's* a hacker?" Diane made a face of disbelief.

"Not in the traditional sense."

"Your friend here better fits that description," Hévin said to her.

"I'll admit I was impressed with your code," I said. "Both the rogue contract and the 'prophecies.'"

"Very kind of you. The overflow attack on the rogue contract. That was you?"

I inclined my head.

"Creative," he said. "And it almost worked." Something held me back from contradicting him. "I suppose my absent friend led you here? Or were you just wandering through the mountains of Switzerland with your hiking partners in the federal police force?"

"We—" I'm not sure what I was going to say, but Diane cut me off.

"Your 'friend' was very cooperative," she snapped at him. To me she said, "We had better let the Swiss police handle this."

Bernasconi walked up to Hévin. Standing over him, he spoke in French. I didn't need to understand the words. He was asking Hévin to come in for questioning. Hévin's amused tolerance suggested that he saw one of his students in Bernasconi's youthful manner. Or perhaps, I thought, he had a trick up his sleeve. He'd demonstrated how quickly he could clamber over the mountain, but I doubted he could outrun Bernasconi. Did he have more cyberweapons at the ready?

"My friend had little time to cooperate with you," Hévin said to Diane, as he stood. "I heard from him just this morning."

"He didn't need much time," Diane replied. "We both know how much he likes to talk."

I didn't understand why Diane said this to Hévin.

Later I would come to appreciate her foresight.

TWENTY-SIX

It turned out the restaurant wasn't far away. Parmalin and two detectives reached us less than ten minutes later, lowering themselves with their hiking poles down the rock-littered slope. With one pair of police behind and another pair in front, and with Diane and me flanking him, we marched Hévin over the path back up the hill.

As the trail entered the woods, he reached into his pocket. A detective barked at him from behind.

"I don't have a weapon," he called out in English, holding up a keychain. "You've already searched me." He pinched a tiny black plastic USB device between his thumb and forefinger, letting his keys dangle. "I was just wondering what this little device might be worth. It's a crypto—"

It slipped from his fingers as he stumbled on a rock. He stooped to pick it up, but Diane dropped to a crouch and snatched it.

"Thank you," she said, as she stood and pocketed the keychain. "We will crack this."

Hévin shook his head indulgently.

"Unfortunately, no, Diane," I said.

"Why not? We have hardware experts."

"I'm giving Prof. Hévin the benefit of the doubt, but I assume it's password protected. And I'm sure he chooses strong passwords." I said to him, "This has the secret key that controls the contract, I'm guessing?"

"That will be an excellent topic for our conversations in the near future."

The negotiations had begun, and my life would depend on them. By now, of course, I was used to being a pawn.

*

We didn't have to walk far. A police car was waiting on the logging road we'd taken on the way up, along with the red Volvo. Hévin was escorted into the police car, while Diane and I climbed into the back of the Volvo. As we drove off, I probed a sunburn on the back of my neck with my fingers. I couldn't imagine how I'd gotten it. Diane produced the wispy olive-green scarf she'd removed for the hike, smoothed her blouse and blazer, cleaned her glasses, gave her head a vigorous shake, fingered her hair, and came out looking as fresh as she had in the morning. Even her shoes showed no evidence of our hike. Silver sparkles must hide dirt.

We drove back to Geneva, retracing our outbound route, but bypassing the airport and heading for a different part of the city. We pulled up behind a neoclassical building spanning an entire block, at the cantonal police station in Pâquis.

The prosecutor from the Geneva Freeport, with the help of the police, had already completed an initial interrogation of Farnese. While the police went off with Hévin, Diane and I watched a video recording of it.

Defying urgent whispers from the attorney at his side, Farnese answered the prosecutor's questions with diatribes that went to the moon and back, propelled by his animated hands. After the preliminaries— name, residence, and so forth—he was asked where he obtained the gold dish. He plunged into the story of a major eighty-year-old collection of antiquities he'd recently acquired from a Lebanese family. He gave what must have been a well-rehearsed sales pitch on the collection's engraved gemstones. Gemstone engraving was a kind of miniature sculpture, a major art form in the ancient world. ("Tiny monuments to beauty!" he exclaimed, pinching together his fingertips.) Today most people are only interested in big, bold visuals on their electronic toys. ("Bits of shit," he said with a grimace.) Before civil war erupted in the 1970s, Lebanon had been the political bedrock of the Middle East for a thousand years. Over the course of half a century, the magnificent collection in Farnese's hands survived the country's breakdown, a feat as remarkable as the pristine condition of its pieces. He told the story of the eagles released by Zeus to locate the center of the world. (He flapped his fingers, thumbs interlocked like a shadow-puppet bird.) This was the myth represented magnificently on the gold dish. He boasted about his work in the International Association of Dealers in Ancient Art. He'd helped the association correct European Commission misconceptions ("lies") about provenance, looting, and the scrupulousness of dealers. Twice shaking off his attorney's hand from his forearm, he concluded with choice words for the Swiss justice system, enlivened by choice gestures. The rest of the video was more of the same.

He reminded me of the CEOs of small tech start-ups I've met over the years. Ask one of them a question, any question, and you'll feel like you've popped the cap off a warm bottle of beer. They too are desperate.

The prosecutor gave Diane a chance to interrogate Farnese. I wasn't invited to watch, but was left alone in a lounge of some kind with a sofa and a Nespresso machine. Determined not to sleep until we returned to the apartment, I rummaged through the basket of shining colored espresso pods beside the machine, hunting for the strongest. I drank two ristretto shots. A home remedy for bodywide cellular depletion.

✳

Diane burst into the room, startling me awake. I gathered my limbs from their far-flung places on the sofa and rose to sit.

She took a deep breath.

"That pig!"

"Worse than expected?"

"Maybe I seemed too eager." She frowned. Given Farnese's defective brain-to-mouth filter, sexist comments from him wouldn't have surprised me. "We need to find his cache before it disappears. The moment his network learns that he's been arrested, they'll scatter like cockroaches when the lights come on."

"You couldn't have done worse with him than the prosecutor did. The Swiss police didn't learn anything more from surveillance? Or from his tablet or phone?"

"Plenty. Enough to send him to jail. Prof. Dassault says that she will be busy for a year. But not what I need to know. They found email showing that Farnese was planning to transport important objects to Geneva, but we don't know from where. If we don't find them soon, they could disappear for decades." She sank into a chair next to the sofa. "Or forever."

"Maybe he just needs time to cool off and have his attorney knock some sense into him." As I heard myself say this, I realized it was drivel.

Diane leaned toward me. "You know the feeling of regret, how it's a kind of torture? Normally it's a feeling about the past. But right now, I'm seeing and feeling the pangs of future regrets. Regrets that will haunt me if I haven't done everything possible. I have to make sure this treasure from Delphi doesn't end up in the wrong hands."

Parmalin walked into the room.

"That man's a fool," he snapped. He said to Diane, "I watched your interrogation. Farnese thinks he'll avoid prison this way. He won't. But perhaps Prof. Hévin will talk. You were smart to make him believe that Farnese was furnishing evidence against him." Then he turned to me, "The prosecutor wants your help with some technical details."

"So Hévin's cooperating?"

He massaged the back of his neck. "He's negotiating."

※

Parmalin brought me to the interrogation room. It was more civilized than I expected. There was a large, frosted exterior window topped by a clear transom. The walls were bare white, with small devices mounted near the ceiling, a camera and what I took to be a microphone. Otherwise, it could have passed for an ordinary if cramped corporate conference room. In the center was a table flanked by chairs on its two long sides.

Marie Fiorina, the prosecutor from the Geneva Freeport, sat at the table opposite the door. She was in her sixties, I estimated. Dark-eyed, with the deeply tanned, wrinkled skin that retirees in the US work hard to cultivate in Florida. Her black suit and black shirt gave her a trim, sober judicial appearance. Two bits of frippery ruined it: her bleached blond mop of cropped hair and a heavy gold-chain necklace.

She had no need to try to look imposing, I soon came to realize. She quizzed me in her raspy smoker's voice about the basics of smart contracts and the particulars of the rogue contract. She was unforgiving of imprecise explanations and she forgot nothing. The only way to parry her sharp questions, I could see, would be to ramble like Farnese.

After twenty minutes, Hévin and a severe-looking woman with her chestnut hair done up in a bun entered the room, along with Parmalin and Bernasconi. Hévin and the woman, his attorney, sat opposite the prosecutor. Parmalin and Bernasconi positioned themselves on the prosecutor's left, while Diane and I sat on her right. The table wasn't meant for five people on one side, so we had to squeeze in.

Hévin was in the habit of lecturing in halls packed with hundreds of submissive undergraduates. In some professors, this experience leaves a permanent podium manner. Hévin had it even under interrogation. I'd have been paralyzed with fear, but he was there to instruct.

"So you've been appointed sheriff's deputy," he said to me across the table. "I believe it's common in your country, at least in the cowboy movies I've watched. But I wasn't aware it happened in Switzerland."

"We hear you want to negotiate," Diane said.

"I'm *willing* to be of service to you." He glanced at his attorney, "Let's start with some important facts. I'll speak in English for the benefit of the sheriff's deputy. Yes? I hope he'll show patience with our *Jeanne d'Arc* English." The prosecutor gave him a look of irritation. "First, I've received no money from Farnese, who is a friend after all."

"There is no motive for any crime," his attorney added.

"That's for us to determine," the prosecutor rasped in her no-nonsense voice.

"Second, my charming friend Giuseppe Farnese has spoken to me often about his Greek treasures."

"You're an expert on ancient Greek art?" the prosecutor asked.

"No, but I would be happy in the spirit of cooperation to entertain you with some of my friend's colorful stories. You'll find them most instructive."

"We found a gold libation dish," Diane interrupted, before the prosecutor could fire off another question, "a *phiale*, in the *Ports Francs* this morning. Do you know where it came from?"

"I don't know exactly where your gold dish came from. But I *do* have almost as accurate an idea as my friend does."

Diane and I looked at one another.

"Finally," Hévin continued, "there's the small device of mine you took the initiative to *appropriate*. It contains a secret key which I understand has piqued your interest."

"That cryptographic key was in unrelated smart-contract code created by Prof. Hévin as part of his research," his attorney said. "Others may have copied his code."

"That's not how it works," I said. "Keys are associated with particular accounts. Either his account controls the rogue contract—in which case he was almost certainly involved in coding it—or it doesn't."

"Can you disarm the contract?" the prosecutor asked Hévin.

"Given the small device in your possession, I believe I can."

"So you admit that you played a role in creating the contract?"

"Yes. So did your deputy."

"I—" I spluttered.

"What does he mean?" she asked me.

"He means . . . he means that I created steel and he forged a gun out of it."

"An apt analogy," Hévin said. "But then I neither loaded the gun nor touched the trigger."

"You knew how it would be used."

"Just as Sig Sauer knows that criminals will use its pistols."

"We're talking about a weapon created for one purpose. And you've admitted you had your thumb on the safety this whole time. You—"

"I created an off switch as a special precaution. I didn't even know the contract would be a real threat. It was only this week that evidence emerged—"

"Evidence?" I yelped. "Evidence?" I gestured in appeal to the prosecutor, whose mouth opened as she considered whether to interrupt me. "Vigàno was murdered. The bounty claim was proof positive of that. The way the contract works—"

"Unfortunately," Hévin interjected, "smart-contract features can be inconvenient. If the contract in question is shut down, someone could simply create another. That state of affairs is not my doing. It would be best if the community works together to prevent a recurrence of this incident. Wouldn't you agree?" *Don't interfere*, his look warned.

Having admitted to the prosecutor that he could shut down the contract, Hévin was now compelled to do it. But he was determined to avoid prison and was issuing a veiled threat. If I derailed his negotiations, he'd find a way to launch a new contract—and he wouldn't make the same technical mistakes twice. Of course, in principle I could equally well put a price on his head with my own smart contract. But he knew that in reality I couldn't, because like most people, I was constitutionally incapable. I knew he could, because he already had. In madness lies power.

"We don't see eye to eye on much," I replied, "but on this one point we agree." I said to the prosecutor, "I've made my point. Prof. Hévin was at least complicit in Vigàno's death and in my view orchestrated it. I've nothing more to say, but I can answer any other questions you have."

"Thank you for your help," the prosecutor said. "I'm sorry if this caused you pain." Then, softly, she said, "You may go."

Hévin watched me as I stood and circled the table on my way to the door. He yawned—at me, if that's possible. Gritting my teeth, I left the room.

✳

I had no trouble staying awake this time. I prowled around the small lounge, asking myself how I should have handled Hévin. Had I kept my cool, I wouldn't have provoked him and borne the humiliation of backing down. What was my goal anyway? Didn't I want Hévin's negotiations to succeed? I had only hours before the contract on my head activated. Didn't I want him to shut it down as soon as possible? What had changed was the prospect of the danger lifting, leaving room for the luxury of vengeful thoughts. I wanted Hévin's smug face behind bars. Above all, I wanted to beat him. And I wanted him and everyone else to know it.

As I paced and fretted, I became aware of a different question yanking on a bell pull in the back of my mind. The gold dish. What did Hévin mean? He said he didn't know where the gold dish came from, but had as accurate an idea as Farnese. How could that possibly be? What was this "Grotto" in Delphi?

✳

Diane returned to the lounge with the strangest expression on her face. Something like her look of sympathy when I was rescued from the kidnappers, but this time brooding and confused. She sat in a chair and motioned toward the sofa. I sat near her.

"We are taking a break from the interrogation."

"I see."

She frowned. "It's clear how things are trending."

"What do you mean? They're going to let him go?"

"Not exactly. Not yet. But it will be hard to build a case against him, unfortunately, and he knows it. To begin with, there are those Russian hackers, suspects we may never take into custody."

"So Walker told me."

"Switzerland doesn't have juries. But smart contracts are so arcane that even judges may struggle to understand them. I certainly do. That's another issue. And Hévin's involvement is indirect and vague."

"He should be charged as an accessory to murder and attempted murder. But I see the problem. What do you think a judge will make of everything that's happened?"

"A judge will think that Prof. Hévin was perhaps complicit in the creation of software used in a rogue smart contract—whatever that is—with parties beyond the reach of the law as part of a plan to solicit murder from parties unknown by methods unknown."

"That bad, huh?"

"I am afraid that it is." She put her hand on my arm. "I want to see justice for Prof. Viganò. And for you. I really do. Badly. But I don't see how that is going to happen now."

"I get the sense you want to ask me something."

"It's not too late for me to try to influence the prosecutor. I can't provide official input to the Swiss investigation, but I think I have some say. This is an international case. We could in principle request his extradition to the US. We could pressure them. I will fight if you want me to. Prof. Hévin—no, I will call him Hévin the way you do—Hévin will disarm the contract. I am sure of that. They will find something to prosecute him for if he doesn't. But if he receives full clemency, he will cooperate in other ways. We don't know what he knows, but he may be able to give us clues about where Farnese is keeping the rest of his artifacts."

"Ah."

"Tell me what you want me to do. I will do it."

Her face was close to mine. I now understood. She was holding back from pressuring me, but her desire was clear. If we lost time now trying to send Hévin to prison, she might also lose her chance to locate Farnese's artifacts.

I stood and stretched. I turned away from her, bowed my head, and thought. Surely I'd get Byron's head on a platter. That was vengeance, but not satisfying, because he wasn't a real adversary, just a vicious, inept lackey. Hévin might or might not technically have loaded the gun or touched the trigger, as he put it, but he was the real puppet master. Even if Farnese provided the money, gave the orders, and masterminded the resurgence of Apollo—which wasn't certain—Hévin was the technical brains of the operation, my opposite number.

My answer to Diane was a foregone conclusion, but I still asked.

"Does clemency mean a public dismissal of the case? Or keeping the whole thing under wraps?"

She pursed her lips. "They prefer to avoid a scandal. It would be bad for his university, which is one of the top in Europe, and bad for the reputation of a small country like Switzerland. Maybe he pays a fine."

"Diane," I said, "It's petty, I realize. But I have to know. In your eyes, have I beaten him?"

She gave me a look of such sadness that I couldn't understand where it came from. "Of course."

I hadn't beaten him. At best, I'd forced him to retreat from the battlefield, and I knew it. But I was willing to settle for the booby prize of having my pride intact in front of Diane.

"OK," I said softly. "Then it's time to beat Farnese." I walked to the door. "Do everything you can." I held it open for her.

She rose and walked over, kissed me on the cheek, and left the room.

TWENTY-SEVEN

"Wake up! We need to go!"

Given the pins and needles I was on, it was incredible that I'd fallen asleep again. Diane was shaking me.

"Go where?"

"Greece."

"Greece? Right now? Are you kidding me?"

"I will explain on the way."

"Remind me not to do a day trip with you again," I groaned.

Parmalin guided us briskly through the building.

"It will be close," he said, "but you'll make it. No problem. I've arranged an escort to the airport for you. You said your apartment is in Plainpalais? Yes? Good. So ten minutes there and then twenty to the airport. You have at least ten or fifteen minutes to pack your bags."

"*Merci pour tout, Roger*," Diane said.

"I wish I could go with you . . ." He shook off a buzzing thought. "I don't want to create an international incident," he chuckled, "but it's like a Tintin adventure."

Right outside the building, a police car with a uniformed driver awaited us. It was a little past six in the evening. The last viable flight to Athens left just before seven thirty.

"Good luck," said Parmalin as we shook hands. He laughed. "And beware the Prince of the Sun!"

"Who's the Prince of the Sun?" I asked Diane as we drove off, siren wailing. We were both in the back of the car. "Apollo?"

"It's from a Tintin story, *Temple of the Sun*. My favorite one, actually. Tintin discovers an outpost of the Incan civilization, which was supposed to have vanished centuries ago. The Prince of the Sun is the high priest of their ancient religion."

"Our ancient religion existed until a couple of days ago." I smirked. "But now Apollo is sitting in a police station." Little did I suspect how things would change that night, how differently I'd come to think of the god. "Look, Diane, you seem confident, but I'm still frankly terrified. The bounty activates tonight. What if they can't get Hévin to use the off switch and shut down the contract by then? Before the secret syndicate of Tintin-like bad guys comes out and knocks me on the head, I need to call Ray and have him divert to Athens."

Diane brought her hand to her mouth, then clasped my arm. "But you don't need to," said, beaming. "How stupid of me not to tell you right away. It's over!" She twisted and hugged me. "They got Hévin to shut it down."

I couldn't check from my phone, so I messaged Corinne.

> Contract may be disarmed. Check please?
>   (In Switzerland. Long story.)

A minute later, I got a thumbs-up. Actually, about thirty of them, and then a voice message I had to jack up the volume to hear over the police car's siren. "You did it! I don't know why you're in Switzerland, but go gorge on some of that famous chocolate! We'll whoop it up when you're back. I'm so—so happy for you!"

"Confirmed?" Diane asked.

"You're right. It really is over." I showed her Corinne's thumbs-up. "What a relief! I think it's a relief, at least. But I can't really say, because I don't feel it yet. Not in my gut anyway."

In fact, the thought of Hévin getting away scot-free sickened me. Farnese and Byron would pay the price because people understood their crimes. But I had built tools in the service of truth and freedom and Hévin had weaponized not just my tools, but my principles. He'd done so in the guise of no less than the Greek god of truth. To me, that was true hubris, a crime far worse than the grasping or violent antics of Farnese or Byron, crimes that were at least human. Hévin had escaped because he'd done deeds beyond the understanding of mere temporal justice. Which goes to show you can never beat a god. Even a false one.

"Your gut is empty," Diane replied. "Do you realize we haven't eaten since breakfast? I have something . . ." She rummaged through her handbag.

"Why are we rushing to Greece?" The police siren made it felt like we were driving there. "And where exactly are we going? What did Hévin say?"

"The Grotto. We are looking for the Grotto. A cave where the artifacts were discovered and where most of them are still hidden. It was found by a local man—one of the looters—a few years ago after an earthquake. Farnese doesn't know where it is because the looters don't trust him. They brought him there blindfolded."

"Then how are *we* going to find it?"

"We have clues. Detailed clues. Farnese told his story to Hévin—many times, it seems—and Hévin told us."

"To get a plea deal?"

"Yes. In part. But I think he told us even more than he needed to. He seemed almost eager."

"Maybe because you convinced him that Farnese betrayed him."

"More than that. At first, I thought it was just because he enjoys lecturing. But remember, he doesn't know how we found him. He knows only that we found Farnese first. So he may also blame Farnese for being careless and getting caught."

"And what did he tell you?"

"The looters would drive Farnese somewhere at night and then walk him blindfolded to the Grotto. We know that it took about forty-five minutes. He told Hévin that they made him leave his phone behind when they started walking, but he recorded the location where they drove him. Roger found a place marker near Delphi in a map on Farnese's phone. We also know the Grotto is near a stream, because Farnese complained to Hévin about getting wet in it. I think we can find it, especially with the help of a geologist and a team to review satellite data on the area around Delphi at night, when the looters work. Farnese was already trying to locate the Grotto himself. That is why he talked so much about it with Hévin. He probably wanted to betray his looters and steal the artifacts."

"Abyss beneath abyss of perfidy," I said. "I can code up something to search geological data."

"I just hope it's not too late. Farnese couldn't have communicated with the looters directly, but he could have had his attorney do it. You saw that attorney in the videotape. He is worse in person."

"I see. Thus the frantic hunt."

She nodded. "I have got a friend in the Greek Archaeological Service who will meet us in Delphi tomorrow morning. He is going to try to assemble a team. We need a geologist, police surveillance, maybe help from the military. The problem is that the looters could clear out the Grotto tonight."

"Does Hévin know what's in this cave? Is . . . is *it* there?" I don't know why, but now that we were getting close, superstition held the word back from my lips.

"There are more gold artifacts. That is certain. If they are anything like the libation bowl—I just can't imagine—it would be an immense discovery. Like the tomb of Tutankhamen. Farnese talked to Hévin about a sacred stone. But when I asked Hévin about the Omphalos, he didn't know what it was. Farnese may not have named it, or Hévin didn't remember the word."

My phone pinged. I slipped it out of my pocket. Lukas. It pinged again. The Priestess. I was about to put it back, but it pinged again. And again. Everyone at Adyton was messaging congratulations. Half of them were offering to buy me a beer after work. I guess Corinne hadn't told them I was abroad.

"You know, thriller movies are silly," I said, showing Diane the flurry of congratulations. "The hero always escapes death with just seconds to spare. In real life, he's got"—I checked my watch—"more than seven hours. And who knows when the assassins would actually have knocked me off."

We stopped at the apartment and rushed upstairs. My bedbug precautions meant I only needed to gather my toiletries. Clothes flying, Diane packed in five minutes.

"I was just going to leave my luggage here, to be honest," she said as we scrambled back into the police car. "But I don't want to waste time trying to buy clothing and a toothbrush in a backwater of Greece."

"All you need is those shoes. The silver stuff is magic pixie dust."

She gave me a not-too-gentle kick.

✳

She was on her phone from the moment we left the apartment, shoving it in her bag only for the security check at the airport, then talking and messaging again as we walked to and reached the gate. She scrambled to get help. She switched between French and English on her calls, and I could swear I also heard her speaking Greek. I heard her press Walker to get a list of sites around Delphi recently visited at night. As I later learned, this meant convincing someone at the National Geospatial-Intelligence Agency—one of those obscure intelligence agencies no one's ever heard of—to comb through reconnaissance data, mainly satellite imagery. She took herself off to a secluded area near the gate before I could hear more.

I went and scrounged for edibles at a bizarre little coffee stand, a tiny faux food truck with a policewoman mannequin at the wheel. I had just enough time to buy a dinner of bananas and chocolate for us before we boarded. We were bound first for Vienna. After a short layover there, we'd hop on the last nonstop flight to Athens.

"I think we have a geologist," Diane reported as we boarded. "A friend of a friend in France. He'll also meet us in Delphi tomorrow. I'm still working on getting an intelligence report. Maybe all we need is the license plate of a car parked at the spot marked on Farnese's phone. We're so close. But unless you're in an inner circle, these things take forever. It doesn't help that I'm trying to orchestrate things by messaging and talking over an open line."

"How did you get a geologist to drop everything and rush to the center of the world?"

"Tintin."

"Tintin? Really?"

She laughed. "A little bit. The call to adventure is irresistible. But also think about what this would mean for someone's career. And for a geologist the area around Delphi is a playground. Geologically rich and seismically active."

The late spring Central European sun was shining when we took off, Apollo still in the sky watching our interminable day.

"If we're going to meet them at Delphi in the morning," I said when we were in the air, "we'll get only four hours of sleep before we have to leave Athens, won't we?"

"We are driving to Delphi as soon as we land."

"What? Diane, that's nuts!" I shot back. The kind of headstrong nuts I find attractive in a woman, I thought. "You booked a hotel?"

"Morning traffic is atrocious in Athens. I want to be in Delphi as soon as possible in case anything happens. My friend is driving to Delphi right now. As I said, the artifacts in the Grotto could even be on the move tonight."

"Then I guess we should get some sleep," I said, less to offer well-reasoned advice than because my eyelids were drooping.

"Yes, we should."

I shut the window, snuffing out the golden flame cast by the low sun onto the seat back in the next row, and settled in for the fitful hallucinations that pass for sleep in economy class.

✻

We landed in Vienna after sunset, just before nine o'clock.

Diane reached across and lifted the shade. I don't know if she slept. The sky was still aglow, a streak of livid red lingering where the sun had set. "*Entre chien et loup*," she said. "That's what we call twilight in French." She sighed. "It's when dogs sleep, wolves come out, and mysterious and terrible things happen." She took out her phone. "*Et voilà*, at last, Walker . . ."

"We've got only thirty minutes to change planes."

"No NGIA, but maybe Air Force Intelligence . . ." She started tapping.

Head down, phone in hand, she followed me the short distance between gates as I rolled our wheelies.

"My friend Ari," she said to me, "the one in the Greek Archaeological Service—he's already there. He drove to the spot marked in Farnese's phone, up in the mountains to the north. He found trails there. There was no one else around, but he didn't want to explore alone. I don't know why. All he needed to do was wait and see if a car appeared. If it were me . . ."

"Couldn't the looters be dangerous? They may park in different places anyway. I would. This is our gate, Diane. We're boarding."

She looked up, bit her lip, and smoothed down her scarf.

✻

We arrived in Athens just after one in the morning. From the plane we went straight to the car rental desk.

Whoever booked our travel—presumably the FBI—had rented us a toy car. I asked Diane if we could upgrade. I didn't relish the idea of navigating the wilds of Greece in the dark and, to be honest, Diane's thick glasses didn't inspire confidence in her night vision. She agreed to get a larger car, but insisted on paying herself. This was now her show. Perhaps she also felt guilty about the thousands of dollars wasted on our Geneva pad.

"Do you want to drive first?" she asked as I loaded our suitcases into the upgraded, still diminutive vehicle.

"I don't drive."

"Not at all?"

"Not cars," I said.

"Do you have a license?"

"Yes, but I'm a New Yorker."

She huffed in exasperation, but an indulgent smile unfolded under the parking lot lights. "I am too by now, you know," she said. "But okay. I will drive. I like to drive."

Before she started the car, she gave her phone one last look. Nothing new.

How does a Manhattanite drive when there's no traffic or stop lights? This was for me a hypothetical situation, a mere thought experiment—a little like the question of faster-than-light travel among physicists—until Diane took the wheel that night. She tore down the multilane highway that cut through Athens. It was as though police sirens were still ringing in her ears as she chased after the looters of the Grotto.

Out of the frying pan and into the fire, I thought, trembling.

TWENTY-EIGHT

It would have been rude to sleep, and I wanted to be sure Diane stayed awake at the wheel, so I nattered away. By sticking her with the driving, I'd forfeited my right to complain about the way she was flirting with the Earth's escape velocity. Since I didn't want to distract her from the road, I commented on the things whizzing by us. How surreal to see Greek letters transplanted from ancient vases to road signs, I observed. Very humane, those high walls and glass barriers to shield nearby apartment buildings from highway noise. We should take up that idea in the States. Believe it or not, according to the map, there's a forest—

"If it's the police you are worrying about," she said, "Greece has high speed limits and lax enforcement."

"That's not what I'm worried about."

"Then what are you worried about?"

Diane's driving, I realized, frightened me, but it didn't worry me. I looked for my usual worries—disease, incompetence, loneliness—in the front-row balcony seats from which they habitually jeered at me. But they weren't there. I was experiencing a strange calm now that my ordeal with the contract had ended. It brought with it a brief moment of wisdom.

"I don't know. All I know is that I worry about all the wrong things."

I couldn't make out her face, but I took her noncommittal "hmm" to mean she agreed.

After half an hour, the streetlights vanished. We were on a split highway, so Diane flicked on the high beams. Beyond the illuminated road and reflectors, the world was pitch black.

I was reminded of my solitary nights on the Bridge, the sense of speed in a world gone dormant. Now, though, there were two of us sharing that lonely world. Silence intensified the feeling. It was like staring into some-one's eyes. I could sense that Diane too felt the electric tingle of intimacy building between us. As it grew and spread, threatening to touch the inner recesses of the self, I became squeamish. When I saw a road sign with arrows for the cities of Thessaloniki and Thiva and a question came to mind, I seized on it.

"Athens means the city of Athena, right?"

"Yes."

"Does Delphi mean anything?"

"Maybe. But it's obscured by legend, like everything else about the place."

"So we don't know."

"We are not certain. But the Greeks believed that 'Delphi' came from 'dolphin.' They are similar words in Greek."

"Dolphin? Why dolphin?" I asked with emotion. "Delphi isn't on the sea."

"I know. And Apollo isn't the god of the sea. It's a strange story. So strange that I think that it must be based on some historical event. It's not the kind of story you would just invent."

"Tell me."

"After Apollo killed the great python, he set up a shrine. But he needed priests to serve him. When he saw a ship sailing from Crete on the open sea, he transformed himself into a dolphin, leaped aboard, and hijacked it. The sailors tried to throw the dolphin back into the water, but it rocked the whole ship and terrified them. They tried to steer the ship to land, but it wouldn't respond to the helm. The ship sailed on its own, far past the city of Pylos, where they had meant to go, on to a port called Krissa, near the place that would become Delphi. There Apollo appeared in a blaze of splendor and commanded them into the mountains to serve as his first priests. They named the shrine after his dolphin form."

Apollo. Dolphins. I fingered the golden brooch inside my jacket and felt the smooth hump of its dolphin. I'd kept the brooch there even after it had gouged me. I believed it had saved my life by distracting my kidnappers. Had it not been there, or had some other brooch been inside my jacket the day I was seized, events would have taken a deadlier turn. Perhaps my quest of many years to reunite the remnants of my grandfather's collection had been needless. Perhaps I had the one artifact that my grandfather, mysteriously inspired, had meant for me to have, and it had played its destined role.

"Other animals were sacred to him," Diane added. "Wolves, for instance. And ravens."

"Ravens?" I thought back to my encounter with Le Chamois, to the huge black bird by the trailhead.

"They were his messengers. And cicadas. And mice. But dolphins were special. The ceiling of the temple at Delphi was full of them."

The highway soon narrowed to two lanes and began to twist. Rocky, scrub-covered hills appeared in the margins of our light-sculpted tunnel. Soon we were on a single-lane highway with no median. Diane slowed to a sane speed.

There weren't many trees by the roadside, just lone cypresses or junipers. I could make out fields, but not what grew in them. Our headlights picked out tiny flashes of red. Poppies. For a while, Diane had to lower the headlight beams every few minutes for a car approaching from the opposite direction. As time passed and we burrowed deeper into the countryside, other cars became rare.

I must have nodded off at some point. I looked up, startled, and checked my watch to discover we'd been driving for an hour and a half. Streetlights and a Shell station were welcoming us now to the small town of Livadia. It was sacred to the ancient Greek god of auto dealerships, apparently. They lined the road. Once we were through the town, the streetlights fell away again and we climbed in the dark. Tall, conical trees stood sentry by the road. We passed through a narrow tunnel under a mountain. The road twisted against a slope, then the ground dropped away on our left, and a guardrail appeared. We were on a mountainside. We passed through the tiny town of Arachova, whose main single street snaked between two- and three-story buildings faced with stucco and rough stone. The last outpost before Delphi.

After that it was all wild dusty scrub and low trees—olives and I know not what else—perched against a slope on one side of the road. The other side was sheer void. A winding, climbing, dizzying way. Triangular road signs recalled and in some cases added theatrical flair to the ones I'd seen in the Swiss mountains. An inscrutable arrow with a half crossbar. A squiggle made by someone trying out a felt-tipped pen. A tilting car, skid marks behind it forming a scribbled X. We looped around a long hairpin turn and just as we finished and my innards caught up with me, another hairpin turn started winding in the opposite direction. Everywhere by the roadside clung vegetation—thirsty, tough, and wizened—rich tangles of spiky plants alternating with tufts of growth in clay.

✳

We were just five miles from Delphi when we saw them.

Small whitish masses appeared every few yards on the road. I felt a tiny bump under the wheels.

"What *are* those?" Diane asked.

I saw one scurry across the road toward the rising slope of the mountain. "I don't know. But whatever they are, they're alive."

"Mice?" she asked with alarm.

"Could be." I squinted. "Yes, could be."

A dirt byroad forked off the opposite side of the road. She swerved onto it and braked. We got out of the car. One of the creatures scurried across the ground in front of the headlight beams. I shuddered. Creepy as the swarm of rodents was, whatever was driving them helter-skelter up the mountain was even creepier.

"We're stopping because of the mice?" I asked.

"Yes. I'm not sure, but I'm worried about something . . ."

She reached into the car and turned off the headlights. We walked several yards down the dirt road, then stopped.

All around us were mountains, mountains we didn't see so much as sense, unfathomable masses heaving against the heavens. Crickets saturated the air with the selfsame trill heard by the ancient Greeks. Overhead was the purest night sky I've ever seen. The stars were so bright and so many, so clear and so tantalizingly close that I couldn't believe a thing like that had been hanging unseen over my head for every night of my existence. What other wonders were the heavens holding suspended up there in silence? Star upon star tickled my retina the longer I stared. That's why it took me so long to notice Diane.

She was craning her head queerly in the direction the car pointed.

263

I looked. Somewhere in the distance—it was hard to tell how far away—lights danced above a mountain. Enormous ethereal columns, the color of flame. Three of them, shimmering into and out of existence.

"What is that? A gas-powered electrical plant? Here?"

"No," she said.

"Then—"

"No, no," she said, her voice rising. "Get into the car!"

She ran back, opened the door, and scrambled into the driver's seat. I hesitated.

"Get in!" she called.

I was still yanking at my seatbelt when she backed, turned, and swung onto the road. She tore off, back in the direction we'd come.

"What? What is it?"

"An earthquake."

"I didn't feel anything."

"Not yet. But soon."

"How can you possibly know that?"

"The ancient sources. They say that before it happened, animals fled into the mountains. There were strange lights in the sky. People call them earthquake lights."

"But—"

". . . and howling dogs, bubbling in the sea, blasts of wind . . ."

"I didn't feel any wind. Couldn't those be myths?"

"Not myths. There are often earthquakes here. I knew someone who was here during one in the nineties. From my department at Princeton. He saw the same warning signs."

"If that's true, shouldn't we sit and wait?"

"Yes. No. I don't know. It could be hours or days. I only have my instinct. To run, like those mice."

"I—"

"I need to focus."

She craned her neck and fixed her gaze on the road. We looped back around the hairpin turns at a speed just this side of nauseating and sped back through Arachova.

We didn't get far past the town before we blew a tire.

That's how it felt, at least. The car juddered and my teeth rattled as Diane worked the brakes and wrestled with the steering wheel. We scraped a guardrail, and it felt as though we might crash through, but Diane managed to maneuver away and slow the car. We were lucky. A small patch of asphalt bulged off the side of the road. We skidded to a stop there. Even then I felt the ground shaking. Bright dust swirled in front of the headlights.

It felt like a long time, but the whole thing lasted for less than a minute. "We should wait," I said. "There may be aftershocks."

We sat in silence. We felt a rumble. Then, for a long time, all was still.

I don't know what gave me the courage to do it—maybe an urgency to live after this fresh scrape with death—but I put my hand on Diane's. She didn't pull away. She took my hand and held it.

As we waited for the wrath of the god to subside, a thought dropped from somewhere above with a faint splash. It coiled and swirled and spread until it tinted my whole mind with certain conviction. Apollo had tricked me and Diane into a false reading of signs and prophecies. I had thought my trials and adventures were about me and the rogue contract, my transgressions and the god's wrath. But I'd gotten it all wrong. In the days of Delphi, Apollo blinded men to their coming doom. He had instead spurred me to action with the illusion of a doom that would never happen. He had made me an unwitting foot soldier in his battle to protect the remains of his godhead, to prevent imposters from seizing the mantle of Delphi in cyberspace and trafficking in his sacred relics from Greece. Which meant, strange to say, that he of the golden hair and glittering bow, the god of light, music, truth, and oracles, had been on my side all along.

EPILOGUE

The Greek Archaeological Service never found the Grotto, the Omphalos, or any new gold artifacts near Delphi. The earthquake had been a powerful one—magnitude 7.1 according to news reports. It severely damaged buildings, opened sinkholes, and triggered rockslides in the mountains. Dozens of people were injured and there were two confirmed deaths. Diane obtained Greek law enforcement reports indicating that a group of four local men disappeared during the cataclysm. All that was found was an empty car on the earthquake-ravaged mountainside. I expect we'll never have proof, but Diane seems certain that on that fateful night, the looters of the Grotto were buried or plunged into the underworld with their secret. I share her melancholy at the thought that the Grotto may now be lost again for years, for centuries, maybe for eternity. At the same time, I can't shake off a belief in divine will behind the incident, that exposing the god's sacred treasures to the world would be wrong, would be—dare I say it—impious. So in the end, I have to confess that I hope the Grotto is never found.

Giuseppe Farnese is at the center of a prolonged extradition tug-of-war involving Switzerland, Greece, and Italy. You'd think it's being played out with actual ropes tied to his body to hear the way he howls in court. At one point he delivered an uninterrupted, three-hour diatribe in which—trying to flatter the judge all the while—he railed against Prof. Hévin for telling lies (out of purported envy for Farnese's rich tenor singing voice), claimed that all of the objects in the Freeport belonged not to him, but to clients asking him for appraisals (though he'd regrettably lost his emails with them), and then turned around and asserted that he was planning to donate nearly all of these pieces to Greek and Italian museums (which would have been a first in his twenty-plus-year career). He ended his speech drenched in sweat, having subjected the court to a snow job of proportions previously unknown even in the alpine nation of Switzerland. The various cases against him could take years to play out. The authorities have confiscated his passport, but for the time being he's otherwise free. It angers me to think that he may be able to hire a fresh gang in Greece to hunt for the Grotto, but at least Diane assures me that he's under surveillance.

Farnese's refusal to cooperate with the authorities has been a thorn in Diane's side. A number of Delphian artifacts had already passed through his hands before his arrest and have surfaced or left traces in the underground market. Diane has helped recover a few. One of these is a gold dish, equal in splendor to the one in the Freeport, that depicts Apollo with a seven-stringed lyre. It's etched with a dedicatory inscription that Diane says may bring us an inch closer to resolving the mystery of when Delphi's most sacred objects were hidden away in the Grotto, if not how. She's been hot on the trail of the other dispersed artifacts for many months now, concocting excuses for her superiors so that she can help with the hunt outside US jurisdiction. Her rescue mission, as she likes to call it, has been a frequent and exciting topic of our dinnertime conversations. Otherwise, we spend a lot of time arguing about what I should be doing to prevent cybercriminals from finding fresh ways to weaponize smart contracts and about the ever-delicate balance between liberty and security.

The press reported that the Swiss police caught the creator of the rogue contract, but that his name would remain confidential "to protect state secrets." They also reported that it was the Swiss intelligence services who had deactivated the contract. By implying that law enforcement was able to hack it, the Swiss authorities hoped to discourage potential copycats. Copycat rogue contracts have still emerged—not generally for assassination, but for crimes ranging from vandalism to cyberattacks. Le Chamois's contract was as potent as it was, however, because of a rare conjunction of deep technical expertise, overweening ambition, and ample resources resulting from outlandish marketing needs. The copycat contracts that surfaced in its wake have been amateurish, often with bounties too paltry to attract much attention.

I gave one of these copycat contracts to Julia to break as an exercise during her internship at Adyton over the summer after my adventures, when Corinne and I mentored her. As we predicted, she found a serious flaw in a matter of days. As we also predicted, Lukas tried to hire her straight out of high school. Happily she's heading to Cornell to study computer science, so she'll have refuge from him for at least four years. She says that her father—wherever he's hiding—is grateful to me for jump-starting her career. I've been hoping for a giant diamond in the mail, but I guess I should just be happy he's not sending flamenco-enthused thugs after me.

As Walker predicted, the Russian government refused to prosecute their local branch of the Delphian gang. The FBI put out arrest warrants, but the gang have either confined themselves to beaches on the Black Sea or gone abroad under aliases. Walker says it's now believed they worked formerly in Russian military intelligence.

You're probably most curious, though, about the real technical master and visionary behind my story, Prof. Alexis Hévin, aka Le Chamois. He struck a bargain with the Swiss authorities, just as Diane expected. He traded my life and his cooperation in the prosecution of Farnese for a fine of a few thousand Swiss francs and the avoidance of a public hearing. At the time we crossed paths with him, he was on the brink of retirement from his university. Most of the people involved in finding and stopping him now imagine that he's out in the mountains of Switzerland, leaping from crag to crag, pausing now and then to sing arias to the valleys below. That he was forced, in short, to retire from his career as a criminal mastermind.

I, for one, am not so certain.

ACKNOWLEDGMENTS

In the dawn of blockchain time (the year 2014 AD), a Cornell colleague introduced me to a technology called "smart contracts." We spent an afternoon brainstorming uses for them and found ourselves focused on and concerned about one in particular: *crime*. We published a paper that warned of the future risks of rogue smart contracts. Happily, the most dangerous rogue contracts of our paper aren't possible today and, if the community takes care, shouldn't be for a long time. That paper, however, germinated into this novel.

From the very outset, I realized that to do nearly anything important, smart contracts need oracles. For the ensuing whirlwind journey through the oracle industry, I owe thanks to many, especially Chainlink Labs' cofounders, Sergey Nazarov and Steve Ellis, with whom a hopeless first meeting over coffee somehow turned into the most thrilling extended collaboration of my career. I'm grateful as well to Lorenz Breidenbach, multifaceted technical wizard, and Adelyn Zhou, prime mover behind the Chainlink community. Hats off also to the Link Marines.

My friend Jeff Edmonds explained to me what he could of the workings of the US intelligence community. Jean-Pierre Hubaux led me up many a Swiss mountain and usually safely down again. He and Laura and Marty Wattenberg gave early and incisive comments on my manuscript, while Lorenz Breidenbach helped game out technical details. Kendra Harpster's excellent critique helped propel my book through the publishing gauntlet. Susan Barnett, my copyeditor, purged some choice bloopers from my manuscript, for which I'm grateful. Special thanks to my editor at Talos Press, Mike Campbell, who took on *The Oracle* despite only being "crypto curious" and masterfully steered it to completion. Any errors or missteps in my ancient world or speculative future one are not theirs, however, but mine alone.

A number of facts and incidents in *The Oracle* draw on historical reality. My many sources notably include works by Pausanias and Plutarch, *Delphi* by Michael Scott, and the scholarship of John Hale and Jelle Zeilinga de Boer. For the incidents involving antiquities trafficking, I made particular use of *The Medici Conspiracy* by Peter Watson and Cecilia Todeschini and *Chasing Aphrodite* by Jason Felch and Ralph Frammolino. Sophos and Symantec reports provided key details in the hunt for the Delphians.

As a scientist in academia, I'm in the business of writing science fiction. Most of it ends up in publications at scholarly conferences. Some becomes reality. Some is woven into *The Oracle*. All of the heavy lifting in my research came from my group at Cornell Tech, past and present: James Austgen, Kushal Babel, Ethan Cecchetti, Phil Daian, Andrés Fábrega, Steven Goldfeder, Yan Ji, Tyler Kell, Mahimna Kelkar, Sishan Long, Deepak Maram, Ian Miers, and Fan Zhang. Thanks also to friends, cofounders, colleagues, and staff in the Initiative for CryptoCurrencies and Contracts (IC3), especially Sarah Allen, Jim Ballingall, Ittay Eyal, Oana Gherman, Sarah Meiklejohn, Andrew Miller, Elaine Shi, Gün Sirer, and Dawn Song.

However long my roll call of thanksgiving to friends and colleagues, there's only one high priestess in my life, my wife. She is present in some way on every page of this book.

ABOUT THE AUTHOR

Ari Juels has a short but hard-to-spell name and a long job title. He's the Weill Family Foundation and Joan and Sanford I. Weill Professor in the Jacobs Technion-Cornell Institute at Cornell Tech in New York City, as well as a computer science faculty member at Cornell University. He cofounded and codirects the Initiative for CryptoCurrencies and Contracts (IC3). He also serves as chief scientist at Chainlink Labs, where his seminal contributions to oracle networks are commemorated in the name of the smallest denomination of the LINK token: a Juel. He is the author of well over one hundred widely cited and influential research publications, along with a previous techno-thriller, *Tetraktys*, published in 2010.